The Wolf

KJ G‌RAHAM

ISBN: 9781077495692 (paperback)

This is a work of fiction. Names, characters, businesses, places, events and incidents are either the products of the author's imagination or used in a fictitious manner. Any resemblance to actual persons, living or dead, or actual events is purely coincidental.

Acknowledgments

George Kean
Lesley Jones

Table of Contents

1

The Warning

N eil Andrews slammed his office door closed as he entered in a mixture of anger and frustration. He had spent the last hour at first demanding then pleading with the prime minister not to go through with
this folly. Jean, his PA, placed a tray on his desk with two cups of coffee
and a plate of biscuits, and waited. 'Two cups, Jean, why two cups?'

Before Jean could answer Bruce Ellis entered unannounced. 'Two
cups because I don't think I will be leaving here until I can talk some
sense into someone in MI6, so refreshments might be called for. How is
my favourite MI6 director getting on? You do know what your government is doing is lunacy? Vadek Volkov as Russian ambassador to the
UK – are you kidding me!'

Neil didn't even have a chance to gather his thoughts before the rant
continued.

'Neil, please tell me this is your PM playing a sick joke on us. If
you don't get back to Number Ten and sort this, my boss is going to be
giving your boss a call – and it won't be a cosy chat. Just to give you a
reminder who you will be letting into your country with full diplomatic
immunity, let me recap on our Russian friend just in case MI6 has been
sleeping on the job.

'Vadek Volkov or, to give him his Russian Mafia name, "The Wolf",
on the surface runs a string of dubious nightclubs all over Eastern
Europe, but in truth he smuggles drugs, weapons, anything that will turn
his company a profit, legal or otherwise.' Bruce Ellis turned, apparently

to make sure Jean had left and closed the door behind her, before continuing. 'Neil, we got a CIA agent into his organisation when we found out he was attempting to sell a decommissioned Russian nuke to the Iranians. Luckily our man pulled the plug on the operation and the nuke was recovered in the port of Baku, Azerbaijan. Volkov smelled a rat and every one of his men, including our agent, was killed to ensure there were no traitors in his team. Neil, buddy, he is real bad news. Whatever he's coming here for you can be sure he's up to no good. Shut the door now while you still can.'

Neil Andrews had tried to shut the door, but he did not want to admit to his American friend he had failed, so he changed the subject.

'So tell me, Bruce, are you still the President's blue-eyed boy? You must have scored a few brownie points with him when you gave him Bin Laden.'

Bruce Ellis must have been aware Andrews was trying to throw him off scent, and went straight for Andrews' Achilles heel.

'Neil, you know as well as I do that in our business you're only top dog until the next crisis comes along and you're thrown back into the mix and told to sort it. As you're in the mood to change the subject how is my favourite British spy getting on? Have you coaxed Samantha into coming back to work yet?'

Andrews sat back in his seat trying not to show that Ellis had hit a raw nerve. 'No. She's too busy playing mummies and daddies in Scotland.'

Bruce Ellis stood up as he received a text. Apparently deciding the meeting was over he shook Neil's hand and headed for the office door, then turned back with one final thought before leaving. 'That's a real pity about Sam, buddy, because if you go ahead and let that Russian asshole into your country I think you're going to need her special talent to get rid of the parasite. See ya!'

Neil Andrews sat deep in thought long after Bruce Ellis had gone. Neil refused to believe Samantha O'Conner was finished with MI6. Since she had gone on extended maternity leave Neil had not had to sanction the elimination of any undesirables; even though she had been gone for over two years, Sam was still the best assassin retained by the secret service. He knew one day he was going to have to lift the phone and have her returned to active duty, whether she liked it or not.

Samantha O'Conner sat perched on a huge boulder that millions of years ago had crashed onto the Scottish west coast beach from the cliff above. Through time its sharp jagged edges had been eroded away by the action of the sea, leaving it a smooth and convenient resting place which, over the years Sam, had become fond of, often stopping after her runs to recharge her batteries and take stock of her thoughts.

Today was no exception. Sam had just finished a six-mile run and before heading back up the zigzag cliff path to Comriach, her glass house on top of the cliff; she had climbed onto the stone quietly with the stealth of a lioness stalking her prey. Only a few metres in front of her a seal sunned itself on a rock, waiting patiently for the tide to return and save it the trip down the sandy beach to the sea.

While watching the seal, Sam let her mind drift to other things. For the first time since her childhood she felt a whole person once more; at long last she had a life and a family, and slowly the bad dreams from her past were receding. Sam did not want the feeling of contentment to ever go; this was home. She had pledged the rest of her life to Adam, the only true love of her life, and their son, Luke.

Little Luke had been born on the island of Arran two years previously, giving Sam and Adam the final piece of their family jigsaw. Sam wondered, while relaxing in the warm sun, who had replaced her at MI6. From time to time agents worked together on cases, but this was not the norm; to maintain security agents were normally kept apart.

Sam knew very few other agents and none like her who had been trained specifically as an assassin. She knew also that MI6 would never admit to the fact that they employed this type of agent, instead referring to them as 'specialists'. Sam wondered how many more of these specialists MI6 had trained – was there a Samantha number two waiting in the wings to step into her shoes?

Sam shivered in the light sea breeze as her memory flashed back for an instant to the bad old days when her only pleasure was the adrenalin rush as she closed in for the kill of her intended target. She dragged herself back to the present just as a grey cloud covered the sun, dropping the temperature noticeably and giving Sam the excuse she needed to get her tight legs working again. She set off up the cliff path in a final sprint, her mind now set on only one thing: her hot shower and then a strong coffee to bring her back to life.

By the time she reached the front of the glass house the sun had once more escaped the clutches of the cloud and Sam admired her house as the sun glinted off the many panes of privacy glass that made up the front of the unusual building built by the Huff company. Sam looked up at the balcony of the house she had come to love, its interior set out with the living area high up on the second floor, its lounge and balcony facing west overlooking the islands of Eigg, Muck, Rum and Skye, a view that, when the sun set, melted the heart of whoever stood on the balcony looking out over the glory of Western Isles. She half expected to see Adam looking down on her as he had done so many times, but today the balcony was empty. Little Luke was with his nanny, Sue, for the afternoon while Adam was busy working on his new pet project with his old army pal, Bob Hunter. Sam had the house and the afternoon to herself and she was going to make the most of it.

Adam and Bob had just finished stacking the sandbags around the end of the new firing range and had stopped for a well-earned rest; Adam surveyed the surrounding area, deciding that his latest project was finally ready for the booked guests who would be arriving later in the week. It was Bob who'd had the initial idea when he retired from the army but, when Adam had offered Bob a security job and his wife Sue the job of nanny to young Luke, they had jumped at the chance of joining Bob's old commanding officer on the idyllic west coast of Scotland. After only a few weeks, Adam and Bob had decided as well as building a lodge house at the foot of the long drive it would also be a good idea to follow Bob's idea and hopefully cash in on the latest leisure craze called Airsoft which, as Adam had discovered, was basically powerful

BB guns, which had replaced paintball as the new generation shoot-'em-up game.

Adam was not the type to do anything half-heartedly and, after a bit of negotiation with the local landowner, had purchased a sizeable piece of land only a few miles inland from the glass house. Although pretty much useless to most people, the marshy ground on the edge of a small loch lent itself perfectly to Adam and Bob's venture. Both men had taken to the project in a big way and while local builders put the finishing touches to Bob and Sue's new gatehouse, Adam and Bob were to be found day after day planning and building their adult playground, felling some of the trees on the land to open the ground up and using the trees to build two substantial log cabins and a series of shacks arranged in a small village setting for use in the Airsoft games.

The first of the log cabins was the reception and armoury while the second building next to the shooting range had been Bob's idea. As well as Bob could remember, it was an exact replica of the killing house that was a feature of training when he had been stationed at Credenhill; it would bring an element of authenticity to the games planned for the unsuspecting guests. With the military precision and planning they had both had drummed into them they checked every pistol and every rifle they had in stock. Luckily for them, a power line crossed the corner of their land – the Airsoft weapons they had chosen were electronic and would need constant charging to keep them operational. The main log cabin had electricity and heating and if the venture failed would be transformed into holiday accommodation as a backup plan.

Adam had just finished checking and marking the weapons so they could be identified if they went missing while Bob ran a stock check on the Airsoft batteries and ammunition, when Sam appeared in her trademark Herbie Beetle.

'So this is where you pair have been hiding for the last week! Sue, Luke and I were about to file a missing persons report with the police. If it wasn't for the unwashed dishes and unmade beds we would have posted you missing.'

Adam said nothing, instead handing Sam one of the Airsoft Glock handguns, which was already loaded with a magazine. Sam studied the Airsoft weapon, loading and unloading it and working the slide as she would have done with the real thing, then she turned her attention to the ten tennis balls that had been secured to the top of ten poles sunk into the ground in front of the sandbagged wall. Without any further coaxing she opened fire on the tennis-ball targets. Her first shot caught the tennis ball on the left and the ricochet spun off, pinging off a sandbag. Sam corrected her aim, hitting the remaining tennis balls dead centre and sending the small round pellets directly back at all three of them. Adam was not surprised by Sam's marksmanship – even with a toy gun she was a force to be reckoned with – but Bob had never witnessed Sam in action and was surprised by her skill. 'Well done, Samantha – not bad for a woman!'

Adam winced at his friend's unfortunate comment; he knew Sam well enough to know what Bob had just said would be like a red rag to a bull. He watched Sam as her eyes flashed anger. She caught Bob's eye and neither one was for backing down. Adam sensed a stand-off coming but did nothing, interested to see who would win the battle of wills.

Sam was the first to break the silence. 'I wasn't aware that having a penis and testicles was an advantage in shooting. You learn something new every day, Bob.'

Before either Adam or Bob could react to Sam's answer her gun hand spun upwards, bringing the Airsoft Glock to bear and firing the instant her target was in the sights. She hit Bob with a shot from the Glock in the middle of his forehead causing him to step backwards. Adam winced in sympathy with his big army pal; he knew that had to have hurt his pride as well as his skull.

Sam did not wait for Bob to recover, winking at Adam as she tossed the toy gun to him, then heading for the Beetle. 'Almost teatime, guys. I'll pick Luke up on the way home. Can you get back home at a decent time tonight, please. Sue can sort that blister on your head, Bob. See you later.'

Adam bent over, killing himself laughing, tears streaming down his face. He stood to see Bob staring in the direction of the retreating Beetle, his cheeks flushed with a controlled rage.

'Mate, if there was a wrong thing to say to Sam, that was it. Holy shit, your forehead looks bad – you look like Frankenstein's monster.'

The big soldier's fury faded as the laughter continued. Adam was glad to see his big mate had eventually seen the funny side of the situation.

Later that evening, after tucking young Luke in and making sure he was settled in bed, Sam and Adam gazed down on their tiny miracle. Luke had his mother's colouring and blonde curly hair; he was slightly on the small size for his age but where he lacked Adam's looks he made up for it with his temperament, refusing point blank to sleep but eventually giving in to tiredness after Adam had paraded him around on his back while Luke squealed with glee and his mother chuckled at the sight of the pair bonding with each other. Eventually Adam and Sam retired to the calm of the lounge, a routine that had not changed since Luke had been born two years previously.

Out on the balcony, toddler clothes set out to dry on a frame whipped back and forward as the westerly wind picked up strength. Far out to sea, clouds were blanking out the silhouette of the islands dotted across the horizon and highlighted by the setting sun; mother nature was warning of an impending storm heading their way. Adam sat upright on one of the couches while Sam lay with her head on his lap, engrossed in a novel she had picked up while shopping in Fort William.

Adam could not let his mind settle and his thoughts turned to how far they had come in only two years of playing happy families. Sam's beloved shooting range had been turned into a toy storage area, every gun except two Glocks locked away in the battery sheds for the solar panels. The gym was now halved in size having been transformed so Luke could play while his mother trained.

Sam herself had changed dramatically since the arrival of Bob and Sue. Now, with more time on her hands, she wanted to use her talent for French and German to give private lessons to struggling school pupils, so she had placed ads in local shops.

Adam studied Sam as she turned the page of her book; she had taken to civilian life like a duck to water. Adam on the other hand had struggled to throw off the past; he still had the haunting feeling that this peaceful existence they were enjoying was only temporary and that evil stalked him, just waiting for him to drop his guard.

This frame of mind had been the reason Bob had joined them. Fearful that their hideaway had been located, Adam wanted more security, and when Bob informed him he had left the special forces Adam offered him a job looking after the security of the glass house and its contents. It was a nice bonus that Bob arrived with his new wife, Sue, an army nurse Bob had bumped into when picking up a squaddie from the Royal Centre for Defence Medicine in Birmingham.

It only took Sue seconds with Luke and one of his beaming smiles to convince her to become his nanny and his best friend into the bargain. Sam was relieved Luke's stubborn temperament had not been put to the test, with Sue being given the seal of approval by Luke.

Adam glanced down at Sam again and found that she was fast asleep with her head on his lap, the pages of her book moving backwards and forwards in tune with her steady breathing. Adam sat studying her face; in Adam's eyes her face was perfection. Only a tiny scar on her lipline told a tale of a previous encounter with an assassin. Sam had been lucky; the German hitman had beaten her to within an inch of her life and had left her face in a bad way. Adam could have sat all night watching Sam but he knew tomorrow was going to be a busy day, so he picked her up and carried her through to the bedroom. Even after two blissful years Adam found it hard to believe he and Sam were still very much in love.

Adam tossed and turned in bed. He was tired, but the next day played on his mind; it was a big day for his new venture. In the morning he had the lads from the hotel bar coming to give the Airsoft site a trial run then in the afternoon he had his first paying customers. Adam knew if anything went wrong in the morning, he had little time to sort it before his customers arrived; there was no point worrying. He would just have to wing it and hope for the best.

Most of Neil Andrews' staff had left for the evening; only Jean remained hovering, waiting to see if Neil needed anything. Andrews had to almost chase her out of the office to get her to go home; he did not want anyone to overhear the conversation he was about to have over the phone.

Neil waited until he was sure Jean had left then dialled the number for the Invermorroch Hotel in Arisaig. It infuriated Neil that Samantha O'Conner refused to allow a phone or mobile in her highland hideaway, and the fact that Sam was not available to take the call did nothing to relieve his rising blood pressure.

'Hello, Paul, I would appreciate it if you could get a message to Mrs Hunter urgently. If you could get her to phone Neil at the office immediately that would be great. No number, Paul, she will know it, thank you.'

Andrews hung up, lifted a file marked 'Top Secret', and pored over the contents for the hundredth time that day. He needed Sam and he needed her now; the contents of the file changed everything – he knew why Volkov was here.

After some time a thought occurred to Neil and he turned his attention to his computer to dig through the personnel files of MI6 looking for a suitable candidate. It did not take him long to find who he was looking for and he lifted the phone. Neil's hunch was correct; the duty supervisor was told to get Callum McPherson down to Neil's office at the double.

Callum McPherson had only started working in Vauxhall Cross six months ago and, as Neil had suspected, being a new start, eager to impress, he had worked on into the evening. Callum knocked and entered Neil Andrews' office and was directed to the chair opposite the desk by the top man.

'Callum, I see from your records that you were invited to join us in the computer division to access your skills as a surveillance officer. It would appear you impressed one of our field teams when you managed to evade detection as you moved across Europe – you have shown good initiative both in the field and here, where you have made a solid start. Callum, I am sure you've had enough of me blabbing on so I will get to the point. I need someone to do a job for me, but not one of our regulars. I need a fresh face – someone who can think on their feet and keep me in the loop. Do you think you can handle that? Say now if you want out because once you're committed there will be no get-out clause.' Neil was a wise old head; he knew dangling a carrot like this would be irresistible to an up-and-coming new start like Callum.

'I'm in, sir, no problem.'

Andrews sat back in his chair studying Callum before continuing. He could see in the young man shades of himself when he had first been recruited from university so many years ago; he knew if he had been offered this chance just like Callum he would have grabbed it with both hands.

'Okay, Callum, I want you to head up to Arisaig on the west coast of Scotland and make it your base. Without drawing attention to yourself I want you to shadow and report back on the actions of a couple called Ann and Allan Hunter who live to the north of the village in a house called Comriach on the coast. Don't drop your guard if you are ever in their presence. They are both clever people. In particular try not to engage in conversation with Ann Hunter – she can literally smell undercover operatives. I want to know who they are speaking with and if anyone is acting strangely. Finally, report to myself and no one else. You'd better get a move on, young man – I want my first report from you in forty-eight hours.'

Neil Andrews stood up to shake Callum's hand and draw the meeting to a close, but Callum had one last question for Neil.

'No problem, sir. Shall I pick up surveillance equipment from the stores or will it be dispatched to me?'

Andrews gave Callum a withering stare. 'You have eyes, ears and a phone. Learn to use them first, son. Call me in forty-eight hours. Goodbye.'

Sam was heading back to the glass house after her morning run when she bumped into Paul Kidd, the owner of the Invermorroch Hotel, coming out of the side entrance to the hotel.

'Ah, just the very lady I was hoping to catch up with this morning.

I was going to pop up to the house on the way to the big Airsoft launch but you've saved me the trip.'

Sam pulled up and started stretching while she listened to Paul. She did not want to be rude but she needed to relieve Adam of childcare duties so he could get across to the game site and ready it for the first guinea pigs.

'Paul, honey, I hope it won't take long. I'm in a bit of a rush – Billy the Kid and his sheriff are desperate to get to the site for the big opening.'

Paul winced. Sam knew he'd be nervous before taking part in the launch.

'Just two seconds, Ann, that's all. I had a call last night asking for you – the chap said it was urgent. I'm sorry – we were run off our feet last night or I would have popped up then. The chap said to tell you it was Neil and to phone the office. He left no number but said you would know it. Sorry if I'm a bit late.'

Sam's mind was already in overdrive. She exchanged a few more words but her mind was elsewhere; she thanked Paul and wished him good luck at the shooting then headed off up the hill back towards the glass house. Sam had dreaded this moment, but she knew it had to come sooner or later. On the run north from Arisaig, Sam went over in her head what she was going to say to Neil Andrews; it wasn't so much what to tell Neil – she had already decided she was finished with MI6 – but she needed to find a way to put it across to him; it had to be put in a way he could not argue with.

Sam arrived at the glass house to find Adam waiting by the car, packed and ready to go. She lifted Luke onto her hip as Adam planted a kiss on her forehead before jumping into the Beetle and vanishing down the hill, intent on getting to his Airsoft camp before his first test pilots arrived.

Sam had no time to say anything about the phone call – not a bad thing, she thought; she had not made her mind up yet what to tell Adam. She had a feeling he would say nothing if told but that it would smoulder inside him. She placed Luke in his playpen with his favourite cuddly elephant and sat pondering what to do over a mug of coffee. Sam was not sure what her reluctance to tell Adam about the call said about her and their relationship. She was sure she wanted to stay here with her partner and her son. but there was a tiny bit of her that yearned for adventure and wanted to remain an MI6 agent rather than the perfect mother, watching her family grow as the years flew by. At the moment it was irrelevant; she did not know yet what Neil was going to say to her. For all she knew it might just be a social call, although she doubted that. Sam checked on Luke before heading to the hall cupboard. After a bit of hunting she returned to the lounge with a box containing a new mobile phone, a sim card and a battery pack. She didn't trust the security of these phones; this one had never been used – she had bought it in case of emergencies. The last thing she wanted was for Luke to become ill and having no way of contacting help.

Sam inserted the sim and battery pack before punching in the number Neil had given her. To her surprise the call was not intercepted by the call centre or Jean, but instead went straight through to him.

'Hello, Samantha, thank you for getting back to me. I trust you're all well up there in the back of beyond?'

Sam was surprised that as well as getting straight through to Neil, he had known right away that it was her calling.

'Impressive, Mr Andrews. How did you know it was me calling considering I'm using a burner phone? How did you manage that one?'

Neil Andrews chuckled. 'That's an easy one, Samantha. There are only two people who have the number I gave you: yourself and the prime minister. As it was not a secure call it had to be you. Samantha, we need to talk urgently and it's not the type of conversation we can have on the phone, if you get my drift. I'll text you where and when so keep the bloody phone switched on. I need to go, Samantha, but be ready. For god's sake don't do a runner on me – this is very serious. You have got to meet with me, I implore you. Got to go. Bye for now, Samantha.'

Sam had no chance to question Neil further; the phone connection was broken instantly.

Adam was aware of a figure standing by the log cabin as he pulled into the car park they had cut into the woods; at first he thought it was one of the locals arrived early for the test session but on closer inspection the young man was not one of his pub recruits.

'Hello there – you must be Allan, the owner here. I'm Callum. I asked at the hotel in Arisaig and they said you might be looking to hire people for your new venture.'

Adam didn't have the heart to reject Callum's offer of help outright, instead ushering the forlorn-looking character into the log cabin before putting the kettle on for an early morning brew.

'Honestly, Callum, I hadn't thought about employing anyone else – after all, we haven't even started in business. I tell you what though … grab a tea or a coffee and tell me a bit about yourself. I'll keep you in mind if it turns out we do need an extra pair of hands.'

Callum volunteered to make the coffee while Adam logged on to the web and checked out the new pre-payment website he had just set up for Comriach Airsoft Ltd. At first everything worked fine but after only a few minutes the screen froze, then, to Adams horror, lost all the information and displayed only a green screen. Adam was in full panic mode; he had the trial this morning, which was a freebie for his local friends, but in the afternoon he had his first paying guests and he had no idea either if they had paid or exactly how many were coming today. It was to be finalised this morning.

Callum turned, coffees in hand.'. 'Problem, Allan?'

Adam thumped on the keys in desperation; the last thing he needed this morning was a computer problem. 'I hate these bloody things. It worked like clockwork all last week and the minute you need the bloody thing it goes tits up. Bloody typical.'

Callum handed Adam a coffee while looking over his shoulder. 'Mind if I take a look, Allan? I did a computer course at uni. You can get other things ready for the big day.'

Adam slid off the seat, letting Callum replace him at the keyboard. He was just turning his thoughts as to where his business partner had got to when the cabin door opened and Bob appeared, flustered and out of breath.

'Sorry, Mac, the missus bolted with the car this morning and to add insult to injury I overslept, today of all days. It's this bloody healthy air up here, I tell you. It's not good for you – I keep bloody falling asleep.'

Adam pointed to the door and led Bob outside, leaving Callum fiddling with the computer. 'I take it you left your brain asleep as well. How many times have I to tell you my name is now Allan, not Adam or Mac or boss, just Allan.'

Bob looked crestfallen. 'Sorry, mate, I'm just not used to this spy business. I'll try not to do it again. Any chance of putting the kettle on while I start looking out the kit? How many toy soldiers are coming today?'

Adam did a rough calculation in his head before replying. 'Set it out for twenty to start with for the morning. I'm not sure for this afternoon – the paying lot have not got back to me with numbers yet. I need to see how the young lad is getting on and I'll put the kettle back on for you.'

Bob stopped, turning back. 'Yeah, I was going to ask where he had appeared from.'

'He's looking for a job. I was going to tell him we were fine until the bloody computer bought it. Now I'm not so sure – an extra pair of hands might come in handy if this thing proves popular. What do you think?'

Bob shrugged his shoulders and turned away before answering. 'You're the boss. As long as you don't expect me to sort the bloody computer – but if you are keeping him tell him mine's tea with two sugars and milk.'

One hour later the locals were starting to arrive. Callum had rebooted the computer, installed new software and booked in the paying guests. Adam patted him on the back, informing him he had the job he was looking for, then sent him to find Bob and assist with any last-minute kit issues.

Adam and Bob had thought out things and decided they did not want to go through a safety briefing every time a group arrived, so they had set up a video warning of the dangers and safety precautions that must be observed by all players.

While the now fully assembled group watched the video, Callum handed out face masks to protect the players' heads from the BB-type ammunition. Adam took the time to study his first lot of game players. There was no one present that overly concerned him; a couple of young lads from the local farm were probably going to need an eye kept on but the rest were more mature adults, with only two girls from the local town making up the female contingent. Once the video was finished Bob took six players at a time to show them how to load and fire their Airsoft guns, then let them loose on the tennis-ball target area where they were warned they had to wear their face masks. During the second group practice Bob found his hands full as one of the older gamekeepers refused to put his face mask on, stating that it was a toy and he wasn't running about with a stupid mask on for anyone. Adam stood back at first, letting Bob continue, but this was not the army now and Bob, without the power of his sergeant's stripes, was unable to persuade the stubborn gamekeeper. Adam could see that this was affecting the mood of the assembled group and wasting valuable time.

Adam marched across to the still arguing pair. He raised his Airsoft pistol when he was ten feet from the gamekeeper then, to everyone's shock, he fired six shots into the gamekeeper's puffed-up chest and waited for the natural reaction of the man – to raise his hand to the target area of his chest – before firing one final shot to the back of his hand. The old gamekeeper went red then paled as the pain of the shot to his unprotected hand started to course through his now swollen hand.

'Sir, the rules are there for a reason. As you can now tell at firsthand these are not toys. We all want to have a bit of fun but if you do not want to play by our rules I must ask you to leave.'

Adam did not have long to wait for the old man's decision; he flung the mask on the ground and stomped off in the direction of the car park, the humiliation and the pain clearly too much to bear. Adam supervised a now very quiet group as they tried their weapons before splitting the groups into ten a side, with Callum ushered into one of the teams to replace the departed gamekeeper. Adam and Bob took one team each and refereed the games, only stopping when time and physical fitness both ran out, just on lunchtime.

To Adam and Bob's great relief, after a ropey start the Airsoft games had gone down a treat with every player promising to sign up for a paying game and to bring their friends with them next time. Two or three locals hung back to talk to Adam and Bob about the games, in particular one man who questioned Bob about the last game of the day, the 'killing house'. Bob had constructed a two-storey building with four rooms on each level; each room contained a tailor's dummy hostage along with various tailor's dummy terrorists. There was even a recording system and the players could buy a video as a souvenir of their time on the course. Adam listened in without speaking at first.

'So, you two guys are both ex-army, but where did you serve? Correct me if I'm wrong, but that is the killing house? I mean, that last game is right out of the SAS handbook. Are you guys ex-SAS?'

Bob caught Adam's eye but Adam said nothing; he had warned Bob that creating the killing house would result in some guests who knew a bit about the Special Air Service posing many questions – and he had been proved correct on the very first game.

Bob was like a rabbit caught in the headlights it was Adam who eventually answered the question. 'Bob here was army but I only did a bit of TA. But you're right about the killing house. We got the plans off the internet and thought it would be a bit of a blast trying out the SAS moves, isn't that right, Bob?'

Bob grinned like a Cheshire Cat having been let off the hook.

The conversation was cut short as first Bob, then all who were still present, watched the arrival of Sam kitted out in her running gear making her way up the forest trail at a steady jog while pushing a baby buggy in front of her, Luke bobbing from side to side as the pushchair made its way over the rough terrain. As the rest of the men split up Adam took Sam to one side out of earshot. Over the years, Adam had become an expert in judging Sam and the minute she had made eye contact with him he knew this was no casual visit, no popping by to see how things were going. Sam was here for a reason and by her body language it was something important.

'Hi, Dad, I thought I would bring your son up here to remind him what his father looked like, just in case he'd forgotten you.'

Adam shook his head, frowning. 'Samantha O'Conner, I wasn't born yesterday. Spill the beans, Missus – why are you really here?'

'Adam, I've been thinking about things. I need to end it with MI6. I have spoken to Sue and she's happy to look after Luke for a couple of days while I go down to London and sort things out with Neil Andrews. You're busy so I'm going to take the car Neil left with us, drop it off, sort things out, then fly back to Inverness. I'll give Sue a call when I get back and you can pick me up – what do you think?'

Adam tried hard to keep the concern out of his voice, but he was worried about Sam's latest revelation. 'Sam, cast your mind back, girl, to the first time we met. It was you who told me that once MI6 had its claws into you there was no leaving. What makes you think anything has changed with them? Would it not be better to let things stay as they are at the moment? After all, out of sight out of mind works for me.'

'Don't worry. MI6 have never had to deal with a field agent who's become a mother before. I'll tell them the truth, Adam – there is no way I can work in the field any more. I am compromised. I will never give a hundred per cent knowing I have a child to care for.' Sam leaned forward and kissed Adam gently on the lips before withdrawing, holding his gaze. 'Don't worry, Mac, I love you. I am not running away – our life is here now but I need to draw a line under my past and move on. I'll be back in two days, you have my word on it.'

Before Adam could come up with a good reply Sam had turned the buggy round and headed back down the forest track. Adam wanted to follow her and try to talk her out of this new madness but he had no time; he needed to clean and charge the Airsoft guns and equipment before the imminent arrival of his first paying guests. He watched longingly as Sam slowly slipped out of sight. He knew instinctively when he arrived back at the glass house she would be gone, off on another one of her own private crusades.

Sam stopped at the lodge to drop Luke and his buggy with Sue before jogging the last few hundred metres up the hill to Comriach. She hurriedly packed an overnight bag. Her last task was a visit to the office where she opened the safe and removed cash for the trip. On top of a stack of notes sat her Glock; she picked the weapon up, hesitating. Her natural instinct was to pop it into her handbag, but she hadn't carried the gun for more than two years and the thought of carrying a loaded weapon had become alien to her. Sam placed the Glock back into the safe; after all, she was only going to London to hear what Neil had to say before handing in her resignation, nothing that she needed to be armed for. She checked her mobile phone before leaving – nothing yet from Neil. She smiled to herself; she would call Neil when she got into London. He was not going to have time to set up the agenda or meeting place; she was going to call the shots on this one.

Adam, Bob and Callum watched as the three new Land Rover Discoveries made their way up the forest track in convoy, pulling into the parking area almost as if choreographed. The driver of the lead Discovery was first to leave the vehicle and made a beeline for Adam, offering his hand as he introduced himself and his entourage who were climbing out of the other vehicles.

'Good day – you must be Allan. My name is Serge, and I must say I and my colleagues are looking forward to this.'

Adam introduced Bob and Callum while Serge introduced all twelve of his friends to them.

Bob took charge, showing the safety video which was followed by the gun hand out and demonstration. Adam took the time to study his newly arrived clients. Serge was a small and wiry man, probably in his late forties; he reminded Adam of a bantam-weight boxer. He seemed to be very much in charge of the group; Daniil and Milad seemed to be his closest friends in the group; they were probably both in their thirties and looked tanned and fit. Callum had struck up a conversation with Daniil while everyone except Serge concentrated on the Airsoft demo.

Adam noted that Serge was far more interested in his surroundings and the three of them rather than watching the safety video. While the party tested their new toys, Adam grabbed Callum. 'I see you've made new friends already, Callum. Did you find out anything about our guests?' Adam had tried to keep the question casual but as he had watched the group his curiosity had got the better of him.

'Yes, a fair bit actually. Daniil speaks good English and is very chatty. They're all Ukrainian, working in Aberdeen training on some new type of oil pipeline they're going to be installing back home. Should be good for business, Allan. Oil workers will have plenty money to spend here, I would imagine.'

This news explained a few things; Serge was obviously their foreman and had taken it upon himself to be their spokesperson. The games began and, while at the start of each game Adam explained the game and its rules, when the game got underway Adam stood back to let Bob and Callum assign themselves one to each group. As the games progressed Adam watched Serge interacting with first Bob then Callum as he swapped from team to team. Throughout the afternoon a nagging feeling persisted in the back of Adam's mind. There was nothing he could put his finger on but there were little things that gave him an uneasy feeling in the pit of his stomach, so much so that when the games reached their climax and Adam had explained the killing house to his Ukrainian audience he almost felt glad that this was the last of the games and he could say goodbye to Serge and his workmates.

After the last game Serge arrived at the office while his mates waited in the Discoveries. Serge assured Adam and Bob that they had had a great time but that they needed to get back to Aberdeen for work the next day. Adam and Bob watched as their first paying customers departed while Callum went about gathering the gear for cleaning and charging.

At first there was an uneasy silence between the pair before Adam broke the spell and spoke out. 'Well, Bob, what did you think of our guests today?' Adam had his own thoughts but he wanted to hear what Bob thought before airing his own views on the day's proceedings.

Bob watched the dust settle as the last Discovery vanished from view. 'Something wasn't right with them, mate. I don't know what it was about them, but something was off.'

Adam nodded; Bob had confirmed his own thoughts.

'You're spot on, my old mate. For a start, how did that Serge guy know who I was? There are no pictures of us in our literature but he came straight over to me and used my name.'

Bob was nodding in agreement. 'Adam, you know in a group that size you usually get at least a couple of guys with raw talent when it comes to shooting. That lot couldn't hit the side of a bloody barn this afternoon.'

Adam was again nodding. 'You're right, Bob. Their technique was good but they couldn't hit a thing. Airsoft guns aren't that bad. Jesus, the guys from the pub in the morning were better shots – we better check that the sights are okay.'

Bob was shaking his head and frowning at the suggestion. 'No way did all the weapons go out of spec. I tell you, Adam, if I didn't know better I would say that our Ukrainian friends were deliberately trying to miss. Don't ask me why, but if I was a betting man that would be my shout.'

Adam mulled over what had just been discussed; it made no sense. Why would a group of testosterone-fuelled guys pay all that money to travel halfway across Scotland to play a game to deliberately lose.

Some time later Adam was still puzzling over the strange encounter when Bob let out a howl of laughter. Adam followed Bob's line of sight, his eyes coming to rest on the arrival in the car park of a pale blue VW camper van. No sooner had it pulled up than Callum jumped from the driver's seat, a look of indignation on his face at Bob's antics.

'Jesus, boss, come and look at this, bloody Green Peace have arrived. Callum, son, you never told us you're one of the peace movement – what's with the flower power machine?'

Callum was pale. Adam could tell from his body language that he was not happy with Bob's derogatory comments about his mode of transport.

'Bob, has anyone told you that you have no tact – or taste for that matter. Daisy here is a stunning 1970 example of a Volkswagen Dormobile and she is a very sought-after piece of history.'

Bob winked at Adam then, despite his tongue lashing from Callum, continued his slagging. 'Daisy? You actually call your motor *Daisy*? Jesus, son, I would love to introduce you to some of my old marine pals. Adam, have you got a pair of marigolds and a pinny young Callum could use? I think he would be more at home doing the dishes than handling firearms.'

'So what's with the "Adam" thing? That's twice today you've called Allan Adam.'

Bob looked away, breaking eye contact with his partner and almost seeming embarrassed.

Adam shrugged his shoulders as he turned and headed for Herbie. 'Slip of the tongue, I guess. You guys can lock up – I'm going to head for home to see if my wife has deserted me yet, and I'll pick up the wee man. See you both tomorrow. We still have lots to do here so get a good sleep – we will be busy.'

Adam picked up Luke and in the process found out from Sue that Sam was gone. He concealed his disappointment from Sue who tried to hang on to Luke, but Adam was having none of it. His partner was missing – at least he could now pass the time with his son, catching up for the weeks he had spent building the Airsoft site.

Adam spent the next hour preparing and making a meal for Luke and himself before getting Luke into the bath. At first Luke had despised the bath but over the last six months he had changed; he now did not want to get out of the bath. This had transformed bath times from a dreaded chore into a happy part of the day looked forward to by both child and parents. Adam looked on as Luke hid one of his ducks among the foam from the baby bubble bath; his mind wandered once again to his missing partner. Although Sam was prone to seat-of-the-pants decisions she had settled down since Luke had been born; secretly Adam hoped that this interruption to family life was the last one before Sam completely immersed herself in her new life on the west coast of Scotland.

2

London

Sam made good time after leaving the glass house, only stopping for fuel and a comfort break just north of Birmingham. It was late evening when she rolled the Scirocco to a stop outside the Sheraton Grand Park Lane. She handed the keys to the valet before heading for her room and a well-earned bubble bath. Tomorrow was going to be tough, but Sam was determined she was going to tell Neil enough was enough – she owed it to Adam and Luke.

Next morning Sam was one of the first people to enter the breakfast area. Although few diners were present, every head turned as she glided into the room, such was her presence. Sam's choice of clothing had not been left to chance; she had power dressed that morning in a black, lightly pinstriped Versace business suit over a plum-coloured Givenchy shirt. On her feet she wore a pair of black patent Louis Vuitton heels and carried a matching clutch bag. Unusually for Sam she had not tied her hair up in a ponytail, and instead had left it in the natural state, highlighting her shoulder-length blonde mane. Sam had chosen fresh fruit for her breakfast and as she worked her way through her food she went over the next stage of her plan in her head. Neil was a creature of habit; Sam knew that in about five minutes Neil would leave Aylesbury, heading into the office accompanied by one of his bodyguards. Sam would wait until he was en route before contacting him on her mobile to arrange the meeting place; she had thought long and hard about this and had decided on a place they both knew well.

Sam waited until the waiter had poured her coffee before dialling Neil's number. There was a short pause before his slightly irritated voice answered the call.

'Samantha, rather early in the morning for you, is it not?'

Sam smiled inwardly. She could tell Neil was already on the back foot; he was far more used to calling the shots from his office than getting out-of-the-blue calls from wayward agents.

'I'm here in London, Neil. Meet me in the park at the spot where we captured Areli Benesch. Be there in one hour, Neil, or I'm into the wind.'

'Now wait just one minute – what the hell are you playing at, woman? I need to see you, but in my office, not some bloody picnic in the park.'

Sam cut him off before he could finish his rant. 'One hour, Neil, better get a move on, tell your driver to get his finger out.'

She pressed the red end-call key before Neil said anything else, then switched the phone off before he could call back. Sam knew from previous encounters that Neil would be raging with her.

In a small office inside the Russian Embassy Ludmilla Berkov, a military strategic analyst, clicked off her Tupolev txr listening monitor and headed for Vadek Volkov's office. During her time at the embassy there were very few records of an uncoded telephone being used to contact a British secret service encoded unit. Not only that, but two of the names Volkov had asked questions about on his arrival here had possibly been used in the conversation. Ludmilla dropped the recording of the conversation off with Vadek Volkov and left without waiting for any type of response. She was glad to get clear of his office as he was a pig of a man; only Ludmilla's fear of him outweighed her disgust of him. His arrival at the embassy had been tainted from only his second day in office when one of the chef's assistants accused him of raping her, an accusation that was quickly swept under the carpet by the security team. Ludmilla herself had to fend off unwanted advances by Volkov as he attempted to slip his hand up her skirt while watching her monitor as he checked on her work.

Ludmilla had had the presence of mind to stab the desk with her paper opener only inches from his free hand, sending a clear message to him that any further advances of his wandering hand would have dire consequences for him. Ludmilla heard no more from him that morning after dropping off the phone conversation file, although she did detect a certain amount of coming and going from his office.

Thirty minutes after leaving his office Ludmilla witnessed the departure by the side entrance of Vadek Volkov and three of his security detail. Ludmilla was no naive young secretary; she knew that her actions against Volkov would have repercussions for her. She seized the opportunity and, grabbing a folder as cover, headed straight up to Volkov's office. Luckily for her, Volkov's PA was nowhere to be found and Ludmilla slipped into his office unnoticed. This man was a pig in more ways than one; his desk was littered with correspondence. Ludmilla suspected none of this would be of great importance, instead targeting the drawer directly in front of Volkov's chair. The drawer was not locked and on inspection of its contents Ludmilla's attention was drawn to the blue personnel file hidden below two other files. As she had suspected, Volkov had not taken her rejection of his advances well.

A paper A4 sheet clipped to her records was a copy of an email sent that morning to the political department in Moscow warning them that members of the London embassy staff had noted that Ludmilla Berkov had been failing in her duties and had become influenced by western culture. Vadek Volkov had requested her return to Mother Russia with immediate effect, where he recommended she be put through a correction programme and inquiry to establish if any classified information had been passed to foreign powers.

Ludmilla was beside herself with fury; she could barely stop her hand trembling as she replaced the personnel file back in the drawer. This monster was going to ruin her career, if not her life, and all because she had defended herself against his unwanted sexual advances. Ludmilla forced herself to calm down trying to think of a way out of this nightmare. It was then she spotted the marking on the top file; the file was Russian military issue and marked 'Top Secret – no copying or unauthorised distribution'. Ludmilla thought for a second; maybe she could use this file to discredit Volkov and land him in trouble for letting the file go public. She quickly thumbed through the file, taking a picture of each page with her phone. The second file had no such markings, but Ludmilla decided to photograph the contents anyway. She was halfway through when she heard voices outside the door. She quickly returned the files to the drawer and headed for the door, exiting just as the building's security chief stopped in his tracks and regarded her with curiosity. Ludmilla was falling to pieces mentally but outwardly she managed to maintain a facade of business as usual.

'Good day, Peter. Vadek is not in, if that is who you are looking for. He left some time ago.' Ludmilla gave no explanation why she had just left his office but brandished the file in front of her, making it obvious that was what she had come for. Peter thanked her then turned and headed down the corridor back the way he had just come. He would not think anything out of the ordinary was happening, she hoped; after all, Ludmilla was a trusted operative with one of the highest security clearances in the building. Ludmilla's legs were like jelly as she made her way back to her office. She had heard the rumours about Vadek Volkov: he was not a man you would want to cross. She had a feeling if she messed this up and Volkov found out she wouldn't need to worry about being transferred home in disgrace. She would be a dead woman.

Samantha O'Conner finished her second cup of coffee, checked her watch, then decided it was time to make a move. After leaving a generous tip with the staff she headed out of the hotel, turning right on Piccadilly and taking in a few shop windows at a leisurely pace, making the most of her return to the capital but heading in the general direction of Hyde Park. Once in the park Sam strolled along the same footpath that only a few years ago she had sprinted along in pursuit of one of Mossad's most dangerous assassins. When Sam had contacted Neil she was aware she was not scrambled and her conversation was open to the world, so her meeting place had been specifically picked so that only four people knew of it; two were now dead, so only Sam and

Neil knew the location of the meeting place. The weather could not have been better as Sam ambled along in no great hurry. If she arrived a few minutes late so be it; today she was setting the agenda. Dictating when she arrived would be up to her and would set the tone for the rest of the meeting.

Although it was still early, Hyde Park was filling up with park goers eager to make the most of a beautiful day. Sam smiled as a couple with their young boy passed going in the opposite direction. The young lad wobbled from side to side on his stabilisers as he struggled to master the art of balancing a bike. Sam made a mental note to return to London with Adam and Luke once things had been smoothed over with MI6.

Some distance behind the family two police officers in high viz jackets patrolled the park walkway; the young male officer took more than a cursory glance as Sam passed. To Sam's amusement his colleague, an older female officer, reprimanded him for paying too much attention to the pretty girls in the park. As Sam walked her mind returned to the present situation. She was sure Neil would try the softly, softly approach to get her to stay at Six first, then when he was getting nowhere he would no doubt use blackmail, bringing up the matter of the ownership of the glass house. Sam was not worried by this; Neil had far too many skeletons in his closet to be throwing his weight around. Unfortunately for him it was Sam who had worked on a lot of Neil's under-the-counter operations. He knew fine well that Sam could do just as much damage to his life as he could to hers, so it was stalemate.

Sam knew in her heart that by lunchtime today she would officially be a free woman – today would be the first day of the rest of her life. The thought of it put a spring in her step and she increased her walking pace in anticipation of her meeting with Neil.

Neil found a bench facing out over Hyde Park just over from a circular park shop. A quick glance around the area told him he had arrived at Samantha's designated meeting place. His driver for today was Alec, a royal protection officer from the Met who had been drafted in as holiday cover. Alec took up position by the nearest tree to get eyes on everyone in the immediate vicinity.

Neil was not a happy camper; yes, he needed to speak to Samantha urgently but he did not like being told what to do. Although professionally they had been together for a long time there was friction between them; it was only because Sam was so bloody good at her job that Neil cut her so much slack. He was reminiscing about the fact that Samantha had almost become his sister-in-law when he spotted her some way off marching towards him. The perfectly still weather seemed to be changing; a breeze had started to ruffle the leaves on the trees. Out of the corner of his eye Neil saw Alec momentarily move his gaze upwards to the sky then, for the first time, Neil's ears picked up the hum from above. He looked up himself just as a camera drone came into view above the trees; it was the downwash from the drone's hard-working propellers that was moving the leaves on the trees, not a breeze as he first thought. Neil was aware of Alec starting to move his way when he heard an audible click above him just at the same time as Alec burst into a sprint, heading his way flat out.

From Sam's vantage point she could see it was too late. The device dropped from the drone, landing nose down less than a metre behind Neil, the pressure cap in its nose making perfect contact with the ground and detonating instantly. What happened next was too horrific even for Sam's trained mind. Neil had clearly been the target and was killed instantly. The fragmentation device was a blunt instrument designed to kill everything in the immediate vicinity. No one at that point could have saved Neil; Sam wanted to look away but she was frozen to the spot, an unwilling spectator in the unfolding carnage. All Neil's bodyguard had managed to do was bring himself within range of the deadly explosion. He was hit in the head by shrapnel and died almost before he hit the ground. An old lady walking her terrier was almost as close as Neil and was cut to pieces in the hail of shrapnel; a jogger and a young couple who were unlucky to be passing at that exact second were also hit and cut down; some others by the coffee shop were wounded, but they were at the limit of the device's lethal range and stood a fighting chance of survival.

For a fraction of a second Sam looked on at the carnage dumbstruck and in a state of shock. Neil was all but gone; only a dishevelled bundle of smouldering clothes lay where seconds ago he had been sitting on the bench. The old lady lay just behind Neil facing upwards, her lower body at a grotesque angle to the rest of her body. She was still clutching a dog lead while miraculously her pet dog howled and whimpered but seemed untouched by the hell that had just been unleashed on the park. Behind them lay a small group of bodies. As Sam approached she could see that at least one of them was beyond help, his lower half twisted and tangled, his legs and intestines not in their natural position. Sam should have stopped to help the others but her head was elsewhere. *Who did this? Where are they?*

Sam had spotted something. She wasn't sure but she knew she had to check it out. Pulling her heels off she took off at a sprint heading to the edge of the park towards the main road. Had it been a branch of a tree moving? She was not sure, but there was no wind. Sam was the only one running that way – people were running into the park to see what had happened. She kept going; just as she was about to give up she was rewarded: an individual in a white hooded overall was loading a black drone into the back of a white unmarked Transit van. It was the drone landing that Sam had spotted in her peripheral vision. The hooded figure spotted Sam exactly the same second she clocked him, and the look of panic on his face confirmed his guilt to Sam. Sam was eighty metres from the van and started sprinting towards it. The hoodie banged heavily on the side of the van before launching himself into the back as the van screeched into life, flying backwards along the street with Sam in hot pursuit. The van carried out an expert reverse turn, almost going over on its side before the driver regained control and thrashed the van away from a standing start.

During the manoeuvre Sam had got close and for a few seconds she managed to maintain the gap, hoping the van would get snarled up in traffic and allow her to make contact with the evil bastards who had just murdered her boss and a handful of innocent bystanders into the bargain. Sam cursed as she ran for not bringing her Glock with her but despite maintaining an Olympic pace over a distance of three streets her efforts were in vain; the van was clear of traffic and gone. Sam stopped on a street corner, holding herself up by a one-way road sign, as grief finally overtook the ebbing adrenalin rush.

Sam sobbed uncontrollably; her perfect morning had just turned to hell and the enormity of what had just happened had started to sink in.

The head of MI6 had been assassinated in broad daylight in the centre of London. The next thought in Sam's head brought her back from the edge of despair; instead the cold chill of fear coursed through her body. There would be a manhunt in the capital for Sir Neil Andrews' killer; the powers that be outside the inner circle of MI6 would find out that it was her who had initiated the spur-of-the-moment meeting and there were plenty of witnesses who saw her in the park, one of whom was a police officer who couldn't take his eyes off her. Also she had run from the scene of the crime and she was well known for having a stormy relationship with her boss. In addition, Sam knew MI5, who would undoubtedly lead the investigation, were aware that she was a trained killer; it wasn't good … Sam knew she could be in big trouble.

It took Sam a few seconds to decide on the only plan that would give her a chance to get her side of the story out before she was captured in what surely would turn out to be a witch hunt.

While Londoners were finding out about the events in Hyde Park, Sam pulled herself together and made her way back through crowded streets towards her hotel. The scream of sirens filled the air. Police car after police car passed, presumably on their way to cordon off Hyde Park. Sam made it back to the hotel to find a group of people watching a news flash on the big screen TV in the foyer. She glanced at the screen as she passed, heading for reception. The banner at the bottom of the screen read 'Terrorist Attack in Hyde Park'. Sam wondered how long it would be before her face ended up on the big screen.

Reunited with the Scirocco, Sam found she had to take a number of detours as roads had been closed to allow emergency services direct access to Hyde Park. On arrival at Vauxhall Cross she pulled up by the barrier where a stony-faced guard regarded her with cold eyes.

Jean had taken advantage of the unexpected free time afforded to her after her boss had called unexpectedly to say he would be late in to-day. She had just left the canteen after finishing a cooked breakfast – the first she had managed in years. She was in the corridor when she bumped into one of the young trainee assistants who had been working with her, who informed her that there had been another terrorist attack in London. She excused herself and hurried back to the office to get things ready for the inevitable explosion of activity.

Jean was surprised not to find Neil barking orders at her. She decided to take the bull by the horns and call him in case he was unaware of the attack. She tried the number three times with the same result: number unattainable. Jean changed her plans; she needed to have things in motion when Neil arrived. The first thing he would want to know was if a COBRA meeting was being called by the PM and if so, when. He would want to speak to his opposite number, Bill Mathews, at MI5 before the meeting.

Jean was about to call the Home Office when her phone rang, Jean half expected Neil to be on the other end of the line, but it was a voice she was not familiar with.

'Excuse me, is that Jean, Jean Mitchell?'

Jean looked down at her phone display to see that the call had been put through from the gatehouse. 'Yes, gatehouse, this is Jean Mitchell, Sir Neil Andrews' PA. How can I help you?'

'Ma'am, I have a woman here seems very agitated … says she's with MI6 but has no ID. I was going to send her on her way but she is very insistent I tell you two words: "Red Vixen". Does that mean anything, ma'am, or do you want me to get rid of her?'

Jean froze. Red Vixen was Samantha O'Conner's emergency call sign. 'Put her on the line, gatehouse, I need to speak to her.' There was a short pause while Jean held her breath.

'Jean, it's Sam. You need to let me in – I need to speak to you urgently. Please, Jean, you know it's me.'

The guard had been correct – Sam did sound distraught. That worried Jean because she knew Sam; it must have taken something big to upset her – normally she was unflappable. Jean had watched this girl having a bullet wound stitched with no anaesthetic and she'd been less concerned than she was now. 'No problem, Sam, we just need to get your ID sorted, then we can have a chat.'

Before Jean could finish Sam exploded. 'No, Jean, I need in now! It's Neil, he's gone. I need to speak to someone now!'

'What do you mean *gone*, Sam, where has he gone?' Jean had a sinking feeling but she refused to believe this mad call without further confirmation

'Let me in, Jean, for god's sake! Someone assassinated Neil. I was there, Jean, and you need to let me in so I can speak to someone.'

Jean dispatched security to escort Sam from the car park to Neil's office. While she waited for the unexpected meeting with Sam she studied her complexion in the bathroom mirror. She couldn't stop her hands trembling as she rearranged a loose hair that had escaped from her tight bun; her grey hair gave the effect of a pale complexion, but this morning she really was grey in the face as well. She heard the outer office door open and close but her legs refused to move. She didn't want to face Sam – she wasn't sure if she could maintain her composure in her presence.

Sam's voice in the outer office startled her back into action. 'Jean, did you know that when my sister was killed and I pestered Neil to train me as an agent it was her call sign that Neil gave me: Red Vixen. It was her red hair, you know – that's where the name came from. He wasn't all that bad, you know. He'll be with her now, together at last.'

Jean walked from the toilet into the office where to her surprise she found Sam standing there, tears rolling down her pink cheeks. Jean said nothing but took Sam's hand. Together they walked into Neil's office where she sat Sam down, then she closed the door. She opened the bureau behind Neil's desk and took out two glasses and a bottle of eighteen-year-old Arran single malt whisky, then poured them a very large dram each. Jean knocked her glassful back in one go. 'Tell me, Sam, the whole story. I need to hear it with my own ears before I drop the bombshell on Downing Street.'

Jean listened intently while Sam told her the whole story from the beginning. Sam came to the end of her tale and both women sat for a second before Jean, who was sitting in Neil's chair, sighed and picked up the phone, pressed a pre-set button and waited while the call was put through. Jean may not have been an agent but when it came to navigating her way around Whitehall, she was a master. 'Hello, this is Sir Neil Andrews' PA. I have Sir Neil on the line waiting to speak to the Home Secretary. Please inform the minister the call is urgent.' Jean caught Sam's eye while she waited on the line and gave her a reassuring wink.

'Good morning, Home Secretary, this is Jean Mitchell, Sir Neil's personal assistant. No, minister, Sir Neil is not here. I used his name to get to you fast. I will not waste time, minister. I have terrible news. Sir Neil Andrews was one of the people killed in the Hyde Park bombing this morning.'

Jean struggled to hold herself together as she spoke, a tear escaping from the corner of her eye; she brushed it away continuing with the conversation. 'No, minister, I do not believe it to be a mistake. One of our agents was due to meet Sir Neil in the park and witnessed the attack. Minister, you need to know that our agent is sure Sir Neil Andrews was the target – the others were purely collateral damage. Minister, I apologise for contacting you in this manner but you will need the information for the PM and the COBRA meeting – someone just targeted the heart of our security services. Yes, minister, I will wait for further instruction. Yes, Samantha O'Conner our agent is here with me. Goodbye.'

3

Bill Mathews

Bill Mathews was having a week off. He had just finished lunch and had returned to his beloved garden to potter about when he heard the screech of tyres outside his home in Merlin Crescent. Bill frowned, making a mental note to have a word with the police commissioner about young idiots with cars in Harrow. Being the head of MI5 had its perks, one of which was when you talked to the commissioner about something it usually got his undivided attention. Bill was deadheading a rose bush when his side gate burst open and four of his MI5 men marched across his lawn towards him.

One of the four was Dan Massey, an agent who had worked with Bill on security assignments previously. It was Dan who spoke before the shell-shocked head of MI5 found his tongue.

'Mr Mathews, you need to come with us, sir, we have a car waiting. This is a matter of national security. The prime minister needs you in a COBRA meeting. We are here to make sure you get there, sir.'

Bill Mathews finally found his tongue after the initial shock. 'Dan, what the hell is going on? I have attended dozens of these things. Never have I been given an escort.'

'Neil Andrews bought it today, sir. We have intel says he was targeted. All agencies are on high alert in case of further attempts on key personnel – you are pretty near the top of the list, hence the reason we are here, sir.'

Bill felt the colour drain from his face; his secateurs fell from his grip onto his manicured lawn. 'Holy shit, who the hell had the balls to kill the head of MI6?What the hell happened, Dan?'

'Let's get you into the car first, sir, then I'll tell you as much as we know so far.' Mathews was about to protest when a fifth agent appeared from inside his house carrying one of his suits and a bag of his clothes. 'Sir, we really need to get going. Phil has packed you an overnight bag and has contacted your wife to let her know you have been called to Downing Street on urgent business. Your wife will have round-the-clock police protection until this mess is sorted out. We're going straight to Downing Street at the request of the PM. I hate to be a pain, sir, but can we get going?'

Bill Mathews spent two hours with the PM and the rest of the COBRA committee before leaving Downing Street headed for Vauxhall Cross. Bill was thankful of the time alone in the armour-plated Jaguar to gather his thoughts. He had started the morning on leave, looking forward to some private time with Millie, and only six hours later he had been asked by the prime minister and the COBRA committee, in light of the grave security situation, to take the reins of both MI5 and MI6 until further notice. Mathews knew this would be a struggle for one person. For some time now he had contemplated retirement; taking on a new challenge was not on his agenda. MI5 alone had become a huge challenge since the rise of Islamic extremism in the UK; looking after Great Britain's security abroad was not a task he thought could be added to his already huge workload.

Jean packed Sam off to the staff canteen to get something to eat; although Sam protested that she had no appetite Jean would not take no for an answer, assuring her that as soon as she heard anything she would send for her. Jean had been sent word that Bill Mathews was on his way and to afford him every assistance he required, and she wanted Sam out of the way so she could explain Sam's presence before Mathews asked to see her. Jean was not sure if the pair had met before, so she needed to warn Mathews of Sam's sometimes volatile temperament.

Jean was in the process of gathering Neil Andrews' personal effects and packing them into a box for storage when she became aware of someone standing behind her; she turned to find Bill Mathews watching her without speaking. Although startled she managed to remain calm as she turned to face MI5's top man. 'I would say good afternoon, Mr Mathews, but under the circumstances I don't think that is the correct phrase. What do you need, sir? Just say the word and I'll get right on it.'

Bill Mathews crossed the room and sat on the edge of Neil's desk, studying Jean before speaking. 'Jean, we have met on a daily basis and yet we don't really know one another. Please believe me when I say I am truly sorry to have lost Neil. He was a huge asset to the security of this country. I can't help feeling that I've been left holding the baby here. It's well known that you have been a great help to Neil and indeed the other MI6 directors you have worked with in the past. You know running both departments is truly an impossible task but for the moment, in the circumstances, we will have to try. I'll need your help to get through this and I'm not just talking about cups of tea here. You know the score and you help run the show here, so I'm counting on you to keep me on the right track.'

Truth be told, Jean had never been a fan of Bill Mathews; she had always found him a sullen, dour character, but then again at first she did not rate Neil Andrews either. He'd had an ego the size of Mount Everest, but over the years she came to admire his devotion to the job and his disregard for political correctness. In the light of Bill Mathews' statement Jean decided to give him the benefit of the doubt and throw her weight behind his efforts to run both security services.

'Mr Mathews, you can count on me. After all, we have to find out who killed poor Neil – the reputation of both Five and Six depend upon it, sir.'

Bill Mathews nodded thoughtfully. He would be under a huge amount of pressure to find the perpetrator of today's terrible act.

'Good, strong coffee and a list of things I need to do here would be good, but first, Jean, can you get me Chris Oliver at Thames House and then the police officer in charge of the Hyde Park bombing. After that I had better speak to Samantha O'Conner.'

Jean nodded without speaking then left the office intent on carrying out her instructions.

Two minutes later Neil's phone buzzed. Bill Mathews walked round the desk, finding it strangely awkward to sit in Neil's chair for the first time.

'Jesus Christ, Bill, am I glad to hear your voice. The office has gone mad – the Home Office has never been off the bloody phone and the place is in total lockdown. We have staff that can't even get near the building. The Home Secretary went mental when she found out you were on leave – practically threatened to have me sacked if I didn't deliver you to her at Number Ten.'

Bill Mathews listened for a second before stopping Chris Oliver in his tracks. 'Listen up, Chris, this is your big chance to shine. A lot of high-ranking people will be watching how we handle this situation. I need you to step up a gear. For the moment I'll be working from Vauxhall Cross – I've been put in charge of Six so I need you to keep things going for me at Thames House: cancel all leave. I need you to get hold of John Sullivan at GCHQ – we need to find out if there's any chatter about Hyde Park, in particular Neil Andrews. No one knows of his death, so any mention of him needs to be investigated. Chris, whoever did this has sent a statement of intent. None of your agents makes house calls unarmed and without SCO19 backup – do I make myself very clear? I need to talk to some people so I need to go. If you need me call here and ask for Jean. She will find me. I made you my number two for a reason – it's time to prove to me I made the right choice. Good luck, Chris, and be careful – we don't know what we're dealing with yet.'

Bill's next call was to Commander Devlin, one of the Metropolitan Police's rising stars who had made his name in the antiterrorist unit as a no-nonsense badass.

'Commander Devlin, I need you to bring me up to speed on the investigation so far, please.'

Devlin wasted no time with niceties. 'Seven dead, sir, a further twelve wounded, three critically, final death toll expected to be nine. We have just found the van abandoned in Croydon. One Asian male was challenged at the scene and was shot dead by SCO19 officers before he could use the suicide vest he was wearing. Bomb squad are en route to make explosives safe. The Hyde Park bomb was delivered by a drone that we've found in the van. The bomb itself was high-yield explosive of military quality. Unfortunately, sir, it has just been confirmed Sir Neil Andrews and Sergeant Alec Davies were two of the fatalities.'

Bill Mathews breathed a little easier at the news of the van and the dead terrorist. 'In your opinion, Commander, was this a terrorist attack?'

Devlin for a second paused before replying. 'Yes, Director Mathews, in my opinion probably Islamic State related, but the investigation is ongoing. We will keep you informed.'

Bill Mathews smiled to himself; Commander Devlin was looking to take all the glory. Mathews was no longer interested in the glory side of things, but he knew from bitter experience that sometimes things got overlooked when the glory hunters took charge.

'No need, Commander Devlin. I will have two of my men, Dan Massey and Phil Thomson, with you shortly. They can keep me informed of progress. Thank you for your time.'

Bill wasted no time calling Chris Oliver back and requesting both agents get themselves to Croydon post-haste to take charge of the developing situation.

Mathews was just about to call Jean into the office when she knocked then entered as if clairvoyant.

'Ah, there you are, Jean. Could you find Samantha O'Conner for me and get her down here.'

Jean walked over to the desk and placed an A4 sheet of paper in front of Mathews while holding on to a rather large portable file carrier. 'Mr Mathews, just a bit of information for you before Samantha arrives. She had arranged to meet Neil privately in Hyde Park to discuss her resignation from the service. Samantha is now a mother – she feels that she can no longer carry on. You did ask for my help. My advice to you would be to tread lightly with her. I can tell that Samantha thinks somehow Neil's death is her doing. As for the A4 sheet, the building is now at security level Black. You will be aware of procedures at Thames House but not here – this sheet details our procedure. In particular, may I draw your attention to the two new security guards in the hall – they may ask for ID because they are covert special forces soldiers. I have seen at first-hand what happens to anyone who ignores their request. We've had to take one of our cabinet ministers to hospital to have his dislocated shoulder put back in after he attempted to threaten one of the guards.' Jean had a wicked twinkle in her eye as she spoke to Mathews but refrained from smiling.

Bill Mathews on the other hand picked up on Jean's amusement at the situation and broke out in a beaming smile as he replied to her. 'I will make sure I treat them with respect, Jean – after all, it wouldn't look good if I ended up frogmarched out of the building on my first day here. Jean, I don't like the look of that file carrier you're holding on to for dear life. Tell me that isn't paperwork I need to sign?'

Jean placed the heavy metal cantilever file carrier on Neil's desk before handing Mathews the key for it. She hesitated for a second before speaking. 'Sir Neil Andrews only ever asked me to do one thing in the event of his death. I know you're up to your neck in it, sir, but Neil implored me to hand over this file immediately to his successor in the event of his death. He never said why but it seemed very important to him. Now I've done what he asked I will leave you and send in Samantha. She will be here shortly – I'll tell her just to knock and come in, sir.'

Mathews toyed with the idea of opening the folders but decided against it for the moment; he was far more interested in finding out details of the Hyde Park incident from the eyewitness account of Samantha O'Conner. The files could wait until later.

Sam had crossed paths with Bill Mathews on a few occasions in her line of work; occasionally MI6 and MI5 conflicted with one another, but it was usually Neil who sorted things out with Mathews. Sam entered Neil's office and sat down, not knowing what to expect; this was her first one-to-one, face-to-face meeting with the MI5 director. Mathews invited her to tell her side of the story and sat quietly taking notes until she had finished before asking her a couple of questions to clarify things. Sam was surprised by his calm, quiet inquiry; she had expected more of a grilling from him. After he had finished questioning her it was Sam's turn to ask the questions.

'Director Mathews, do you have any intel on the attackers yet? I was thinking about contacting drone manufacturers – that one looked a bit special – it might give us a lead, you never know.'

Mathews was shaking his head. 'No need, Samantha – we have the drone, the van and one of the attackers. They were found this afternoon by a police arms unit in South Croydon. Unfortunately the attacker tried to detonate a suicide vest and was shot and killed by the police – early signs point to an Islamic State sponsored attack.'

Sam shook her head at the last statement. 'I would doubt that, sir. Since when did Islamic State start recruiting Europeans to their cause?'

Mathews had been studying his notes while Sam spoke; he stopped and looked up at Sam, a worried look on his face. 'The man the police gunned down was Asian, Sam.'

Again Sam shook her head, this time more vigorously. 'No, sir. The two men were European and were wearing white coveralls. There were no Asian men with them.'

Sam was waiting for Mathews to question the reliability of her statement, but instead he reached over the desk, a thoughtful expression on his face as he buzzed for Jean. Before he had a chance to say anything further Jean was by Sam's side.

'Jean, can you arrange for Samantha to stay somewhere tonight and we'll start again fresh tomorrow? Samantha, I want you on top form tomorrow. You will have mugshots to look at and I want you to help with an artist's drawing of the two men you saw in the van.'

Sam was about to complain when she felt Jean's hand on her shoulder silently telling her to politely wind her neck back in.

'Mr Mathews, Sam will stay with me at my house tonight – I'll feel safer with her there after today. If they can get to the director what hope have any of us if we become a target.'

Mathews nodded in agreement and said goodnight to the two women. Just as Jean and Sam reached the office door he spoke again. 'One last thing, ladies. I might not have the charisma that Neil had, but I am good at my job. We will work as a team and we will get these bastards. Get some sleep tonight – we have a busy day tomorrow, all of us.'

Mathews returned from the vending machine brandishing a large can of Red Bull. As he had suspected, the forensic reports on the crime scene and the findings so far on the van and the bomber were waiting for him; his men had pushed the investigating team to the limit. Tomorrow, when the world found out that the head of MI6 had been assassinated, things would get crazy and he needed to have answers ready for all the relevant people.

After a troubled read of the new documents Mathews at last turned his attention to the files that Jean had handed over to him from Neil Andrews. He was not sure what he was going to find as he cranked open the locked folders. He started at the front, intending to work his way back through the packed folders. Each folder had a heading tab attached and Mathews noted that more than half of the files were labelled with people's names. The first name was the prime minister's; it turned out the folder was a dossier on the past misadventures of the PM. Mathews thumbed through the names: politicians, royals, police, secret service, judges, lords. There were names in these folders from all sections of the upper echelons of power in Britain. Bill pulled file after file, each one packed with unsavoury information about the person in question. Mathews was shocked at some of the revelations unfolding before his very eyes; realisation of the power he held in his hands was also starting to dawn on him. No wonder Neil Andrews was so good at this power game – he had held all the aces in the form of these files.

Mathews' eyes came to rest on one particular file which bore his name. With some trepidation he pulled the file; he was fairly certain that Andrews had nothing on him, but if so why the file? To Mathews' horror he was looking down at pictures of himself and a young woman sitting on his lap as he stared longingly into her ample cleavage. It only took a millisecond for him to realise the pictures had been taken at an office Christmas party where he had ended up very drunk. The pictures were accompanied by a copy of an official government complaint and report of misconduct issued against him by presumably the owner of the cleavage. He had known nothing about any of this; not surprisingly the civil servant who had investigated the fictitious claim was himself the subject of one of Neil Andrews' naughty boy folders, having been removed from a brothel by the boys in blue. Putting two and two together there was no wonder he had forged the report to save his own neck. Mathews was raging; if Andrews had lived he would have received a punch in the mouth for dragging his name through the mud and using concocted evidence to do it.

After the revelations of the first half of Neil Andrews' folder, wild horses would not have stopped Mathews from trolling through the rest of the files. As Bill worked his way to the back of the file it became clear to him that the files pertained to past 'need to know', under-the-counter operations that MI6 had been involved with but had never been recorded in official paperwork; it became clear to him that Samantha O'Conner featured heavily in these files. More than once Mathews had to stop and reread certain paragraphs in wonder and sometimes in disbelief. It was no surprise that they had been filed away; if these files had reached the public domain many heads would be on the chopping block and number one would have been Sir Neil Andrews, closely followed by Samantha O'Conner.

Sam was awake early and tiptoed down Jean's stairs in an attempt not to wake her up. Jean's house was beautifully decorated and spotlessly clean, if somewhat dated. Sam had noted that the house phone was located in the hall on a period table. She had discovered on her way back from Vauxhall Cross that the battery of her mobile phone had drained, so any thoughts of calling to first find out how Luke had been getting on without her and to get Sue to ask Adam to get in touch with her urgently had to wait. To Sam's dismay when she had awoken the battery had taken no charge and had died again the minute it was switched on. She had decided the next best course of action was to borrow Jean's house phone to make the call from the hall. Sam had no sooner sat quietly down at the phone table when a voice behind her startled her.

'Good morning, Samantha, the kettle is on if you fancy tea. If I were you I would think long and hard before using an unprotected phone line. I take it you were about to call home? I think after the events of yesterday and a new boss in charge it would be advisable to toe the line, at least for today. Come on, let's have breakfast then head into the office before things get mad. You can call home from a protected line before the big news about Neil Andrews breaks today.'

Sam thought for a second then nodded without saying anything; she followed Jean into her kitchen. Over breakfast the talk was polite if a little strained. Sam had never considered Jean a friend, although she had high respect for her professionally. There was an age gap and a line Jean apparently would not cross; Sam on the other hand had crossed many lines and until now had never been afraid to risk everything in pursuit of her objective. Both women had made considerable sacrifices for MI6. Jean had never married, instead working long hours as personal assistant to a string of MI6 directors. She had never put her life on the line like Sam, but her private life had been more or less destroyed by her devotion to her work, a fact of which Sam was well aware. Although not friends it was this mutual sacrifice for a cause they both believed in that bonded them.

Transport in the city that morning had ground to a halt as the two women travelled together to the office. Security checks at many buildings had been increased since the government announced it had introduced the highest terrorist threat level.

As Sam and Jean listened to the morning news in the taxi on the way, the reporter live in Hyde Park queried why this had happened, adding that Downing Street was about to make a statement on the Hyde Park bombing that morning.

Jean decided a few streets from Vauxhall Bridge that they should complete the rest of their journey on foot to speed things up. As soon as the pair entered the building they were approached by one of Jean's colleagues who informed them that Bill Mathews wanted to see Sam in his office the minute she got in. If Jean was surprised he was in before them she said nothing, but Sam quietly fumed; yet again her plans to phone home had hit the rocks. God only knew when she would get out of there; all she wanted to do now was go home to Luke and Adam.

4

Uncovered

S am knocked then entered the office in search of Bill Mathews.
She was somewhat taken aback by the scene that greeted her. Bill
Mathews was in his shirt sleeves with no tie; three empty coffee cups
adorned his desk. He was pale and dark rings had formed under his
heavy-looking eyes. It was clear to see that he had not beaten them in
this morning; the fact was he had never left.

'Ah, Samantha, there you are. Pull up a chair – we have a lot to talk
about.'

Sam sat down after taking off her coat while Bill buzzed Jean on the
intercom and asked her to get them both coffees.

'We have three main areas we need to talk about this morning so
first I'll bring you up to speed on the investigation. The Asian male shot
dead was called Aifa Jiskani, a Pakistani national here on a student
visa. He has been linked by GCHQ to the Syrian warlord Tarek Attar
and his murderous group the SAR Mu Haar Ib. These people are our
sworn enemies and I have no doubt that given the opportunity they
would strike us down. But you know, Samantha, it's all a bit too neat
for my liking – there are a number of things that do not tie up. You said
yourself that the two men you saw were not Asians. Also a drone strike
– not their style I would have thought. But the most damning evidence
was what killed poor old Neil.

'The explosive was a modified anti-personnel mine dropped from
the drone. The mine was of Russian origin – in itself inconclusive, but

both the drone and the type of explosive used points the finger firmly at the Russians. Not only that, examination of the suicide vest Aifa Jiskani was wearing tells a strange tale: there was no way he could have detonated the vest because its manual controls had never been connected. It was rigged to blow by remote control. Luckily for us, Aifa in his haste to put the vest on dislodged one of the control wires. We were bloody lucky – there was enough Russian DSA2 explosive in the vest to bring down a building or, as we now suspect, to obliterate any evidence from the Hyde Park assassination. I have spoken overnight with Bruce Ellis of the CIA and we both agree that this operation bear all the hallmarks of a Russian undercover operation.

'So I think we will let the Russians and the public believe we have bought the story they're trying to make us swallow. I have instructed my counterpart at GCHQ to leak to the press some of the information about Aifa Jiskani and his friends. If the Russians think we've bought the story maybe they'll drop their guard long enough for us to nail the real bastards who thought they could get away with this.

'And that is where you come into the story, Miss O'Conner. We will need our very best people on this and that includes you. Extended maternity leave just finished, it's time to polish up those skills of yours that made Sir Neil Andrews rate you so highly.'

On hearing Bill Mathews' last comment Sam shot to her feet. Her coat, which had been across her knees, fell to the ground and for a second the old Sam was back ready to fight her corner. 'No, Mr Mathews, that will not be happening. The only reason I agreed to meet Neil was to hand him my resignation. Nothing you say will make me change my mind, not even Neil's death will bring me back. I have a young child and a partner in my life. I'm finished with MI6. I'm sorry, but that is the way it has to be.'

Sam had expected an equal reaction from Mathews over her decision but to her surprise he took her outburst very calmly, too calmly.

Mathews leaned under his desk and retrieved two folders. 'I suspected as much, Samantha, but I think you may wish to change your mind shortly. Please let me explain. Last night I came into possession of Neil Andrews' files. On examination of these files I discovered why Neil Andrews was so desperate to meet up with you, even to the extent of breaching protocol to meet you, at your request, in the park, a fact confirmed to me by a friend at GCHQ who intercepted your non-scrambled call to Neil that morning. The reality is that GCHQ were not the only ones listening that morning – that's how they knew he would be in the park – maybe not the exact location, but FSB knew Benesch was captured in Hyde Park. You gave the Russians a window of opportunity and a defined area to search. I think you owe it to Neil to help find his killers because you most probably put him in great danger by your actions, but you're not a stupid girl. I think you already knew this.

'Anyway, to get back to the point, some years ago you embarked on a mission to eliminate a Russian drug ring operating from Iceland bringing in drugs and the occasional Russian undercover agent. You were successful in doing this and the group were eliminated. The woman in charge of operations, who you killed, was Alina Orlov. Her husband Alexi Orlov was also eliminated in Moscow by a fellow field agent, bringing their illegal operation to a close. I'm sure these names will have jogged your memory. I can tell from your expression that you're wondering what that has to do with anything.'

Sam nodded hesitantly in agreement with Bill Mathews' observation.

'It was Neil who put two and two together before the shit hit the whirly thing, only I think they got to him before he got to you. Have you heard of the new Russian ambassador to the United Kingdom, Vadek Volkov?'

Sam shook her head but still said nothing, wondering where this was going.

'No, I didn't think that kind of information would bother you out in the sticks. Apart from the fact that he comes with a bad reputation it didn't bother me much either, but it bothered Sir Neil Andrews big time. You see, he knew something no one else knew: Alina Orlov, before she was married, was Alina Volkov, Vadek Volkov's baby sister.'

Sam was frozen to the spot. She could feel her blood running cold and her dark past rising from the ashes to confront her.

'Ah, I see that touched a nerve, Samantha. Please let me continue for there is more, much more. Vadek Volkov is a drug dealer and a club owner who has moved into the arms business, not exactly what you would call a suitable candidate for ambassador to the UK. It would appear that he has some hold over the Russian premier and demanded the post be given to him.

'Samantha, the penny dropped with Sir Neil. Volkov has no interest in the Russian Embassy or the role as ambassador. He came here for one thing and one thing only: he is here for you, Samantha. He wants revenge for his baby sister. Somehow he has found out it was you who killed her and he's after you – that was what Neil Andrews was about to tell you before he was killed. I can't prove it yet but my gut feeling is telling me Volkov will let no one stand in his way in his pursuit of his vengeance for his sister's killing.'

Before Sam could recover from the shock of what she had just heard, Bill Mathews handed her a set of photos taken in an airport lounge. Sam sifted through them but recognised none of the men portrayed in the pictures; she handed them back, puzzled. 'Should I know any of these men? You'll need to give me a clue as to what you expect me to tell you about them.'

'I don't expect you to know them, but I do want you to remember them because it could be the difference between life and death for you. To the untrained eye they could be businessmen, holidaymakers, travellers, but in reality they all have two things in common: they are all Russian Spetsnaz soldiers, some GRU, some FSB alpha group, and all were recruited by our friend Vadek Volkov or, as his Russian friends call him, "The Wolf". These men arrived in the UK by different routes but all have visited the Russian Embassy and left there as a team.

'Also contained in our late director's files were notes and documents relating to various high-profile people, dirt that if let out in the open would finish the careers of all the people in the folders. It was hardly surprising to find a folder for both you and your partner among the files, considering the nature of the work you carried out for Neil. You, for example, according to the files, now live in a luxury mansion on the

Scottish west coast that once belonged to the very person we have been talking about. Samantha, Alina Orlov was a drug trafficker. The proceeds of her crimes should have gone to the state, not to the person who ended her life. Samantha, we both know that is the tip of the iceberg. You are an assassin – there are people you have disposed of in other countries that have extradition treaties with the UK. I only need to lift the phone and you'll spend the rest of your life rotting away in some godforsaken hole in a foreign land. You killed people our government knows nothing about and never sanctioned.

'Your boyfriend murdered one of the IRA's top men, which directly led to the IRA's bombing spree on mainland Britain as retribution, for god's sake. You were both out of control and you should have been brought to task for your actions. Only Neil Andrews stood between you and prison, Samantha. I am a reasonable man and I know Sir Neil would have put you under great pressure to carry out his wishes. I am prepared to make a deal with you. Give me your word that you will toe the line and work for me and I in turn will continue with Neil Andrews' deal, making sure both your files never see the light of day. Cross me and you will both be front page news. Do we understand each other?'

For a second Sam said nothing; she knew her plans for the future had just been sunk, but she could not yet bring herself to agree to Bill Mathews' request without checking all the angles for any way out of this mess. If it had been Neil on the other side of the desk things would have been different, she had just as much dirt on him as he had on her, but Bill Mathews was another story. She had no leverage on this man; he owed her nothing and he knew everything. Her blissful life had just ended. In her mind she could hear herself telling Adam a long time ago that once MI6 got its claws into you there was no leaving; over the last couple of years she had dared to think she had escaped their clutches but in truth she had only been kidding herself.

Mathews was speaking again. 'Samantha, I see from one of the files that during your probation, working alongside Agent Kent when you first joined us, you were assigned to Diana's MI6 protection detail when she was out of the country.' Sam had not expected this line of questioning and struggled to hide her horror at where this might lead. Mathews continued, not giving her the chance to think.

'The file says that you were returned to England for a change in duties but it did not say why. Samantha, you will find when you work with me that I try to leave no stone unturned. That's why I checked with passport control – the final pages of the file did not specify when you returned. Also GCHQ were kind enough to check stored MI6 phone logs for the dates around the time you flew back into Heathrow. It showed you were ordered to leave France immediately and your passport was scanned on 30 August 1997. You see, Samantha, and I am positive you do not need to be reminded of this, but the fact is you were assigned to Diana's protection detail in France and you were removed the day before she died. I would like to know what was so important that you had to leave that day. Can you tell me, Samantha?'

Samantha avoided eye contact with her new boss; it was not fear of the man that was causing her sudden agitation, but the subject he had brought up made the hairs on Sam's neck stand on end. For many years Sam had tried to bury that weekend away in the back of her mind. In truth there was nothing Sam could tell Bill Mathews, only that her own enquiries into the very same question Mathews had asked had borne no fruit, and the more questions Sam asked the more people wouldn't speak about it. Eventually Sam had been pulled up before Neil Andrews and ordered to drop it or be transferred out. Sam could feel Bill Mathews' eyes boring into her skull as the silence in the office became awkward.

'Mr Mathews, on the subject of the house you've got me. It was wrong and I knew it. As for everything else, all I can say is I followed orders from my superiors. I couldn't give a damn if they were sanctioned or not, I followed orders. As for your questions about the goings-on in 1997, I am sorry to say, sir, I can shed no light on the matter. At the time I asked the same questions and was told to forget about it. If I were you, sir, I would speak to my handler in France at the time, Peter Kent. I have never broached the subject with him because I was ordered to leave it alone, but he may know why we were returned to England when we were.' Sam slumped back in her chair, resigned to await her fate at the hands of Bill Mathews.

Sam watched Mathews as he shuffled through the Diana file which, from where Sam was sitting, looked incomplete. He closed the file and placed it to one side; it looked like that was one secret that Neil Andrews may have taken to the grave with him. Sam sensed for the moment at least the subject was closed. Without saying anything Mathews handed Sam a photo he had been holding on to; he let Sam study the picture for a second before explaining what she was looking at.

'It would appear Neil had one of his agents placed near to you. These pictures were taken from his phone – that is your partner Adam McDonald talking to members of Vadek Volkov's Spetsnaz team.'

For the third time that morning Sam had been struck dumb. She instantly recognised Adam and Bob at the Airsoft site talking to the Russians. It only took milliseconds for it to register with Sam that her partner and son, if not already dead, were in mortal danger and it had been she who had caused this god-awful mess. Sam sprang to her feet to leave, but Mathews for the first time raised his voice. 'Samantha, I am ordering you to sit down. Hear me out before you go charging into the unknown. I have spoken to our agent who took those pictures. As of this morning all is quiet at your home. You can phone home when you're finished here. I've ordered the agent up north to assist your partner in whatever he deems as fit in the circumstances, but you are not going charging off into the heather to save him. I need you here, I need to know for sure if Volkov is behind this, and as you are number one on his attention list it would be mad not to use your talents to find out for sure.'

Sam sat back down on the edge of the chair; she was not sure what Mathews had in mind but she was going to give him the benefit of the doubt for the moment. She had no option; she needed him to say his piece so she could get to a phone and warn Adam to get Luke away from the area and find some place safe until Sam found a solution to the problem.

'I have cleared a desk upstairs for you to work from. You will have access to every piece of information on Volkov and all current Russian intelligence we have – our Russian specialist has been informed to help with anything you need. I suggest you get up there make your call home then get your head buried in those files and find a way to infiltrate Volkov's little operation. Let me know the minute you figure it out. Tell Jean to pop in when you leave please.'

Sam was speechless; she had waited patiently for Mathews' master plan, only to find out he expected her to come up with the plan. She had just found out one of the main differences between Bill Mathews and Neil Andrews.

Mathews expected his people to come up with the big ideas then agree or disagree with the plan, while Neil Andrews had been a control freak giving orders that were to be followed to the letter – his ideas, his game plan. His people were treated more like pieces on a chessboard than free-thinking agents. It was not lost on Sam that Bill Mathews had overlooked the part where her job prior to his arrival had been purely as a specialist finisher; she had not been active as a field agent. Her speciality was after all else had failed and the problem still remained, her job was to eliminate the problem, a task she had excelled at. For the moment though the new task she had been given would have to wait. Adam and Luke were her priority; she needed to warn them of the impending danger they were in.

Sam needed to speak to the field agent who had taken the pictures and there was one person Sam was pretty sure would know how to get hold of that agent. She picked up the phone and dialled Jean's office number.

Adam became instantly awake, checking his surroundings before moving. In Sam's spot on the bed a small body wriggled then lay motionless, his small chest rising and falling as he slept, his eyes moving behind their eyelids, his lips sucking on an imaginary dummy as he dreamed baby dreams. Adam watched his son, running his fingers gently through his golden curls. He was not sure if it had been Luke's movement in the bed that had woken him, but now he was wide awake his mind turned back to the events of the last few days and the encounter with his first paying guests. A strange feeling again came over him; something was wrong and for the life of him Adam couldn't put his finger on what it was that was spooking him so badly.

Try as he might, sleep would not come as his mind turned things over in his head. He was missing Sam badly; he had become used to her presence and her counsel on things he needed to talk about. If she had been here she might have been able to shed some light on why Adam's guests had spooked him so badly. From the bedroom window Adam watched the sunrise as its golden rays turned the colours of the bedroom furniture into a golden hue; in the middle of the double bed his son's little angel curls resembled those of a boy god, gleaming like a golden halo. The sea was as calm as a millpond; it looked like today was going to be a day to be savoured.

Adam finally gave up on sleep and transferred his still sleeping babe back to his cot before heading to the kitchen to prepare breakfast for himself and Luke.

While he was preparing breakfast a gentle knock came from the front door. Adam's heart jumped into his mouth. Who was knocking at this early hour of the morning? On the way down the spiral staircase to the door Adam gave himself a good talking to; he was losing it. Why he was so jumpy he had no idea, and he was not liking the new sensation one little bit.

From the bottom of the staircase Adam could make out the figure of Bob standing by the front door trying to see in through the one-way privacy glass.

'Morning, boss, sorry to bother you this early but I couldn't sleep. Truth is, mate, something is eating at me. Just popped by to say I was going to do a full sweep of the area. I haven't done one for a while with the building work up at the shooting site and security has kind of taken a back seat. I wondered if you fancied breakfast down at the hotel this morning – young Callum is meeting me there after I've given the perimeter a checking over. Are you game?'

Adam was about to reply when he heard rumbling about coming from upstairs. 'Thanks for the offer, Bob, but I need to sort out the wee man's breakfast. By all means have a rake about. I'll give breakfast a miss, but I will join you for coffee once I've dropped Luke off with your good lady. I need to go before shorty upstairs stages a breakout from his cot. Catch you in a bit.' Adam sprinted up the stairs just as Luke teetered on the edge of his cot, foiled again.

Adam polished off two slices of toast and jam while Luke played with his baby porridge while watching Adam enviously, seeming desperate to get his hands on the toast.

Again Adam heard the front door. This time the knock was loud and Adam detected a certain agitation in the way the knock was performed. He lifted Luke clear of his high chair and placed him in his playpen while he set off once more down the stairs to discover the source of the new knocking.

Big Bob almost fell through the front door as Adam opened it; his eyes were wide as he pushed the door closed behind him and entered the garage area. He looked like he had just seen a ghost.

'Jesus, Bob, what's the hurry? What have you been up to?'

Bob took a second to catch his breath and gather his thoughts. 'I knew it, Adam, I fucking knew it – those bastards at the Airsoft site. Oil workers my arse!'

'Woah, slow down, Bob, rewind. Start at the beginning. What are you trying to say? Calm down, man, for god's sake.'

'Sorry, Adam. I started my sweep of the area on the far hillside looking across to Comriach. At first everything was kosher, but I thought I had broken my bloody leg in a rabbit burrow I stood in by accident. On closer inspection it was clear no rabbit had made that – it was an observation hide skilfully made. I reckon two men have been carrying out surveillance on this house – and not too long ago either. Adam, that hide was not constructed by amateurs. I would put money on special forces of some type. Someone wanted eyes on you – what the hell is going on here? What the hell have you and Sam been up to?'

Adam was at a loss to say who had targeted them but he knew right away Bob was correct. He trusted his judgment about the hide and he'd had the same feeling as Bob that something was wrong. If only Sam had been here. He needed to speak to her urgently, but first he wanted Luke out of harm's way. Bob was dispatched to find Sue and get her back there while Adam tried to think of what to do next.

In the basement of the Russian Embassy a meeting that could not be held in the open was taking place, hundreds of miles from the glass house, but Sam and Adam were high on the agenda.

Vadek Volkov had called the meeting between himself, his head of security, Peter Sokolov, and his intelligence chief, FSB Agent Vasily Kurmich. Sokolov had been Volkov's chosen man from his business empire but Vasily Kurmich had been forced on him by the Kremlin because he was the highest-ranking agent based in the UK and well placed to assist the new ambassador. Vadek Volkov was no fool; he knew as well as assisting him he was there to keep an eye on him. Volkov had already intercepted two messages bound for the Kremlin and destroyed them; nothing was going to get in his way. Volkov was in a rage but for the moment he locked it away until the facts had been explained to him.

'Gentlemen, I want to know why I was the last person to find out that my target had moved. Not only that but in Hyde Park we had her in the palm of our hands. What can you tell me to explain your incompetence?'

Volkov stared from man to man. Sokolov had seen him in full flow before and Volkov was therefore not surprised Sokolov chose not to make eye contact with him; he would have an idea what might follow and was bracing himself. Kurmich, on the other hand, was a problem. Volkov could feel a murderous mood swing coming over him as the arrogant fool stared defiantly back at him. He had no respect for him although he had been ordered by Moscow to comply with the new ambassador's requests. Volkov had waited long enough for an answer and continued.

'Has the cat got your tongues? So, my friends, let me help you. Feel free to correct me if I get my facts wrong. Kurmich, you were tasked with destroying the van and our terrorist friend so nothing could be traced back to us. Only the DNA of a known terrorist should have been found, but instead the British have the van intact and clues that may lead them back to us. Kurmich, it was your team in Scotland who placed the trackers on our target's cars and were to keep them under surveillance until I paid the bitch and her family a visit. Instead I find from an office junior that your idiots let the bitch slip away and then did not track her. Now she is holed up at MI6 headquarters after almost foiling our removal of their meddling head man. Two things are obvious to me: our performance was poor and you, Kurmich, you were in charge of the poor parts of the operation.'

Volkov spun round, his eyes burning into Kurmich's skull. In his right hand he was holding Peter Sokolov's Grach pistol; without hesitation he fired, hitting Kurmich in the stomach. Kurmich curled up, a look of disbelief on his pale face, his lips emitting a low groaning noise.

'Kurmich, consider yourself relieved of duty. They tell me a stomach wound is agony. Would you like me to be kind and finish you now or let you bleed to death? I think I will leave it up to my friend here to decide. Goodbye, comrade.'

Volkov walked Sokolov to the basement door before handing him back his weapon. 'Get that sorry piece of shit out of here. I want you to finish him then dump the body for the British police to find. Spread the word that our agent has been assassinated by the British agent Samantha O'Conner – an unprovoked attack on a Russian diplomat. Let us see if we can draw the bitch out of her den.'

Sokolov nodded while watching the death throes of his work colleague; luckily he had survived another of Volkov's punishment exercises. 'What do we do with the woman's family in the north?'

Volkov thought for a second; he had wanted to execute them in front of Samantha O'Conner, but things had changed and he had lost the element of surprise due to the incompetence of Kurmich. Again his rage overtook him and he ran across the basement; he launched a series of kicks to the stomach of the fatally wounded Kurmich, who screamed in pain, unable to defend himself against Volkov's rage. Volkov walked back past Sokolov, readjusting his tie and smoothing down his hair in an attempt to calm himself. 'The bitch's family in the north – obliterate them. No one lives. They must die at any cost. Do it and do it right this time, then I can look the bitch in the face just before I take her life and tell her I have taken her family just as she took mine.'

Volkov walked from the room and two steps from the stairs he heard Sokolov's gun fire once more. He smiled to himself as he took the stairs; he had stopped the flow of information to Moscow and the death of their agent would give him an excuse to kill Samantha O'Conner. As far as they were concerned, Sir Neil Andrews had been targeted by SAR Mu Haar Ib, nothing to do with him.

Adam sat watching Luke in his playpen while waiting for Bob and Sue to return to the glass house. It was then he had an idea; he spent the next few minutes digging through drawers before eventually coming up with what he was looking for. He had once seen Sam using the little meter he had found to check for bugs and tracking devices; he started in the lounge, completing a sweep of the top floor before turning his attention to the ground floor. The needle didn't flinch once and Adam was thinking about changing the batteries as he passed his green Aston Martin heading for the gym and playroom. The needle spiked for a fraction of a second then fell back to rest. Adam stopped dead in his tracks and took a step backwards; as he did so the needle started to lift. It only took him a few seconds with the help of the meter to find the small silver tracking device attached to the inner passenger wing of the car. He continued his search indoors but came across no other devices. He turned his attention to Sam's Beetle parked by the front door; again the needle jumped into life as Adam approached the rear wing. He was about to launch the trackers over the cliff onto the beach when he thought better of it and retraced his steps into the house. Adam headed straight for the bedroom and the bedside cabinet; he removed the Glock and ammunition from the drawer and loaded a clip into the grip of the weapon. He did not know what was going on but the feel of the Glock in his hand eased the sense of foreboding that had come over him. He needed to think, and fast; what would Sam have done?

He heard the sound of engines approaching the glass house. With some trepidation Adam headed for the lounge that led to the balcony; he reckoned this would give him the best firing position on the front door and the surrounding area should the vehicles prove to be unfriendly.

To Adam's relief the first vehicle to arrive at the front of the glass house was Bob's old Discovery, closely followed by Callum's VW camper van. Adam breathed a sigh of relief and headed down the spiral staircase to open the front door for his friends. He opened the door and Sue bustled past him in search of her little buddy. Bob's and Callum's faces were not pictures of happiness. Adam was somewhat surprised by Callum's demeanour; he suspected Bob must have told him about the hide he had found but before he could speak Bob beat him to it.

'Boss, I think you'd better listen to what this lad has to tell you. I think it will go a long way to explaining things that have been going on around here lately.'

Adam turned to Callum, who had turned a whiter shade of pale; something was obviously bothering him big time.

'Where to begin, Mr McDonald – yes, I know who you are. I work for MI6. Neil Andrews sent me up here to keep an eye on things and report back to him. I know this will come as a big shock to you. Director Andrews was assassinated two days ago. I have been in contact with his replacement, Bill Mathews. Since talking to him and your partner I now know the reason I was sent up here. The people who were at the Airsoft site are Russian special forces under the command of Vadek Volkov, the Russian ambassador to the UK. Samantha says to tell you that this man Volkov had Director Andrews killed because he had found out Volkov's reason for coming here was to kill her and everyone connected to her. She has tried to call and warn you but could not get through to you or Bob's wife, so in desperation she contacted me. She says the Russians are well trained and if given the green light will kill without hesitation. They are too dangerous to engage. She has been given orders to remain in London until Volkov is dealt with. She needs you to get Luke to safety – she will find you as soon as she can get away from London.'

Adam sat on the bottom step of the spiral staircase, shocked at what he had just been told. For the moment he had nothing to say to the two men standing in the garage; his head was spinning. It was hard to take in – Neil was no longer alive; Adam had known him since their school-days. As for the Russian wanting Sam dead – that was not surprising. Sam had made many enemies throughout her career; what she had done to this Russian must have been bad for him to go to these lengths to get her. What was a surprise to Adam was that Sam had obeyed orders and stayed in London rather than heading home to her family.

Adam looked on as Sue, Bob and Callum rounded up a few essential things. His head was in a bad place but he knew he needed to come up with some sort of plan urgently.

Sam had excused herself from her desk and headed for the one place in Vauxhall Cross that she could get peace to think things through. She signed out a Glock from the armoury then waited patiently for a firing booth to come free. Sam had never been a religious person but for the first time in her life she found herself praying that the message she'd got to this guy Callum had reached Adam before it was too late. Callum had been her only hope; he was the only one with an encrypted mobile phone and after the disaster with Neil she was not about to trust a normal mobile – she was now sure her every word would be monitored. As for Callum, Sam had little faith in him. She had dug out his file to find that he was a probationer who had arrived only six months ago; worse still he was not a field agent, only an analyst. Sam even doubted if Six had let him carry a weapon, never mind fend off a Russian Spetsnaz unit. Adam's only hope was to run and hide before Volkov unleashed his men.

Sam was still mulling things over in her head as she entered the now vacant booth. She slid the clip in then checked the slide before punching the ready button with her thumb. At the end of the range a paper bad guy moved from side on to full view. Sam fired twice at the target which after only one second once again turned side on, not allowing a shot; this was a new system that had been installed since Sam was last here. It was designed to test your reflexes as well as your aim. Sam waited for the target to make itself visible again; she could see from the monitor that she was high to the right with her first shot and her second had missed. Sam cursed for not keeping the shooting range at home working just as the target reappeared. She fired twice again; this time her first shot was still high but closer to the paper bad guy's heart. Her second nicked the side of the target but missed the bad guy's body by two inches. It was fair to say that her full concentration was not on the target as again one shot hit high, the second missing. She should have been adjusting things in her head but instead she was worried sick what Adam would think of her abandoning her lover and her child to an unknown fate at the hands of Russian madmen while she hid in the bowels of MI6.

She had thought this through again and again and it kept coming out the same; better to hope Adam could get to safety with Luke than go against Bill Mathews and end up in jail while Luke was given away to a foster home. Sam couldn't bear to think of that happening. No. She would do what she had been ordered to do and things still had a chance of working out. If the unthinkable happened and she lost Luke and Adam the shit would hit the fan: first she would kill the Russian bastard, then she would kill Bill Mathews for not letting her go to them. After that it didn't really matter because her life would be over. Sam decided to pack it in when Jean arrived to escort her home for the evening.

On the way back in the cab Sam was silent even when Jean produced a new battery for her phone. She could not raise her spirits; only a brief 'thank you' escaped her lips. She was struggling to see what difference having a battery would make; she could not use the phone in case it alerted her new and very deadly enemy. As a courtesy to Jean she loaded the new battery and thanked Jean for getting it.

Outside Jean's house Sam was deep in thought as Jean searched for her front door key in her large handbag. Sam felt her phone vibrate. She froze; no one but Neil Andrews had this number. She became even more concerned because the screen showed no number although the phone continued to ring. Sam pressed the green 'Call Accept' button, holding her breath while she listened. While Jean looked on Sam heard only breathing at the other end of the call. She was about to hang up when a woman's voice spoke with a heavy Russian accent. 'The owner of this phone used it to arrange a meeting. Meet me in the same place tomorrow at noon if you want to know the truth. Come alone and unarmed.'

Before Sam could speak the woman hung up. Jean regarded Sam quizzically as if waiting for an explanation. Sam walked past her heading for the door. 'Bloody double-glazing salesmen. No wonder I hate bloody phones.'

Jean shrugged her shoulders without saying a word.

The minute Sam arrived at her desk the next morning she checked with her colleagues for any word from Adam or Callum; her heart sank. Again nothing had been heard from Scotland.

Sam didn't waste time at her desk. Instead, armed with her shiny new ID badge, she paid another visit to the armoury where she signed out a new Glock, four spare magazines and a couple of boxes of shells. She was glad to see as she arrived at the firing range that only one other booth was occupied. She busied herself stripping and checking the new weapon before loading all five clips with bullets. The next thirty minutes were spent getting used to the feel of her new gun before deciding she was happy with the balance and accuracy of the weapon. Sam was happier with her performance; the new gun had helped. The voice on the phone had said no weapons but Sam was happy to ignore the request; she was not about to let some Russian hitman have a free shot at her – if he did she would make sure she was not the only one dodging bullets in Hyde Park today.

Sam arrived early and entered the park some distance from the ill-fated area where Neil had lost his life. She wanted to carry out her own surveillance of the park before meeting the owner of the voice on the telephone. Sam was acutely aware that the call could be a trap by Vadek Volkov to lure her into the open where his men could deal with her; alone with only a Glock, a throwing knife and no back up she stood little chance against trained Russian operatives but she was in a desperate situation. She needed to get Volkov sorted out one way or another so she could get out of the capital and go to the aid of her family. Sam told herself if it were a trap, at least it would keep Volkov's attention away from Adam and Luke.

Sam checked out her reflection in the window of an unmanned police car parked inside the park. Its occupants were busy talking to park visitors, presumably in connection with the recent so-called terrorist attack. Sam gave them a quick glance to check she was not the object of their attention. She was wearing grey shorts and hoodie sweatshirt topped off with a pink baseball cap and matching pink Ray-Ban sunglasses; her right thigh and knee were heavily bandaged. Sam had moved the usual position of her ankle holster to the bandage on her knee; if she needed to draw the weapon it would be faster from her knee than her ankle. Sam had studied Russian special forces training and she knew how good they were; she knew every split second could mean life or death in an encounter with Spetsnaz operatives. She gave the throwing knife taped to the inside of her left forearm a quick check to make sure it was secure before heading of running with a noticeable limp.

As Sam approached the now tented and taped of area where she had witnessed the carnage her eyes, hidden by the Ray-Bans, were out on stalks checking faces and positions. She ran past without checking her pace, stopping some distance away to stretch and check for anyone tailing her before heading off into the distance. Reasonably happy with her first pass, Sam checked her watch by the boundary wall before removing the hoodie and turning it inside out. She now wore a white hoodie, her baseball cap was tucked in her waistband, and her blonde mane was released, held back only by a white headband.

Sam's second pass was faster without the limp. She had almost gone past when she spotted a woman jogging in front of her; it was clear to Sam's trained eye that running was not what was on this woman's mind. Sam slackened her pace, keeping a distance between them and observing the woman as she looked left to right in search of something. Sam needed to know if she had any accomplices with her. One hundred metres past the police tape the woman turned to run back the way she had just come when she collided with another jogger; she started to apologise to Sam. The minute Sam heard her voice she knew she had found the mystery caller; the Russian accent was unmistakable.

Parked on the pavement not far from Marble Arch, Dan Whittaker sat in the back of a lookalike BT repair van. His surveillance equipment was state of the art. Unknown to MI5 he had piggybacked his monitor system onto their camera system, watching what they were watching and listening to their commentary from their own equipment.

In Dan's opinion, as one of the CIA's top surveillance officers, their filming of passers-by at the scene of the Hyde Park atrocity was clutching at straws. If it was a deranged madman then yes, he might return to the scene of the crime, but this was no deranged madman; it had been planned and executed by pros. Dan knew there was no way in hell they would be back for a look. It was only his boss sitting next to him today that persuaded him to appear interested.

Dan was trying hard not to fall asleep when Bruce Ellis leaned forward, squinting at the monitor. 'Back, Dan, back it up a bit.' Dan carried out his boss's request, puzzled by his sudden interest. Ellis slapped the counter, stood up and headed for the door. 'Samantha O'Conner. I knew it. If she's here something is going on. Find her and track her, Dan, I'm going in on foot. Keep me informed and don't lose her, Dan, she's as slippery as an eel.'

Sam helped the other jogger to her feet, smiling for the benefit of anyone watching; still smiling she made eye contact with the woman before speaking. She needed to judge the woman's reaction to her next words carefully; if it was some type of trap she would give it away in her eyes.

'I am the one you called to tell me the truth. Run with me as if we're friends jogging. Let's get moving – come on, move.'

Sam set off away from the blast site, the other jogger matching her pace after only a short time. Sam had answered a few questions in her own head about this unknown woman. She was no field agent – her running was laboured and her fitness was poor. Sam's fear of an ambush had diminished; the woman was a wreck mentally – even jogging Sam could tell something was eating away at her new friend.

As Sam passed a big oak tree the woman gave up running, using the tree as a prop while she tried to regain her breath and her composure. 'I take it that you are Samantha O'Conner, the person who called your director to arrange the meeting here. Please believe me – I had nothing to do with his killing. I am so sorry for your loss.'

Sam stopped and moved behind the cover of the big tree before stretching, which gave her time to think of how to tackle the Russian woman. 'You seem to know who I am, so if you don't mind please tell me who you are and what is this truth you talk about?'

The Russian looked like she was about to burst out crying but rallied and held it together. 'I am Ludmilla Berkov. It was my shift when you called your director. Your name was one of two names given to me by my ambassador to listen for and report to him. I had no idea why, I just did my job. I'm sorry. Ambassador Volkov is a very nasty man – he gives our country a bad name. He is about to have me returned in disgrace to my country with my career in ruins. The reason I have called you is to warn you that while I was in his office I came across a file in his desk about something that is not in the Russian people's interest to let happen. I am no traitor, but this man Volkov has decided to deal with enemies of both our countries, so you must be warned. He is in collusion with a terrorist called Tarek Attar – I have read our FSB file on this animal and he is a man with no morals and a deep hatred for everything that is not part of his religion. You must tell your security services to stop this man – your capital is his next target.'

Sam shook her head. Vadek Volkov had already used this smokescreen to hide his own men. 'We already know that Tarek Attar and his SAR Mu Haar Ib organisation have been used as patsies to cover up the attack on our director. They are not the threat.'

Ludmilla's eyes were on fire. 'No, you must listen to me – this is no smokescreen. I have seen the documents – Tarek Attar has paid thirty million dollars into Volkov's Swiss account. Volkov is supplying a weapon to be used here in London, but the deal is he must wait until Volkov has finished his business in London and is safely out of the country before deploying the weapon. This is no joke – you must find Attar. These fools will start World War Three between our countries. These men are mad. Please believe me – for thirty million dollars you can be sure Attar has bought something very, very bad.'

Ludmilla was shaking with a mixture of fear and rage. Sam was in deep thought for a second. 'So you don't know what the weapon is, where it is, or when it's going to be used?'

Ludmilla shook her head, looking crestfallen. 'No, I did not have time to take pictures of all the documents. I was disturbed and had to leave Volkov's office. I am sorry.'

Sam thought again for a second before speaking. 'Okay, Ludmilla, we are both in the shit here, so this is what we're going to do. You will go back to the embassy as if nothing has happened. You will find a way to get me into your embassy. When you do, call me at the same time as you called before. I will make sure the phone is on – now get out of here before we are seen.'

Ludmilla hesitated. 'But if I do manage to get you in, what will you do?'

Sam made eye contact with her. 'I'm going to kill Vadek Volkov, then you can show me the documents you talked about. Easy, isn't it? Call me tomorrow, Ludmilla. I need to get this done quickly. Now go that way – stay away from the blast site. Go!'

Sam watched the Russian woman jog away while she still remained by the trees, and then turned to start jogging in the opposite direction. She'd only passed a couple of trees by the path when a voice startled her. She looked instinctively to see who the voice belonged to; a figure sitting on a bench by a tree stood up and walked in her direction.

'I said nice day for a run.' Bruce Ellis had a wicked twinkle in his eye as he walked over to Sam, smiling. 'We meet again, Samantha. I hope I didn't startle you? It's just that you look a bit like a rabbit caught in the headlights. Who's your friend?'

Sam cursed to herself; Bruce Ellis had the uncanny knack of turning up at all the wrong times. 'Hello, Bruce, I had no idea you were in town. I take it you're on a break and popped out of the embassy for some fresh air. Better be careful – haven't you heard Hyde Park is not good for the health of security chiefs.'

Ellis touched his forefinger against his earpiece. Sam watched as his brain took in what he was hearing on his headset. Ellis removed his hand, a puzzled look on his face. 'You were speaking to the Russians?

The girl is Ludmilla Berkov, she works at the Russian Embassy. She's an intel officer with the second highest security clearance. Why, Sam? It was the Russians that took out Andrews. Care to share?'

Sam cursed under her breath; the last thing she needed was the CIA poking their nose into her business. She knew from bitter experience that once Bruce Ellis was involved he would not take no for an answer. 'Bruce, just leave it, we've got this one covered. The woman was the FSB's attempt at misinformation. She's been trying to tell me that Tarek Attar was the mastermind behind Neil's death and is planning more atrocities in the UK. It's bollocks, but if you feel the need you can check him out. We already know Volkov's men have tried to frame Attar's group and take the heat off themselves – today was just another sad attempt to deflect the blame. We have it covered, Bruce, so you can tell the CIA to stand down. This is our backyard and we will take the rubbish out. We don't need any help this time, my friend.'

Ellis seemed about to object, but then said, 'We were all sorry to hear about Neil – he was a good guy in a bad world. I have a feeling you're going to miss him, Samantha, he was your guardian angel. I don't think Bill Mathews will cut you the same slack as your old buddy did. Listen, I got to shoot, but if you change your mind or need my help just say the word. Got to fly – see ya!'

Bruce Ellis bounded away to an exit on his right where a BT van had just pulled up. To Sam's surprise Ellis jumped into the passenger seat and waved back at her as the van pulled out into the heavy traffic. Sam watched him go, knowing she had missed a perfect opportunity to ask Ellis to send backup in case Adam was in trouble. She knew if she confided in Bruce Ellis about the truth of what was happening her new boss would not be happy at her breach of security protocol, but deep down, although she cursed herself for being so stubborn, she knew her pride would not let her accept outside help. Ludmilla was going to have to come up with a way into the embassy so she could kill the Russian bastard and stop this nightmare.

5

Ambush

Adam smiled; Luke chuckled and gurgled with pleasure as Sue tickled him under the chin, then got him into his travel suit ready for a trip into the unknown.

Bob had left Callum a list of things to get before heading off, this time armed with an MP5 for one last visit to the Russians' observation dugout to make sure the unwanted visitors had not returned.

Adam finished writing a note for Sue then folded it and put it in an envelope. He was still not sure if he was doing the right thing but he could not sit and do nothing while waiting for his Russian friends to make the first move. To have any chance he needed to be at least one step ahead of them at all times; all their lives could depend on it. Adam passed Luke sitting up in his carrycot and gave him a pat on the head, then avoided eye contact with Sue. He headed for the door to check that Bob was okay and on his way back to the glass house. He met him at the top of the zigzag path to the beach and stopped him; what he was about to say was better said out of earshot. Adam could not be a hundred per cent sure the glass house was bug free.

'Okay, Bob, this is what we're going to do. We're going to head for Area One. You and Callum are going to run interference in the camper to keep the Russians off my tail. I've left a note for Sue with instructions – she doesn't need to be part of this.'

Adam stopped speaking. Bob was shaking his head a look of bewilderment etched on his weather-beaten face. 'I've never been to Area

One, but I have spoken to a few guys from the regiment who have. Adam, it's miles away – how do you propose to hold off a determined attack with a bloody camper van? Are you mad? It's too risky – there has to be a better way. Think of your son, for god's sake. If anything happens to Luke Sam will kill you if the Russians don't get you first.'

Adam clenched his jaw while fixing a cold stare on Bob. 'You let me worry about Sam. Have you no faith? Remember, you're talking to the man that dragged your sorry arse halfway across Kuwait on a moped to get you back in one piece. We get to Area One and not even a Spetsnaz unit would dare to try anything. Trust me, old friend, we will be fine. We don't even know if our Russian pals are still here – after all, no one has seen them since the Airsoft game.'

Bob and Callum watched Adam from the front seats of the camper as Adam handed Sue the letter. They couldn't hear what was being said but from the concerned look on Sue's face they weren't discussing the weather. Sue had tears streaming down her face as Adam gently loaded the carrycot into the passenger seat of the big green Aston Martin. Bob watched as Adam said a few more words to Sue before heading for the camper van side door. By the time Adam opened the door, Sue had vanished back indoors without making eye contact with Bob.

Adam placed a holdall on the rear floor of the camper van then handed Bob one of the handheld two-way radios from the Airsoft site.

'What did you say to her, Adam?' Bob was going nowhere until Adam answered him.

'She isn't coming with us, big guy. You may have signed up as my security and Callum here has signed up through joining Six, but Sue did not and I will not let her get involved. I've given her instructions in the envelope so she can get away from here safely.'

Bob slammed the palm of his big hand down on the camper's dash in frustration. 'Adam, this is madness. For god's sake just call the police, man.'

Adam's stare was piercing as he regarded his mate with calculating eyes. 'And what are they going to do – arrest them for digging a hole?

No, Bob, we go now while we still can. If you want out, leave with Sue, if not, follow me, I'm on channel 7.'

Adam slammed the side door shut, giving Bob one last cold stare before sliding into the driver's seat of the Aston Martin and pulling away from the front of the glass house. Bob sat in silence for a second or so watching Adam disappearing down the drive. 'Don't just sit there gawping at me, Callum, get after the bloody fool.'

Callum and Bob had been travelling south for some time behind the Aston Martin. The familiar sound of the Volkswagen's engine was all but drowned out by the deep exhaust note of the leading vehicle. Bob heard the faint bleep of the two-way radio over the engine noise; he picked up the unit and listened for instructions from Adam.

'Bob, we will be in Fort William in a minute or two. Look in the dashboard cubby box – you'll find a silver magnetic metal disc. When we hit the first traffic lights, nip out and stick the tracker disc on the back bumper of that builders' merchant's truck. Hopefully if we are being tailed it will split up our Russian buddies and send a few of them to Inverness on a wild goose chase.' Bob said nothing for the moment; he was too busy raking about for the disc in the camper's dash.

At the traffic lights Bob sprinted forward and clipped the disc on just as the driver engaged first gear and started to pull away. Back in the camper Bob contacted Adam. 'Okay, boss, the disc is fitted. Two questions: how can you be sure the truck is not going the same way as us and why do you think it will split the ruskies up? Won't they all follow the signal?'

Bob could hear Adam laughing on the other end of the line.

'Bob, that is the reason you made sergeant and I made captain. Read the van: "Superline Builders, Inverness" – enough said. And they will split up because I have the second tracker with me in the Aston. Divide and conquer, mate.'

Bob just about dropped his radio when he realised what Adam had said.

'Jesus Christ, Adam, what the hell are you playing at? Have you lost your marbles completely? Get rid of it before they find us, or at least give us young Luke and you can sprint away. They'll never catch your Aston Martin – you can lead them away from Luke.'

For a second there was silence over the airwaves. Bob thought that maybe he had got through to Adam and he was considering his plan. The radio crackled once more and Bob waited anxiously for Adam's response.

'Not a bad idea, Bob, but I'm one step ahead of you, mate. Do you really think I would risk Luke? The cot was for the benefit of prying eyes – it's full of goodies to play with if our Russian friends catch us before Area One. Your good lady has a note to take the wee man down to the hotel. I've asked Paul and Margo to take Sue and the wee man up to their holiday cottage in Ullapool. They'll be safe there until we can go get them. Now, can we get on with sorting out our Spetsnaz friends?'

Colonel Serge Macinko studied the road map on the leading Discovery's satnav screen from the comfort of the passenger seat as they approached the target area. Although they had carried out intensive research on Vadek Volkov's targets he had been led to believe this was in preparation for a capture mission rather than an execution of the family. Macinko had spent the morning arranging for his team's extraction after the capture scenario had changed to a hit; he knew that the UK would be no place to stay once he carried out his mission. His men had already been caught out when the woman had left unexpectedly, and he was keen to complete the rest of his mission without further complications.

He went over a few things in his head: although the big man named Bob was not family he had clearly been employed as security; Moscow had accessed the British MOD records and confirmed he had been a member of their special forces. Macinko had targeted his elimination first; his wife would be in the vicinity and would also have to be eliminated to avoid her raising the alarm. Macinko steeled himself to what he considered the hardest part of the mission; he had been ordered to kill the child as well as the adults. He would carry out this part of the mission himself; he did not want to have to order one of his men to kill a child. He was fairly sure he was going to burn in hell for his actions anyway, but if he ever got the chance he would like to arrange for the bastard Volkov who had given these barbaric orders to join him.

Only one thing remained a mystery. Alan, the woman's husband, came across to Macinko as a military man but Moscow could find nothing about him; he had mentioned that he had been part of the UK's part-time soldiers but again Moscow could find no record of him. He was a mystery; Macinko just had to make sure he was going to be a dead mystery.

All three Discoveries arrived at their intended target and the Spetsnaz troops moved into a slick, well-rehearsed operation. One Disco and its troops stopped, blocking off the road so nothing could get in or out of the glass house approach road. Macinko and the lead Disco powered up the hill to the glass house while the second Disco stopped outside the lodge house.

Macinko and his driver placed a charge on the glass house door while the two remaining men circled the back of the building.

The charges went off, blowing the big glass door inwards, followed seconds later by stun grenades thrown through the open door. Macinko could hear exactly the same operation going on at the lodge house at the foot of the hill; to their surprise no one was home at either property. Macinko ordered the third Discovery up to the glass house where he pulled the comms officer out of the back of the vehicle by the shirt; he only just managed to keep hold of his laptop as he struggled to remain upright.

Milad Kirov's hands trembled as he carried out a system reset to his tracking screen, which showed the tracked vehicles of their targets still parked outside their home. Macinko hovered over him like the angel of death, feeling pure rage. The screen blinked then returned with no targets present anywhere. Macinko was about to curse when two red flashing dots reappeared on the screen; they could both see that the dots were some distance to the south. Macinko roared at his men to get back in the vehicles then turned to Kirov. 'Milad, your vehicle will lead. For you own good health, comrade, do not lose them this time or I will hand you over to MI5 myself.'

Paul Kidd had just finished reversing Sam's Beetle into a wooden lock-up behind the Invermorroch Hotel as requested in the letter, while his wife Margo was busy fussing over young Luke.

Paul noticed three black Discoveries approaching from the north at high speed; the vehicles made no attempt to slow down for the Arisaig thirty miles per hour speed limit. Paul shook his head and headed back to the hotel; he had read the letter from Alan Hunter and was somewhat concerned. He was happy to take Sue and little Luke up to his cottage in Ullapool, that was not a problem, but Paul made a mental note to confront Alan and Ann Hunter. There had been far too many strange things going on with the couple, and this request had been the straw that broke the camel's back.

Adam pulled the Aston Martin off the road at Tyndrum, stopping at the Green Welly service station and visitor centre to give the thirsty V8 a refuel. While Adam paid for the fuel Bob placed Callum on stag duty while he set about modifying the tail window of the camper van with duct tape bought from the store. Callum had been concerned as to what Bob was up to with his pride and joy but when Bob explained to him that he was taping the catches open so he could open the back window instead of blowing it open if he had to return fire Callum accepted his reason, if somewhat pale-faced at the thought of someone shooting his beloved camper.

Colonel Macinko had instructed his men to drive the Discoveries to their limit; cyclists, tractors and Sunday drivers were shown no mercy as the three large four-by-fours carved their way through the traffic at breakneck speed. Inside all three Discoveries men dressed from head to toe in black, were busy making ready the PP91 submachine guns and P96 pistols that had just been distributed to them; although not their weapons of choice they were well used to chopping and changing fire-arms and could use any to maximum effect.

On entering Fort William town centre the two lead Discoveries broke right, heading south following one signal, while the last Discovery took the north exit from the roundabout to investigate the other signal position. A few miles further on Litvak's group spotted that the signal had stopped moving; they had almost passed a war memorial car park when Litvak realised that this was where the signal had stopped, and he dragged the four-by-four into the car park.

There was screech as the black Discovery skidded to a halt diago-nally behind a parked lorry. Before the driver could react his door was flung open and one of Litvak's men pulled him from the cab by his right leg and arm. Unable to support himself the driver crashed to the ground with a sickening thud. He was still trying to sit up when Litvak's man dragged him backwards until his back rested against the wheel nuts of his truck's front wheel. The Russian was joined by Lieutenant Daniil Litvak who looked down with pitiless eyes on the old man they had pulled from the cab of the truck that carried the homing beacon; he was not who they were looking for and was now only a hindrance. Daniil ordered his sergeant to deal with it and made his way back to the Discovery to report his findings to his commanding officer.

Clear of Fort William and with sparse traffic the two Russian Discoveries really started to stretch their legs. Macinko looked on ap-provingly as leaving Glencoe village the speedo needle touched one hun-dred miles per hour, the big four-by-fours devouring the road in front of them. A quick look at the laptop confirmed Macinko's thoughts: the distance between their position and the flashing red dot had narrowed significantly; it would not be long until they were on top of their prey.

Adam glanced in his rear-view mirror to see where the lumbering camper van was, then back to his dashboard to check his speed – or the lack of it; the Aston burbled along at sixty almost on tick over as the old camper struggled to keep pace even at this speed. As he approached the fork in the road at Crianlarich he had a dilemma on his hands. He had originally planned to ditch the tracking device here but he wanted to keep the attention of the Russians well away from Sue and Luke; he needed to buy them as much time as possible to make sure they got well clear of the area. He made a split-second decision to carry on until Tarbet then attach the tracker to a vehicle heading west towards Carndow and Inverary while he headed south to Area One. So far, so good; for all he knew the Russians might have packed up and gone home. He had seen nothing of them since the day of the Airsoft game.

The wheezy camper engine struggled to climb the incline out of Crianlarich. Bob watched in despair as the speedo dropped to twenty-five and the rear of the Aston Martin started to disappear over the rise. He lifted his handset and made the call.

'Boss, you'd better ease up on the throttle. This old girl is struggling on the hills – either that or the driver is a big girl's blouse. Either way ease off on the loud pedal.'

Bob looked straight ahead, avoiding eye contact with Callum after his dig at his driving, smiling and waiting for Adam to come back to him.

'Come on, you pair, fling some more coal on the boiler. We're not far from Area One – keep your eyes peeled for our friends from Russia.' Bob clambered into the back of the camper and pulled something out of his holdall. Bob loaded a magazine into a fancy-looking rifle. He then pulled down two legs of a bipod on the front of the weapon before pointing it backwards into the empty road behind them. Bob spotted Callum watching his preparations in the rear-view mirror and explained what he was doing. 'Some would say I should use the MP5 machine gun, but if I'm firing at a vehicle I need accuracy and penetration – the L96A1 gives me both. I have an MP5 here, but go blasting that off where the general public are about and someone perfectly innocent could get shot by mistake. If I'm going to take out the driver I want to be sure the bullet will penetrate the windscreen. With the MP5 there's a chance the bullets may be deflected. The L96A1 is a sniper rifle, and at this range it will take out the windscreen, the driver, and the passenger behind him. You just do the driving, Nigel Mansell, and I'll do the shooting.'

Callum was not put off by Bob mocking him as he buried his foot to try and keep in touch with Adam. 'One question for you Bob: Area One. What is Adam talking about, or is that to confuse the Russians if they're listening?'

'No, Callum. If you'd worked for MI5, not Six, you might have known about it. Area One is the most sensitive military site in Britain. It's basically a network of underground tunnels – it's where the Royal Navy store their arsenal of nuclear missiles for the nuclear subs. Coulport is their munitions base but the nukes are kept apart. You'll find no military road sign going to that base, but what you will find and what Adam is counting on is a base that has SBS and SAS on permanent deployment. Even Russian special forces would be mad to attempt anything. I know from speaking to my mates who have been deployed there that they're authorised to use lethal force to maintain perimeter security around the tunnel complex. Let's just hope if we get there they don't use it on us.'

On the road from Crianlarich to Tarbet they had left a reasonably straight section of road and had come across the older section that twisted its way along the edge of Loch Lomond. As it cut its way through stone cliffs, the road narrowed so that passing traffic had to take care not to hit each other on the treacherous road. As Callum negotiated the bends Bob thought he had caught a glimpse of a vehicle coming up fast, but before he could be sure the next corner of the gorge cut off his view.

While Callum held his line on the twisty bends, Bob was aware they had company, and the metallic click from his rifle signalled things were about to go pear-shaped.

'Callum, lad, just drive, but don't let those pricks get alongside. Here we go, son.'

Bob waited for the right moment then let go a piece of string he had used to hold the rear window down. As the window lifted he had a clear shot of the front of the Discovery. Instead of aiming for the driver, Bob fired into the radiator grill. The discharge from the rifle magnified by the interior of the camper almost burst his eardrums. Clouds of steam enveloped the front of the Discovery, for a second or two causing it to drop off the tail of the camper.

As the steam cleared a little the Discovery accelerated in pursuit of its prey. Bob watched through his gunsight as a black-clad figure leaned out of the passenger window, bushes and trees skiffing against his gun arm as he took aim at the old camper.

Again there was a crash like thunder, but this time it was not aimed at machinery. The large-calibre round from Bob's rifle hit the Russian soldier just below the breastbone, shattering his torso before severing his spine as it departed his body. Bob looked on as bodies inside the Discovery tried to grab him but in truth there was nothing left to grab. The lifeless body fell from the lead Discovery like a bag of bones hit by an express train.

Adam heard the gunfire as it echoed around the cliff walls; what he had dreaded had just happened. He knew he should stick to the plan and head for Area One, but he was torn with guilt. He had put Bob and the young guy in great danger; it did not sit well with him that he was running while in all probability his friends were dying trying to save him. Adam cursed, pulled hard on the steering and flipped the back of the Aston round to face back towards his friends. With one hand he tossed the tracker out of the window while his left hand searched the carrycot. He removed an MP5, loaded it and clicked off the safety, setting the weapon to automatic; things were about to get messy, very messy.

The big car tore round a blind bend straight into a scene of carnage; the camper had been run into the crash barriers, which had managed to stop it from falling into the loch. In the middle of the road was a black Discovery, steam rising from the radiator area, its nearside front wheel all but torn off. Its driver's door was open and the driver was firing a handgun at the camper using the step of the Discovery to give him height and a superior firing angle. Adam floored the throttle and the Aston Martin rammed the driver's door closed, crushing the driver's legs in the process. As the Aston passed through the bank of steam from the wounded Discovery a second Discovery came into view. All its passengers were out and had opened fire on the old camper van and its unfortunate inhabitants. All was not lost, however; Adam could hear the short, controlled bursts of fire from Bob's MP5 being worked by his friend. The driver of the second Discovery was the closest to him and the first to turn to face the new threat, but even before the Aston had come to rest, Adam was firing in an attempt to gain the advantage of surprise.

The Russian had used the cover of the door, but from Adam's angle straight on it provided little safety. Adam's burst of MP5 shells cut through the thin metal of the Discovery door skin; the door glass exploded, sending splinters into the face of the Spetsnaz soldier. Two shells cannoned through the door; one was deflected by the soldier's body armour but the second caught him in the groin, dropping him instantly. Adam knew instinctively he would be a dead man if he stayed back there by the second Discovery; he rammed the Aston into reverse, the big rear tyres screaming in anger, and Adam flew back the way he had just come, away from the inevitable hail of bullets.

As he passed the stricken lead Discovery Adam slammed the brakes on, coming to a halt by the nose of the camper. He sprinted sideways, laying down a volley of covering fire into the curtain of steam still rising from the front of the destroyed Discovery and masking his movement to the front of the camper. To his dismay he found that although the camper was still taking hits it had been abandoned. Adam gave the interior a quick once over, picking up a flash bang from the floor and lobbing it in the direction of his attackers to buy a little time. The back of the camper, although peppered with gunshots, was clear, but the driver's area was another matter; blood was sprayed over the windscreen and dash. Callum had definitely been hit and from the amount of blood it looked terminal.

A quick dash to the twisted barrier by the far side of the camper gave Adam the answer he was looking for; he spotted Bob halfway across the shallow head of the loch swimming for the far bank, dragging Callum's body behind him. He decided he could do little more now other than keep the Russians' attention until Bob made it across to the far bank. He ran back again, firing in the general direction of the Discovery and heading for the cover of the Aston Martin just as a Fiat 500 appeared round the bend and screeched to a halt on the cliff side of the abandoned Aston. Adam changed direction and reached the Fiat just as a terrified woman stepped out of the driver's seat. Bullets were already hitting the Aston, the cliff walls, and now the Fiat – its windscreen turned white, hit by a burst from beyond the steam curtain. Adam grabbed the screaming woman by the coat collar and dragged her across the road to the crash barrier where the destroyed camper van gave them cover from the murderous hail of bullets; he literally threw her over the rail, screaming over the gunfire for her to get to the bottom of the bank and curl up in a ball until the shooting stopped. Satisfied there was nothing more he could do for the unfortunate woman he loaded a new magazine into the MP5, lay on the ground and sent a burst of fire under the floor of the camper before sprinting back to the Aston for one final retaliation before calling the retreat.

A quick rummage in the carrycot served the purpose, then Adam got himself behind the Aston for cover as once more the hail of bullets bounced all around him. He pulled the pin on both grenades and lobbed them as high and as far as he could. Through the dissipating steam Adam saw that his actions had been just in the nick of time. What were left of the Russians had regrouped and were moving forward when the first grenade landed behind them. The man Adam assumed to be the commander and his men hit the ground just as the grenade detonated; the lead soldier had just got to his feet when he spotted the second grenade just in front of them. He threw himself on the grenade just as it went off, saving the lives of his fellow soldiers but condemning himself to death.

Adam ran to the driver's side of the Aston. He had played his last card and needed to get out of there having done everything he could. He was about to step back into the Aston when he spotted a movement by the stricken Discovery door. The soldier he had rammed with the

Aston was crawling from the side of the vehicle; his legs were shattered but he was Spetsnaz and still a threat, legs or no legs.

Adam fired from only feet away, ending the torment of the wounded soldier and removing the threat. He then launched himself back into his car, praying that it was still capable of getting him out of this hell.

The big V8 roared into life like a wounded bull. Adam backed it up slowly at first to clear the Fiat abandoned by the inner cliff face, then full throttle leaving two black strips of rubber before flinging the nose round in an attempt to get away from the scene of destruction. For a second Adam thought he had escaped the clutches of his Russian pursuers but his heart sank as on moving forward the Aston started to vibrate and grind violently, the front end of the car shaking badly. Adam was only travelling at walking pace but he knew it would not be long until the Russians got their act together and gave chase once more. He didn't need to stop; he knew the front offside corner of his beloved car was jammed hard against the wheel, caused by the impact with the four-by-four. He was not far from Area One but he was not sure how long it would be before the mangled bodywork finally cut its way through the front tyre.

As the gunfire ceased Macinko counted the cost of the encounter; he had lost four of his men while one other had been wounded. This was getting out of hand. Macinko knew that to go back now without completing his mission would be very bad for both his and his men's health. Failure was not an option in Spetsnaz units; from now on it was do or die, there was no other option left.

Volkov had not been straight with him; this was no ordinary mission. You don't lose a third of your unit to supposed civilians, a fact confirmed to him as he searched the camper van to find an Accuracy International L96A1 British army issue sniper's rifle, but where were the people that had manned this camper van? Macinko picked up the weapon, using its telescopic sight to scan the surrounding area.

On the far side of the loch Bob had pulled himself from the freezing water but he was having problems pulling Callum's inert body from the swirling waters of Loch Lomond. He had watched the Russian soldier in black pick up his rifle and use it to search for them but as yet he had not turned his attention to this side of the loch. Bob badly needed to get Callum out of the water and behind the nearby bushes before they became target practice for the black-clad figures. It was then for the first time Bob noticed that he had not walked away unscathed; to his horror blood was running down his leg and dripping into the loch. He was numb from the cold water but his rapidly stiffening leg told him all was not well. Further investigation found a neat hole in his upper thigh; there was no exit wound so the bullet was still lodged somewhere in his thigh. Bob had no recollection of being hit but in the heat of things he had been too busy trying to get the lad out of the death trap to notice anything. With one almighty heave Callum's body finally slid onto the blood-soaked embankment. Bob watched warily as the Spetsnaz leader on the other side of the loch looked south down the loch-side through the telescopic lens of a sniper's rifle; the heavily damaged Aston Martin was making a slow withdrawal. In the foreground at the water's edge a pale-looking woman got to her feet; she had just drawn out her phone and was punching in numbers. Bob spotted her at the same time as the Russian. He wanted to scream at the woman to get down but there was no time. The Russian slid a shell into place, corrected his stance, leant forward and fired. Bob watched in horror as the woman's head exploded just before the crack of the sniper's rifle reverberated around the hills and cliffs surrounding them. Bob felt the adrenalin pulse once more through his weary body – he wanted to swim back across the loch and kill the black-clad bastard with his bare hands. The poor woman had done nothing more than be in the wrong place at the wrong time. Only his fear for Callum's life stopped him; he needed to find help and fast.

While Colonel Macinko rounded up his men the third Discovery arrived in the area after its detour. Senior Lieutenant Daniil Litvak ordered his driver to pull out past a group of stopped vehicles headed by an articulated lorry. The driver, who had a bullet hole in his windscreen, had obviously come into contact with the mayhem ahead and was stopping traffic from going any further. As the Discovery pulled alongside, Litvak waved his pistol at the driver causing him to step aside in shock.

When the Discovery pulled up next to Macinko's Discovery it was Litvak's turn to be shocked; it looked as if his team had been ambushed and not the other way around. Macinko bellowed at him to follow and sped away from what could only be described as a war scene.

Adam had limped the Aston as far as Tarbet. As he turned at the junction the grinding increased dramatically, followed by a loud bang as part of the Aston's front spoiler detached itself, allowing the front wheel rotate slightly more freely. Adam checked his rear-view mirror anxiously and pressed on, pushing the car as fast as he dared. Adam threw the Aston onto a farm track just as the front offside tyre finally said enough was enough and blew the sidewall out with a huge bang. Normally the car would still drive on three good wheels but the combination of the damage the car had sustained and the uneven surface of the dirt track road caused the nose of the Aston to dig into the dirt like a snowplough. The further Adam went the deeper the nose dug in until finally the clutch exploded, leaving the car with no drive.

Adam wasted no time as he scrambled round the front of the stricken car. He slipped a Glock into his jacket pocket and slung the MP5, complete with his last full magazine, around his neck and set off at a jog up the muddy wet farm track. He didn't want to sprint; if he remembered correctly the Area One base was some way off. He needed to preserve his energy in case the Spetsnaz troops found him.

After a few minutes hard driving along the twisty loch-side road, it finally opened out as it reached the small village of Tarbet. Macinko drove the lead Discovery while Litvak monitored the situation from the passenger seat of the second vehicle. Macinko was about to swear as they reached the road junction in Tarbet. With no idea or tracker to say which way the man they knew as Alan Hunter had fled, it was Macinko who noticed the green headlamp bezel from the Aston Martin fifty yards from the junction. Macinko smiled as he thrashed the Discovery onwards following the bodywork clues. A few minutes later Daniil Litvak spotted the stranded Aston Martin only a short distance from the road on a muddy farm track; he screamed at his driver to stop and the Discovery stood on its nose then reversed at speed. Litvak's vehicle was the first to arrive behind the Aston Martin. Litvak ordered his driver to drive around the stranded car but was not prepared for what happened next. The big Discovery's front wheels sank into the moss-covered boggy ground until it bellied out. Macinko arrived on scene and seeing Litvak's predicament tried the other side of the stranded Aston Martin without slowing down. The result was much the same although Macinko's vehicle sank so badly that it was impossible for them to open the doors; they had to exit the vehicle through the windscreen area, which had been already removed by gunfire courtesy of their enemy. With the brute strength of seven men they managed to recover Litvak's Discovery to the safety of the hard ground behind the Aston but Macinko's machine was too far off road to attempt recovery and was left sinking into the scenery.

Adam heard engines revving in the distance behind him and put two and two together. The engine noise came no closer so for the moment he was content that they would have to follow him on foot. He had climbed a small rise in the track before dropping down into a hollow so he was for now well out of sight from the area he had left the car. He racked his brain trying to remember how far Area One was from the road. It had been years since his short visit to the site; he had been flown out of there after he was ordered to flee from Northern Ireland. He was top of the IRA hit list and MI5 had taken no chances, moving him to one of the most secret sites in the UK, well away from the public.

Adam was glad he had chosen a green raincoat that morning. Its camouflage properties could well be put to the test if his Russian buddies caught up with him. He desperately wanted to pull up the hood, because the Scottish weather in the form of a heavy drizzle was now making its way down the back of his neck, but he needed all his senses; he needed to hear where his pursuers were. Adam looked back with some trepidation. The men who were about to give chase on foot were probably some of the toughest special forces soldiers on the planet. He had no doubt that if he did not find Area One very soon he would stand little chance alone with these men. As he scanned the mist-covered hillside for movement his only comforting thought was that he had bought enough time for Sue and Luke to get away. He hoped if he died now Sam would take comfort from the fact that he had done so saving their son.

Adam shook his head, flinging off the gathering rain droplets; he had to stop thinking like this. 'Who dares wins' – for god's sake he was SAS – it's not over until it's over. He needed to keep going and if it came to it he would take a few of these black-clad bastards with him to hell.

Adam cut across the path onto the moor, heading for the nearby treeline; he knew it would slow his progress massively, but the open farm road was far too exposed to be caught on. In the gloom of a rainy Scottish day he could vanish into the mist-covered scenery. Another fifteen minutes stumbling and stepping through the uneven boggy ground, threading his way through the treeline as fast as he could move, and still no Area One. Adam was beginning to doubt himself. Had he had picked the correct track? After all, this area was riddled with forestry tracks. He swore silently under his breath, stopping for a second to take a breather and listen for his pursuers. Somewhere in the distance multiple sirens were wailing; it was safe to assume they had found the camper. Very soon there would be a massive manhunt for the parties involved in the loch-side debacle. Adam wondered if it would be possible to signal to the police helicopter – it was sure to be called in to assist the operation. For a second his spirits rose but then he remembered the hunting pack behind him; they would have heard the sirens too, which would drive them on to finish him and escape before they were cornered. He switched his attention back to the way he had just come and the summit of the rise he had crossed five minutes ago. The mist had started to drop and the track on the horizon was partially obscured by dense fog; for a second Adam scrutinised the misty track then his eyes picked up movement just below the horizon, coming in his direction. He counted eight black ant-sized figures evenly spaced and zigzagging their way towards his position. Slowly Adam backed himself further into the edge of the adjacent forest then, when he was sure he was hidden, he charged headlong through the trees knocking rain from the branches onto himself in his haste to keep a gap between himself and the Russians.

6

Area One

Adam leapt at full speed in the mist over a tree stump and straight into a chain-link fence. He sat back looking up at the obstacle he had just run into. On top of the fence rolled razor wire stretched into the mist. This was no deer fencing; to his right a grubby white sign proclaimed 'Ministry of Defence Property. Keep Out'. He had found his target. No fancy signs – Area One blended into the scenery; even the trees were not disturbed to avoid giving the base away from the air.

Adam had a new dilemma. Did he try to follow the fence to the gatehouse or did he risk being shot by his own regiment if he crossed it? Adam was not sure how far the gatehouse was and made the split-second decision to take his chances and jump the fence here before the Russians arrived on the scene. He used the fence support and a tree branch to force the razor wire down; he was about to jump when he heard a voice commanding him to halt and freeze. Adam looked up from his efforts to scale the fence. A young man in his early twenties stood dressed in outdoor climbing gear – no uniform – an M4 shouldered and pointing directly at him. While he kept eye contact Adam ignored the young man's order, slowly using his thumb and forefinger to remove the Heckler and Koch MP5 from around his neck, letting it down by the strap before allowing it drop inside the fence. Adam's brain was racing; he needed to pick the right words to say to the young lad. If he said the wrong thing his next movement could be his last.

'I need to speak to your commanding officer urgently. I'm going to reach inside my coat pocket and remove my Glock with my fingertips and drop it with the MP5, then I'm going to jump down and you can pat me down and take my weapons. I must speak to your commanding officer. If you shoot me you will be shooting a MI6 operative. Tell me, how do you think that will go down with your boss if you shoot me?'

The young soldier was rattled but he kept the gun sight trained on Adam and said nothing. Adam was acutely aware the Russians must be closing in; he had no more time for talk. Slowly he removed his Glock and dropped it before following it down, rolling to take the shock out of his legs from the jump. As he stood up he was patted down by the serious-looking young man.

'I don't know who you are, mister, but you better be telling the truth. Get moving that way and remember, one fuckin' step out of line and you get a bullet in the back quicker than you can say MI6 – you got that?'

The young guy was busy talking to someone on his head mic when Adam heard the thud of a shell hitting a body. He turned to see the look of shock on the young lad's face as he fell forward. He heard another shell whistle past his ear as instinct kicked in and he hit the ground just behind a large tree root. He grabbed and pulled the young guy over the root with him to give him some cover. To Adam's relief it had not been a kill shot; the shell had hit the soldier high on his arm, rendering the arm useless. The soldier transferred the M4 to his other hand and sprayed the area beyond the fence with a burst of automatic fire before sinking back down behind the root system, his face racked with pain. Adam ripped the cord from his hood and grabbed the lad. He made a basic tourniquet to stem the flow of blood while the young guy roared into his head mic. 'Code red, code red. Hostile fire Area 9 north-east perimeter. Man down, repeat, man down. Require assist.'

Adam was leaning forward to retrieve his MP5 when he felt the wet warm barrel of the M4 touch the back of his neck.

'Don't even fuckin' think about it. You had better tell me what the fuck is going down here or I swear the next bullet is for you, arsehole!'

Adam released his grip on the MP5 and slowly slid further down behind the tree root while keeping a close eye on the perimeter fence for visitors. 'Okay. The men attacking are Russian special forces – they're after me. There are eight of them outside the fence and as we sit here in the pissing rain debating they will be flanking us on either side to make sure we don't get help. We need to get going.' Adam went to make a move but again the M4 was pressed against his head.

'Listen, spook, I'm the fuckin' boss out here and I say we stay put until my buddies arrive.'

Something in Adam's head snapped and he grabbed the muzzle of the M4, forcing it away from him while getting up close and personal with the young soldier. 'Listen very carefully. You are hit, in shock and slowly bleeding to death. You couldn't hit a barn door with your M4. Before I was a spook I was 22SAS, so don't just sit on your yellow arse – get up and get moving before I take your M4 and beat you to death with it.'

Adam groped around for his MP5, found it and crawled past the dumbfounded soldier who fell into line, moving awkwardly because of his wound.

Captain Fiona Malden sat in the back of Area One's control room studying her flight plan while she waited for Major Daniel Lucas to finish his inspection of the facility. Malden had spent the last week ferrying Major Lucas around the country, checking security at all the strategic bases in the wake of the MI6 director's assassination. This was not her idea of fun and the fact that Lucas treated her like a school-girl did not help things. Since joining 658 Squadron Fiona Malden, whether training or on missions, had proved to her colleagues that she was one of the best pilots in the Joint Special Forces Aviation Wing and one of the few to have been awarded the DFC for her efforts. She had recently turned down promotion and a desk job in favour of her adrenalin-fuelled missions with special forces – she was not quite ready to hang up her flying helmet – but her latest task, combined with the fact that she had worked with the late Neil Andrews, had put her into what was for her an unusually depressed state of mind.

Malden was daydreaming about getting out of this crappy Scottish weather and heading home to her cottage in Tillington and her beautiful Audi R8 that she'd had little chance yet to play with, when the sound of machine-gun fire echoed around the base. Fiona Malden was used to gunfire. She had worked in Afghanistan where she regularly had to put up with ground fire directed at her aircraft, but she was not sure why this would be happening in Scotland. She looked at Major Lucas, who in turn looked at Duty Sergeant Powers quizzically, but Powers had no explanation. After a second the desk mic crackled into operation. All three listened to the code red message transmitted by Steve Turner. Malden waited for a reaction from her commanding officer as Sergeant Powers grabbed the desk mic, flicking it to transmit all.

'Code red, I say again, code red. This is not a drill. I repeat, this is not a drill. Wilson and Mathis proceed to Area 9 with caution. All others to hold station and await further orders.' Powers switched off the mic and Major Lucas loaded a clip into an M4 he had just removed from the gun rack in the corner of the room. Fiona was awaiting her orders but for the moment it seemed that her talents were not required.

'Try to get your man back on the radio and find out what's going on. I am heading to Area 9 to see for myself. Look after Fiona until I get back, there's a good lad,' Lucas yelled as he left to head in the direction of Area 9.

Two soldiers who had been in the canteen on a break appeared and Powers wasted no time sending both men to double the guard on the entrance to the tunnel leading to the underground complex that contained the nuclear weapons with instructions to take out anyone coming within fifty metres of the complex entrance. Sergeant Powers was considering his next move when his corporal checked in on the radio, his voice no more than a whisper.

'Be advised, multiple intruders confirmed Area 9. Moving to intercept. Out.'

There was a set procedure to follow but Powers had been holding off, hoping for the situation to resolve itself. This latest message gave him no choice; he knew once he hit the alarm button all hell would break loose. SBS troops based in and around Faslane would seal off the base. Royal Marine commandos based at Coulport and reinforcements from the commando base in Arbroath would be heading their way very soon.

Adam had stopped for a second to let the wounded soldier catch him up; just as the soldier reached his side Adam noticed movement to his right. He had already started to take cover when there was a burst of automatic fire from the left. For a second Adam was confused; a body burst out of the undergrowth to his left, firing again to his right. There was a return of fire but it was short and stopped abruptly as the black-clad figure of a Russian soldier broke cover and fell forward, hit multiple times by rounds from an M4 wielded by someone Adam couldn't see. The new arrival stepped forward firing a final burst into the inert figure, making sure his target was finished and no further threat.

Almost simultaneously a major in uniform and two soldiers in civvies arrived on the scene. The major introduced himself as Major Lucas and was in the process of examining the dead Russian soldier when the group came under fire from two directions. Lucas ordered covering fire while he and Adam dragged the now struggling wounded soldier away. Lucas turned to give one final order as Adam felt and heard the hit. At first he thought he had taken a round, but the shock wave had passed through all three men's bodies, arm in arm as they were, helping the wounded soldier; it was soon apparent, though, that Major Lucas was the one who had taken the hit. He was struggling to stay upright and stumbling forward. Adam wanted to stop but when he slackened pace Lucas roared at him to keep going. The three remaining soldiers laid down murderous covering fire, turning the immediate wooded area to firewood.

Lucas guided the three of them out of the scrub past the tunnel entrance to their far left, past the canteen towards the control room. The door opened and to Adam's surprise Fiona Malden, who he had worked with previously, appeared, followed by a sergeant, M4 at the ready. Lucas and the wounded soldier sank to their knees. The young guy propped himself against the wall of the office, struggling for breath, while Fiona and Adam dragged Major Lucas to a sitting position so they could examine his wounds. The bullet had caught him low in the back on one side and, as Fiona pulled his shirt clear of the wound, dark blood flowed freely onto his already saturated trousers. Adam was no medic but he had seen this type of wound before in the battlefield. He doubted if even a medical trauma team would be able to do anything. He looked first into the eyes of Major Lucas, trying to hide his despair, then at Fiona Malden. It was clear to see that in his blood-spattered and muddy condition she had no clue who he was. Adam had recognised her instantly but Fiona did not click. Adam watched as slowly, in a state of shock, recognition began to dawn on her.

'Jesus Christ, Mac, how? I mean, what the hell are you doing here?'

Fiona continued to hold a pressure on Lucas's wound while Sergeant Powers tried to bandage him up. Powers was still struggling with the field dressing when Fiona called a halt to the proceedings, rechecking the major's pulse in his neck before satisfying herself that he was gone. Powers turned his attention to the young guy who was as white as a ghost and shaking badly. The gunfire to the east had slowed to the occasional burst as Fiona re-entered the office in search of more medical kit. Adam joined her in the search.

In a ditch on the far side of the mud track Colonel Serge Macinko's mind was in turmoil. He needed to complete the mission assigned to his unit but his military mind was telling him to get the hell out of the predicament he found himself in.

In all his years in charge of the FSB alpha group he had never been led on such a merry dance. The husband of the woman who was the main target was not known as military, but he had ambushed his unit, then led them to this unknown military camp. One of his men had just reported back saying he had spotted a heavily guarded tunnel in the hillside. Macinko knew they were in the same area as the British nuclear submarine fleet; he had studied Faslane and Coulport in great detail previously, so he knew if this base was connected in some way he had very little time until British forces arrived in overwhelming strength. His men, if ordered, would fight to the death, but this so-called hit would then become a major international incident, one that his government would not be able to talk itself out of. Macinko feared that his actions could start a war neither country wanted.

Grudgingly he admitted this unknown stranger had him in check in this all too real game of chess. Macinko gave the order to pull out, telling senior Lieutenant Litvak to get what was left of the unit to the extraction point; he would not be joining them. It was not quite checkmate yet; he wanted to give his men time to get out while he had one last crack at taking down this deadly stranger.

Captain Fiona Malden had the turbine engine of her Gazelle AH1 running as she watched Adam help Steve Turner into the chopper for his trip to Faslane. She had left Sergeant Powers in the control room to tell the Faslane trauma suite they had a casualty inbound and provide them with his blood group so they could be ready.

There were two rapid bursts of machine-gun fire from the gatehouse – Fiona heard them over the whine as the turbine engine of the Gazelle warmed up. She hoped that the gunfire came from British guns defending the entrance; she needed to get her machine into the air pretty damned quickly. Their position was far too exposed and the Gazelle would make a prime target for their attackers if they caught it on the ground. As if someone had read her mind there was another burst of machine-gun fire, this time much closer. Fiona realised her machine had been hit as she felt the vibrations through the superstructure and closed down the engine, at the same time drawing her Beretta and thumbing off the safety catch. She remained on the far side of the stricken chopper trying to catch a glimpse of the enemy. Adam was not so lucky; as he turned round from loading the now unconscious soldier into the chopper he was confronted by a black-clad figure.

Adam recognised his cold blue eyes and slight build from the Airsoft game. He thought about trying to engage him in conversation, but he knew this man was Spetsnaz and he had no intention to do anything other than kill him. Macinko only hesitated for a fraction of a second to say one word as he squeezed the trigger. Adam froze to the spot; he knew he had finally run out of luck as he heard the words from the Russian soldier: 'Checkmate.'

Sergeant Powers fired through the window of the control room just as the Ninja-type character raised his weapon to shoot the blood-spattered stranger by the Gazelle. The stranger was still frozen to the spot as Powers kicked the control room door open and put two bursts of machine-gun fire into the head and body of the Russian special forces soldier. As he lay on the ground, blood starting to pool around him, Powers wanted to make very sure he was a dead man. He felt no remorse; he had just spotted the bodies of two MOD police officers sprawled on the road by the gatehouse. Karma was his only thought as he kicked the Russian's body over to inspect his handiwork. Powers was about to speak to the stranger when Corporal Armstrong radioed into control.

'Sarge, we've spotted six of the bastards bailing out heading east. Permission to intercept?'

Sergeant Powers placed the M4 on the table, shaking his head as he replied. 'Negative. Secure the perimeter. That is our job here and our only job. We have enough casualties without adding to them. Remain at Area 9 until relieved.'

Adam entered the control room while Fiona Malden checked on the condition of the two MOD officers at the gatehouse. He stood quietly listening to the sergeant updating the base commanders at Faslane and Coulport; he wanted to but in when he described the incident as an attack on the base but decided to wait until he had his full attention.

The sergeant finished his report and was advised SBS would be with him in five minutes. Captain Kemp from M group would assume command for the moment while 43 Commando had recalled all personnel and both bases were locked down until further notice.

Adam waited until the sergeant had switched off the mic before speaking. 'I don't know your name, but I would like to thank you for saving my life.' Adam went to shake the sergeant's hand but he was met with a steely-eyed stare and no attempt to take his hand.

'I don't know who the fuck you are, pal, but you have one hell of a lot of explaining to do, so sit over there and shut your mouth until someone asks you a question. Do we understand one another?'

Adam was not having a good day; he needed to explain the situation and the red mist was starting to descend. This was the last thing he needed right now. 'Listen, soldier, it is very important that you listen to me. I have information that you need to know now, not in an hour's time when someone gets round to talking to me. These men are Russian special forces. They are not attacking the base – they were after me. I am the target, not this base or any other base. The target is myself and my family, nothing else. The man you shot was the leader of a twelve-man Spetsnaz unit.'

The sergeant had picked up a brush and had started to remove some of the shattered glass littering the control room floor. He stopped and shook his head. 'Bullshit. Are you telling me you all just happened to be passing this base? As the Scots say, do you think I came up the Clyde in a banana boat, son? I've never heard so much bollocks in my life!'

Fiona Malden walked back into the office just as the sergeant finished speaking. 'The MOD guys are both dead. Sergeant Powers, if I were you I would listen to what Adam has to say. I can vouch for him, we have worked together before. I am pretty sure he will be telling the truth – he's not the type of guy who talks bullshit.'

Fiona was still speaking as the sound of revving engines and the unmistakable sound of Land Rovers with off-road tyres howling in protest at being worked hard on tarmac roads broke the tension that was building in the control office. Three 110 Land Rover Defenders screamed into the parking area between the disabled chopper and the control room. Men were pouring from all three vehicles, armed to the teeth with various types of military hardware. Adam watched the men take up defensive positions around the compound before their leader and his second in command appeared satisfied they had secured the area and came looking for answers in the control room.

Captain Kemp listened first to Sergeant Powers then to Adam's version of events before dispatching his second in command to check in with troops guarding the perimeter. Kemp sat down wearily, looking out of the control room window and studying the scenery, clearly trying to make up his mind on the next step.

They did not have to wait long until he was on his feet again. 'Sergeant Powers, you will accompany your wounded soldier to Faslane. You will also take Mr McDonald here with you. Until further investigation I am placing him under military arrest – you will supervise his detention at Faslane. Captain Malden, you can hitch a lift to Faslane where you can contact your commanding officer to arrange your pickup. I suggest you get a move on – your man has lost a lot of blood. M group will take over security here for the moment until further orders come in from higher up the tree.'

Fiona came to Adam's defence. 'Captain Kemp, there is no need to place Adam under arrest – for god's sake, he's one of yours. He was special forces when you were both wet behind the ears. He can be trusted, I swear it.'

Kemp's clenched fists gave away what his face did not. 'It would be better if you kept your personal thoughts to yourself, Malden. No one knows the truth yet. I prefer to let military intelligence carry out an investigation before jumping to conclusions. You obviously have personal feelings for McDonald. You'd better be careful not to get dragged into this with him.'

Sergeant Powers had to physically stop Malden from grabbing Kemp. 'If you are addressing me it's Captain Malden, and don't talk to me like I'm some office girl fresh out of school – we are the same rank. Have you any idea who the man you're about to arrest is? He has powerful connections in London who will have your resignation for this.'

Malden turned her attention to Sergeant Powers who was still holding on to her arm. 'Are your ears sewn on, Sergeant? Take your hands off me. Touch me again and I will have you on a charge for assaulting an officer.'

Fiona Malden's dark eyes burned into the back of Sergeant Powers' skull. Powers apparently decided not to test her and she marched out of the office. 'Adam and I will get the wounded lad into the Land Rover. You pair can do as you wish. Let's get going before you decide to stab anyone else in the back!'

Adam followed Malden out of the office to help her transfer the young soldier from the Gazelle. 'Fiona, thanks for backing me up in there, but if I were you I would distance yourself from me. I could be in a lot of bother here – unregistered firearms and breach of the Official Secrets Act are just two things that spring to mind. On top of that I don't have Neil Andrews to watch my back this time. They could lock me up and throw away the key if they wanted to, you know.'

Fiona turned to him as they reached the far side of the helicopter. 'Adam, where are Samantha and Luke? You might need her to pull some strings for you this time.'

Adam shrugged his shoulders, trying to hide his dejected mood from Fiona. 'God knows, Fiona. She went off to London on one of her crusades just before all this shit started. She managed to get word to me about the Russians just in time. Luke and his nanny are safe, I hope. I led the Russians away from them so they could escape. I know nothing more – I think the Russians have killed the MI6 agent Sam was in contact with. He was up here helping me.'

After a bumpy trip west in the Defender they were ushered in by a heavily armed guard at the gates of Faslane naval base. The young squaddie, who was dipping in and out of consciousness, was rushed away by a medical team. Powers led Fiona and Adam into a room with no outside windows, then stood by the open door. 'Are you coming out while I lock the door, *Captain* Malden, ma'am?'

For a second Malden said nothing, weighing up the situation. 'If you're going to lock Captain McDonald up you can lock me up as well. Just make sure when you contact my base commander at Credenhill you tell him where I am, and why you have locked up Mac. That will be all, Sergeant. You can go.'

Powers slammed the door before turning the lock. His footsteps faded into the distance as Adam and Fiona were left alone in the locked room.

It was Fiona who was first to break the silence. 'I don't think Sergeant Powers is a big fan of women in the military, especially ones who outrank him.'

Fiona looked round at their sparse new surroundings while Adam sat on the edge of one of the two beds – the only furniture in the room. He was still finding it hard to come to terms with the fact his world had once more been turned upside down. His home abandoned, his son in hiding, Bob possibly killed or wounded, his Aston Martin destroyed and Sam gone walkabout, as his Australian pals would have said.

He knew Fiona was trying to take his mind off the bad place he was in when she spoke. 'I wonder whose room we've stolen. By the looks of things I don't think they'll miss the room that much.'

Adam eventually replied without looking up, his head still in his hands. 'Rest rooms for the divers, I suspect. When a sub is in port it has divers in the water constantly. They take shifts guarding it so I reckon this is one of their rest rooms.'

Fiona Malden was shaking her head in disbelief. 'Lovely – swimming about in a Scottish loch in the middle of winter. They couldn't pay me enough to do that job. I'll stick to my helicopters, thank you very much.'

Adam was aware Fiona was still trying to lift the mood in the room and with a conscious effort he tried to put his own problems to the back of his mind. 'Well, we have time to kill, Fiona. What do you suggest? Tell me what you've been up to for the last couple of years.'

Fiona rolled her eyes before speaking. 'Locked in a room with only beds and all you want to do is talk. Yip, that's Mac for you, no sense of imagination. It's okay, Mac, honey, you're safe. I've seen Samantha in action and I for one would not tangle with that lady. Adam, don't worry too much about Sam. Remember, I was in the hospital when you were in a coma and if there's one thing I know for sure – that girl was worried sick. As sure as day follows night that girl is head over heels in love with you. Who knows what she's up to, but I know she will move heaven and earth to be with you. I'm not sure you know that, though. Cheer up – you're a lucky man. You've found your perfect partner. I'm still single and looking for Mr Right.'

Adam stood up and started pacing backwards and forwards, feeling like a caged lion, then walked over to the door to make sure no one was outside. He perched on the side of Fiona's bed. 'Fiona, I need you to do me a couple of big favours. I reckon it won't be long until they're told to get you back to Credenhill. When you get out I need you to check out a few things for me. As well as the MI6 lad, one of my old colleagues, Bob Hunter, was involved in the shoot-out with the Russians. The last I saw of them he was dragging the body of the MI6 guy across the loch. I need you to find Sam and get her to go and look for Bob. He might be in big trouble – that is if he made it.'

Fiona sat up, crossing her legs on the bed, and put her hand on Adam's shoulder. 'Of course I will. But where will I find Samantha? I mean, I can't just waltz up to MI6 and ask to speak to Samantha O'Conner, can I?'

Adam reached up, removing Fiona's hand from his shoulder. At the same second footsteps outside were followed by the door being un-locked. Sergeant Powers entered without invitation.

'Captain Malden, there will be a Chinook here in fifteen minutes dropping off reinforcements from 45 Commando. You need to be on the Chinook. Apparently our commanding officer has arranged for you to brief him on the situation here. The helicopter's not stopping so I would advise you to say your goodbyes to your cellmate and get mov-ing.' Although nothing more was said it was very clear Sergeant Powers was not happy about the evolving situation.

Adam stood up to give Fiona room to get to her feet in the tiny room. She was about to walk out but turned and gave Adam a peck on the cheek. 'Don't worry … I'll find her.'

Malden turned towards the door and Powers' disapproving gaze.

'Don't worry, Sergeant, we're not dating or anything. The man pulled me unconscious from a sinking helicopter and saved my life. I think a little kiss is the least he deserves. Bye, Adam.'

Malden walked past Powers, flicking her jet-black bobbed hair back as she adjusted her collar, causing Powers to shuffle out of her way to avoid being hit by her elbow.

7

The Embassy

Sam woke from a troubled sleep to find the glass of water by her bedside vibrating. As she watched it stopped then started again; it took her a few seconds to realise that her phone was vibrating next to the water. Sam grabbed the phone then checked the screen; no caller, it had to be Ludmilla. She clicked the green button and listened, holding her breath.

'Tonight, 9 p.m., a minibus from the Elsa Novak Studios will drop off a group of girls at the ambassador's residence. Make sure you are one of them. I will meet you there.'

Sam had no chance to cross-examine Ludmilla; she had already gone.

It seemed an eternity until Sam was alone at her desk. She punched in Elsa Novak Studios and came up with a website for glamour models, but she smelled a rat. A bit of digging, a call to the Met vice squad, and Sam was given the password and alternative website of Elsa Novak Studios where young girls were paraded on screen wearing very little, some nothing: call girls for clients to pick and order online. Vadek Volkov was obviously a good customer if he could afford a bus load of these girls. Sam was noting down the address when Jean appeared by her shoulder.

'Thinking of a new career, Samantha? I don't think Adam would be too impressed with that one – don't you agree? I tried to call but you were engaged. Bill Mathews would like to see you. He has a COBRA meeting in an hour so I would imagine he's looking for a progress report. Best not to keep him waiting – he's under a lot of pressure.'

Ten minutes later Jean ushered Sam into Bill Mathews' office. Mathews was not the only one whose nerves were frayed. Sam had not spoken to Adam for days and it was starting to eat at her. Jean apparently thought she could defuse the atmosphere with coffee and biscuits. Bill moved his mug to the side and looked at Sam as she sat cupping her mug in both hands.

'Well, Samantha. How is your side of the investigation progressing? I need to speak to the PM shortly – can you give me anything to keep him off my back?'

Sam cursed to herself. She did not want to tell Mathews anything but she needed to keep him sweet for the moment. She decided to give him a few crumbs without giving away her real intention. 'I have a contact inside the Russian Embassy who's doing some digging for me. They seem to think this Syrian warlord Tarek Attar is planning some type of attack. I'll know more at the next meeting.'

Mathews was frowning and fidgeting with his hands. 'Not good enough, Sam, not nearly good enough. I want proof Volkov was behind the assassination. I couldn't give a damn about this Attar rumour – you need to get your finger out and step up a gear.'

Sam was getting close to the edge but with great effort controlled her temper. 'Have you heard anything from Scotland yet? Have you sent anyone to help?'

Mathews stopped twiddling his fingers and gripped the edge of the table, his fingertips going white with the pressure; veins started to show on his forehead as he lost his cool. 'For god's sake, Samantha, forget about events in Scotland. I need you concentrating one hundred per cent on matters here. That is an order. Do you get that or shall I send you a memo?'

Sam placed the cup of untouched coffee by the side of her chair her hand shaking with fury. She then leaned forward, her eyes wide with the madness in her head. 'Time for some home truths, my friend. If you care to revisit my file you will note that I am a finisher – MI6's politically correct name for an assassin. If you want field work, get a field agent. I'm doing what I can. I have to meet my contact tonight at the Russian Embassy and hopefully the situation will resolve itself.

'If you want to replace me, feel free, so I can sort out my life. If not, get off my back and let me do my job. Just remember, if anything happens to my family it won't just be the Russian who will pay a terrible price. Got that, or shall I send you a memo?'

Sam started for the door, intent on leaving.

'Samantha, did you just make a threat on my life?'

Sam turned back just as Bill Mathews stood up. The tips of their noses almost touched as she leaned over the desk and spoke through clenched teeth. 'No, Bill, not a threat, never a threat. It's a promise from me to you. Got it? I'll put that in the memo too.'

Mathews shouted after her as Sam left the office. 'Do not do anything other than speak to your contact, and I want you in my office first thing tomorrow morning.'

Sam's taxi pulled up on Greenhill in Hampstead. She paid the driver and although he had dropped her outside the Elsa Novak Studio she walked along the street checking window reflections and passing cars for signs of a tail. After a few minutes she doubled back along the smart-looking street. Sam was pretty sure that the beautifully decorated Novak Studio had the local population fooled into thinking it was a photographic studio. After all, anyone would expect a stream of pretty girls going to and from the studio. She entered through a marble-clad archway that led to the back of the building. On arriving at reception the page three model behind the desk asked if she could help. Sam could tell from her attitude that she was used to turning away Elle McPherson hopefuls. Sam asked to speak to Elsa Novak regarding Vadek Volkov's account; she was pretty sure that would get her attention. Three minutes later Sam was ushered past a large bouncer type, who was loitering in the hallway, and shown into a maroon leather-walled office where no expense had been spared on the decor. Behind the huge desk a woman with short blonde hair wearing a business suit sat regarding Sam over the top of a pair of designer glasses.

'Good morning. I believe you have something to do with Ambassador Volkov. Is that correct?'

Sam shook her head, walking into the middle of the room, her hands in her pockets. 'There are two ways this can go. Let's hope we can come to an amicable agreement. I work for a government agency and you are going to smuggle me into the Russian Embassy with your call girls tonight.' There was silence in the office; you could have heard a pin drop. The blonde woman stood up and removed her glasses, then shouted, 'Ronnie, can you come in, love, and take out the trash.'

The door opened and the bald bouncer walked into the office, an evil smile on his face. 'Pretty girl ... I hope you put up a fight. I like fighters.'

'I don't know who you are or what you want, love, but I have friends in high places. You don't worry me. Ronnie will see you to the door. For your own health I would go quietly – Ronnie had a fetish for beating up tarts with big mouths.'

The woman sat down again, replacing her glasses, and returned her attention to the paperwork on her desk. Sam turned to face Ronnie. 'Listen, mate, do yourself a favour and take an early lunch break while I speak to your boss.'

Ronnie said nothing but removed an old Browning pistol from his belt as he headed for Sam. He was bringing the pistol to bear on her when she leapt, kicking the gun from the hand of the mesmerised minder with her right leg. She landed like a cat just as Ronnie bent down to pull his backup revolver from his ankle holster but again he was no match for Sam. Once more she leapt but this time she spun high above the desk. Ronnie was just rising from a crouching position as Sam spun clockwise in the air, the speed of her spin trebling the force with which the heel of her right foot made contact with Ronnie's jawbone. There was a sickening crack as Ronnie's jaw parted company with his skull and the big guy crashed forward, landing on a nest of ornate coffee tables and turning them instantly to firewood.

Sam replaced her hands in her pockets and walked round to the side of the shocked woman's desk. 'Poor Elsa. You have no idea what you've got yourself involved in, have you? Humour me, Elsa, and switch your computer on. Check all your bank accounts, and yes, the Russian account, the Swiss account, and your safety deposit bank as well.' Sam wandered round the room checking out the paintings on the wall while Elsa checked her bank accounts.

Eventually she looked up, her eyes narrowing. 'What have you done with my money, you evil cow?'

Sam smiled at the last reference before replying. 'Elsa, here is what is going to happen. You will drop me off with the girls as planned at nine – easy, no hassle – that's all I want. If everything goes to plan, your accounts will return to normal in the morning.' Sam stood up as she talked and walked over to the far side of the room, picking up a cushion and the Browning, which she had kicked from Ronnie's hand. She placed the pillow on Ronnie's chest, pushed the Browning hard into the pillow and pulled the trigger. Ronnie's unconscious body gave a jerk as the muffled thud fired a bullet through his heart. Elsa gasped, stood up and knocked her chair over in her panicked attempt to leave the room. Sam wiped down the Browning and grabbed Elsa by the hair as she tried to make her escape. With the safety on, Sam forced the hysterical woman to hold the discharged gun before dropping it into a plastic bag.

'If anything goes wrong I will make sure this gun, with your prints on it, is handed in to the police. My friends will make sure that Ronnie here has all your stolen money in his account and that is why in a fit of rage you broke his jaw with the gun then shot him. You see, my dear, if I wanted to I could make it look like Mickey Mouse shot Ronnie. As I said before, you have no idea who you are dealing with. I will be outside walking the street at eight thirty. Remember, no mistakes, Elsa, or you are history. Now, sort yourself out. After all, you're meant to be a hard-nosed brothel madam, tough as nails, not a blubbering wreck.'

Sam spent the next few hours shopping for clothes to wear that evening. She spent some time with Sally, one of the younger shop assistants, who helped her pick an outfit for what Sam had led her to believe was going to be a hot date. Sam had been closeted away on the west coast of Scotland for the last two years and had more idea about which type of nappy was best than what the current fashion trends were in the capital. She finally settled for a purple wrap silk dress, long black suede boots, and a black waterfall jacket. Sally watched Sam as she modelled her new outfit, adding that the only thing needed was for Sam to have her hair done in curls to finish off the look. Sam then found herself two doors down from the clothing shop in Sally's sister's hair salon.

While the girl worked on her hair, Sam turned things over in her head. She'd thought that her life had moved on from her murky past, but in truth she had just proved deep down she was still a cold-blooded killer; she had killed the minder without even a flicker of emotion. She had needed to prove to the woman she was capable of anything. For Adam's and Luke's sakes she needed tonight to go as planned; she could not afford Elsa Novak talking to Vadek Volkov and the only way to do that was to make Elsa more terrified of her than of Volkov. Billy in IT at Six had provided the final incentive for Elsa Novak; her life revolved around money. Billy had worked his magic with her accounts, making them seem empty. Elsa could not have known that they would return to normal at the next security sweep by the bank's IT system.

Sam found a coffee shop near Jean's house and parked herself by a window table, thinking things through for tonight and watching the world go by. She used her mobile to call the Invermorroch Hotel, but her usual source of gossip had left the temporary staff to run the hotel while she took a break. Sam ordered another cup of coffee; she had decided she was not going back to Vauxhall Cross until she had been to the Russian Embassy – she did not want Bill Mathews screwing up her plans for the evening.

Bill Mathews was reading a report supplied to him by his second in command at Thames House when he stopped abruptly, rereading the name listed in the surveillance team's report from Heathrow Airport. He picked up the phone and dialled directly to his office at MI5 headquarters. 'Hi, Chris, how goes it at Thames House? Listen, I have the copy report from Heathrow. Are you sure you made positive ID on Tarek Attar?'

'One hundred per cent, sir. He tried to disguise himself as a businessman called Suleiman El Mahdy, but we took DNA from a glass he used at the bar. Just got the results back – it's a match to a sample Interpol have. Didn't want to pick him up just yet. Thought we might see who he's talking to these days. You okay with that, sir?'

Mathews was more worried than intrigued; Sam had been right all along. 'Okay, Chris, let's see what he's up to. Double your teams following him and make sure your best people are on him. We can't let him out of our sight – he's a dangerous man. Keep me informed.'

Mathews hung up then called Jean. 'Jean, can you get Samantha down to my office immediately please.'

There was an awkward pause before Jean replied. 'Sorry, sir, she's out of the office. She hasn't been allocated a safe phone yet. The quartermaster says there's some kind of hold up with the contract. I'll get her to contact you the minute she's back.'

Bill Mathews shook his head as he put the phone down and studied an email request by Brigadier Wilson of the Army Intelligence Corps requesting that MI6 send someone to investigate one of their people who had been accused of breaching security protocol at Area One and to arrange a meeting urgently to discuss the problem. Mathews switched off his computer, shaking his head. Agents with no phones, brigadiers with an axe to grind: Mathews had had enough. He hadn't been home that week and his wife was waiting for him; he was going to go home and take his poor wife out for a meal. Tomorrow was another day.

Sam checked her reflection in a shop window while she waited for Elsa and her girls to show up. Her camouflage seemed to be working – she had already received a number of wolf whistles from passing cars. She had also been accosted by a scruffy-looking youth who wanted to know if she fancied a party. Sam informed him she was an undercover vice cop and asked if he wanted to continue the party at the station.

Sam's outfit didn't scream 'prostitute', but it didn't make her look like she was Mother Teresa either. Her thigh-length black boots concealed her Glock while her dress would keep the guards' eyes off her boots. Herjacket lining concealed two spare magazines for the Glock. Sam's blonde mane was now curly and hung down over her shoulders; her black silk clutch bag held no secrets as it was sure to be checked by security. Her make-up, although subtle, was applied slightly more heavily than usual, so that when she looked again in the shop window at her reflection she almost did not recognise herself, such was the transformation.

To Sam's surprise it was Elsa herself who pulled up in the Transit minibus. Elsa said nothing as she climbed aboard but her look of hatred said it all. Sam studied her minibus companions. If it had not been a life or death situation for her she would probably have wept. Sam was by far the oldest present; in fact it was safe to say that most of the girls were young enough to have been her daughters, in particular one oriental girl who looked like she was still a schoolkid. Sam was worried that when things got nasty these girls would be caught in the crossfire. She focused, telling herself what she was about to do was for her son; nothing else mattered.

The van passed by the embassy and continued on to the ambassador's residence where two heavily built bodyguards stood guard by the front doors. Sam hung back as the girls trooped out of the minibus while Elsa sat by the controls not moving, almost as if she were cast in stone. Sam wanted to see what the guards were checking, if anything, before committing herself to a check. She picked up a movement in the corner of her eye. The window on the ground floor to the left of the entrance was not lit, but a figure stood in the darkness looking out at the minibus. Sam could just make out the ghostly white face of Ludmilla Berkov staring out at her in the darkness; she was clasping a folder to her chest with crossed arms.

Sam had watched the guards intermittently lift a handheld metal detector and sweep it over the girls as they passed. She slipped something into her mouth as she approached the guard head down, avoiding eye contact. She wasn't having much luck; as well as being stopped by the guard to her right he swept the metal detector over her; as she had expected it started beeping. The guard stepped forward to frisk her but Sam gave him the best puppy dog eyes she could muster, breaking into a beaming smile to reveal the braces on her teeth. The guards burst out laughing, pointing to the metal braces, and waved her through, smacking her on the backside for good measure as she passed. Sam thought she had done it as she stepped inside the big Kensington residence, but waiting inside the door was another man Sam recognised from pictures she had studied at Vauxhall Cross. He was Peter Sokolov, head of security and a far tougher test.

Sam watched as Peter Sokolov stood in the hallway directing the girls to where he wanted them, so she was prepared for the attention as Sokolov stopped her. He asked her to open her clutch bag and poked around looking for something that shouldn't be there, but nothing would have stood out: make-up, condoms, wipes, deodorant, pretty much what he might have expected to find. Sam was questioned but her answers would only confirm why she had never been seen here before – a divorced mum just arrived here from Birmingham, and Elsa had sent for her to fill a gap in her escort service. Sokolov was watching her all the time, but Sam was as cool as a cucumber. He was clearly still weighing her up when a roar came from the rear of the building. Sam could see Sokolov was rattled by the outburst and wanted to find out for himself what was going on. He told Sam to go to the drawing room and wait with the other girls he had sent there.

Sam started to make her way to the rear of the house where she had been told the drawing room was situated, but the minute Peter Sokolov vanished she retraced her steps and entered the room on the left of the entrance hall. The room was in darkness when Sam entered and it took a few seconds for her night vision to start working in the dark room. She found herself standing in the dining room; in the far corner of the room Ludmilla Berkov stepped out from behind the heavy curtains. Her eyes were like saucers and she was shaking uncontrollably.

'Pull yourself together, Ludmilla. I can't do this without your help. Tell me, do you ever meet with Volkov in this house?'

Ludmilla froze, thinking for a second, then moved round the dining table to join Sam by the door. 'I have only met with the pig once across the hall in his library, why?'

Sam put her arm around Ludmilla's shoulder to comfort her and guided her to the door. 'Okay, here is what I need you to do, then it will all be up to me and your job will have been done. Take the folder with you, go to the guards at the front door and tell them you have an urgent message from Moscow. Tell them it can't wait until morning, that you need to speak to Volkov and that you will wait for him in the library as usual, got it?'

Sam almost had to push Berkov out of the door, then, when she started heading for the front door, Sam darted into the library, her fingers searching in the dark for the light switch.

Once inside Sam used her time waiting for Ludmilla to return to get ready for her assault. She removed the braces from her mouth then retrieved the Glock 17 from her right boot, operated the slide and checked the magazine was secure. She slipped her spare mags from the lining of her jacket and tucked one in either side of the folds of her dress. She had just finished removing the throwing knives from the sleeves of her jacket when the door slipped open and Ludmilla Berkov stepped into the room. Sam positioned her on the far side of the room to await the arrival of her target.

Vadek Volkov sat in the corner of the conservatory with his newly arrived guests. Volkov rocked backwards and forwards on the edge of his seat in a trance-like state as Senior Lieutenant Daniil Litvak described Major Macinko's attempt and his subsequent death as he tried to eliminate Samantha O'Conner's partner in the north of Scotland. Volkov for a second time let out a roar of fury; he was in a state of shock. His carefully drawn plans to send the bitch and her family to hell were in tatters. He was a worried man; he knew when Moscow found out that his men had unwittingly attacked a British military base he was going to be in big trouble, possibly even a dead man walking.

Volkov was still thinking about his next move when he was

approached by one of the security officers who explained he had intelligence officer Berkov waiting in the library with an urgent communiqué from Moscow. Volkov's heart sank; they had already found out about the attack in Scotland. Wearily he got to his feet and headed for the library.

Peter Sokolov had been watching one of his men starting to undress the young Japanese girl when he noted his boss leaving the room. In the back of Sokolov's mind something was still bothering him about the blonde call girl he had stopped at the front door. He decided to tear himself away from the entertainment and head for the study where he had sent the blonde and some of the other girls. He wanted another look at her and to take a few pictures of her so security could run her face through their database of undesirables.

Bruce Ellis opened a can of Coke as he studied the latest document to cross his desk. It was from Captain Joshua Tracey, commanding officer of the USS *Alaska*, one of the navy's Ohio class ballistic missile submarines. Captain Tracey had filed a report that when he had visited Faslane naval base, security levels at the base had been raised to critical. Captain Tracey had no details of the risk but had raised security levels on the *Alaska* and had cancelled all shore leave. He was asking for clarification of his next actions from naval command.

Bruce Ellis knew Josh Tracey personally; they were good friends. Josh was a cool head and Bruce knew he would not have sent that report if it was just a peace demonstration. Something had happened in Scotland that had worried his friend. Bruce called a number at the Pentagon and was put through to David Hollinger in military intelligence. David had been designated military liaison at the White House situation room, sitting next to Bruce Ellis on occasions.

'Hi, Bruce, how goes it in the UK? We've been missing you in Washington. Rumour has it you've been a bad boy and got sent away – care to comment, buddy?'

Bruce Ellis smiled to himself. The one thing he did not miss about

Washington was the gossip and rumours that were part of everyday life in the capital. 'No, bud, I'm still in the good books. Just keeping an eye on our interests here. The Brits have a few nasty problems. David, what can you tell me about a problem at Faslane? Do you have any intel you can share?'

'I take it you're talking about the report from the *Alaska*, Bruce. Yeah, the British army are playing their cards close to their chest. They scrambled two crack commando units to their nuclear bunker that supplies Faslane. There's been talk of a Russian attack on the base, but we have spoken to contacts in Moscow and they had nothing to do with it. The UK media is being fed a story about gangs. We suspect terrorist activity, but our analysts put the risk to our sub as low. So there you go. Time to get your CIA colleagues up to Scotland for a wee holiday and find out what the hell the Brits are up to.'

Ellis had just replaced the receiver when Dan Whittaker called. Bruce was about to leave for the evening but decided to take Dan's call before heading off.

'Sorry to bother you at this late hour, sir, but I have a couple of things you might be interested in. You asked me to look into Tarek Attar. I did, and he's here in London, just arrived. MI5 are tailing him – they spotted him at the airport.'

Bruce Ellis was surprised by the revelation but said nothing yet. He needed to think things through.

Whittaker waited a second or two before continuing. 'The other thing is – remember the broad you spotted in Hyde Park? One of our remote covert cams outside the Russian Embassy just picked her up going into the ambassador's residence with a bunch of chicks. If she is secret service she has big balls snooping about in there.'

The hairs were standing up on the back of Bruce Ellis's neck; he was well aware that Sam did not do field work. He was not sure what was going on but he had a bad gut feeling about it.

In Switzerland he had witnessed at first-hand what Samantha O'Conner was capable of. If for some reason she was let off the leash inside the Russian Embassy the political fallout would be immense. She had been lucky to escape alive in Switzerland; she would almost certainly run out of luck if she tried anything foolish tonight.

'Dan, pick me up with the van at the front of the embassy like yesterday. We need to stop her.'

Two phone calls later and a lot of string pulling and Bruce Ellis waited impatiently as his phone called Bill Mathews.

Mathews answered the call sounding weary; apparently he was at home.

'Bill, it's Bruce here, Bruce Ellis. Listen, this is very, very important, so just tell me the truth. What the hell is going on between Sam and the Ruskies? Just in case you're wondering, this isn't a social call.'

There was a tense silence for a few seconds while Bruce Ellis waited for Bill Mathews to speak.

'Bruce, I understand your concern, but it has nothing to do with the US. It's a domestic issue.'

Bruce Ellis climbed aboard the BT van that had just pulled up before launching a verbal broadside at the MI6 director. 'Listen up, Bill. Someone sneezes in the Kremlin and the Pentagon are up all night analysing the consequences. Don't hit me with it has nothing to do with you shit. You get into a fight with them and we are duty bound to step into the ring with you, so quit stalling and tell me what Sam is up to.'

Mathews seemed to hesitate before saying, 'Okay, you win. Neil Andrews ordered Sam some years ago to close down a Russian drug operation, and in the process Sam eliminated a woman. It turns out that the woman was Vadek Volkov's younger sister. It would appear Volkov has found out and is here for vengeance. Sam was meeting a contact outside the Russian Embassy tonight to obtain evidence so we can petition the Russian premiere to have Volkov removed and punished for his actions.'

This time it was Ellis who went quiet for a second or two. 'What were you thinking, Bill? This is Samantha O'Conner we're talking about. She's not going to take a statement or look for evidence, Bill, she is a killing machine, and she just walked into the Russian Embassy ten minutes ago. This ain't going to end pretty, Bill. No one wins here.

We got to stop this. I'm on my way – you better get back to your office. I think you're going to have a busy night.'

Sam watched the expression on Ludmilla's face change and she could feel the presence of someone in the open doorway as she stood behind the door, her Glock held at the ready in both hands. Volkov stepped through the door and crossed to the middle of the room before speaking. 'Ah, Miss Berkov, have you come to join our little party? No, I didn't think so. Well, don't just stand there like a dummy – what do you want?'

Things started to move in slow motion for a fraction of a second. Ludmilla Berkov's eyes looked past Volkov, fixing on the Glock 17 that was sweeping upwards to a firing position. Volkov turned, following Ludmilla's stare, to look straight into Sam's eyes. She knew he'd recognised her instantly. Sam's gun sight picked out Volkov's chest but the open door smashed into her arm and head as she fired. Her first shell hit Volkov high in the chest, smashing through his ribcage and exiting through his shoulder blade. Sam lost her balance and went down behind the door just as Peter Sokolov dashed into the room laying down covering fire. He grabbed his boss by the ankle, firing again as he pulled Volkov's body clear of the library. Sam was not in a position to stop their escape as Sokolov screamed for his guards. She was dazed from being hit by the door. As she got to her knees by the doorway her next actions were pure reaction to movement. The first guard charged through the open door; for a second his silhouette was captured in the door frame and Sam fired, diving forward onto her belly then rolling sideways. A second guard arrived to find his colleague falling forward, hit twice in the chest; he lifted his pistol but Sam's head had cleared and she shot him between the eyes. His body fell backwards into the hall then slid down the wall, his brains and blood making a grotesque collage. Sam was about to move to the hall when she heard a cough and wheeze from the other side of the room. In the heat of the action she had forgotten about Ludmilla. Her eyes searched around, but Ludmilla was not in view. She darted across the room, where she found Ludmilla propped up against a bookcase. Her eyes were wide and her hands were clasped to her belly where a trickle of blood escaped and ran down between her clasped fingers. She tried to talk but no words came out. Sam lifted her fingers then replaced them quickly as the blood started to ooze from a torn area of her waistband.

'Don't talk and don't move. Just keep your breathing normal until someone comes. I need to leave you, Ludmilla … I need to make sure I got the bastard.'

A tear trickled down Ludmilla's face as she nodded in agreement. Sam picked up the folder Ludmilla had dropped, gathered up her coat, rearranged her hair quickly into a ponytail and walked out into the hall clasping the folder in front of her.

Sam made her way from the library towards the rear of the building. One advantage she still held was the fact that only Sokolov knew what she looked like; any other witnesses to her arrival were either dead or wounded. If she was quick she could still use this to her advantage. It didn't take long for her to test her theory. Two security officers had made their way towards the front of the building following the trail of blood. Sam watched as they headed towards one another. She made a show of carrying the folder. She addressed them, speaking in their native tongue, and asked for help, saying there was a madman in the library. The lead man lowered his Tokarev pistol, pointed to the back of the building and told her to go with the other women. Sam slid her Glock from its hiding place in the folder and fired twice. Both men went down without managing to fire a shot. Sam stepped over them, finishing the second man with a shot to the head.

She found herself at the bottom of a large staircase. She could hear running, screaming women and shouting men coming from all around as panic set in. She checked her gun, slipping a fresh clip into the hot weapon. Sam sensed movement above her, then the handrail to her left exploded as a 9mm shell narrowly missed her. She spun upwards, her sight looking for the target, just as a suited figure leaned over to see if he had hit his own target. Sam fired, hitting the suit in the head; if Sam's shot hadn't killed him the fall from the staircase finished the job.

His body crashed through an antique smoked-glass table, cutting him to pieces; a dark stain started to spread towards Sam's booted feet. She cursed to herself as she moved back out into the open; her original plan was to shoot Volkov, grab Ludmilla, kill the two front door guards and get the hell out of there, but her plan had been compromised the minute Sokolov hit her with the door. Any normal person would have cut and run, but Sam was no normal person; she had come here to kill Vadek Volkov and until she knew he was dead she would not stop.

Sam picked up the blood trail where Volkov had been dragged to safety, but the trail passed through a closed door. She could hear voices on the other side of the door. Entering could be suicide for her, so she decided to cut right through an open door then try to cut back to the left and trace Volkov's whereabouts. Entering a large room facing the gardens Sam spotted a makeshift stretcher heading for the rear door as she emerged between the conservatory and what looked like an art gallery leading to the back garden of the residence. It could only mean one thing: Volkov was still alive.

Sam realised instantly this was make or break time. She flung the folder to one side and dived onto the floor, minimising herself as a target, then opened fire on the stretcher party. For the first second or so Sam had the advantage and two bodies went down, one of which was a stretcher bearer. The group came to a halt as Sokolov's men stopped and fired on their target. Sam ducked back towards the door but bullets were exploding all around her. She felt the thud and shockwave as she was hit, but she continued firing. Her aim was now compromised by the need to move backwards looking for cover. One more of the Russians went sprawling face down, his pistol discharging into a nearby canvas. As Sam moved she was aware that she was dragging herself through something wet. It was only when the slide on her Glock stopped moving that Sam's foggy mind realised she had run out of ammo; she retrieved the last magazine from her waistband and as she looked down it dawned on her the wet stuff all around her was actually her own blood.

Sam's senses returned just in the nick of time; after loading the clip she looked up to find two men charging her position. With only six feet to spare Sam discharged her Glock into the chest of the charging guard. She was finding it hard to hold up the Glock now; everything was an effort, she was so tired; she just wanted to put the gun down and go to sleep. Suddenly there was a blinding light. Sam's ears felt like they had exploded; she was in agony, falling forward. She lost her grip on the Glock and it was gone. She curled up in the foetal position; her oxygen-starved confused brain could not analyse what was happening.

Sam started to come to what she initially thought was hours later but in reality was only seconds from the flash bang explosion. The first thing she saw was the face of the dead guard she had just shot in the chest only inches from her own face, then someone in a black ski mask was shouting at her. At first there was just ringing in her ears, then the eyes behind the ski mask started to look familiar. She picked up on some of the words ski mask was shouting at her: 'Sam', 'leave', 'hit'. Then the words started to register.

'We need to leave now. Can you walk? You're hit. Come on – if you want to see your son again we have got to get moving. Sam, can you hear me?'

Sam shakily got to a sitting position to find bodies rolling about in the same agony as she had experienced. She had never been near a flash bang explosion before. Luckily the Russian stretcher party had taken the full force of the blast and were still disorientated. Sam spotted a second black-clad figure covering them both as his friend tried to get Sam to her feet. She whispered to ski mask to get the folder. She spotted the danger just as her new ski-masked friends were gathering the spilled contents of the file. The second guard who had charged at her was close by and was starting to recover; he was heading for her dropped Glock. She recognised Peter Sokolov as he got to his knees picking up the discarded Glock 17; the look in his eyes was of pure hatred. Sam fell forward. Using what little strength she had left assisted by the forward momentum she threw her knife. The blade was razor sharp and hit Peter Sokolov in the throat just above the Adam's apple, cutting deep into his windpipe. Sam had used every last ounce of her willpower; she was finished, and fell into the black abyss of unconsciousness.

8

Agent Down

B ruce Ellis was a worried man. He knew that Sam was badly wounded and manoeuvring her body through the hole cut in the hedge at the back of the tennis court had to be done carefully, but they had minutes, if not seconds, until the Metropolitan Police and the Royal Protection Group closed down the whole area. Already sirens had arrived at the front of Harrington House and Met Police firearms officers would be making their way through the building. At last Dan managed to thread Sam's lifeless body through the hedge past the security wires that had been cut to gain entry. Dan lifted Sam into the back of the BT van and Ellis slowly pulled away, drawing as little attention as possible to himself. At the end of the service road gates stopped their exit onto a busy street. Ellis pulled the BT van over by a hedge and once again Sam's body was fed through a carefully cut hole, this time into a public car park. After placing Sam's body in the back of a replica London ambulance both Dan and Ellis stripped off their black coveralls to reveal paramedic uniforms. On exiting the car park Bruce Ellis's decision to use two decoy vehicles was vindicated; further along the street armed police had blocked off the service road exit. There would have been no way the BT van, even with its urban camouflage, would have escaped the scrutiny of the road block.

Bruce Ellis switched on the lights and sirens and turned left, heading for his old friend in Harley Street. The wailing sirens and lights blended in with what had now become the epicentre of police activity in the capital.

Bernie Edelstein was a Harley Street consultant who had been placed and bankrolled by the CIA. He was in the middle of entertaining a group of wealthy businessmen over dinner when his phone pinged in his pocket. A quick look at the screen showed a one-word text: 'Patriot'. Edelstein, frowning, excused himself then talked with the hotel manager before returning to the dining table. 'Unfortunately duty calls, my friends. I have an emergency that needs my urgent attention. I have asked my friend Mario to look after you all in my absence. Feel free put anything you desire on my tab. Good night, folks. I look forward to working with you all in the near future.'

Bernie Edelstein took a cab back to his office where he found an ambulance double parked, its engine still running. He paid the cab then approached the ambulance with some trepidation. He knew who had sent the text and he was not looking forward to finding out what was to be asked of him this time. As Edelstein approached the doors opened and Bruce Ellis and one of his men lifted out a stretcher bearing the body of a blonde-haired woman. Bernie could tell from the body language of the two men that things were not looking good for the girl. All three men entered the building without speaking, Edelstein leading them through to the rear of the building where he had a small emergency room and two recovery rooms.

Edelstein examined the woman and found two bullet wounds on her body. For the first time since arriving he spoke to the two CIA men. 'Bruce, this girl needs a transfusion urgently and then surgery. You need to get her to hospital.'

As Bernie stopped speaking they heard a car screech to a halt outside the building.

'Bernie, I took the liberty of checking our records on Samantha here and got one of my people to acquire blood for you. I think it just arrived. As for the hospital, that ain't going to happen. I need you to fix her up, buddy, so let's get busy, my friend.'

Bernie Edelstein shook his head. 'Bruce, she needs a trauma team – the bullet hole in her thigh is bleeding too badly. I suspect, although it can't have ruptured the artery badly, simply because she would be dead by now, it has possibly nicked the femoral artery. If I go poking around and cause more damage to the artery I don't have a team to back me up – she would be dead in seconds. We need to get fluids into her and get her to accident and emergency urgently.'

Bruce Ellis walked over to Edelstein, getting into his personal space before speaking. 'Every A&E in the country will be checked for gunshot victims tonight. She takes her chances with you or she dies, no arguments. You've operated on men in the field with more severe wounds. What's wrong, Bernie? Life too easy here – removing moles, the odd tummy tuck all you're good for these days?'

Edelstein was furious with Ellis but he started getting things ready for Sam's operation as he spoke. 'Okay, big mouth. You'll find overalls in the cupboard. Get scrubbed up – you're going to help me and if the girl dies it will be on your conscience, not mine.'

Edelstein set up a drip and heart monitor before giving Sam the anaesthetic; he made a vertical incision through the bullet wound and after fighting his way through Sam's toned quadriceps he found that his initial suspicions were correct. He felt beads of sweat forming along his hairline. He closed off the artery then gingerly removed a fragment of the bullet that had punctured the artery. With great precision Edelstein brought the edge of the artery back to its natural position. Edelstein's steady fingers repaired Sam's femoral artery using a suture, then released the clamp returning blood pressure to the repaired artery. He swabbed away lost blood, studying his handiwork to make sure the repair was holding. Satisfied he had plugged that hole he turned his attention to Sam's second wound.

A second bullet had caught Sam in the side, passing between two ribs and damaging the cartilage between them before exiting without hitting any major organs. A quick check on Sam's blood pressure and heart rate showed that Bernie's repair to her artery was starting to help her recovery; already her heart rate had stabilised.

If her body survived the shock and sepsis did not set in she should be okay.

Edelstein set about cleaning out the wound on Sam's side and patching it up; he fretted to himself as he worked. His patient had an almost perfect body and given the time and the correct equipment he could have repaired the wound so it would have been almost invisible, but here he was back to his old army ways – patch them up then throw them out. Sam was going to have a nasty scar to remember this night by. Edelstein gave her a couple of injections then applied dressings to each of the wounds before standing back, mopping his sweat-covered brow while watching his new patient's chest rise and fall in a steady rhythm.

Bruce Ellis removed his coverall and replaced it with a jacket before giving Sam the once over. 'Well done, Bernie, you've saved the day. We need to go. The office will be bouncing after the events of tonight. You earned your pay check tonight, buddy.'

As Ellis made for the door Bernie Edelstein intercepted him, feeling panicked. 'Where the hell do think you are going? The girl may be patched up but she's not out of the woods yet. She's going to need constant monitoring for the next couple of days – you need to take her to a hospital.'

Bruce Ellis turned back to face Edelstein looking mildly annoyed. 'Bernie, remember that big fat check you get every month from Uncle Sam? That is your retainer for when we need you to do things like this for us. How many times do you need to be told she can't go near a hospital? Cancel your dinner dates and do the job we've paid you for – and for your own safety I would tell no one who you have here. I'll be back in the morning to see how our patient is doing. See you then, doc.'

Edelstein watched Bruce Ellis jump into the passenger side of the ambulance, closing the door as it pulled away. He was a worried man; outside he could hear London erupting. He headed for his study and switched on his TV to find a newsflash just starting on BBC1. He listened and watched as images of ambulances, police cars and high-ranking police officers filled the screen. First reports had come in that

Kensington Palace had been attacked; the police officer was telling the reporter that this information was wrong, but as a precaution the Royal Family living in Kensington Palace had been evacuated and that an incident at Harrington House, the home of the Russian ambassador Vadek Volkov, which was near to Kensington Palace, had been the scene of possibly a terrorist attack although it was too early yet to say for sure. What had been confirmed by a reporter outside the Royal London Hospital was that there had been multiple fatalities and a number of casualties, one of whom was the Russian ambassador himself, whose condition was described as critical. The screen then cut to a reporter based in Moscow who was talking to Dimitri Panoz, the Russian Federation minister of defence, who looked sternly into the camera saying that an attack on an embassy was an attack on Russia itself and that Russia would not rest until the perpetrators of these atrocities were found and dealt with.

Bernie Edelstein had an uneasy feeling in the pit of his stomach as he dialled the number of a friend who was a surgeon at the Royal London.

'Hi, George, sorry to bother you. I hear you're having a busy night. Just wanted to touch base with you about badminton – I've forgotten when you booked the court for. Was it Thursday or Friday? How's things at your end? Not having to operate on any terrorists, are we?'

'It's Thursday, Bernie – just don't forget it's your turn to pay for dinner, old boy. Yes, it's a bit manic at the moment. As for terrorists – what a lot of bollocks. Someone farts now and it was the terrorists. As far as I can make out it was a madwoman with a gun, according to some of the victims. Terrorist my hairy arse. Must dash – see you Thursday and don't forget your wallet.'

Bernie put down his phone. For the first time that evening his hand was trembling. He checked on his patient, who was still out. He was about to head for a coffee but then a thought occurred to him: if this was the madwoman did he want her to wake up? He played safe and increased her sedation before leaving the room; the quicker he got rid of her, the better.

It was late when Dan Whittaker eventually dropped Bruce Ellis off on Vauxhall Bridge. Ellis had had to stall Washington, promising to give them a full report in the morning. He had washed and changed into a suit but he needed to speak to Bill Mathews before deciding on his next move. Although it was late he was sure Bill would be in the office looking for answers to this latest attack. As he walked over the bridge the silhouette of the MI6 building stood out dark and imposing on the London skyline. Bruce was in a world of his own when the woman's voice broke through to him.

'Hello there, fancy meeting you again.'

Ellis turned to look at the woman in the raincoat he had just strolled past in a dream. She was medium height with short jet-black hair that even in the dark had a sheen. Her facial features were sharp but her large green eyes gave her the appearance of a modern Cleopatra.

'You don't recognise me, do you? Fiona, Captain Fiona Malden. Remember Arran, covered in blood? You were there with Sam.'

Suddenly it clicked – the chopper pilot who had been shot. He'd been too busy dealing with Sam to study her at length.

'I'm sorry, Fiona, I'm kind of in a bit of a dream tonight – lots of things on my mind.'

'It's Bruce, isn't it? Are you looking for Sam too? I need to speak to her urgently. Do you think you can get us into MI6? I tried but they were having none of it. Maybe you can pull some strings. I really need to speak to Sam – it's desperate. What do you say, Bruce? Will you be my knight in shining armour?'

Bruce Ellis smiled, taking Fiona's arm. 'Fiona, walk with me to the security gate and tell me what is so desperate that you need to get hold of Samantha at this ungodly hour, and I will see what I can do.'

By the time the pair had reached security at Vauxhall Cross Bruce had stopped en route twice to cross-examine Fiona Malden. He already knew what Neil Andrews had discovered previously; Volkov was on a crusade to wipe Samantha O'Conner and her seed from the face of the earth. It was no wonder she had risked everything to kill him. Ellis needed to speak to Bill Mathews and Mathews needed to hear what Fiona Malden had told him about events in Scotland.

After some negotiations with security Bruce Ellis was finally told to wait while Director Mathews was found. It was almost half an hour later when Ellis escorted Fiona Malden into Bill Mathews' basement office.

It was Mathews who started the conversation. 'I must say, Bruce, I'm intrigued. How did a CIA special investigator and Army Air Corps Captain Fiona Malden, DFC, end up calling me at midnight? I must apologise for the delay. Jean, my PA, is not here and things tend to go to hell in a handcart when she's off. I took the liberty of looking at your file while I waited on your arrival, Fiona. By the way, Bruce, when we're finished here can you hang on for a bit? I need to speak to you about the Russian Embassy carry on.'

Ellis pulled up a chair and signalled Fiona to sit down before joining her in with a second seat. 'Oh, I think when we're finished here, old buddy, you won't need to ask about that. First I would like you to listen to what Fiona here has to tell you. You see, her story, my story, and your story are all going to join up and make sense. Fiona, you have the stage. Please, continue.'

Bill Mathews said nothing but under the table his hands were restless, a sure sign that his stress levels were high; he had a feeling they were just about to get higher.

'Mac asked me to get Sam – he's being held at Faslane by the army. To let you understand, Sam managed to get word to Adam that they were being hunted by Russian hitmen. Adam led the Russians away from his kid, but they caught him en route to Area One.

'There was a shoot-out. Adam managed to get away and find Area One where he was seeking sanctuary. I was at Area One with my commanding officer when Mac arrived with the Russians in hot pursuit. There was a firefight and the Russians left after failing to kill Mac. He has been arrested pending a military investigation and he thinks the MI6 guy you sent and his mate Bob Hunter may be wounded or dead. He wanted to tell Sam so she could help.'

Fiona's version of events jogged Bill's memory about the request from the army about someone they were holding; he should have followed it up. He put it to one side in his mind for the moment – he was more worried about Samantha O'Conner; Adam could wait. Sam was missing. The last thing she'd reported was that she was meeting someone outside the Russian Embassy. Mathews knew she had been inside when all hell broke loose; he needed to know where she was. He thanked Fiona then turned to Bruce.

'Okay, Bill, before I start I got to say you had this coming to you, pal. If you'd told me about Volkov's agenda I could have told you what would happen if you dropped Sam in the mix. Fiona, I haven't told you the whole story. I'm sorry, but I had to find out what you knew.

'When I heard Sam was heading into the Russian Embassy I had a bad feeling. If I'd known from the beginning Volkov had sentenced her family to death I would have tried to stop her. Bill, Jesus, what did you think Sam was going to do – discuss things with him over a cup of tea? You should not have used her. She was compromised, for god's sake, she was never going to follow your orders – she's a killing machine.

'Anyway, enough of that. This is what happened tonight: we were hanging around the back of Kensington Palace by the hedge that marks the boundary of the Russian ambassador's residence when the shooting started. I took the decision to intervene. We went in through the hedge that led to the tennis courts. By the time we got inside Sam had dropped Volkov and a bunch of his men. We could see she was hit badly but refusing to run until she finished the job, so we rushed them with flash bangs and grabbed her before they killed her. We managed to get her out before the Met closed the area down. Sam is with one of our doctors – she was in a bad way – we had to operate on her leg to repair a damaged artery and she took another bullet in her side. She's been patched up and is safe for the moment. I think MI6 owe my team big – what do you reckon, buddy?'

There was an awkward silence in the room. Bill Mathews was thinking of the political implications Sam had caused by her reckless actions; the fallout would be huge. Heads were going to roll over this one. He was aware that one of Bruce Ellis's great strengths was being able to read other people's thoughts – it had served him well many times – and tonight was no exception.

'You're very quiet, Bill. I don't blame you, buddy. All those years climbing to the top of MI5 then handed the top job at MI6 for it all to come crashing down around you. The PM will ask for your resignation to appease the Russians and for the first time both MI5 and MI6 will be left without an experienced person in charge.'

Mathews shifted uncomfortably in his seat. He nodded in agreement without speaking. He knew Ellis was correct – it looked like his retirement would be in disgrace. He had misjudged Samantha O'Conner; he thought she would obey his orders but in the end she chose a kamikaze attempt at saving her family.

Ellis spoke up again. 'I have an idea that could solve your problem. Hear me out and think about it before you make any decisions. We both need to stick to it once we start – there'll be no turning back or it will be both our jobs on the line. Volkov has had all surveillance equipment removed from his residence – with ladies of the night visiting you can see why he did it. The top men in Moscow wouldn't be happy if they found out Volkov was using his residence as a brothel.

'Sam arrived in a van. No one saw her before the attack other than her contact in the embassy and she won't say a word. Yeah, sure, the Russians will put two and two together, but if Samantha O'Conner is in America on a training exercise how can she have carried out the attack? Without Sam or surveillance evidence, eyewitness statements during the attack will count for nothing. You backdate the paperwork and I'm pretty sure I can make Sam vanish.'

After a few seconds Bill Mathews leant forward clasping his hands in front of him. 'If I were to agree to this madness, and I haven't said I will, how do you propose to get Sam out of the country without anyone finding out?'

Bruce Ellis stood up unexpectedly and headed for the door. 'Buddy, it's late, and this gal needs to be escorted home. I have an idea but I need to run it past a few people first. Sam isn't going anywhere fast and neither is Adam by the sounds of things. Let's sleep on it and tomorrow we will meet and I will tell you what I have in mind. In the meantime, let's see if our misinformation departments can blame some nasty terrorists for attacking the Russians. Goodnight, Bill.'

Outside Fiona Malden waited as Bruce dialled a number then pressed a second button turning the screen and buttons red. He spoke for a few moments then hung up and turned back to Fiona.

'Sam is stable and still under sedation – I thought you might like to know. Looks like you ain't going to be speaking to her for a bit yet, Miss Malden. Can I interest you in a drink, my treat? Sort of an apology for not telling you the truth when we first met – what do you say?'

Fiona hesitated for a second before taking Bruce's arm. 'Okay, but let's get a couple of things straightened out. I don't like being lied to. I am not a miss, just call me Fiona. The drink will be fine, but first I need to find a hotel for tonight. I didn't plan to be in London this long. Any ideas, Bruce?'

'My hotel is ten minutes' walk from here. I'm sure I can talk the night manager into giving you a room. We can have a drink at the bar before you go up to your room, what do you think?'

Bruce seemed genuinely shocked to find out from the hotel's duty manager that there was not one single spare room available anywhere in the building. His embarrassment was compounded when the manager suggested in the circumstance he was willing to turn a blind eye to Fiona sharing the room with him. Fiona watched with some amusement as Ellis was initially lost for words. To make matters worse she could see Bruce was struggling to make sense of why she was finding the situation amusing.

'Come on then, lover boy, you win. Take me to your room.'

'Fiona, I had no idea, I mean, I didn't plan this. I wasn't trying to trick you. I don't want you wandering about looking for a hotel at this hour, though. I'm a bit embarrassed for putting you in this position.'

Fiona said nothing, but smiled and pointed to the elevators. She followed Bruce up to his penthouse suite and watched while he fumbled with the key entry card. Fiona decided to have a bit more fun with Bruce, who was obviously still struggling with the situation.

'You'd think you had never taken a girl back to your room before, Bruce. Your hand is shaking trying to open the door. Here, let me do that for you.' Fiona took the card, swiped it, then held the door open for Ellis. As he walked past her she continued with the taunting.

'Bruce, you'd better calm down, mate, things are going to get worse for you shortly. Remember, I didn't plan this visit. I have no overnight bag with me and I am not sleeping in my clothes, so if you get embarrassed inviting a girl into your room you're going to be in a bad way when I get my kit off.'

After a few minutes fumbling about Bruce produced a large gin and tonic for Fiona before sitting opposite her clasping a bottle of beer in his hand. Fiona was still in a mischievous mood and set about winding up her host.

'So, what's with the fear of women? You're acting like a sixteen-year-old virgin – tell me you're not still wearing white socks?' Bruce had an idea what Fiona was on about but he had never heard that turn of phrase before.

'If you're asking if I'm still a virgin, no I am not, but if we're going down that road – are you?'

Fiona unconsciously touched the watch on her arm before replying. 'I'm a widow, Bruce, so no, I lost my white socks some time ago. My hubby was killed in the first Gulf War. It's been a lonely life without him.'

Bruce had touched a nerve with Fiona and for the moment she dialled down the wise cracks, not sure where to go next with the conversation.

'You know, Bruce, you're not a bad-looking fella – you should have no problem getting a girl. Don't wait for the right time, life is too short. Enjoy yourself while you can, live for today, is my motto.'

Bruce handed Fiona another G and T before removing his tie and taking a swig from his second beer. 'I hear what you're saying, Fiona, but I am so darned busy. There's always another gangster or terrorist to chase, then when you do bump into a nice girl your mind starts playing tricks with you – is she a plant, a spy, an assassin, who is she working for – it's the job I'm in, it makes you paranoid. I'm so tired of trying to second guess everybody. It's a lonely life, the secret service.'

Fiona got up. 'Look on the bright side – you get to chase bad guys. You know you can really make a difference to people's lives in your job. Changing the subject, would you mind if I went for a shower or do you want to talk a while longer? I'm okay with that if you just want to talk.'

Ellis checked his watch before replying. 'No, you go for your shower. I have to make a few calls home so you go right ahead.'

Ellis had just finished his third call to Washington when Fiona Malden appeared from the bathroom sporting only a small bath towel. Bruce was having a hard time trying to not find Fiona's curvaceous figure interesting, which amused her.

'Sorry about the small towel but it's the only size in there. I did try to find a bigger one so I wouldn't embarrass you.'

Bruce was obviously getting used to Fiona's sense of humour. He looked her up and down before replying. 'No, I would say that pretty much looks good on you. I missed a trick – I should have left out only hand towels. Nice tan, by the way. I see you've been hitting the sunbeds.'

Fiona made her way over to the huge double bed, stopping at the foot of the bed. 'No sunbeds needed. I just finished a tour of Cyprus and Syria. It's amazing how many quiet places you can find to sunbathe when you're off duty. It's a pity about the bloody bullet hole in my belly. Scar tissue doesn't tan – what a bummer.'

Fiona dropped the towel by the foot of the bed, revealing a perfectly tanned body spoiled only by the repair work carried out to her bullet wound, before climbing into the huge bed.

It took Bruce Ellis a few seconds to recover from Fiona's full frontal. 'Well, there's something you don't see every day. Looks like I'm on the couch then?' The way Bruce had phrased it, it was more of a question than a statement.

Fiona patted the bed in response. 'Don't be silly, Bruce. Come to bed if you're finished with your calls. We can talk for a bit.'

Bruce was smiling as he unbuttoned his shirt. 'Yeah, we could talk, or you could show me what you mean by "enjoy yourself, live for to-day" – I think that's what you said.'

Fiona said nothing as she switched off the light.

Next morning Bill Mathews was surprised to find Fiona Malden still accompanying Bruce Ellis as they sat down. Jean fussed about serving them coffee and biscuits before retiring to the outer office. Bruce Ellis seemed to have a new spring in his step as he took charge of the meeting while Fiona Malden passed round the biscuits.

'Okay, Bill, I called in a few favours last night. This is what I propose to do with our wayward British agent. We have the USS *Alaska*, one of our submarines, currently on a visit to your Faslane base. She is due to rotate home to her base in Georgia, leaving today. The *Alaska* has been told to hold station for the moment and to hand over temporary command to the CIA, namely me. What I need you to do is get Adam McDonald released into my custody at Faslane. Fiona here has volunteered to fly Samantha O'Conner from her base at Credenhill to Faslane. You will need to get permission from the army because they'll need to give Fiona one of their Chinooks to do the job with. We will load them on the sub and no one will see a thing. As if by magic Sam is in America. If anyone tries to point the finger at MI6 we're all in the clear.'

Bill Mathews was in the middle of dunking his digestive in his coffee when Ellis finished speaking. For a second he stopped, staring at Bruce Ellis as if he was mad; only his digestive vanishing into his coffee snapped him out of the trance.

'So let me get this right. I have to borrow a Chinook from the army then tell them to hand over Adam and forget all about everything. Are you mental?'

Bruce Ellis was smiling. 'Come on Bill, man up. All you have to do is borrow a chopper and tell the army to mind its own business – start throwing your weight about, man. If I can steal an Ohio class ballistic missile nuclear sub armed to the teeth with trident missiles from the navy, surely you can come up with one helicopter – you don't even need to find a pilot.'

Bill Mathews had few options left. The PM wanted a briefing on the Russian Embassy incident and it was make or break time. He had to lie his ass off or come clean and almost certainly be asked to go; he was beginning to see why his predecessor had taken so many risks previously. Reluctantly he agreed to call Bruce when he had things sorted with the military.

Bruce popped into the embassy to finalise a few things and check up on Sam. Edelstein was very dry on the phone. He had sent his staff home and locked himself in with Sam, who was still sleeping, but her stats were improving hour by hour. He wanted to know when his guest would be leaving. Bruce promised to visit later to discuss Sam's transfer out.

Ellis joined Fiona for lunch at Maggie's, a theme pub Bruce had become fond of when staying in London. It served great food and its layout let him watch the entrance while being hidden by large wooden seating. If he was attacked there was plenty of cover he could take, and only one entrance meant he could keep an eye on who was dining in the same place as him.

Both Bruce and Fiona were in good spirits as they tucked into steak and chips. Bruce was not sure how he had fallen under the spell of the bubbly dark-haired army officer but he was having trouble keeping his mind on his job when Fiona was around, a problem he had rarely experienced with the opposite sex. After lunch Bruce was contemplating his next move when Fiona dragged him into a fashion boutique, which to Bruce was bad enough. He watched as Fiona bought a new outfit to replace the clothing she had worn now for the second day. His CIA training did not help him as to his horror Fiona, with the shop assistant in tow, approached him with two sets of lingerie.

'What do you think, Bruce? Which set do you like?'

Ellis just wanted the ground to open up and swallow him as the shop assistant looked on, a twinkle in her eye.

'Sorry, Fi, not really my area of expertise – it's not me wearing it. I'm sure you would look just fine in either set.'

Fiona picked out the white lace set and the assistant headed off to remove the tags and bag the garments. Fiona leaned closer to Bruce, lowering her voice, her big green eyes overflowing with mischief. 'Play your cards right this afternoon and I could do a bit of modelling for you, big boy! That is if you can sneak me past your hotel manager again.'

Bruce checked his phone; still nothing from Mathews. 'Well, Bill hasn't called yet and we have time to kill. Has anyone told you that you're a bad influence, Fiona Malden?'

Fiona winked at him before heading for the checkout. 'Many times, Bruce, many times.'

Back at the hotel Fiona flung herself onto the bed, kicking off her shoes.

'Oh my god, how can anyone wear heels? My feet are killing me – give me army boots any day.'

Bruce Ellis sat down on the edge of the bed studying Fiona before speaking. 'You know from certain angles you could be Elizabeth Taylor's twin sister? When she was younger, obviously.'

Fiona sat back up, massaging her feet. 'Yeah, a few people have mentioned it. Their guide dogs agreed with them. Has anyone ever told you from certain angles you look nothing like Richard Burton? I'm going for a shower before I get my new gear on.' Fiona got up, grabbing her bag of new clothes before blowing Bruce a kiss as she headed for the bathroom.

Bruce wandered over to the window, studying a grey London landscape while he checked his phone for messages. His eye caught the blood-spattered folder on the chair by the window.

In his rush to change and get to Vauxhall Cross after rescuing Sam he had forgotten about the folder she had been carrying when she was gunned down. Bruce sat in the chair and started sifting through the folder. It was not a complete dossier but rather a collection of memos and receipts. At first Bruce made little sense of what he was reading until he found one particular piece of paper – a note written by Volkov as a reminder to himself. It was a scribbled payment reminder with a date, an amount of money and a name. It was the name that stopped Bruce in his tracks.

Volkov had just paid the Russian defence minister 80,721,945⊠. Bruce did a quick calculation in his head; over $1,500,000 had been handed over. Alarm bells started to ring; when his team had intercepted Volkov's attempted nuke sale to the Iranians there was some talk that Dimitri Panoz had been involved. Unfortunately his team were murdered before they had proof of this.

What worried Ellis was that the date of the alleged money transfer was two years after the Baku incident. If there was lesson Bruce Ellis had learned from his time at the CIA it was that leopards never change their spots; could Volkov be up to his old tricks again, and if so, who was buying the nukes this time?

Bruce Ellis started studying each piece of paper in minute detail.

A delivery note from the Norwegian boat builder Marex made no sense but could be a piece of the jigsaw. Ellis switched his phone to scramble and called Frank Deangelo at the Pentagon's Russia desk. 'Hi, Frank, this is very important. Have any Russian nukes gone AWOL in the last six months? I can't remember any memos but can you think of any?'

Frank Deangelo sighed audibly before replying. 'Well, yes and no. On paper they're all accounted for at the moment, but there was one incident that didn't smell right. The cargo ship *Nizhny* went down with three tactical nukes, part of her military cargo. Our navy have confirmed the ship did sink, but conveniently it lies at the bottom of the Norwegian trench, too deep for a proper inspection. The weather was good that day, no mayday call went out, and as yet the Russian authorities have never said where the cargo was bound for. Don't know if that's what you wanted to hear. As far as I know that's the only nukes not found.'

Bruce Ellis didn't like the sound of what he was hearing and decided to do a bit more digging. 'Frank you don't have the file to hand, do you? I need to know who it was that signed off on the cargo transfer.'

Bruce could hear Frank clicking through files on his computer while he mumbled to himself looking for what Bruce wanted. 'Captain was Oleg Malovich. Nope, he hasn't signed the inventory. Hold on, I might have the original cargo inventory from the Norwegian coastguard. Yip, here it is, yes. Signed by D Panoz, it looks like, that's the name. Any help, buddy?'

Bruce Ellis thanked Frank, promising to take him for a beer when he got back to Washington, then the minute he hung up his head was back in Sam's folder looking for more information. His next find was a bank fund transfer from Volkov's Swiss bank to a Cayman Islands account for $1,000,000. Ellis placed a call to the CIA financial unit based in Switzerland where first he gave the Cayman Island account number, which belonged to a holding company called Bernstein and Hollinger, but after speaking to his counterpart in Switzerland the account's real owner was revealed as none other than Volkov's Syrian friend Tarek Attar.

Bruce Ellis was puzzled. If Attar was buying weapons, possibly nukes, it made no sense why Volkov was paying him; something strange was going on here.

Dan Whittaker was next on Ellis's call list.

'Hi, boss, am I glad you phoned. I'm going mad sitting about doing nothing. Please tell me you have something for me to do.'

'Dan, remember you were telling me MI5 were tracking Tarek Attar? Do you think you could break into their system to see if they recorded any phone conversations involving him?'

'Shouldn't be a problem. The Brits may be good at surveillance but they're not so good at securing what they have. Gimme five and I'll get back to you. If I get anything I'll forward it on to you in a sound file, later.'

Bruce started pacing backwards and forwards. His investigator's nose was telling him there was something going on here. What had he stumbled upon? He had a hollow feeling in the pit of his stomach.

The shower had stopped and Fiona was giving it large with the hair-dryer as Ellis's phone pinged to tell him he had a message. Dan's text contained a sound file and a brief explanation. 'No phone calls, boss, directional mic recording from a meeting with unknown in bar. Attar never spoke once but his friend had plenty to say!'

Ellis downloaded the sound file then turned up the volume so it wasn't drowned out by the noise of the hairdryer in the next room.

'I take it you have the funds transferred. Good. I have here the codes for your little toy – they are simple enough to understand. My boss said to remind you that he does not want you starting the game ahead of time – no cheating allowed. He will be out of town soon enough and he wishes you good luck and happy sailing when the game starts, my friend.'

To most people the conversation would not make any sense; MI5 would know it was a coded conversation, but unless they had the jig-saw pieces that Bruce had in Sam's folder they would be in the dark. Bruce Ellis was starting to piece together a picture that could lead to something truly terrible. He was up and pacing again, talking to himself, beads of sweat breaking out on his forehead: missing nukes sent by Dimitri Panoz, who was paid by Volkov; a boat bought in the same area as the Russian nukes went missing; a Syrian warlord paid by Vadek Volkov, and now against all odds in a country that would arrest him for war crimes.

It was all circumstantial evidence but if he had put the pieces to-gether correctly in his head, and taking into account the first attempt by Volkov to put the blame for Sir Neil Andrews' murder on Attar's group, it looked like Volkov was trying to bring a nuclear device to London, probably by boat. Ellis knew Volkov was bad news, but would he be insane enough to detonate a nuclear device in London and try to blame the Syrians? Things were dropping into place as Ellis waited for Jean to put him through to Bill Mathews.

Sam had told him the Russian woman from the embassy had tried to warn them about Tarek Attar; she had put two and two together and did not want her country implicated in the madman's plot. Volkov may have wanted Sam and her family dead, but Sir Neil had given the order and he had paid Volkov's price for it. If he had already targeted two MI6 members then a bomb in a boat made perfect sense – the MI6 building at Vauxhall Cross was on the banks of the Thames. It was the work of a madman, and Vauxhall Cross would be ground zero, wiping of the face of the earth the organisation that had killed his baby sister.

The only saving grace at the moment was that Volkov was still in town; as long as he was here the people of London were safe.

Ellis was given the polite brush off by Jean who was not letting on as to the whereabouts of her boss. Bruce felt panic rising in his stomach as he called Frank Deangelo back. 'Hi, Frank, it's me again. Listen, buddy, I forgot to ask what size are the nukes that went down with the boat?'

There was silence as presumably Deangelo checked his computer. 'That's a difficult one to answer, Bruce. The Russians are very cagey about that kind of stuff. They're listed as Mirov class airborne weapons systems, nothing else listed, but they're typically between one and five-kiloton yield, depending on their theatre of war.'

Ellis was almost frightened to ask the next question. 'Frank, if a bunch of lunatics got their hands on one and detonated it in a city how bad would it be?'

'Bruce, what are you telling me? Tell me you're kidding, man. Catastrophic, if it has a five-kiloton yield, and you have to bear in mind that this weapon is designed as an air burst device, not on the ground. That would reduce its effectiveness, but you're still talking about say wiping Manhattan off the face of the earth, nothing left, or in your case if it's London the city centre would be gone and the radiation would render the rest of London a no-go zone.'

Bruce thanked Frank, hung up, then called the Royal London Hospital. He was just putting down the receiver as Fiona appeared by his side. For a second his mind was in such turmoil he did not realise she was modelling her new lingerie for him.

'Well, what do you think? Does it meet with your approval?'

Bruce Ellis's tried to be enthusiastic, but he was not the same man

Fiona had left in the room less than an hour ago. He felt the blood drain from his face, he was sweating profusely, and he stared into space.

Suddenly, as if engaging another gear, he snapped back and straight into action. 'Very pretty, Fiona. Get your clothes on quickly – we need to go now. I need you to pick up your car then drop me at Vauxhall Cross. We need to hurry.'

Bruce could see Fiona was puzzled by his behaviour; he doubted if anyone had ever failed to pay attention to her charms before.

'What's the problem, Bruce, why the hurry?'

Ellis walked towards the window, playfully smacking Fiona's bottom on the way past and turning back. 'Hurry, kid, we need to go. Vadek Volkov has just been transported by private air ambulance to Switzerland for further treatment. We need to hustle – I'll explain in the car.'

By the time Fiona had retrieved her Audi R8 from the multistorey car park then fought her way through the afternoon traffic another hour had passed. Bruce spent the time in the passenger seat barking orders to his London-based team; he needed to find the boat Volkov had purchased in Norway. Bill Mathews would need all the help he could get if they were to track down this very credible threat. If there was an explosion there were thousands of Americans in the UK capital at risk of being incinerated; it was his duty as much as the British secret service to stop this madman.

By the time Fiona pulled up outside the MI6 building Ellis had still not confided in her, although she must have realised from the phone conversations something big was going on. Bruce stopped just short of the security barrier; he did not want her parking.

'Sorry, Fiona, but you're not coming in with me. Drop me here then get out of here and back to Hereford. I'll get you clearance for the Chinook and let you know when we'll be dropping Sam off. I hope to god I'm wrong, but I think Volkov is about to hit the MI6 building with a stolen Russian nuclear warhead of some description. You don't want to be anywhere near just in case he pulls it off. Need to get moving, Fiona – get out of here. No stopping until you're clear of London – now go!'

Bruce leaned across the Audi cabin and gave a shell-shocked Fiona a peck on the cheek before grabbing the bloodstained folder then exiting before Fiona could ask any questions.

Jean seemed surprised to discover Ellis was waiting downstairs. Only an hour or so ago he had been told Bill Mathews would not be available for the rest of the day.

'Hello, Mr Ellis. I'm sorry, but Bill has only just come back from Downing Street and has a busy afternoon of meetings. Can it wait until the morning? I'll arrange a working breakfast for you both.'

'Sorry, Jean, but this can't wait. I need to see Bill urgently – and as for the meetings, I would cancel them. I bet you twenty bucks when your man hears what I have to tell him meetings will be the last thing on his mind.' There was silence on the other end of the phone. Ellis sensed Jean was still not on side. 'Jean, listen to me. I have always been square with you guys. Please listen when I say this is probably the most important meeting Bill will ever have: trust me, please.'

'Oh, very well, Mr Ellis. I can give you ten minutes with him, but please don't make a habit of jumping the queue.'

9

Volkov's Revenge

Bruce Ellis talked Bill Mathews through the folder as he moved from page to page studying the documents Sam had almost given her life for.

By the time he was finished and Ellis had completed his thoughts on the situation he was a worried man. Ellis was no fool and he was the CIA's top man; he didn't get there by accident – it was his team that had found Bin Laden. Mathews had to agree it did look like Volkov had completely lost the plot; he felt the colour drain from his face. Even if Ellis was wrong he had to act now; he had to find out either way.

Mathews saw Bruce Ellis out, both men promising to keep one another up to date with their manhunt.

Call after call went out and then, as news broke in the various departments of the government and the military, Jean's phone lit up like a Christmas tree.

It was Bruce Ellis's team in cooperation with Interpol that came back with the first important piece of information. Volkov's boat had left Oslo the same day the Russian ship had gone down. His boat, a cream and burgundy Marex named *Valhalla Express*, had not returned to port. In London this new information caused an explosion of activity; the Home Secretary ordered the Thames flood barrier closed until further notice in an attempt to stop any more river traffic from moving towards the city. All available SAS and SBS were ordered into the city while police forces were ordered to supply officers to search the River Thames for any sign of the *Valhalla Express*.

To Bill Mathews' disgust, MI5 had lost track of Tarek Attar and his two companions, last seen on the A2 dual carriageway heading out of town.

Almost in a state of desperation Bill Mathews studied the area where Attar had thrown off his MI5 tail. Five minutes later he was on the phone to his number two, Chris Oliver, who was holding the fort at Thames House.

'Hi, boss, how are things at Six doing?'

'Jesus Christ, Chris, what are you doing to me? I bloody well told you not to lose him and what have your team done? Not only that – he is loose on our watch with a bloody atom bomb. You better tell your team to extract the finger. I want him found before morning or I swear to god every single agent involved will be lucky to get a job as a car park attendant by the time I'm finished with them. Your men lost them on the A2. Looking at the map it's not that far from the Thames. There's a marina at Gravesend – I suggest you start looking there and don't stop until you find the slippery bastard.' Mathews slammed the phone down without waiting for a response from his number two.

Bill was angry at himself for losing his temper with Chris Oliver. He was acutely aware how much pressure he was under – an atom bomb in London and the security services on their knees, their old director murdered and their top agent out of action, he was stretched to the max trying to run two departments. Mathews had a bad feeling about it; this could be the time the good guys didn't win.

Bruce Ellis entered his office at the US embassy and immediately placed a call to the situation room at the White House. After informing those present, including the President, of the situation in London, Ellis was given a list of Americans who were to be evacuated immediately, one of whom was Ellis himself. Bruce did not argue with the order; he arranged for the people on the list to be rounded up and flown home under the pretence that they may have been infected by a fictitious character who was targeting American citizens with a bio weapon. The last thing Ellis wanted was the population of London finding out that there was possibly a terrorist loose in London with a nuclear device. Bruce clicked on the TV in his office to see what the press were saying about the situation. Obviously the story was big; the BBC had moved their anchor newsreader out into the streets of London away from his desk, which usually only happened when a big story broke. Between the death of Sir Neil Andrews and the gunman attacking the Russian Embassy the news anchor had not been at his desk much in the last few weeks.

Bruce was amused by the latest fairy tale dreamed up by the Home Office to cover what was really going on. Apparently there had been a huge underground earthquake in the North Sea and combined with unusually high tides the government had taken the decision to close the Thames flood barrier and deploy hundreds of police officers to the banks of the Thames to supervise flood defences. The anchor pointed to a map showing possible flood damage to the London area in the event of a freak wave caused by the deep-sea disturbance and coinciding with high tide. The people of London could rest easy knowing the government had the situation under control. One of the lesser stories was the hunt for an escaped prisoner; the public were asked to be vigilant but not to approach the man. Ellis looked up as a picture of Tarek Attar was displayed on the screen. Ellis shook his head in disapproval; it may help in the search for Attar but if he didn't know there was a manhunt for him before, he sure as hell did now. Not the thing you wanted to do if the man had his finger on the trigger of a tactical nuke.

The fog slowly started to clear; voices came first, then bright lights, then pain – a horrible gnawing, burning pain that threatened to make Vadek Volkov scream. He could not move, he could not tell anyone of his agony. As his senses returned, so did the intensity of the pain, so much so that he wanted to die.

Only one thing made him fight on – his all-consuming hatred for the people who had murdered his little sister. It had taken him years to find out the truth and more years of planning his revenge on the British secret service. He could not die – he must not die until he knew those involved had paid a terrible price for their actions. A beautiful blonde angel who turned for a second into a nurse appeared and gave Vadek an injection that took the pain away and then, shortly after, robbed him of his consciousness.

These events recurred over and over, but gradually the pain levels dropped and the consciousness became clearer and longer, until one morning Vadek Volkov woke up as if he had just had a bad dream. He was stiff and sore but he was alive and his hatred still burned brightly.

He sat patiently while the Swiss doctor explained his injuries to him. The first bullet was the one that had almost killed him; even although the shooter had been hit by the door her bullet had been deflected by his ribcage, shattering and firing slivers of shrapnel into his heart and left lung, while the main part of the bullet exited high on his back, badly damaging his shoulder muscle. One of the bullets, fired while he was on the stretcher, had passed through the neck of one of his stretcher bearers and had ricocheted down, smashing Volkov's left ankle to pieces. He sat calmly while the doctor explained that he had managed after three operations to remove all the shrapnel from Volkov's upper body, and that it would take time and complete rest for his organs to recover from the major surgery. As for his ankle, the doctor had managed to save his foot but the ankle itself was held together by steel pins. The doctor doubted if Volkov would ever have full movement of the joint again. Volkov thanked the doctor and his team for their efforts then asked if any of his staff were present. To Volkov's surprise, Lieutenant Daniil Litvak joined him in his private room. Volkov had expected his friend Peter Sokolov to have been in charge of his security as usual; he was shocked to find out that Peter had died at the hands of the woman who had shot him.

Litvak spent the next two hours going over everything that had happened; for the moment Volkov's memory had deserted him. Only one name and one face remained to haunt him: the woman who had come so close to killing him. Samantha O'Conner's face as she fired her weapon was burned into his memory and his hatred for her was so great now that it almost hurt him.

He was contacted by Dimitri Panoz who, when finding out about the attack, promised to demand the British government hand the perpetrator over for trial in Russia. This did little to quench Volkov's thirst for revenge.

He recalled Litvak to his bedside. 'Daniil, I am making you head of security. I have advised Minister Panoz of this and he has agreed to my request. I would like you to leave me one of your men for security and take the rest and any more freelance people you may need and go and hunt down this bitch Samantha O'Conner. I will personally pay any costs incurred. Tell your people whoever kills O'Conner will win a bounty, which again I will pay myself. Tell them I will pay five million dollars. I don't want her captured. I want her dead.'

Next morning, after little success in finding either Tarek Attar or the elusive boat, Bill Mathews was draining his coffee cup when a call came through from the Portsmouth customs office. The phone ringing had almost made the cup in his hand fly from his grip, such were the conditions of his frayed nerves.

Fifteen minutes later, watching the monitor in front of him, Bill Mathews knew he was about to make the most important decision of his entire life. Although he had just finished a coffee his mouth was as dry as parchment and some invisible force was tightening a steel band around his head: as he watched the monitor the figure of Tarek Attar wandered around behind a lorry driver in the lorry park for trucks leaving for the continent.

Customs had informed him Attar, using the alias Mohamed Mooshan, a French national, was travelling to Cherbourg as a passenger on board the Scania truck pictured on the screen. Attar had obviously decided that he did not need to become a martyr for the cause just yet – he had left his colleagues to sacrifice their lives while he crawled under another stone and lived to fight another day.

Bill Mathews had dilemmas by the score; he could not contact the PM or the Home Secretary because they were on a conference call with the Kremlin, but he needed to act quickly. The lorry was due to board the ferry shortly, but also Attar had never removed his hands from his pockets. If he was carrying a remote, one wrong move could be fatal for many Londoners.

Unknown to Attar and the rest of the car park travellers police, backed up by the local commando unit, had blocked off the area a few hundred metres from the car park. Mathews had Superintendent Brookland on the end of the phone, who in turn had a marksman waiting for instructions on a nearby rooftop. So many things were going through Mathews' head: what if Attar's men found out he had been killed and triggered the weapon? Who else, if anyone, had control of the weapon? What would the PM say if he acted? What would Neil Andrews have done? With a heavy heart he lifted the phone.

'Superintendent. If the target removes his hands from his jacket and they are empty your man has permission to shoot. To be clear, in the absence of higher authority I am authorising shoot to kill. You must be sure he does not have a detonator to hand before firing.'

There was silence for a second. Neither he, nor, Mathews suspected, the superintendent, was used to cold-bloodedly taking a human life. Yes, Mathews by his indirect actions had taken many lives, but never so clear-cut and in HD right in front of him on the monitor.

'Director Mathews, will you put those instructions down in writing for me, just to keep things in order?'

Superintendent Brookland was clearly making sure his arse was covered in the event of a major cock-up.

'Just get on with it, man. Let's sort the paperwork after we kill the bastard.'

Brookland did not respond but Mathews could hear him giving the kill order to his officer as he contacted him by radio.

Mathews turned his full attention to the monitor. Attar continued to stroll up and down as the truck driver checked the security of the straps holding his load before the ocean trip.

For seconds nothing happened. Bill Mathews was at screaming point, such were the state of his nerves. He was cursing Neil Andrews for leaving him in this position just as Attar removed his hands from his pockets; he moved them towards his mouth to blow on them as if to warm them.

It was like a scene from a bad dream, made stranger by the absence of sound from the monitor.

Attar's head was forced backwards by the shock, then his knees crumbled. The back of his skull was gone. Arterial blood sprayed into the air, his heart trying to feed what was left of his shattered brain. It was over in a fraction of a second. The lorry driver was still reacting to the noise as armed police poured from every building, forcing the bewildered driver face down on the ground. Mathews watched as the driver, in a state of shock, was cuffed and bundled into a waiting police van.

Mathews turned his attention to the search of the River Thames for the boat and its suicide crew. His desk phone rang and Jean put Brookland through to her boss without questioning him.

'Director Mathews, we have searched the body and his belongings. He was clean – no detonator or even a phone.' Mathews thanked him and hung up, looking at the monitor showing the Thames Barrier but not really seeing anything, his mind computing the latest news. It was more or less what he had thought; Attar had been far too calm to have been holding the detonator, so either the bomb was on a timer or Attar's friends were going to detonate it by hand. His train of thought was once more interrupted by the phone.

Air Marshal Sir Bernard de Voight had asked for a moment with Bill Mathews. 'William, we speak once more. As per your request, your pilot has picked up the Chinook and we have cleared a flight plan with air traffic control. Anything else you require just give me a call – glad to be of service. Happy hunting, my good man. I shall bother you no more. The Chinook will be with you imminently. Goodbye.'

De Voight hung up and for a second Mathews did not pick up on what had just been said. Suddenly it clicked, but over the monitor speaker a crackly message burst into the room: 'Be aware, target acquired. I say again, target acquired, heading west. The boat has just passed Tower Bridge. It was moored east of Tower Bridge among a group of barges. The boat has two visible occupants. Now passing out of my range.'

There was a tense silence for a few seconds until again the boat was picked up by the next shore patrol. 'Alpha control. Boat inbound, two males visible. Please advise course of action.'

Mathews knew his phone was about to ring and pre-warned Jean to put it through. It only took two seconds for the expected call to come in.

'Good morning, Director Mathews. I trust you are following events on the Thames at the moment. The target boat is approaching Blackfriars Bridge. I have two of my best marksmen positioned before Waterloo Bridge. May I suggest we take them out before they get as far as Westminster?'

Mathews had already deployed two fast attack boats from the Royal Marines but they would be crucial minutes from the target. 'My dear Commander Devlin, it is immaterial. The minute that boat got past the Thames Barrier the city centre was doomed if they were to detonate the weapon. You have permission to take them down. I have Royal Marines on their way. For all our sakes, don't bloody miss.'

Mathews was watching the action unfold via a long-range camera fitted to a police helicopter some distance away from the river. For a second the target was obscured by high-rise buildings until the camera operator reacquired his target. Mathews was still trying to understand what had happened when the radio crackled back into life. 'Alpha control. Targets down. Repeat: targets down. Two navy boats moving to intercept from Westminster direction. ETA thirty seconds.'

Mathews was having problems remembering to breathe as the two fast navy boats turned, waiting for the sleek Marex to pass between their craft; as it approached they gunned their boats up to speed. Mathews breathed again as he watched three navy bomb disposal men clamber onto the Marex deck. One sailor stepped over the dead body of one of Attar's disciples to close down the throttles of the cruiser and bring it to a halt for a hasty inspection by the munitions experts.

For minutes nothing happened as Mathews looked on. Such was his concentration that when the phone rang once more Mathews had to sit down. The vision that would not leave his head was the mushroom cloud he had seen so many times in documentaries; would his name go down in the history books like the *Enola Gay* if he triggered this atomic explosion by his actions today?

Commander Devlin was talking to him, telling him about Attar's men they had just eliminated, one of whom had been knocked overboard by the head shot. His men had started to search the river for his body. Devlin asked if Mathews had arranged for the helicopter. As if planned a Chinook appeared and slowly lowered itself above the captured Marex cruiser.

As Bill looked on at events unfolding on the screen, Jean burst through the door. 'Director, I have an emergency call for you on line two. You need to take it, sir.'

Mathews did not reply but dived for the control panel to switch incoming lines.

A familiar voice filled Bill Mathews' ear. Mathews had expected the prime minister, not his American friend.

'Listen, Bill, before you blow a gasket it was me who talked Captain Malden into this.'

From the corner of his eye Mathews saw two figures standing on the now open tail door of the big Chinook. One was waving in the general direction of the camera while holding a phone to his ear.

'Bruce, for Christ's sake what are you doing? This is not a CIA problem. What do you think you're doing? You can't lift the nuke – if it explodes airborne the devastation will be much greater. Stand off and let the navy do their thing. That's an order.'

Bill Mathews watched helplessly as Bruce Ellis conversed with one of the navy men before lifting the phone back to his ear. 'Bill, I don't think we have time to debate this. If you think I'm going to stand back and put thousands of Americans in London at greater risk, think again, buddy boy. Your man doesn't think he can defuse the bomb. Its control panel has been activated and it's in Russian. We got to get that baby on the chopper and fast – we don't have time to sail it out. It has to be the chopper. I'm taking one of the navy dudes with us. Bon voyage – say one for us, buddy.'

Bruce Ellis clicked off his phone then pulled on a headset. 'Okay, Captain Frilly Pants, let's see how good you really are. The navy guys are getting the baby out of the cabin but they say it's a heavy little bitch. I need you to put the tail door of this bad boy onto the rear deck of the boat, so let's start by dropping her down say five feet.'

Ellis watched the deck of the Marex loomed closer and, just as he was just about to yell *stop*, the tail door stopped less than a foot from the deck with almost perfect timing. Dan Whittaker and the three navy men emerged carrying a large green missile supported by a makeshift cradle crafted from the boat's bedding. For the first time Ellis could see the exposed control panel, green lights blinking menacingly as the weapon of death was manhandled towards the waiting Chinook's tail lift. With a huge effort the tactical nuclear weapon was lifted on board the Chinook. Bert, the oldest member of the navy team, joined Dan and Bruce in the Chinook hold, and the second the weapon was secured Bruce clicked his mic back on. 'Okay, baby girl, let's get this thing out of here, full throttle please. Oh, by the way, compliments to the captain. That was a nice piece of flying. Well held.'

Fiona Malden was pouring with sweat – a horrible, cold, clammy sweat – and her mind was racing. She was trying to calm herself down by telling herself that every mile she managed the more people she was saving from a terrible death. She could hear Bruce attempting to take her mind off what she was carrying by trying to inject some humour into the situation, but it was not working. At least when the weapon did detonate she would be vaporised instantly; she would know nothing about it and would not suffer. She increased power to the Lycoming engines of the twin-rotor helicopter and watched the air speed started to pick up as the army chopper headed away from the centre of the capital, its rotors beating the air and echoing through the tall buildings of London. Malden watched her gauges as the Chinook approached its top speed of 170 knots. In her ear air traffic control were telling her to climb to fifteen thousand feet. Fiona was having none of it. 'Control, this is army flight Charlie Tango One. Cannot comply. Repeat, cannot comply.

Requesting emergency procedure. Require air traffic cleared from my flight plan. Repeat: emergency.' Fiona switched off her comms. She was not in the mood for an argument with air traffic control; they would just need to do their job and clear her a flight path out to sea. After all, what did it matter if they took her pilot's licence – she probably only had minutes to live. Fiona could see the coastline on the horizon. All she needed was a few more minutes and she would save hundreds of thousands of innocent lives.

Fiona listened in on the comms as their new friend Bert explained to Bruce and Dan that any Russian tactical weapons he had been trained on the control panel could be removed and the unit disabled, but with this particular nasty the control panel was part of the casing. Bert seemed to reckon that the only way to access the internals was to remove the nose of the weapon, a task he thought would be suicide once it was armed. Bert thought the Russians could abort the weapon remotely but as green lights were still flashing it would appear the weapon was live, with nothing to tell when show time was likely.

While Dan and Bert sat helplessly mesmerised by the flashing green lights Bruce decided nothing more could be done in the hold and headed for the cockpit.

Fiona was shocked as she caught her reflection in the Chinook's side window. Her normally pale complexion was grey and she looked like someone had just chucked a bucket of water over her. She smiled and gave Bruce a cheeky wink as he clambered into the co-pilot's seat.

As the coast approached Malden changed her course to north-east. She searched for Bruce's hand and gave it a squeeze. 'Not long to the coast now, Bruce. You get back with the guys and I'll take us down just off the coast. You guys don't need to be here. I will hover for a second and let you drop into the sea.'

If Bruce Ellis had suspected Fiona might come up with something like this he hadn't mentioned it so far. 'Captain Malden, if you think we're going to jump out of a perfectly good helicopter into the North Sea you must be mad – we could die of hypothermia. No, I think we'll continue our little trip further north, then you can take us down to sea level and we can drop off our nasty little package before heading home for tea and crumpets, or whatever you Brits do to celebrate. That sounds far more appealing to me, don't you think?'

Fiona saw Foulness Island disappear over her left shoulder as in front of them now nothing but North Sea was visible. For the next twenty minutes she watched the English coast vanish while checking the fuel situation of the Chinook. She carried out a quick check on her position. 'Okay, let's dump this bad boy and get out of here. What do you say, Bruce?'

'Okay, let's do this.'

'I'm taking her down. You go help the boys get that thing to the door.'

Fiona was skimming the top of the waves as she lowered the rear door, then shouted for them to go for it. She could hear her own heart beating as she waited for some kind of response from the guys in the hold. After what seemed like minutes the radio crackled into life.

'Okay, Fi, bomb's away. Let's get the hell out of here before that thing decides it doesn't like swimming and causes a stir.'

Fiona Malden's adrenalin surged at the thought of survival. She checked her coordinates in case she was asked where she had dropped a nuclear bomb. She knew she would remember those numbers for the rest of her life – assuming she lived: latitude 55.81, longitude 3.03. Anyone wanting to fish here might get a nasty surprise. She closed the tail door then turned the big machine for home, lifting its nose slowly as once more the Chinook built up to its top speed, heading directly west and UK landfall.

Whether it was the timer or whether the nuke was pressure sensitive no one would ever know, but as the Chinook made its escape, deep in the North Sea a nuclear explosion superheated the water, sending it at supersonic speeds to the surface where it broke through into the atmosphere, turning the surrounding sea to a boiling cauldron of white water and the air to fire.

The shock wave hit the Chinook from the rear, lifting its tail high in the air and pointing its nose down into the cold grey North Sea. Fiona

Malden's reactions were lightning fast – they had to be to stop the machine diving to destruction. At first she thought she'd lost her engines as her cockpit instruments died. Her flight controls seemed ineffective, but Fiona was not ready to give in. She screamed at the Chinook as if it were a naughty pet animal; she refused to let the nuke win as she fought to regain control of the helicopter. Slowly the big machine started to respond as she levelled it out only feet from the sea; she was not sure how badly damaged the Chinook was or how long she could keep it in the air.

Only Fiona had been strapped in. Bruce Ellis had been thrown forward, hitting his head on the superstructure of the chopper. He wiped blood from his eyes as he staggered back to the hold to check on the other two. Dan was helping a pale-looking Bert to a sitting position. Bert had been holding on to some netting and had tried to keep hold when the shock wave hit, but had damaged his shoulder in the process.

Although the Chinook seemed to be flying, Fiona Malden had lost every instrument on board. Most she could do without, but the one that was worrying her was the fuel gauge. She had been pretty critical on fuel to make it back but now, flying blind with no instruments – that could prove disastrous. There would be no fuel to search for somewhere to land and no warning the fuel was running out. Fiona had no option but to continue blind, at least until she sighted landfall – she hoped.

Bruce sat in silence next to Fiona. They both spotted it at the same time; land was in sight and the mood lifted as they realised they might just make it. Fiona planned her landing on the first available field but, when she spotted the familiar terrain of the Humber estuary and its landmarks, she knew to fly over the hospital then the airport was only a hop away for a Chinook. Fiona carefully put the Chinook down on the vacant Air Sea Rescue landing pad, much to the surprise of the ground team who were at a loss as to why the big military machine had landed without authority.

Jean Mitchell burst into Bill Mathews' office, a beaming smile on her face. She had joined Bill Mathews as they had watched the navy guys lift the missile into the back of the helicopter, then there was nothing other than air traffic control reports. Two hours ago, GCHQ had sent a report stating they were picking up chatter from various places stating that there had been an earthquake in the North Sea, and one report from a ship stating that there had been a massive explosion at sea. But there still had been no radio contact from the Chinook. Fearing the worst, Bill Mathews had contacted the PM to inform him of the joint SIS–CIA operation to remove the nuclear threat from London. He had warned the PM to expect the worst for the helicopter team and that he may soon have to contact the President to inform him of the missing CIA agents.

Jean slapped the telephone message down on the desk, clearly unable to keep the good news to herself. 'They made it, sir. I've just had a call from the search and rescue station on the Humber. Captain Malden has made an emergency landing there. Seems they had a rough time. Chief Petty Officer Robert Prentice and Special Agent Bruce Ellis have been taken to the local hospital for treatment. The army helicopter was damaged in the blast and has been grounded awaiting repairs. Captain Malden has requested a replacement helicopter – she seems to think she still has a mission to carry out for you, although she refused to fill me in on the details. Would you care to fill me in so I can organise whatever Captain Malden requires?'

Bill Mathews breathed a sigh of relief. His gamble of going it alone without authorisation from Downing Street had paid off.

'Don't worry, Jean, I'll sort out transport for Captain Malden. If you could get me the PM on the blower first, then Air Marshal de Voight. While I'm speaking to them could you find out how our two invalids are doing from the Chinook?'

Although Bill Mathews thought the call to the air marshal would be awkward as he explained the grounded Chinook he had borrowed, he was expecting a better result from the PM – after all, his team along with the CIA had averted a nuclear disaster in the centre of London.

Although initially the PM did thank his team for their efforts, he soon moved on to the subject of the attack on the Russian ambassador's residence. The Russian premiere had demanded that MI6 hand over the agent named by Vadek Volkov to the Russian defence minister for interrogation. Although the PM did not agree to that it had been agreed that a Russian team could cross-examine Samantha O'Conner here in the UK.

Director Mathews placed a few things in his briefcase and pulled on his jacket, feeling morose. Jean entered the room. 'I have just been on the phone to a very nice doctor. Good news again, sir. Bruce Ellis has been discharged and has already left the hospital. He had six stitches in a head wound. Petty Officer Robert Prentice has a broken collarbone and will be discharged within the hour – his CO is en route to pick him up. Will there be anything else, Director?'

Mathews started to make his way out before replying. 'If you could contact Captain Malden and congratulate her on a superb job. Tell her she has a Lynx on its way to her – the fly boys seem to be a bit short on replacement Chinooks. Once you've done that get yourself home – that's an order. We've all had one hell of a day. I'm going to see if my poor wife is still speaking to me. Goodnight, Jean.'

Fiona Malden had showered at the Air Sea Rescue station and borrowed a spare pair of overalls. She had tried to sleep while her new transport was sourced but the adrenalin was still coursing through her veins. She sat in front of the big TV in reception as the evening news came on, tucking into a fish supper that had been brought in for her. To her amazement the main news had nothing about the day's events in the capital other than the London flood barrier had been reopened to river traffic. Apparently the geological event and high tide had passed without incident. Nothing terrorist related, only a French national Mohamed Mooshan had been shot in Portsmouth after he brandished a weapon at armed police officers carrying out a customs search.

On the later local news a geological survey team working in the area had reported a huge underwater disturbance, possibly an earthquake or volcanic activity.

Fiona could not believe no one knew what had just happened; for the first time she understood how Adam McDonald must have felt after Ireland and Kuwait. He had given so much with no recognition and here she was in the same position. Only the people at the highest level would ever know what risk she had placed on her life today. She was still glad she had stood up to the challenge and she knew in her heart that her team today had saved millions of lives, but she could never speak about it; she could never tell anyone how close Britain came to disaster. She wondered how many unsung heroes the country had produced and how many would never be able to tell their story, gagged by the Official Secrets Act.

Captain Andy Cook, one of Fiona Malden's fellow pilots, arrived in a Gazelle eventually to take Fiona back to Credenhill where a Lynx had just been dropped off for her. Andy made fun of Fiona's predicament but Fiona knew he was tentatively trying to find out what she had been up to when she was supposed to be on leave, and how she had piloted the damaged Chinook. Fiona took the abuse from her colleague without divulging what she had been involved in. The adrenalin had finally worn off; all Fiona wanted to do was climb into her bed at home and sleep for a week.

Bruce Ellis rang the doorbell for the fourth time. He was not feeling at his best; his head throbbed and his stitches felt as if they were about to burst open. Eventually Bernie Edelstein opened the door. Bruce had no time to waste; behind him the ambulance sat ticking over, Dan Whittaker waiting at the wheel.

'Holy shit, am I glad to see you. Where did you steal the ambulance? I hope the police ain't tailing you.'

Bruce Ellis brushed past Edelstein; he did not want to be seen outside this residence. 'Good morning, Bernard. I trust my patient is alive and kicking. The ambulance is my company car. I know you probably expected a silver Aston Martin complete with ejector seat but that's too British, my friend. An ambulance can move about London virtually unnoticed – you get to double park and no one can see inside – the perfect CIA company car. How is Samantha?'

Bernie rolled his eyes at Ellis. 'Oh, I think she's recovering. Boy, am I glad you've come to get her. I was thinking of getting a gun and shooting her myself – I've had one hell of a time keeping her here.'

Bruce Ellis entered the recovery room to find Sam wrapped only in a bed sheet hobbling round the bed towards the opening door. 'Bernie, give me my fucking clothes or I'll—'

Sam stopped dead in her tracks.

'Wow, girl, what the hell are you doing out of bed? Get your ass back in the bed and I'll get Bernie and your clothes. That's some reception for the guy that saved your butt.' Bruce waited as Bernie appeared with the evening clothes Sam had been wearing to the embassy.

'Second thought, Bernie old buddy, could Sam borrow a set of your scrubs? Where she's going, evening dress might not be the best idea.' Bernie left without speaking.

'Bruce, thanks for pulling me out and patching me up, but I am going no place with you. I need to find Adam and Luke. God knows where they'll be or if they're alive.' Sam wiped away a tear.

Bruce was glad Sam was recovering from her wounds but she looked depressed. She must have been worried sick about her family. He pulled a grey wig and glasses from his pocket and flung them onto the bed next to Sam. 'Adam is fine and I'm pretty sure, knowing him, he'll have made sure little Luke is safe. Put the wig and glasses on and I'll take you to him. No tricks … trust me. You will see Adam soon.'

Sam looked at the wig quizzically then turned to speak but Ellis had read her thoughts and beat her to it.

'Sam, did you really think you could shoot the shit out of the Russian Embassy and walk away without repercussions? The Russian premiere is after your blood, and you can bet your last dollar London is, as we speak, crawling with FSB agents, all looking for a blonde assassin. Get your granny wig on and let's go.'

What seemed like many hours later the ambulance pulled up at the gatehouse of the Credenhill army base. Bruce spoke to the duty sergeant, who seemed somewhat surprised at two Americans in an ambulance pulling up, but he had obviously been told to expect Ellis and let him pass. Bruce was given directions to the landing area where Captain Malden was waiting for her passengers.

Bruce was glad to see Fiona Malden had recovered from her brush with death and was eager to get the show on the road. Bruce and Dan unloaded Sam from the back of the ambulance. She was pale, her eyes were sunken in her skull and she had the haunted look of a woman on the edge. She was wheeled to the chopper in a wheelchair for her flight north. Fiona gave her a hug and Bruce a more intimate cuddle before helping to get Sam loaded into the back of the borrowed Lynx.

Bruce sat next to Fiona in the co-pilot's seat, leaving Dan to head back to London with the ambulance.

Once airborne and Fiona had finished talking to air traffic control Sam, although not her normal self, had a dig at Bruce Ellis.

'So, Bruce, how long have you been fraternising with the enemy here? Does your boss in the White House know you have a British army girlfriend?'

Bruce's eyes made contact with Fiona Malden's big green ones; she gave him a saucy wink as he turned to face his accuser in the back of the chopper.

'Considering I saved your life, am taking you to find your family, and am going to smuggle you out of the country before they hang you in the Tower of London for your attack on a foreign power, I think you're skating on thin ice, girl. Captain Malden and I are just good friends – that's what I'll be telling my boss if he asks. If anyone asks, I would appreciate it if you back me up on that. After all, you owe me a quite a few favours. If you know what's good for you, when I need your services you will pay me back for all my kind help.'

After Sam's initial comments she fell silent. She looked drained and within twenty minutes was asleep, her body hard at work trying to repair the damage.

10

The Uss *Alaska*

A dam McDonald had slept late; he had lost track of time, confined to his room and allowed out only with a commando guard for exercise once a day. It was the multiple footsteps that alerted Adam to the arrival of guests outside his locked door. He listened as the door was unlocked then, unusually, there was a knock. Adam was surprised but shouted to his unknown guest to come in.

A tall thin officer entered and closed the door behind him. He introduced himself as Colonel Davis, officer commanding 43 Commando Faslane. Davis shook Adam's hand then asked him permission to sit on the opposite bed.

'I trust that your stay with us hasn't been too terrible. I have been speaking with the Ministry of Defence, MI6 and, I believe, a friend of yours who has cast some light on matters. They have confirmed your identification, Captain McDonald. Although your decision to seek help at Area One was questionable, I can see why you did it. If the Spetsnaz troops had engaged you in a populated civilian area the death toll could have been significantly higher. That said, I see no further reason to hold you in detention, although I would advise you to remain on base for a couple of reasons. The police have requested an interview with you over the gun battle fought at the roadside by Loch Lomond. Also the press are hanging about at the gatehouse.

'A helicopter is arriving here from London and Director Mathews of MI5, acting director of MI6, has requested that I give you any assistance you need.'

Colonel Davis stood up, intent on leaving, but Adam needed a couple of questions answered. 'Colonel, my friend you talked to, was it Fiona Malden?'

Colonel Davis walked to the door, opening it before replying. 'No, Captain McDonald, I spoke to Sergeant Hunter. I believe he said you both served together with 22 SAS. He too is sheltering here from the attentions of press and the police – he's waiting for you in the canteen. Please feel free to go and join him. I believe he is desperate to get in touch with you.'

Adam walked into the canteen to find Bob Hunter sitting by the window, gazing into an untouched cup of tea. He lifted his head, and the minute he spotted Adam he jumped to his feet. In the joy of seeing his friend he apparently forgot about his leg wound, and sat back down quickly. Normally Adam would have at best shook his hand, but he had been cooped up worrying about Bob and Callum for days, so he gave the big ex-marine a hug before sitting opposite him, anxious to find out about Callum.

'I knew you would be okay, Bob, but I need to know what happened to the young lad. Did he make it?'

Bob nodded. 'A couple of hikers found us and carried Callum north along the West Highland Way trail until we found a cottage. I thought the young lad was a goner, but we hit it lucky. The cottage owner was a doctor. Between us all we managed to keep the lad alive until an air ambulance arrived and rushed us both to hospital. They operated on the lad immediately and removed three bullets from his upper body. The young guy was lucky – not one shell hit a major organ. Once I knew he was out of danger and they'd sorted me I legged it when I noticed the policemen waiting to interview me were too busy chatting up the nurses.

'I thought they might bring you here so after a ding-dong row with the gatehouse they finally let me speak to the boss here. He has told me I have permission to be here but if the police come looking for me I'm on my own.' Adam explained what had happened at Area One and how the love of his life, his big green Aston Martin Vantage, had met with a muddy end on the farm track. Bob nodded in sympathy with Adam's description of the big Aston's last movements.

'Yeah, I'm sorry about your car. I had a look under the tarpaulin – it is a bit of a mess.'

Adam was amazed, delighted and dismayed all at once.

'What? You didn't know your car was in the car park?'

Within five minutes Bob and Adam stood in front of a blue tarpaulin, Adam reluctant to lift the cover on his once pristine Vantage. It was Bob who pulled the cover off, revealing the extent of the damage to the big British supercar. The driver's side had taken the biggest beating. Its handcrafted aluminium wing had been smashed into the front suspension, the radiator grille and bonnet had two or three bullet holes, and the offside wheel and sill had been damaged from the trip down the farm track before the clutch said enough was enough. The pair were in the middle of a debate as to whether the Aston could be repaired when Adam heard the beat of a rotor blade coming from the south. Both men turned instinctively to watch for the approaching machine. Slowly the dot in the distance transformed into the familiar shape of a Lynx. The chopper turned in an arc out over the loch then without hesitation swung round, dropping towards the helipad on the north side of the Faslane base. Adam had seen this fast, accurate type of flying before; he did not need to wait for it to land to find out who the pilot was. It had all the hallmarks of Captain Fiona Malden; the question was who she had brought with her.

Adam and Bob made their way to the helipad, Adam wanting to get there as soon as possible, but Bob had a heavy limp and was still making heavy weather of getting around.

As they approached the now stationary helicopter Adam's prediction about the pilot was proved correct. Fiona removed her helmet to reveal a jet-black head of hair; she threw her head back to rearrange her helmet hair before spotting them and waving. Adam's eyes were drawn to the figure of Bruce Ellis who was busy working at the rear of

the chopper; it took Adam a few seconds to figure out that it was Bruce
– he was the last person he expected to see getting out of a British army
helicopter. To his surprise he was folding down a wheelchair, then he
lifted down a blonde girl. She looked up and spotted Adam just as
Bruce placed her gently into the wheelchair. The second their eyes met
Adam realised the blonde was Sam. It was if he had just had an electric shock; his heart almost exploded when he saw her, then the penny
dropped: she was in a wheelchair. His mood swung once more like an
out-of-control pendulum and he took off like an Olympic hundred metres runner towards the trio by the chopper, leaving Bob to hobble on
alone.

Adam was taken by surprise as Sam launched herself into his arms
from the wheelchair. She sobbed into his chest and asked where Luke
was.

In truth Adam did not know for certain if Luke and Sue were okay;
he had been detained and had no further knowledge of their situation. All he knew was he had done everything in his power to lead the
Russians away from their son and Sue, giving them the best chance to
escape north.

'They will be fine. When I got your message I sent Sue north with
Luke. I sent Sue down to the hotel with a note asking Paul and Margo
to take them up to Ullapool to their holiday home out of the way until
I had dealt with the Russians. What the hell happened to you?'

Adam felt Sam sag in his arms and spotted a change in her colour. He knew she was struggling, and helped lower her gently into the
wheelchair. After a second or so back in the chair she rallied and as
they headed for Bob and the admin building she cross-examined Adam.

'So you thought it was a good idea to leave our son with Paul and
Margo? We need to go and get him before the Russians find him.'

Once inside the admin building Bruce Ellis left the group with
Colonel Davis who had arranged a buffet for his new guests. Adam
longed for the time when he could be alone with Sam. For the moment
he had to make do with holding her hand as she leant her tired head
on his arm.

Sam used the time inside the building to study the people around her. Fiona Malden had been unusually quiet; she too was checking everyone out. Sam had already noted Fiona watching her and Adam, but had not decided if her interest was curiosity or possibly jealousy. It was clear to see that Fiona was very much in the market for a relationship. Sam's thoughts turned to the object of Fiona's latest attraction. Bruce Ellis might not be able to match Adam in the looks department, but he wasn't an ugly guy by any measurement; he was witty, and Sam sensed in him an honest but very clever and cunning mind. She decided that Fiona and Bruce would make a good couple and if she got the chance she would encourage the relationship, if only to make sure Fiona stayed away from Adam.

Bruce Ellis returned to the room with Captain Tracey, a US navy officer. He introduced Tracey to the assembled group, explaining he was the captain of the USS *Alaska*, which was visiting Faslane at the moment. Bruce noted Fiona Malden regarding the new arrival with interest; he had a feeling he was being compared to his friend as Fiona studied them both without commenting. Ellis knew in the looks department he was outgunned by Josh Tracey – he had the advantage of a dress uniform and, for a submarine officer, he had a great tan. Bruce decided that it must be his natural skin tone as he was pretty sure the USS *Alaska* wasn't fitted with sunbeds.

Bruce took advantage of a quiet moment to allow Josh Tracey to question him.

'Okay, buddy, let's have it. How the hell did the CIA, namely you, manage to get the Pentagon to hand over one of their missile boats to you? For god's sake, Bruce, tell me you haven't got some crazy mission planned. My guys are tired – it's been a long tour. You do know when we leave here we were meant to be going home, not on some mad CIA adventure.'

Bruce did not want Josh making a scene. He noted Josh's voice starting to increase in volume as he questioned him. 'Josh, it's me you're taking to. Don't worry, my friend, you are going home. All you have to do is make room for a few extra passengers, that's all. The girl in the wheelchair, her partner, their kid, and me. There, you see, it wasn't that bad, was it?'

Josh Tracey stared at Sam in her wheelchair, clearly unsure how to respond to this latest piece of information. 'Jesus Christ, Bruce, what the hell was wrong with British Airways? They fly to America, you know.'

Bruce patted his buddy on the back. 'Come on, Josh, think about it. You know I can't tell you why. All I'm going to say is the reason that girl is hitching a lift home is so important it was the President that signed over your boat to me, not the Pentagon. Now if the Commander in Chief is willing to take one of his ballistic missile subs out of service to act as a taxi, you can bet your last buck it's pretty damned important, buddy. Now you go and sort things out and I will break the news to the folks that they're going for a sail in one of Uncle Sam's most expensive machines.'

Bruce Ellis knew what he was about to suggest to Sam and Adam was going to be a hard sell, but he was determined to get them aboard the USS *Alaska*. Bob, Fiona and the colonel were engaged in conversation while Adam and Sam had stolen a quiet moment and were over by the exit. Bruce seized the chance and asked the pair to pop outside for a second while he had a word in private with them.

'Sorry to break up your reunion, folks, but I need to tell you what is going down here. Sam, you're in a lot of hot water over the embassy thing. Adam, I know you're out of the loop – Sam can fill you in later – but, take my word for it, if Sam doesn't toe the line now she could be in a world of trouble. Director Mathews and I have agreed a plan of action that will take the spotlight off you, Sam. You and Adam are going to be guests of the American government for a while until things blow over here. We are leaving today with Captain Tracey and the USS *Alaska*.'

Bruce Ellis had not finished speaking but Sam let him go no further. 'No, Bruce, no way. I am going to find my son and that is the end of it. I'll take my chances with the embassy thing but I must find Luke before the Russians have a chance to regroup.'

Bruce had expected nothing less from Sam and he had already prepared his next exchange. 'Samantha O'Conner, listen up, girl. In thirty minutes your ass better be on that sub. Now listen up, and no butting in before I'm finished or I'll carry you onto the boat myself. Director Mathews has told the Foreign Office and the Ruskies you are on a joint training mission in Nevada with American special forces. Also at the moment you are in no fit state to open a can of Coca Cola, never mind fight off another Russian attack. You will be safe in America. Word on the street is Volkov, who unfortunately survived your assassination attempt, has put a price on your head. He is happy to pay five million dollars to the man that kills you, so I think you might have more than the Russians after you. As for your kid, tell us where he is and we will go get him. Come on, Sam, you owe me big. I have arranged all this – don't make me look like an idiot. For god's sake, Adam, you must see she is in no fit state to defend her family. Come with us and we'll look after you until you're well again.'

Sam was still having none of it but Adam had obviously been shocked by her frail condition. Bruce knew Adam did not trust him, but surely even he had to admit any further encounters with the Russians would almost certainly end badly. There were still at least six Spetsnaz out there somewhere, and if they had just put a five-million-dollar bounty on Sam's head it was clear they were not giving up any time soon. Sam fought verbally with Bruce, but she was tiring.

'For the last time, I am telling you I am not getting on your bloody submarine. Adam and I are going to get our son. Even if I agreed to get on the damned boat there is no way we can get Luke on board and that, my friend, is a deal breaker.'

Adam intervened. 'Right, you pair, give it a rest. Maybe there is a way to sort this out. Listen up, Bruce. Here's the deal. Sam and I will get on board, but there are two conditions: we head for Ullapool where Luke is in hiding. I go ashore and get Luke, but if for some reason he isn't there or I can't find him you must agree to leave us there to find him. That is the deal. That is the only way you have a chance of getting us to go to America – all three of us or none of us.'

Bruce Ellis was escorted on board the USS *Alaska* by its executive officer, Mike O'Brian. He found Captain Tracey in the sonar room talking with two of his men. Josh Tracey smiled at his old buddy as soon as he spotted his arrival. 'Gentlemen, I would like you to meet our new skipper for our trip home, Special Agent, Pentagon and White House Liaison Officer for the Central Intelligence Agency Bruce Ellis. Well, Agent Ellis, where are our guests? Mike has kindly volunteered to give up his quarters to your friends for our trip home. As for you, you can bunk down on the floor of my cabin, and if you think you can outrank me and take my bed it isn't going to happen. You have stolen my boat, but I draw the line at my bed, pal.'

Bruce Ellis shook the hands of all present before replying to Josh Tracey. 'Don't worry, guys. I'm not about to take command so I'm afraid you're stuck with Captain Tracey. We have one stop to make, and then take a couple of my friends back to Kings Bay. That is all I ask of you. Sam and Adam, my friends, are saying their goodbyes and tidying up a few loose ends before joining us shortly, then we can get going.'

Sam and Adam had just said goodbye to Fiona and Bob and were heading towards the sub when Bruce Ellis passed them, making for Fiona. Adam was about to stop pushing Sam's wheelchair and wait for Bruce when they were accosted by a small stocky American sailor.

'Hi, guys, you must be Samantha and Adam. I've been sent by Mike our executive officer to find you and escort you to the USS *Alaska*. I'm COB Cushe, but just call me Nathan. Not many folks get to ride on the navy's finest boat – you must be kinda special, I guess.'

Nathan Cushe took over pushing duties from Adam and started them towards the sub.

'So, Nathan – remind me again what COB stands for – is the *Alaska* a good sub to be on?'

Nathan Cushe puffed out his chest in pride as he answered Adam's questions in a friendly and informative style. 'Okay, guys, sorry. I was forgetting you're not navy. COB is short for Chief of the Boat. The captain may be the boss, but it's the Chief of the Boat who runs things, and what a boat she is. The USS *Alaska* has won about every award there is to win: the Omaha Trophy, the Battenberg Cup. You name it, she's won it. She is the number one Ohio class ballistic missile submarine in the Atlantic fleet. When you picked a boat to go for a sail in you picked the best damned boat in the US navy.'

When Adam and Sam reached the watertight door of the sub Cushe offered to carry Sam on board, but the medical centre at the base had supplied her with a pair of walking sticks so she politely refused, saying that she would manage by herself, if a little slower than the rest of the crew.

Cushe led the way, clearly fretting over Sam's every step, while Adam folded up the wheelchair and brought up the rear in case Sam needed help. The stairs posed a problem but, with a steadying hand from Adam, Sam finally arrived at the executive officer's quarters where she put on a brave face for the benefit of Nathan Cushe.

'Chief, thank you for your help. Can I ask an awkward question?'

Cushe stopped in his tracks and turned to face Sam. 'No problem, honey, you can ask me anything you want. Fire away.'

Sam crunched up her nose, holding it with her fingers to emphasise the point. 'What is that smell? It's a cross between ammonia and sulphur. Will it always be like this?'

Cushe chuckled as if he had been expecting a far worse question. 'Don't worry, honey, give it an hour and you won't notice it. It's the chemicals we use to remove the carbon dioxide from the cabin air – you get used to it. My missus cracks up when I get home – it takes her weeks to get rid of the smell from my clothes. I need to get the guys ready to get underway, but if you need me just ask for the Chief. Speak to you later, folks.'

Bruce Ellis had been so focused on getting Sam on board the sub that he had almost left without speaking to Fiona Malden. He told the executive officer to get ready to go and he dashed back past Sam and Adam in a desperate attempt to find her before she left the base. To his great relief she was still with Adam's mate and the base commander.

'Boy, am I glad you're still here, Fiona. I was so busy with the sub I almost left without speaking to you. Listen, things have been crazy – I never did tell you how much I owe you. I need to get moving ... I might be picking up the wrong vibes but there is still a thing between us, you know, sort of unfinished business. Tell me if I'm wrong and I'll back off.'

Fiona appeared calm, but it was hard to tell if Bruce's stumbling attempts at defining their relationship were working.

'Listen, Bruce, I'm sure you have a girl in every port, but if you're trying to say should we see each other again, you've got my number. If you're back in London call me – just make sure this time it's not to pick up a nuke.'

It was as if a great weight had been lifted off Bruce's shoulders. 'I swear, Fiona, there's no one else. It's just me rattling about in my old ranch talking to the furniture. We don't need to wait until I'm back in London – come out to visit. It's an open invitation, any time is fine by me.'

Fiona squeezed his arm as she leaned forward and gave him a kiss on the cheek. 'You look after my friends and I'll give you a call soon to arrange a visit to this ranch of yours. Bon voyage.' Fiona turned away, giving Bruce a saucy wink as she left. 'I need to go and check on my chopper. See you soon!'

Bruce Ellis joined Josh Tracey in his cabin as the XO got the *Alaska* underway.

'Okay, Bruce, where are we making our stop? I have a little task to perform first if you don't mind. Intel reckon there's a Russian sub sitting out in the inlet and we have a British Vanguard class sub just about to leave on patrol. We've arranged to leave at the same time and I've agreed to get the Russians' attention so that HMS *Vigilant* can head north without a Russian tail. I take it you have no objection to this?'

Bruce Ellis studied the chart of the Scottish west coast, tracing the coastline with his finger until he found Ullapool. 'This is where I need you to go. We'll need to go ashore for an hour or so, then home. No more stops. I have no problems with you helping the British Navy, but out of curiosity – how are you going to fool the Russian boat?'

Josh Tracey was smiling as he pointed to the chart. 'I'm just about to head to the control room, but as we speak HMS *Vigilant* is alongside us. To the Russian sonar we look like one boat. The dilemma for them is which one is which? We'll head for the Ayrshire coast where if our timing is correct we'll meet the ferry from Ardrossan heading for the island of Arran. Both our boats will travel under the keel of the ferry, destroying Russian sonar capability. As we approach Arran I'll take a sharp turn south at full speed. HMS *Vigilant* will remain under the keel of the ferry for as far as possible and while we lead the Russian away the British boat will go quiet of the coast of Arran, where it will remain overnight until the coast is clear. As for the Russians, they're welcome to follow us all the way to the good old US of A if they want to. We are going home – nothing for them to report back to Moscow worth talking about.'

Captain Tracey found his XO, Mike O'Brian, in the control room. He had worked with Mike for the last seven tours; the men said very little, both knowing how the other worked. Josh Tracey passed the coordinates for Ullapool to O'Brian, who studied them on his chart without commenting. When the time was right and both nuclear subs had travelled some distance under the hull of the big ferry, Tracey gave his XO a nod and without hesitation Mike gave the helmsman the order, 'Hard to port and all ahead full.' Josh needed his boat to make as much disturbance in the water as possible so that the Russian sub would pick it up over the turbulence of the Arran ferry's propellers and change course to follow him. He gave the order to set course for the destination he had given his XO and left the control room, happy in the knowledge that his unusual visit to the Scottish fishing village would confuse the hell out of his Russian friends.

Bruce Ellis sat by himself in Josh Tracey's cabin thinking things through. He had not planned for the chance of the *Alaska* being shadowed by a Russian sub, but it was not a problem. In fact, the Russians finding out that Samantha O'Conner had picked up her kid and escaped to America had played right into his hands.

The President had set him an almost impossible task, but things were at last starting to fall into place. Hopefully Samantha's arrival in the States would trigger his end game; his plan had to work – he had no backup plan.

Sam had put on a brave face in front of the Chief of the Boat but alone with Adam, although he knew she wanted to talk to him, the waves of tiredness quickly overcame her and within fifteen minutes of arriving on board she was asleep, still holding on to Adam's hand.

Adam decided that with no place to go, curling up next to Sam was the only option, although unlike Sam he could not sleep. He played the last few hours over in his head. It was good that for the moment they could rest easy, knowing Vadek Volkov could not touch them, but he was worried that the evil bastard had somehow managed to find Luke. For the moment he put the thought out of his head; there was nothing he could do for the next few hours until they reached Ullapool. Adam's thoughts turned back to Bruce Ellis. Adam couldn't put a finger on it, but something was wrong with this situation. He knew, since Ellis's team's capture of Bin Laden, the man had real power behind him in the shape of the White House, but it could not be possible that he had the capability to redirect one of America's ballistic missile submarines to help a British agent reach safety in America. No, something was wrong here and, although Bruce Ellis was good at his job, Adam had detected a hesitation in some of his answers, as if he was either making them up or checking what he was saying was believable.

Adam was gently shaken awake by Mike O'Brian. Sam was still sleeping as Adam left the cabin with Mike. It was dusk as the submarine broke the surface of a calm sea only half a mile offshore from the village of Ullapool. A well-drilled crew had, to Adam's amazement, just finished assembling a small sailing boat complete with a tiny outboard motor. Adam wasn't sure about getting into the tiny boat next to the sub. It looked so fragile, as if just one freak wave would smash it against the hull of the *Alaska* and turn it to driftwood instantly.

'It's fine, Mr McDonald. It's the skipper's little toy for playing about with when we're in port. It's well tested – you'll be fine in it. I'm coming with you to sail the little guy.'

Adam was not convinced but nodded. 'Mike, do you have a side arm I can borrow? I don't know how much you know, but there's a small chance we might just run into some nasty Russian special forces who have an axe to grind with Sam and I. It would be better if we were both armed just in case.'

Mike O'Brian said nothing but disappeared back into the sub, returning with Bruce Ellis. Ellis handed Adam a Glock and two spare mags. 'Sorry, not even I can authorise the XO to carry a weapon. Captain's orders. He will ferry you across and wait by the pier for your return. Let's hope you don't have to use the gun – and good luck.'

The trip, using the little electric outboard motor, took only ten minutes. Mike positioned the little Seahopper collapsible boat next to the ladder on the north side of the pier. Although Mike had been ordered to wait by the boat, he tied it up and joined Adam as he scaled the pier. Adam was racking his brain to try and remember where the holiday cottage was; he had been in the pub when Margo had given directions to her friend who was going up to the cottage for the weekend. Mike and Adam travelled at speed, climbing away from the seafront until they came to the second street. Adam knew the cottage was close to the end of the street; it was white with a porch and had a palm tree growing directly across from the entrance. Adam spotted the palm first and increased his pace along the street until he stood outside a white cottage, ringing the doorbell inside the porch. His heart sank when there was no reply. He checked the house sign: *Tigh Geal.* He was sure this was the name of the cottage. While Mike kept watch Adam made his way to the back of the cottage, treading carefully in the dark because his night vision was poor. As he turned the corner of the building the cold metal barrel of a gun was pressed firmly next to his ear, followed by the metal click of the hammer being pulled back into the firing position.

Instinctively Adam froze to the spot; he had been outmanoeuvred. His fingers were touching the butt of his Glock but he knew he would never be quick enough to respond before the bullet penetrated his skull.

'If you even breathe too hard you're dead. Get your hands on your head where I can see them, and do it slowly if you know what's good for you, dickhead.'

Adam's heart almost stopped, then his brain registered and it was all he could do to stay still. 'Jesus, Sue, I almost shit myself. Be a good girl and put the gun down gently. You're a nurse, not the bloody Lone Ranger. I take it Bob gave it to you?'

The gun was hastily removed and replaced by a torch in Adam's face. 'You almost made me have kittens, you big idiot. What the hell are you doing creeping about the back of the house in the dark?'

Adam removed the gun from Sue's hand before replying. 'I did ring the doorbell. Anyway, forget it, how is my wee pal doing? Has he been okay up here?'

Adam introduced Mike to Sue as she let them in through the front door. When Adam told her why they were there, Sue was shocked that they planned to take Luke away that night. As she bundled the sleeping toddler up in his blanket her eyes were welling up.

'How long do you think you will be away for, Mac? I'm going to miss the little munchkin. You take good care of him, do you hear me, Adam McDonald? Watch out for the sun – he'll burn easily.'

Adam was amused at Sue's mothering instincts; he knew the pair had formed a bond the minute they set eyes on one another. 'Listen, Sue, we can never repay you for what you've done, but I'm going to say it anyway: thank you from the bottom of our hearts. Anyway, do you not want to hear what's become of your loving husband? The poor guy got shot trying to save my backside – he'll be fine, but I think he's going to need some pampering. Are you up for the job?'

Sue snorted, her mind off little Luke for the moment. 'That big nanny goat will get no pampering from me. If he's stupid enough to get himself shot that's his problem. My job here is done, so I'm going to do a bit of retail therapy in Inverness before I head back to the lodge house, and Bob better not think he's hiding at the Airsoft site. Margo tells me those thugs have made a mess of my front door, so he better get well quick – he has house repairs to be getting on with.'

Adam would have liked to have talked to Sue for longer, but he was mindful that only a short distance away the American sub was waiting for their return. He gave Sue a big hug before heading off down to the pier, Mike carrying an armful of baby bags while Adam carried a still sleeping Luke wrapped up in his blanket in his car seat. Getting Luke from high on the pier to the little dinghy proved challenging but with Mike's help to steady the tiny boat Adam descended the ladder until Mike could take the car seat from him.

On the trip back to the sub Adam had time to reflect on things. Volkov had failed miserably in his attempt to kill Sam and her family, but, although the threat had been lifted, deep down Adam knew this was not over. He knew Sam too well; when she recovered from her wounds it would be time for Vadek Volkov to be afraid; he had made a bitter enemy of Samantha O'Conner. She would not rest until she had hunted Volkov down and sent him on his way to hell. Sam may have been a mother, but she was a professional killer first.

The trip across the Atlantic proved uneventful. After a day of rest Sam started to use the walkways to exercise her wounded leg. She was pale and had lost weight, but Adam had seen that look in her eye and he knew all too well that she was using Vadek Volkov to focus her hatred as a tool to help her recovery. Only when her energy ran out did she sit in the cabin playing with Luke while Adam studied her. Sam had previously been the perfect mum, but watching her now it was as if she were going through the motions. This latest encounter had reawakened the killer in her; even when she was playing with Luke, Adam could see her mind wandering: that terrible flash of anger in those cold eyes was there only for a second until Sam remembered she was a mother, but nonetheless it was there, lurking in the background of her soul, waiting like a lioness stalking her prey. Vadek Volkov was a dead man.

Five days later the USS *Alaska* docked in Kings Bay, Georgia. Bruce Ellis had already arranged for a short-term stay for Sam and her family in St Mary's, only a stone's throw from the submarine base. But if Sam thought she was going to be left alone she was mistaken. Ellis arrived the next morning and escorted Sam to the medical centre at the base, where she was poked, prodded and X-rayed. Although the doctors were happy with her wounds, they were not happy about her blood. She spent the afternoon receiving blood transfusions before being wheeled to the pharmacist where she was handed a cocktail of drugs and instructions when to take them.

The next morning, while Sam and Adam were trying to coax Luke to eat his breakfast, there was a knock at the door. Before Adam could answer Bruce Ellis appeared in the kitchen, a habit that Adam was not fond of, but to keep the peace he stayed silent and allowed Sam to do the talking.

'Morning, Bruce, you're early on your rounds this morning. Can we get you some breakfast?'

Bruce pulled up a chair and gave Luke's hair a playful ruffle, which earned him a beaming grin from Luke who was doing anything to get out of eating his porridge.

'Don't worry about me, guys. I just popped in to let you know I'm off to Washington for a couple of days. Here are a couple of numbers – if you need anything these guys will sort you out until I get back. Unfortunately the doctors have given you a red card for the next couple of days, Samantha, at least until your blood count is rechecked. I was thinking, when I get back and you get the all clear from the doc we could take a flight to my place in Arizona – I have an old ranch house out there. I think we all need a break to recharge our batteries.'

Sam nodded without speaking, while Adam continued in vain to try and feed Luke his porridge. He didn't speak or make eye contact with either Sam or Bruce.

Bruce said his goodbyes and left them trying to coax Luke to eat.

With only three spoonfuls left Adam decided Luke had won and threw in the towel. He popped Luke into the brand-new playpen with price tags still attached. It was obvious to see their arrival had been hastily arranged; everything in the house was new and looked like it had been purchased yesterday, giving the house a cold, unlived-in feeling. Adam handed Sam a fresh cup of coffee and joined her again at the kitchen table as she watched her son investigating the sales tags on the playpen.

'Sam, I don't trust Bruce. What's in it for him to help us out like this? Remember, he's still CIA. I don't know what, but he's up to something.'

Sam took a slug from her coffee and downed a cocktail of drugs, swallowing before replying to Adam. 'Of course he's up to something – you saw how anxious he was to get us on the submarine, and as for being safe, if that's the case why do we have two guys on a twenty-four hour shift watching the house? The blue Dodge sedan parked two down on the far side of the road has been there since we arrived, but the two men in it have been rotated. The first passenger was bald and smoked, while the passenger in it now chews gum, is constantly on his phone and has hair. FBI or Homeland Security, I would imagine.'

Adam breathed a sigh of relief, knowing that Sam was singing from the same hymn sheet as him. He walked across to his jacket then returned to the table. 'In that case, one for you and one for me.'

Adam placed the Glock and the two magazines on the table next to Sam and the Beretta where he sat. 'Bruce forgot to ask me for the Glock back after going ashore to pick up Luke, and I borrowed the Beretta from Sue.'

Before Adam had sat down, Sam had the Glock stripped to check and clean the weapon.

Adam headed out first, pushing Luke in the buggy. He waited on the sidewalk as Sam locked up and followed him across the street. It had been Sam's idea to get some fresh air and see a bit of the town. He let Sam take the lead; she was leaning heavily on her walking stick and having trouble maintaining a steady pace. She headed straight for the unmarked surveillance car parked in the street. Adam watched the man who appeared to be the senior of the pair in the car turn to face away from the sidewalk, making as if he was deep in conversation with the driver. To their apparent dismay, Sam knocked on the car's side window. Hesitantly the passenger powered down the window.

'Hi, guys, I'm Sam. Adam and I were just discussing which agency you guys are from. Adam reckoned Homeland Security, I thought maybe FBI. How about settling a small bet we had and telling us who you work for?'

Sam smiled sweetly as the two agents racked their brains for an answer that would not give away too much, but they had been rumbled and any answer now other than the truth would have just made them look stupid.

'Hello, Miss O'Conner. I am Officer Lacey of the ONI. This is my partner, Officer le Clerk. Ma'am, we have been posted to make sure you all stay safe. Anything you need, just let us know.'

Sam looked up, catching Adam's eye. He could tell by now when Sam had mischief on her mind and he was pretty sure she was not finished winding up the agents.

'My goodness, guys, St Mary's must be a hotbed of trouble if we need Naval Intelligence to stand guard for us. Do you think it will be safe to visit the shops?'

Lacey pointed to Sam's walking stick. 'Miss O'Conner, can we offer you a lift to the store? You need to take it easy with that leg of yours.'

Sam thanked them but refused their offer. She continued walking with Adam and Luke; she'd told Adam she hoped the fresh air and exercise would help her recovery. Sam put on a brave face on their return from the shop, but Adam watched her slip into bed covered from head to toe in a cold sweat. Within five minutes she was asleep.

Bruce Ellis entered the situation room of the White House to find that the two most powerful men in the country were waiting patiently for his arrival. The President signalled Ellis to sit down while the Chairman of the Joint Chiefs of Staff stood at the head of the table, hands clasped behind his back. He was not a man to hang about and, while the President listened, he immediately launched into the reason for the meeting.

'I take it you have the British woman here. The President and my-self would like you to talk us through this plan of yours once more.'

Ellis had gone over this very plan twice over the phone but decided not to bring this fact up, instead rewinding to the start of his thoughts. 'Very well, General, here we go. As you know, we have had no luck in finding our Russian mole or, as his file states, Agent X. We suspect, due to the nature of information landing in Russian hands, our leak is from a military background rather than a civilian one – so far our armed forces have been the target in the vast majority of cases.

'As recent events in England have shown, Vadek Volkov has left no stone unturned in his quest for revenge: Samantha O'Conner was part of an MI6 team that assassinated his younger sister and her team of drug dealers. It has also been confirmed his contact and probable partner in the Kremlin is the Russian defence secretary, Dimitri Panoz. I am pretty sure when Volkov finds out Samantha is here in America he will ask his friend the defence secretary to contact Agent X to try and find where we have hidden her. We have narrowed our suspects down and we have a specialist team in Europe who have Panoz under constant communication surveillance. I plan to leak where O'Conner is hidden on an individual basis to our list of suspects, so that when Agent X does contact Panoz, although we may not be able to break their code and listen, we will know who we've leaked the information to at that time, giving us the identity of Agent X.'

For the first time in the meeting the President spoke. 'Bruce, have you told the woman that you are using her as bait to capture a spy? I say this because if anything happens to her, it's me who will have to explain to the prime minister what went wrong. I feel that task would be easier knowing the British agent was assisting us and not being exploited by us, don't you think?'

For the next hour the three men went over various details of Bruce Ellis's plan to find Agent X, before Bruce was shown to the situation room door by the President himself.

'Remember, Bruce, tell the woman what is happening. At least give her the chance to defend herself should the situation arise. If it were you in her shoes wouldn't you want to know? Keep the general informed of progress and stay safe, my friend.'

On the way back to the airport Bruce turned over in his head how he was going to break it to Sam that she was a pawn in a deadly game of chess. He had the feeling he would have to be very careful; his dealings with Sam had taught him she was somewhat volatile.

The flight back to St Mary's went without a hitch and Bruce left his pilot refuelling and filing a flight plan for Flagstaff Airport, Arizona.

Adam was washing up while Sam dried the dishes when there was a knock at the door followed by the now familiar voice of Bruce Ellis. Sam dried her hands and shuffled through to the lounge where she found Bruce on his hands and knees playing hide and seek behind the couch, while a giggling Luke looked on from his position in his playpen. Although Sam had her reservations about the American agent she was amused that a man in his position could crawl about on the floor playing with her son; as she watched Luke laugh and hide behind his teddy, copying Ellis's actions, she could see Bruce was good with kids and Luke seemed to accept him without hesitation. Sam reckoned he would make a good dad, given the chance. Bruce spotted Sam standing by the kitchen door watching his antics and got to his feet, dusting down his trousers before giving Luke a high five on his way to the kitchen.

In the kitchen Bruce announced that they were going to Arizona, letting it sink in that he was here to pick them up and take them to the airport where their plane to Flagstaff, Arizona was waiting for them. An hour later Sam checked on Luke, who had just missed take-off and was fast asleep as the Lear jet climbed to its cruising altitude, next stop Flagstaff.

11

Spy Catcher

'Okay, Bruce, time to have a wee chat. Sam and I did not come up the Clyde in a banana boat. You don't just borrow a sub then fly us around America out of the goodness of your heart, so cut the bullshit and tell us what the hell you're up to.'

Bruce was puzzled; the banana boat comment made no sense to him, but he knew by Adam's tone of voice this was crunch time.

'Okay, folks, you're right. I have been holding out on you. A couple of years ago it became apparent that America has a Russian spy in our midst. Despite FBI and CIA investigations we have never been able to find the traitor, who has been code named Agent X. Because the vast majority of information passed to Russia is military, we suspect Agent X is from a military background. After recent events in London it has become clear that the Russian defence minister is heavily involved with Vadek Volkov, and being one of the inner circle of the Kremlin faithful will almost certainly know of Agent X.

'Using Sam over here was my plan to draw Agent X out into the open. I have a gut feeling that when he finds out you're alive and well in America, Volkov will ask his buddy the defence secretary to enlist the help of Agent X to track you down, so his friends in the Russian special forces can pay you a visit. I reckon if we release Sam's whereabouts at certain times to certain people we will be able to identify Agent X by a process of deduction.'

Sam said nothing, but Adam was clearly not happy that his family were once more going to be put in danger.

'So you drag us here with no consultation and expect us to risk our lives on the off chance you might catch a spy. Not exactly a great way to get us on board your little scheme. Sam's not able to defend herself, never mind look after Luke. What happens if your plan backfires and this Agent X of yours manages to get a message to those bastards who attacked us in Britain? Have you worked that one into your little plan?'

There was no love lost between Bruce and Adam, ever since their fateful encounter on the Arran beach when Adam had just found Smithy's body; that day Ellis had seen in Adam's eyes that if he had been given the chance he would have killed every American present, Ellis included. Ever since then Adam had treated Ellis as an adversary rather than a friend.

'Don't worry about that, Adam, you will have round-the-clock protection, and anyway there is no way those thugs are getting into America. There is no place safer for you guys. Just think of it as a vacation with us picking up the bill. You know it makes sense. Would you rather still be detained by the army while your girl faces extradition to Russia and your son is hunted by Russian hitmen in the UK?'

Adam was about to reply but Sam reached over, putting her hand on his and giving it a squeeze before speaking for the first time. 'Tell me the truth, Bruce. Did you hatch this plan before or after you pulled my ass out of the Russian Embassy?'

Bruce Ellis was shaking his head almost before Sam had the sentence finished.

'I swear on my momma's grave that was not the reason I pulled you out. It wasn't until you were laid up with your leg that it occurred to me the Russians would do anything to find you, including contacting Agent X. The embassy thing was a seat-of-your-pants moment – no planning. You gave us no warning – we just rolled up and did what we could, and luckily it worked out.'

Sam sat back, smiling, letting Adam's hand go before replying to Bruce.

'Yeah, I'm pretty glad it worked out. I owe you one, so bring it on. Let's go catch us a Russian spy, then when my leg is better you can point me in the direction of Vadek Volkov – it's time for that particular type of wolf to become extinct.'

Adam was left with little option but to go with the flow, but had apparently decided a few more searching questions were called for. 'Okay, I suppose if Sam is okay with this then I'll go with it. You said round-the-clock protection. What do you have in mind, and where is safe enough to stop a Russian attack?'

Bruce had expected Adam's cross-examination; after all, he had been British special forces and was no fool when it came to close protection. Bruce took a sip of his mineral water before continuing. 'I spoke very nicely to the President, who let me borrow four secret service agents from his own protection detail. They will be joining us at my ranch and will be with us until we have Agent X in custody. I also took the liberty of hiring a housekeeper, who is also a childminder. Hopefully you should get along well with Lauren – she should have arrived from LA yesterday and the added bonus is she is a Scot, just like yourself, Adam.'

Adam said nothing but Sam was obviously thinking ahead. 'We will need access to weapons. Can you arrange that, Bruce? And while we have your undivided attention you can tell us a bit more about the area we'll be staying in. Did you grow up on the ranch?'

Bruce knew even although Sam was injured she would not tolerate being without a weapon, and saying no to her would be a lost cause.

'I have a few handguns back at the ranch you're welcome to borrow, but if you go out with your bodyguard leave them at home. I don't want the local sheriff throwing you in jail because you have no permit. No, I didn't grow up on the ranch, I stumbled upon it when I was on a couple of days off work. Back then I was head of security at Groom Lake or, as you guys know it, Area 51. I was off doing a bit of exploring when I found Trappers Creek and the old ranch house. The rest is history. I paid way over the score for the site and spent four years and every penny I had making it habitable. I continue even today to invest every penny I make in my little bit of Arizona in the hope one day I can find a good woman and retire to my ranch house in the hills.'

The flight took a little over four hours. The later part was taken up keeping Luke, who was now wide awake, amused while Bruce joined the flight crew for the last part of the trip across America.

Within seconds of the jet coming to a halt at Flagstaff Airport they were met by two black Ford MPVs complete with privacy glass. Sam, Adam and Luke were ushered into the first van along with Bruce and one of the suited and sunglasses-wearing secret service agents whose face was blank; only his eyes moved, partially hidden by his dark glasses, darting from object to object as he checked every possible potential threat while the vans remained stationary. Sam and Adam saw little of Flagstaff as the MPVs made a rapid exit, heading north-west out of town, eventually leaving the highway and joining a winding mountain road. They turned off at a large pair of stone pillars, through a shaded wooded drive that twisted back and forward through the trees, climbing as it went, before breaking out into a large clearing with a large half stone, half timber ranch house and three outbuildings. It was clear to see that true to his word Bruce Ellis had spared no expense and, although the building had many traditional features such as a wooden porch and small windows, it looked like it had been built yesterday. As the vans pulled up outside the front of the building for the first time the outbuildings came into full view on the left side of the main house, set out in such a way that they formed a courtyard, the buildings joined at each corner by glass atriums in the middle of the group of buildings. The courtyard contained a large square swimming pool looking out onto the sprawling front lawn and drive. The large solid wood front door was opened by a blonde woman wearing jeans and a sweatshirt. She stood while the poker-faced agent opened the sliding door for Sam, Adam and Luke to climb out, followed by Bruce Ellis who was busy giving his home a quick visual check.

Adam studied the woman as she stepped forward to introduce herself to them. 'Hi there, I'm Lauren. You must be Samantha and Adam, and this wee man here will be Luke. Hello, my wee pal, you're a right wee blondie, aren't you? Welcome to the wild west.'

Adam let Sam go ahead with Lauren as she showed them around the house. Bruce was talking with the secret service agents, presumably going through procedures and various scenarios before eventually joining them along with Lauren and Luke, who had decided sitting on Lauren's lap was a better option than his father's, and was busy wrapping Lauren's hair around his little fat fingers. It was clear to see that Bruce Ellis was not used to having company; although he joined in conversation Adam could tell his mind was elsewhere. He seemed relieved when Sam excused herself saying her leg was playing up. She headed for the guest bedroom for a rest, closely followed by Adam and Luke, leaving Lauren to buzz around, making sure everyone had all they needed.

Bruce took the chance to head for the two guest bedrooms in the rear building of the ranch complex. He had outlined the need for their presence but he wanted to make sure the secret service knew what they might be up against if the shit hit the fan. He called an informal meeting in the first of the two bedrooms designated for the agents.

'Guys, if you need anything just ask Lauren – she will sort you out. I need to go into things in a bit more detail so you will be correctly prepared for any eventuality. My guests have a contract out on them and to make matters worse the Russians would like to have them deported as their guests, which means you might be up against anything from a bounty hunter to Russian special forces. If you think that last statement is a bit far-fetched then think again. A Russian Spetsnaz unit tried to capture them in the UK on their home turf, so I need you guys to be at your very best. Nothing may happen, but if it does I want you prepped and ready for the worst – do we understand each other?'

Bruce let Dan Trudo, who was the quartet's team leader, continue the briefing, ready to add his thoughts if needed. The fact that the Russians had already made an attempt on their protection subjects was information that had not been passed to the secret service. Bruce could tell from the serious faces around the room they didn't like what they were hearing. Dan Trudo requested that they review and upgrade their firepower first thing in the morning, then decided to hit the ground running. Bruce waited as he barked orders to his agents.

'Okay, men, listen up. Four-way radio contact at all times. If it comes to it these guys will be every bit as well drilled as us, so stay sharp. Something doesn't look right, shout it out. No one goes anywhere without my permission. Brian and Ricky, I want motion sensors working tonight. Pete, you and I will get video surveillance up and running and check out the house and perimeter areas. Let's get to it, guys.'

Bruce Ellis showed Dan Trudo and Pete Linn around the house and outbuildings before returning to the lounge area where he found Sam, Adam and Lauren tucking into coffee and cake while they watched Luke astride a wooden rocking horse, giggling and squealing 'Hoss' at the top of his baby voice as he rocked back and forth to the amusement of all present.

Lauren had strategically placed cushions from both of the big sofas all around the base of the rocking horse, with extra cushions at the hearth of the huge stone fireplace for extra protection. Sam studied Lauren as she played with Luke. She had only met the woman hours ago but she was already at ease in her company. Although she had fed and watered everyone, including the secret service agents, she still managed time for Luke, who had decided earlier that sleep was not on his agenda. Sam left Adam in charge of Luke and headed to the kitchen with the dirty cups, giving her the chance to stretch her stiff and sore leg. She was joined by Lauren.

'Samantha, you should have let me take the cups. You look like you could do with your bed. You've had a busy day travelling – between your leg and carrying the wee man about you must be whacked. You get yourself to bed and I'll finish things up here. When would you like your breakfast tomorrow?'

'Don't worry about us, Lauren. We'll get ours when we've sorted out Luke. He can be a bit unpredictable so we will be fine. You sort the agents out.'

Lauren had started rinsing the cups as Sam headed to the door.

'Samantha, you decide how much help you need. I'll go with whatever you decide, but by the looks of that broken leg you're going to have to spend a bit of time working it until it's better. I'd be delighted to look after the wee man – after all, it keeps me from cleaning. Remember, just say the word.'

Sam walked slowly to the door, turning back towards Lauren before leaving the room. 'Thanks, I'll see how it goes. It's not broken, by the way, it's a bullet wound. I don't know what Bruce has told you, but staying around us might not be too good for your health – you might want to reconsider your offer of help. Please call me Sam – Samantha is my Sunday name. Sweet dreams, see you tomorrow.' Sam left, heading for bed. Lauren was correct, she was knackered; she had a long way to go before she could pay Vadek a visit.

It was a warm muggy evening as the sun sank below the horizon, casting long shadows from the huge shipping cranes over the port of Ensenada.

Daniil Litvak was the first of the group to descend from the gangway of the merchant ship, MV *Hanarath Goss*, and stand on Mexican soil. He was followed by the same five men who had been part of the Scotland team; the only new addition was his kid brother, Anton Litvak. They made their way cautiously to the end of the pier, and a white van flashed its headlamps four times as planned to tell them they were safe to approach. Litvak climbed into the passenger seat while his colleagues loaded their bulky luggage into the back of the van. Daniil was the only member of the team who knew Ensenada; he had used this route once before and knew they had a long hard drive ahead of them before they reached the safe house in Ramona. He had authorised his men to carry their handguns because the next and most dangerous part of their trip to America was to cross the border at Tierra Del Sol; the last time Litvak had crossed to America there was little security and only a section of poorly maintained fence to overcome. His enquiries with his friend in Russian intelligence told a different story this time; border guards had been increased and there was a new mood in

America focused on keeping Americans safe. Daniil had no doubt this time the crossing would be a much more difficult task. Five miles from Ensenada Litvak asked the Mexican driver to stop so he could empty his bladder.

Daniil had guessed the driver would use the opportunity to get out for a smoke; he did not have to take aim, he was so close. He sent a bullet through the base of the driver Jorge's skull before calmly holstering his Beretta. He grabbed Jorge's feet and dragged his dead body down by the roadside and into a storm drain. He removed the envelope and the two thousand dollars he had paid him to taxi them, kicked some dirt over the pool of Jorge's blood and rejoined his team, this time behind the wheel of the van.

Daniil had timed his arrival at the border on an overcast night with little moonlight. He studied the section of new fencing through night sights and as he watched he spotted a group of Mexicans making their way to the fence. He saw an opportunity unfolding and ordered his men to join them while he and Anton climbed back into the van.

Daniil picked a likely spot, jumped clear of the van and watched it smash into the border fence, stopping with a grinding shudder as the engine stalled. Anton and Daniil charged after it, Anton carrying a large petrol can, while Daniil set a small detonator. Anton soaked the fence and the van in petrol, then both men left, heading north some distance away. Daniil triggered the detonator and watched the dark sky turn orange as the van burned brightly. Only a few minutes later they joined the small group of people, some Mexican and some his men. With some effort, Daniil held the Mexicans back while he waited for the inevitable arrival of the border guards. Sure enough, a few minutes later the quiet night air was shattered by the roar of a V8 pickup making its way quickly to the scene of the fire. The minute Daniil was sure the coast was clear his men cut through the fence and Daniil sent the Mexicans through first to test the water, so to speak. He watched their slow progress, heading for a nearby field, before taking aim with his sniper rifle. Picking the biggest and fittest man he shot him between the shoulder blades; he watched the man drop and the remaining Mexicans take flight into the fields. Daniil was happy he had done enough to confuse the American authorities and signalled for his men to cross, then head due north to their pickup point. Overhead he could hear the distinctive note of a drone somewhere in the darkness. Probably an American military drone, he thought. He was unconcerned; he was pretty sure their agent would take care of it, and as he listened the drone changed direction, heading away from their position. The Americans would find the Mexican bodies and trace the van and for at least some time they would think it was a Mexican attempt to enter America that had gone sadly wrong.

It would give Daniil the time he needed to find Samantha O'Conner, kill her and claim Volkov's reward money.

Sam had woken early, sore and grumpy after tossing and turning. Unable to get back to sleep she had sneaked out unnoticed, intent on finding out how good her security detail were. First she saw Bruce Ellis leave followed shortly afterwards by Dan Trudo; next from the corner of the barn she watched another agent finishing his rounds checking cameras. His body language when he spotted Sam gave away the fact he was not happy that she had slipped out. He headed straight for her. Sam was in no mood to be ordered around as the agent was soon to find out.

'Ma'am, I would be much happier if we could go back indoors. It's best for you and your family.' The agent gently put his hand on Sam's shoulder to coax her to move towards the front door; it was not the wisest thing he had ever done. Sam may have been wounded but she still had her core strength. In a sudden burst of speed she grabbed the agent's arm, pivoting under it and locking his elbow before using his forward balance and his locked arm to push him face first to the ground. His face made contact with the ground a fraction of a second before the barrel of Sam's Glock rested against his earlobe.

Sam hissed through clenched teeth in his ear. 'What's your first name, Agent? Mine is Sam. I would appreciate it if you called me by my first name and I will call you by yours. I may be wounded but as you have just found out a wounded animal is just as dangerous. Quit with the orders. I know what the risks are – you're not talking to some dumb blonde.'

Sam stood up and tucked the Glock into the back of her trousers, her mood changing as she watched the agent get to his feet and dust himself down.

'My name's Pete, and that was pretty low. If you had been a threat you would never have got near me to pull that little stunt of yours. You took advantage of the fact I was not expecting your challenge.'

Sam was shaking her head in total disagreement. 'Listen to me, Pete, and listen good. Do you think the Russians will drop us a calling card if they come? Remember, I'm an agent too, so don't go looking to protect me. Just make sure my son is safe, that's all I ask. I'll look after myself. Now, if you really want to help, give me a hand to find where the garbage is kept.'

Adam and Luke were asleep when the gunfire started. Adam was in-stantly awake. He checked on Luke, who was still asleep, before flinging a T-shirt on with his boxer shorts and pulling a Beretta from the bedside cabinet. He clicked off the safety and headed for the bedroom door. Outside in the hall doors were opening, agents were flinging clothes on, and Adam was immediately confronted with Lauren in her PJs.

'Where is Samantha?' Lauren didn't wait for a reply as she charged into the room, gathered the sleeping toddler up in the bed sheets and headed out of the room in the opposite direction to the gunfire. Adam and the two remaining agents made their way cautiously out and round the front of the ranch house towards the rear of the buildings, Adam's heart in his mouth. Dan, Pete and Sam were all AWOL. He knew Sam was normally a match for any man, but wounded and with her family holding her back she had a serious disadvantage.

Sam replaced the empty magazine, took aim once more picking the target to her left, and then gently squeezed the trigger. The bullet hit the empty Coke can on the base just off centre, sending the can spinning into the air. On Sam's left, Pete's actions were almost a blur; drawing his Sig from its holster he fired twice in rapid succession. He hit the can twice before it hit the ground. Sam was impressed but not surprised. Pete and the other agents were some of the finest shots in America; you didn't get to guard the President for your good looks.

Sam spotted movement behind her; she had been banking on this and checked her watch before turning along with Pete to greet the new arrivals. Brian and Ricky were not happy and their faces gave away their thoughts on Sam's shooting practice. Adam was smiling. Sam knew he was well used to her unpredictable actions and seemed to be enjoying the fact she was testing out her bodyguards.

Sam noted the two agents' reactions and did not want them blaming Pete for his lack of discipline. 'I can see from your faces, guys, you didn't like my little game. Stupid bitch attracting attention to where we are, I bet you're thinking. Well get over it, guys. You took over four minutes to get your fannies into gear – this isn't going to be some halfwit with a grudge against the President you'll be sorting out.

'If it happens you will be dealing with a professional hit, and a four-minute response is not good enough. Don't worry about me, but if one of you fucks up and they touch my son you better hope the Russians get you first, because I will not rest until I am dead or until I have taken an eye for an eye. Speech over, guys. Adam, where are Lauren and Luke?'

Sam and Adam left the three agents talking among themselves and headed back indoors to find Lauren and their son.

Adam and Sam searched every room in the main building but came up empty handed; Lauren was no place to be found. Adam was for starting to search in the grounds but Sam had been keeping a close eye on the Scottish girl and had already formed the opinion that she was no fool. Sam did not think she would have left the security of the ranch to go charging into the wilderness with a toddler, not knowing where the bad guys were. Adam for a second time turned the kitchen upside down, noting that a large carving knife was missing from its magnetic board; only a white silhouette remained showing the shape of the large knife. In the centre of the ranch stood an original circular stone feature, possibly a stone watch tower from a period before the ranch, half in the lounge housing the large fireplace; the other half of the structure was a feature in the hall. It had had a door carved into the stone which Sam was analysing. Sam had already looked inside the door but all it housed was a storage cupboard for cleaning utensils. She stood back, looking at the structure again. There must be more to the old tower. She revisited the cupboard, moving things away to check the back of the cupboard, but there was no door; the back wall was fixed. Sam was about to leave when she heard a muffled voice and started to smile; faintly from beyond the cupboard she had heard Luke asking for Hoss, and a whispered voice trying frantically to hush him. Sam shouted to Lauren things were okay and a few seconds later Lauren's voice could be heard just behind the door telling Sam to put the light switch in the cupboard on and off three times. Sam did as she was told and the cupboard, as if in a James Bond movie, rotated. Sam found she was standing in a small room at the back of the fireplace. Lauren was still holding the carving knife at the ready in case any nasties had accompanied Sam from the hall.

Sam smiled at the situation as she looked around the dimly lit room. On the walls were racks with shotguns, automatic rifles, night-vision glasses, and a selection of handguns and ammunition. In the middle of the room Lauren stood defiantly, still holding the carving knife at the ready, clearly not sure if Sam had been sent in first by the bad guys. After a bit of coaxing she put the knife down and followed Sam and Luke, who was now fully awake, back into the kitchen where the two women made breakfast for the team. Adam retired to the bedroom to shower, shave and dress.

Out of earshot of the main ranch house Pete was trying to quash a rebellion from Brian, who was the newest in the team and the one with the biggest mouth.

'I don't know about you guys, but I am not going to stand here and let that chick boss me about. She opens that big mouth of hers one more time I will tell her where to go. I didn't join the secret service to babysit some lame-ass Brit agent.'

Pete didn't want Dan arriving back to a full-scale mutiny and decided he needed to wade in before things got out of hand.

'Just you pair remember that you serve at the pleasure of the President, and if he tells us to guard Mickey Mouse then that's fine because that's what we signed up for. If you must know, Samantha is no lame ass. Dan told me she fought her way into the Russian Embassy after her target. She took out eight FSB bodyguards and hit her target before being taken down. Tell me, Brian, do you think you could do that? Dan says the Russians are pissed. I would imagine if they find out Samantha's whereabouts we might have a fight on our hands, so instead of shouting your mouth off it would be better if you did your job.' It was clear to Pete that Brian knew he had gone too far, and he marched off to check out the drive and examine the motion sensors without another word.

Ricky had a puzzled expression on his face; he had remained silent throughout Brian's rant. 'How the hell did Dan find out about the Russian Embassy? I already asked Bruce Ellis about the British agent and her family and was told any discussion about her was out of limits.'

Pete's mind was far away, thinking of any scenarios not previously discussed; it took a few seconds for him to gather his thoughts on Ricky's question.

'Dan says he has a contact at the Pentagon who told him about the Russian Embassy. I was just thinking – you saw what went down today. I suspect if there is a situation the housekeeper will probably do what she did today and grab the kid. You heard what the lady said about looking after her kid. If anything goes down, I want you to shadow the housekeeper, keep her safe so she can grab the kid and get him to safety.'

Dan arrived back later that evening. He had missed Sam and Adam who had turned in for the night, taking Luke for his bath and bedtime story. Lauren made Dan some supper before locking up for the night. He finished his supper before checking Ricky who was doing the evening rounds; he then joined Pete and Brian in their room for a catch-up.

Pete let him know about Sam's little game to test them, and Dan smiled knowingly; Sam was everything he had been warned about.

'The woman is no pushover, that's for sure. Her partner seems to be the weak link, although he comes with a reputation for being a tough bastard as well. Anyway, just to let you know, after finding out about the Russians I decided we might need a bit more firepower, so today I took a trip to Creech Air Force Base in Cook county. I have a buddy there who happens to be the commanding officer. I've had a word with him and he has agreed if we need air cover he can have aerial backup here within half an hour of my call.'

In Ramona the phone rang twice then stopped. Daniil made no attempt to pick it up; instead he pulled a jacket on, grabbed a Beretta and tucked it into his waistband. Outside he climbed into a dusty old Ford pickup. The engine fired first turn of the key and Daniil headed out onto Montecito Road to a destination only a short distance from Ramona airport. Outside in the car park, well away from security cameras, Agent X was waiting for Daniil's arrival and climbed into the passenger seat the minute Daniil parked.

Daniil had met Agent X once before when he had been smuggled into Edwards Air Force Base to photograph new stealth technology and fit one of the Spirit stealth bombers with a tracking system. Daniil had never trusted the man; he had betrayed his country for money and Daniil knew he would only be loyal to the highest bidder. It would not take much for him to turn Daniil and his men over to the Americans. If he was not so important to the Russian defence ministry he would have happily put a bullet in his brain before leaving.

The American was a man of few words. His baseball cap and sunglasses masked his eyes, and it was difficult for Daniil to study him as he spoke.

'The woman and her family have arrived – they are staying not far from Flagstaff. I will find you suitable accommodation in Flagstaff but it may take some time to do this without arousing suspicion. For the moment you will be safe here in Ramona. When the time is right, you and your men will fly from here to Flagstaff Airport. Until then, relax and enjoy your free time. The next time I call, bring your men and their equipment with you to the airport. I must go before I'm missed. Goodbye, my Russian friend.'

Daniil made a show of leaving the airport car park, but once Agent X was out of sight he doubled back, parked the pickup and watched from the boundary fence as Agent X climbed on board a twin-engined Piper Seneca. Daniil waited until the twin-engined machine was airborne, heading north, before returning to the pickup. His team would not be happy that they would have to wait before being allowed to carry out their mission.

In Washington Bruce Ellis had set the trap for the person he considered the most likely candidate for Agent X. General Anthony Brubaker had been a special advisor to the President before his career took a turn for the worse; his son, who was a marine, had gone AWOL which, considering his father's position, was not a major problem. The problem came when the military police found him drunk and in the company of a prostitute. When the police officer got heavy handed with his paid girlfriend the general's son had come to her rescue; during the scuffle that ensued one of the military police officers had his face glassed, sealing the fate of the general's son.

It was felt in higher circles that the bad press surrounding the general and his son might rub off on the President and the general was moved out of the situation room. Brubaker took this badly and things went from bad to worse. It was known on the Pentagon grapevine that General Brubaker was actively trying to undermine the authority of the White House by leaking military problems to the press.

Bruce Ellis had worked with Brubaker in the situation room and used this to his advantage, appearing to accidentally bump into the general in a restaurant.

At first the general was distant, but when Ellis informed him he too was no longer in the situation room Brubaker warmed to him. By the end of the evening Bruce Ellis had explained he had moved out of his apartment in the capital to make way for a British agent who was convalescing after a brush with Russian security in London. The general's staff car dropped Ellis off outside his hotel, both men promising to keep in touch.

Bruce Ellis continued with the illusion and headed to the room rented for him. Ellis had never had any intention of telling his enemies where Samantha O'Conner was hidden away; he had set up video surveillance on his apartment in DC and when Agent X took the bait and contacted his Russian pals he would have fallen into Bruce Ellis's electronic trap. Any attempt to storm his apartment on Fourth Street South would be recorded, and anyone acting on the false information supplied by Agent X would be detained for questioning.

Ellis put a call through to a cell phone informing his three NSA agents monitoring the general that he had started the ball rolling. From now on every call Brubaker and the Russian defence minister made or received would be captured; although the calls would most likely be scrambled or coded, the NSA would still be able to tell if Brubaker was the call sender or receiver.

Agent X had been responsible for the deaths of many American soldiers and agents betrayed on the battlefields of the Middle East. Ellis needed to take him out of the game once and for all. His only worry was that he did not know if he would be able to control his urge to shoot the bastard when he finally had the proof of his treachery.

Before leaving the room Bruce sifted through his mail, which had been redirected to maintain the illusion that he had moved out to accommodate the British agent. Bruce pocketed an invitation to a party at the White House, examined a couple of bank statements, and finally came across a handwritten letter addressed to him at the Pentagon and redirected to his home address.

Bruce tore the envelope open with his thumb and studied the note inside; he smiled, slipping the note in his pocket next to his invitation and left, heading for the hotel restaurant. Over supper he took the note back out and read it once more. He was not sure why but his mood had lifted and for a few moments he forgot about Agent X and Sam and

Adam. Fiona Malden's note stated she had taken time off and would soon be heading to Las Vegas for a break; she asked if Bruce would be around to show her the delights of Vegas. Bruce would be the first to admit he was no expert on relationships, but he was pretty sure he had scored with Fiona. All he had to do was lock up Agent X, put Sam and Adam on a plane back to the UK, and he would be free to explore his relationship with Fiona. Bruce turned his attention back to Agent X. He went over things again; for the moment he could do nothing more than wait for his target to make the next move.

Two weeks later Ellis was beginning to think he had made a mistake but decided to give it one more week before crossing General Brubaker off his most wanted list and moving on to his next most likely candidate for Agent X.

After almost three weeks together things at the ranch house had fallen into a familiar routine, and that was one thing Agent Trudo did not like. It was too easy for anyone carrying out surveillance to monitor and use to their advantage.

After breakfast Sam, Lauren and Pete would set up the cans. Trudo would watch as Sam and Pete taught Lauren how to handle a gun and, as usual, Pete could not resist showing off to the women.

Adam would spend this time in the pool teaching Luke to swim before Sam joined them and Lauren left to start preparations for lunch. In the afternoon Sam exercised, accompanied by Pete, but today Dan Trudo decided to mix things up a bit, sending Pete on a perimeter check while he accompanied Sam on her walk. Her limp was almost gone, only reappearing when she was tired and sore; he noted that even here she carried a weapon concealed in her sweatshirt. They had walked for an hour and were heading back to the house when there was movement in the trees on their left. Trudo instinctively went for his weapon but Sam was faster – she was already on her belly, weapon drawn, covering the moving undergrowth. Just to their left a coyote broke from its cover. They watched its black-tipped tail vanish into the scenery some distance down the track; then and only then did Sam relax her grip on the Glock.

Trudo holstered his gun and gave Sam a helping hand to get back on her feet, grudgingly having to admit that her reactions were superior to his.

'Jeez, that's not good for your blood pressure. I don't know who got the bigger fright – us or the coyote. You okay, Sam?'

Sam dusted herself down, giving the track another look over to make sure the coyote had gone before replying. 'I'm fine, thanks. Was that a coyote? I've never seen one before, I thought it was a wolf. I'm glad it ran away though.'

Trudo smiled at Sam's last comment. 'Trust me, if it had been a wolf you would have known. They are much bigger animals. Coyotes are not much bigger than a dog – wolves can be as big as a lion.'

'Dan, I was meaning to ask you, what do you think of Lauren and I doing a bit of shopping and sightseeing?'

Dan thought for a second; he knew saying no would only make her more determined to go ahead anyway. 'I suppose we could sort something out, but we don't have enough agents to cover everyone. If it was, as you say, the housekeeper and yourself, okay, but not all four of you. Two at a time we can manage. I will need to know in advance where you want to go and for how long.'

Back at the house Sam checked on Luke who was fast asleep after his swim. Adam was engrossed in a magazine, so Sam went in search of Lauren and found her in the kitchen.

Sam joined in with preparation for supper.

'I was talking to Agent Trudo when I was out for my exercise this afternoon. I think I've talked him into letting us get out for a bit. How do you fancy some girl time, maybe do a bit of sightseeing or shopping – do you know any good places in Flagstaff?'

Lauren stopped peeling the potato in her hand to think about Sam's proposal. 'A wee break from peeling spuds might not be a bad thing. There are lots of good places in Flagstaff, but I was thinking maybe we should check out a town not far from here. Williams is a good place to have a poke around – plenty of souvenir shops and some nice Native

American jewellery shops. We could go and check out train times – they have some lovely old steam engines. The wee man would love to get a hurl in one of those, wouldn't he?'

Sam said nothing, but every time she spoke with Lauren she was a little more impressed with her. She had talked about a girls' day out without saying a thing about her son; Lauren had put him before her own enjoyment. Bruce Ellis had picked well when he employed Lauren.

12

Old Joe's Warning

Two days later, after a bit of gentle persuasion from both Lauren and Sam, Trudo finally agreed to let Sam, Pete and Lauren leave for the afternoon. Pete was under strict instruction not to let Samantha O'Conner out of his sight. Sam promised to bring Adam a present back because he was left holding the baby, literally, a task he was more than happy to undertake.

When they'd first arrived, Adam had flinched at every movement, fearing the worst, but as the weeks passed the atmosphere relaxed and Adam almost felt as if he were on holiday. Only the prowling watchful eyes of the secret service agents reminded him things may change in the blink of an eye. After watching Sam and the others leave Adam decided because it was a particularly hot day to give the pool a miss and set up Hoss for Luke to play on.

This went down well with the two remaining secret service agents because they were a bit stretched since Pete had left with the women and Trudo had again done one of his disappearing acts. Adam checked Luke was okay before getting back into his latest book about the local Native American tribes of the area.

On arrival in Williams Lauren left Pete and Sam studying the shops while she made her way to the railway office to find out about train trips from the town. Williams was a busy little town; most of its visitors today were tourists of all nationalities. Pete explained to Sam that

Williams was popular for its rail excursions out to the Grand Canyon. After visiting a few souvenir-type stores, Sam found one of the Native American shops. Pete gave it a quick once over but finding no other entrances and only one person and the young Navajo shopkeeper inside he elected to remain outside watching the entrance and passers-by. Sam wandered in, browsing the jewellery section as an elderly woman left clutching her purchase. As Sam wandered round she noticed that the young Indian shopkeeper had left the counter. Sam was near the back of the shop by the handwoven rugs and furniture when a voice startled her; she had been studying a handmade shirt and had not noticed the old man sitting in a beautifully carved rocking chair, his frail legs covered by an ornately stitched blanket depicting a warrior on a pony hunting down a large black buffalo.

Now he had Sam's attention the old man spoke again. His voice was not what Sam would have expected of a frail old man; it boomed out over the quiet shop, although his eyes remained tightly shut as he concentrated on something deep within himself. Sam could almost feel the air around her chill as the old man spoke.

'I see only the body of a woman in front of me, but her shadow in the great fire of life is the shadow of a great warrior.'

Sam was not sure what to say to the old man but before she could react he spoke again.

'Your heart deceives you: it is strong with your kin but the peace you seek is not here. The shadow of the great timber wolf is upon you and yours. Great danger is close at hand, my child. You must leave this land or turn to dust and be consumed by the sands of the desert. May the great eagle carry you on its wings to safety. You must go now.'

Sam was not sure if this was some kind of joke. She tried talking to the old man but he seemed to be in some type of trance. Fearing he was having some kind of stroke Sam entered the storeroom from behind the front counter, looking for the young storekeeper. She found him heading back to the counter carrying bottles of water. Sam asked for his help with the old man, saying she feared he was having a stroke. The young man followed her to the back of the shop to where the rocking chair stood.

Sam stopped dead in her tracks then turned through 360 degrees looking for the old man; she pointed to the chair. 'He was here only a few seconds ago.'

Sam started to describe the old man to storekeeper but he was smiling and shaking his head. 'Lady, who put you up to this? Was it the kids from school? Because it's not fair to use old Joe like this.'

Sam was stumped; she had no idea what he was talking about. She was halfway through a description of the old man once more when the storekeeper stopped her, walked over to the wall above the rocking chair and pulled a framed photo down. He handed it to Sam.

'It's easy to make it up when you have his picture to go by.'

Sam stared at the photo of the old man sitting in the rocking chair. It had been taken from a local paper, and it was the same man who had talked so strangely to Sam, but the note below the photo made no sense.

Old Joe or, to give him his correct Navajo name, Hok'ee Hatathli, had been a valued member of the Williams community until two months ago when he had passed away quietly in his sleep.

'So you see, ma'am, it's not nice to make fun of the dead.'

The young man started to walk towards the front door to show Sam out, but she stopped him. 'This is no joke. On my life, he was sitting in the rocking chair with that blanket over his legs and he talked to me … he told me things.'

The shopkeeper hesitated. 'Okay, say I play along with this madness. What did Joe tell you?'

Sam repeated as best she could what the old man had said, then waited for the young guy to speak.

When he did find the words his attitude had changed. 'Tell me truthfully, lady, did old Joe's words mean anything to you?'

Sam nodded but said nothing.

'I don't tell many outsiders these things for they would laugh and think it was a stupid conman trick, but I think after your encounter today you may believe me. Hok'ee Hatathli was a Navajo shaman or, as you would call him, a medicine man – probably the greatest shaman the Navajo or indeed any of the other tribes have ever seen. There were many false shamans but Joe was the real deal, for sure. He had the second sight, you know. He attended the great Sundance gathering where he tried to tell the other tribes the only way ahead was to integrate with the white men, but he was shunned and cast out. The other shamans had the taste of blood and thought they could fight back. They were proved wrong but it was too late and all Joe's predictions have since come true.

'He turned his hand to carpentry until he became too old to lift his tools. He was my old friend. He would pass his time sitting in that chair talking to customers and telling them of the old days when he was young, but occasionally his talent as a shaman would show itself. He once told a tourist she was with child. She laughed at the old man but a month later the shop received a letter addressed to the old Navajo gentleman stating that she was twelve weeks pregnant. She asked if he knew the sex of the baby. Joe stated that it would be a boy and that in two years' time he would have a sister to play with. I sent a letter back and last year the woman sent a picture of her family: a four-year-old boy and a two-year-old daughter. She'd enclosed a one-hundred-dollar bill. Joe told me to put it in the cash register because it was of no use to him.'

Sam wanted to know more, but Pete interrupted telling Sam it was time to go. She was about to object but Lauren had arrived and reluctantly she said goodbye to the young man. On the way back to the ranch house Sam was quiet. Lauren showed her some tickets she had bought for a train ride for Luke. Sam thanked her but returned to her thoughts, frightened to tell the others she had been talking to a ghost in case they thought she was losing it.

Later that night, while tucked up cosy in bed with Adam, Sam told him what had happened in the craft shop. Next morning she woke up to an empty bed. She found Adam in the lounge with a pile of Bruce's books by the side of his chair; on spotting Sam he picked up a book and waved it at her as she approached.

'Ha, ghost, my backside. So Joe attended the great Sundance gathering, did he? Rubbish. I've found a book that mentions the great gathering of Native American tribes, only your young friend messed up his fairy tale. The Sundance gathering was in 1876, which would make Joe about 160 when he died. Your young friend can't count. It's just an old wives' tale to attract the tourists.'

Sam couldn't argue with the maths, but it did not explain the meeting or the fact that his words had real meaning. Sam had a feeling there was more to this than just a tourist hoax.

Lauren's tickets were for the steam train trip to the Grand Canyon, three days from the purchase date. At first Dan Trudo said no, but Bruce Ellis arrived to check on his guests and agreed with Sam and Lauren that it would be a good idea for everyone to get out for a bit. If they missed this trip they wouldn't have the opportunity again in a hurry because the steam engine rarely came out to play; normally the train was pulled by a diesel locomotive.

Sam waited until they were all on board safely before announcing she would meet them back at the station because she had unfinished business with a Native American. Adam told her to forget it but he must have known before the words left his mouth he was wasting his time.

Sam disembarked just as the train was about to leave; she waved as Lauren held Luke up to wave to his mum. Sam was disappointed to miss the trip but knew Lauren had it in hand; she waited for the train to depart and was about to head off when a figure appeared on the opposite side of the track. Pete had not said anything, but Sam knew he was good at his job and had second-guessed her intentions. Pete crossed over, joining Sam on the town side of the track. They walked together, Sam passing the occasional comment as she window-shopped.

On the train Luke sat on Lauren's lap, fascinated with the passing scenery. Bruce Ellis looked away from the view to see that Adam had taken the opportunity to sit next to him.

'Well, Bruce, as I have your undivided attention for the next few miles, care to tell me where Dan and Pete have vanished to, and how you're getting on with your spy hunting?'

Bruce had suspected it would not be long until he was asked these questions. 'Pete is providing close protection to your partner. We had a hunch she might rebel at some point at being followed everywhere. Dan is in the town shadowing them. Like us he knows Samantha O'Conner could start trouble in an empty house. Unfortunately I have no satisfactory answer for the spy problem. Our most hopeful suspect has so far has proved fruitless. It's time to move on to our next suspect – a soldier with too many expensive hobbies for his salary. That's part of the reason I'm down here. I plan to bump into him in Vegas.'

Sam tried the door to the craft shop but, as the sign on the door said, it was closed. Pete looked on from the other side of the street watching the passing traffic for anything sinister. Sam knocked on the door in the hope that someone was inside and had just not opened up yet. She was about to give up when she spotted the young guy from her previous visit hurrying to open the door.

'Good morning, Miss O'Conner, am I glad to see you. Please come in. My name is Cheveyo, by the way.'

Cheveyo closed the door behind Sam, leaving the closed sign in place. Sam was not sure how the young man knew her name because she had never given it to him. She followed Cheveyo through to the back office where he offered her coffee. She politely refused; she wanted to ask the young man some questions about old Joe, but it seemed that it was her who was about to be questioned. Sam decided to get her questions in first before she was sidetracked. 'The other day, after I spoke to the old man who you think was Joe, you said he had attended something called the Sundance gathering. Did I mishear you or is that the correct name?'

Cheveyo smiled. He nodded without speaking, letting Sam get to the point of the questioning.

'That can't be right – the Sundance gathering is in the history books. It's very famous and it was in1876. There's no way anyone who attended that could have survived until now – they would have been more than a hundred and fifty years old. Tell me the truth – is this some kind of entertainment for your tourists?'

Cheveyo said nothing but headed across the room to a shelf containing various old books. He pulled one down and flicked through the pages before handing it to Sam, pointing to a section for her to read. While Sam studied the book Cheveyo returned to the shelf, searching for another book.

Sam read the section pointed out to her. It was a list of chiefs and warriors who attended the Sundance gathering of Indian tribes. Listed was the Navajo-Dine' shaman seer Hok'ee Hatathli.

Sam had just finished reading the chapter when Cheveyo handed her a second book, *The Life and Times of Geronimo*. The book was open at a page showing a photo of a gathering of men attending the funeral of Geronimo, dated 1909, followed by a list of those in the picture. On the right of Geronimo's nephew stood Hok'ee Hatathli, his dark eyes staring out of the page at Sam. Again Sam had just finished studying the picture when she was handed a third book, *The US Marines, World War Two*. It was open at a photo page showing a group of men, all Native Americans. At the centre of the picture and listed below it was GI 'Joe' Hatathli. The picture was taken in June 1946 and was of a Navajo code talker unit somewhere in the Pacific. Again Joe's dark eyes stared out of the picture, older and wiser, but the same eyes.

The last thing Cheveyo produced for Sam to study was a newspaper clipping dated October 1987, when Joe Hatathli was voted onto the Williams town council. His dark eyes stared into the camera as he shook hands with the local sheriff, surrounded by his council colleagues.

Sam wanted to argue that this could have been the son of the original Hok'ee Hatathli, but the man in the 1909 picture was middle-aged, and it was the same person in all the photos. Sam studied all the evidence for signs of forgery but they seemed genuine. If it was true, why had no one picked up on the old man's incredible age?

Before Sam could ask Cheveyo he answered her question. 'You're thinking if this is true – why did no one know. Joe never wanted the limelight and, to be honest, in modern America sadly it is far too easy for an old Native American to go through life unnoticed. Joe had no family to tell, but for some reason he saw something in me. He coached me on life, said I was a special type of Navajo, a modern warrior – one who would fight for our people, not with bullets or arrows but with pens, computers and my brain. He made me swear to him I would do everything in my power to become a lawyer. So here I am, working in my family's shop to earn enough to get to college. Anyway, enough of that. I have much more important news for you. Joe has given me strict instructions not to let you leave the shop today without hearing them.'

Sam wondered if the enthusiastic young man had been taking something.

'Joe is no longer here. Isn't that what you've been trying to tell me since I saw him? Is that not correct?'

'His spirit speaks to me while I sleep. Please listen to me, and if you think it's rubbish, so be it. Walk away if you must, but hear me out – for old Joe, if nothing else, please.'

Sam was starting to feel like she was having her leg pulled but nodded for the young man to continue.

'When the next moon reaches its fullness for the first time, the great wolf will send its pack to attack your bloodline. Joe said you must trust Luke with another and fight by Adam's side if you hope to prevail. I have no idea what I have just told you but I hope it is of use to you.'

Sam was in shock. Not even a trickster could have found out what she had just been told. Suddenly she was cold; there were not many times Samantha O'Conner was lost for words, but for the moment she could not talk. She was trying to calculate the next full moon when again Cheveyo came to her rescue.

'I have made tea – I think you may need some while you figure out the message. The only part that I understood was the moon part. In case you're wondering, the next full moon is in two nights' time. I'll be back in a second with your tea.'

Sam's mind was racing; how could this be true? How could she make plans when her information came from a dream about a ghost?

If she told the secret service they wouldn't be able to shoot straight for laughing at her. Sam was not sure how she was going to play it, but one thing had already been decided in her head: she did not want Luke here if there was going to be trouble.

If the ghost of Joe was correct, and Sam had to admit to herself it was a big *if*, then they were in all kinds of trouble. Bruce Ellis had told them that morning about his apartment in Washington being the real target to lure the bad guys, so if Volkov had found them in Arizona it could only mean one thing: Ellis had a leak. Someone he trusted had betrayed him to the Russians; if this was true Sam did not know who to trust.

Cheveyo arrived with the tea as Sam made a spur-of-the-moment decision. 'Cheveyo, tell me, do you believe a hundred per cent that Joe spoke to you? Be honest now.'

'Yes – one hundred and ten per cent. Joe has never been wrong for as long as I have had the honour to know him.'

Sam took a sip of her tea, mulled things over for a second, then put the cup down. 'Cheveyo, I want you to do me a huge favour. Do you have transport?'

Cheveyo nodded uncertainly.

'I want you to shut up shop, follow me home, then I want you to take my son and our housekeeper to Los Angeles. I want you to stay and look after them until I come for them. Here is some money to pay for fuel and food. If you do this for me, my partner and I will pay for your training as a lawyer – you have my word on it. So you see old Joe will get his wish, and you yours, if you help me.'

Sam regarded Cheveyo as he took in what she had just said; she was not sure what his reaction would be. 'Miss O'Conner, Hok'ee Hatathli always said there would be a way to become a lawyer but I thought old Joe was trying to keep me out of the gutter by giving me a goal to aim for. I doubted it would ever come true, but it looks like Joe Hatathli has once again seen the future.'

When the train arrived back from its visit to the Grand Canyon Dan Trudo bundled everyone into the MPV for the trip back to the ranch house. Sam explained to Dan that the old Chevy following them had been arranged by her.

Dan was not happy, but Sam promised to explain everything when they got back. Adam said nothing but made eye contact with her. She gave him a wink, knowing he would wait until they had a moment alone before tackling the subject.

Sam asked Adam to take Luke inside the ranch and give him his supper while she had a word with Lauren. She was not sure how Lauren would react to her suggestion that she take Luke and go.

'Lauren, I have a terrible feeling something bad is about to go down here. I'm not sure who is on who's side. What I am sure of is that you would do anything to make sure Luke is okay. Lauren, I need you to go with my friend Cheveyo. He will take you and Luke home to LA, and when I'm sure it's safe I will come for Luke. Will you do this for me?'

Lauren said nothing for a few seconds, seconds that seemed like hours to Sam as she waited to see if her plan was going to get off the ground.

'Okay, Samantha. Are you sure the young lad can be trusted? I will take the wee man home with me, but for his sake you need to get out of whatever you're involved in. The wee guy needs a mum, not a grave with your name on it to visit.'

Lauren and Cheveyo went about the task of gathering what they needed for the trip to LA while Sam called an impromptu meeting between herself, Adam, Bruce Ellis and Dan Trudo.

The trio stood speechless after she announced that she was sending her son away. Sam did not want to say too much while Dan was there. She knew Adam and Bruce could be trusted but Dan had not won her trust; it was only when he left to speak with his agents did Sam tell Adam and Bruce of her suspicions.

'Listen, guys. I suspect that our location has been compromised. I suspect the Russians know we're here, which means, Bruce, that at least one of the people you trusted with our location is a traitor. I am not about to risk my son's life and I am not about to go into hiding again.'

Bruce interrupted before Sam could go any further. 'No way, Sam.

I don't know where your intel came from, but it's flawed. Dan, his team, two people in the White House situation room and the President are the only people who know about your stay at the ranch. Any misinformation passed about your whereabouts has been regarding my apartment in Washington. Where did this information come from?'

Sam knew this question was coming but she felt they would take her more seriously if she kept her source a secret.

'A hunch, intuition, sixth sense, call it what you want. Bruce, you and I have been at this game a long time. I'm asking you to trust me on this.'

Bruce Ellis threw his hands up in the air in frustration. 'My god, Sam, no wonder Neil Andrews said you were a nightmare to work with. Have it your way. Unfortunately I can't hang around to watch you make a fool of yourself. I have to set up the sting for our next suspect and I've arranged to meet Fiona Malden in Vegas, so I'll be gone for the next few days. I'll instruct Dan to follow your orders and when Fiona and I get back here I will expect a grovelling apology when your hunch doesn't pay off.'

Sam watched from a distance as Dan stormed off in a rage after being told by Bruce of the new situation. She turned her attention back to Lauren, Adam, Luke and Cheveyo, who had formed a little huddle around Cheveyo's old Chevrolet.

Lauren had Luke wrapped round her neck; Sam couldn't help feeling an inadequate mother once again as she ran her fingers through Luke's golden curls, kissing him on the head in a sudden wave of emotion. Cheveyo unfolded a piece of leather and handed Adam a grey-coloured object. Adam looked at the young Navajo and then at the object he had been handed.

'Last night in my dreams Hok'ee Hatathli, the great Navajo shaman, spoke to me and instructed me to give Life and Death to the great white warrior from the land far away, where they fling trees to the skies, drink firewater and dress as women. You are Adam, son of Donald, are you not? For your face fits my dreams.'

Adam McDonald seemed too mesmerised with the work of art that had been handed to him to reply, so Cheveyo continued with his little speech to the small group.

'You will now be the keeper of Life and Death, for no man truly owns it. Many great warriors have carried it and no Navajo will ever stand in your way while you are its keeper. It belongs to this land and was here even before the palefaces found our lands. Hok'ee Hatathli was the last to be entrusted with its power. It now passes to you, son of Donald.'

Adam turned the strange metal tomahawk over, studying its beautifully crafted carvings. On one side of the main shaft was a pair of entwined snakes. The weapon had a razor-sharp polished curved blade with an inscription carved into it; on the other side was the head of a pipe with a second inscription. Cheveyo translated both inscriptions for Adam as Sam listened. The inscription on the blade side said simply 'death'. The pipe, which could be smoked from the tip of the serpents' tails, was inscribed with a prayer to Ussen, the life giver. Cheveyo explained he was the Apache god of life.

Adam studied the tomahawk in great detail. Sam could see he was speechless, probably struggling for the right words to thank the young Navajo man. Sam came to Adam's rescue, enlisting his help in loading up the old Chevrolet Citation, although in the back of her mind, looking at the state of it, she was not sure she should be letting their son near the thing, never mind whether it would make it all the way to LA. Sam took Cheveyo to one side and gave him Bruce Ellis's cell number, with strict instructions only to call him in an emergency and to speak to him and no one else. She was in tears as she gave Luke one last big hug and kiss before handing him over to a very pale and quiet Lauren. Adam gave Luke a cuddle and Lauren a hug before shaking hands with Cheveyo, thanking him for helping Lauren. Adam hugged Sam as they watched the old car, followed by Pete and Bruce Ellis, vanish down the drive heading for the highway. Pete had been drafted into drop Ellis at Flagstaff Airport for his trip to Vegas.

From his position high up in the trees Daniil Litvak watched the two-car convoy leave. He had spent most of the last four days and nights mapping out the ranch, its defences and its defenders. He had carried out the same reconnaissance in Scotland at the glass house before his targets had bolted, leading to the chase and the disastrous attempt to carry out their mission. Daniil cursed, watching the two cars leave; he did not want his plan wasted. For a second time he was going to have to bring his attack forward – as soon as he possibly could. Now that he worked for Volkov and not the army a second failure could seal his fate and would not be good for his health. Volkov was not a man who tolerated failure.

Daniil Litvak's speciality during his time with the Spetsnaz units was working behind enemy lines for long periods without detection, a task he excelled at. Although the secret service agents were on top of their game, Daniil had spent many hours watching and noting their procedures. He knew where they had placed motion detectors and surveillance cameras and at no point had he so much as disturbed a leaf or left a footprint on the ground; not one of his targets had any idea they were being monitored. Daniil felt at last their luck was changing. Only one day after moving into the old barn on the outskirts of Flagstaff his kid brother Anton had spotted the woman entering a tourist shop in the town of Williams while he was out searching for them. He'd had the good sense to mark the target's vehicle with an invisible paint used to mark targets for rocket attacks rather than alert the secret service by following them. Daniil had then contacted Agent X, who searched by satellite for the paint-marked people carrier, coming up trumps with the ranch house. The only time Litvak had been discovered was not by humans; he had been followed by a curious coyote who after watching him climb into a tree had continued with its hunt for food. After the two-car convoy had left, Daniil carefully made his way out of the target area leaving no signs for the secret service agents to raise the alarm.

While Dan Trudo was speaking to his agents Sam took the opportunity to drag Adam into the circular room where Lauren had hidden with Luke. She needed to speak to him and try to explain sending Luke away and she wanted to do it where no one could overhear them.

'You're going to think I've lost control of my senses, Adam, but I need to tell you the truth. Cheveyo showed me and told me things today that my head says can't be true, but there's something – call it a hunch or intuition – but I believe what he said, and if it is true there can be only one conclusion: there is a traitor in Bruce's team. I can't risk leaving Luke here if Cheveyo is correct and the Russians are going to strike the night after tomorrow.'

'Okay, so how did Cheveyo find out? Where did he get his information from, and is it a reliable source?'

Sam was not sure how Adam was going to take her confession and avoided eye contact as she ran things through in her head before speaking. 'Well, it's kind of hard to tell if the source is reliable – he's been dead for a couple of months. Cheveyo had a vision in his sleep. Old Joe told him we were in danger and that the wolf would send his men against us on the next full moon.'

Although Adam said nothing his body language and facial expressions spoke volumes to Sam. She knew she was nearing the point where his loyalty to her would be overtaken by his need to tell her she had it all wrong. For the moment he was sitting on the fence, and Sam could tell she was testing his patience to the limits.

Adam helped Sam browse through Bruce Ellis's personal weapons stash in the round room, a collection which included two M4 carbines, two Sig Sauer XM17 pistols and a box of assorted grenades. Sam stripped the carbines and unloaded their magazines, then reloaded and rebuilt them while Adam worked away in silence stripping the two Sigs before excusing himself and retiring to their room. Sam, having dispatched Lauren, took over dishwashing and cleaning duties in the kitchen; although Adam said nothing she knew he was not happy with her decision to send Luke away.

What Bruce Ellis's home lacked in TV and video it made up for with a large library of books, which took up one full side of the ranch house wall from floor to ceiling. Adam removed a large section of American history books before heading to the bedroom. He studied the books, looking for any mention of Hok'ee Hatathli, but there was nothing. It was by pure chance that while looking for the elusive medicine man he stumbled across a very early picture of Geronimo. Adam studied the men around him and the inscription at the bottom of the page, but there was no mention of old Joe. He was about to turn the page when something caught his eye.

Geronimo was pictured in his early years in talks with a US cavalry officer. It was not this that stopped Adam in his tracks, but what was tucked into his belt. Geronimo's hand rested on his tomahawk Life and Death. Adam glanced across at the bedside table where he had placed the gift from the young Navajo. He stared back at the faded picture; there was no mistake – the two weapons were one and the same.

After this discovery Adam decided for the moment to forget about old Joe and concentrate instead on the tomahawk Life and Death.

After checking a few more books he decided to borrow Bruce's laptop to continue his search. To his surprise his web search proved fruitful and he found that Chief Sitting Bull had been the custodian of Life and Death before it had passed to Geronimo. Adam was amazed at what he had found out about the ancient Native American artefact, but it was the final web entry that hit him hard.

A web article from the *Arizona Daily Sun* reported the burial of a Navajo legend on that particular day. It went on to tell of Joe Hatathli's war record and said he had been buried with a prized Native American relic as a mark of respect for his dedicated service to his beloved people. It explained how Life and Death, a ceremonial tomahawk, had been handed down from chief to chief regardless of tribe, given to whoever was championing the Native American cause at the time.

Two questions formed in Adam's mind and no matter how he tried they would not go away: was the tomahawk he had been given the real thing or a replica? And why, if it was real – or even a fake – give it to him? He picked up the tomahawk and studied it in great detail, from the serpents' entwined bodies to the pipe head, which was stained with use and probably age. Its ornamental beauty changed as he turned it round to examine the business side of the weapon. He picked up a piece of paper and used the razor-sharp edge to slice the sheet of paper in two. The metal itself was strange; it wasn't aluminium but it was light and very strong. Although it looked old, its material seemed almost space age. That was strange enough, but the feeling it gave Adam as he held it was worrying; he felt almost compelled to throw the weapon. It was an urge that only receded after he placed the tomahawk down on the bedside table.

By the time Sam arrived in the room Adam was no longer sure that she had made a mistake; he didn't know what to believe any longer.

Next morning Adam woke to find once again Sam's side of the bed was empty. He threw some clothes on to go in search of his restless partner, and for some reason he could not explain he lifted the tomahawk and tucked it in the belt of his trousers. Adam did not have to travel far to find Sam; she had held on to one of Lauren's swimsuits and was trawling up and down the pool, pushing herself to the limit while Pete kept a close watch for any nasties. Adam joined Pete by the barn door.

Adam noticed Pete looking at the tomahawk in his belt. Pete smiled. 'Are you planning on chopping some wood for the fire this morning, Adam?'

Adam studied the young secret service agent's freckled face before replying. He knew that Sam had taken a shine to him; it was easy to see why out of the four agents he was by far the easiest to get on with and, unusually for the secret service, he was pretty laid back.

'No, Pete, just looking after it until I can find its rightful owner. How long has madam had you out here?'

Pete checked his watch before replying. 'She's been in the water for an hour—'

Before Pete could finish his sentence a voice from the pool interrupted. 'Fifty-six minutes, actually. Adam McDonald, if you call me madam again you will be sleeping on the couch tonight.'

Adam smiled at Pete before turning and making for the poolside. Sam finished the length she was doing and then stopped next to Adam's feet, folding her arms on the edge of the pool. Adam sat down beside her, dangling his feet in the chilly water. He was deep in thought.

Sam was first to speak. 'Do you think Bill Mathews knows what's going on here? How long before things calm down and we can go home?'

Adam looked into her grey eyes, wanting to reassure her everything would be fine, but he knew Sam better than that. She wanted the truth, not some Alice in Wonderland fairy tale.

'You told me years ago when we first met that MI6 never let anyone go. I think you were right. I know one thing for sure: when the Americans are finished with us, whatever happens they will use us as a bargaining chip to feather their own nests. I spoke to Dan Trudo after Luke and the others left yesterday. He checked discreetly with the FBI – there are no reports of any Russians entering the country. He thinks you're nuts, for the record. He thinks you're suffering from a type of PTSD after the embassy thing.'

Sam's expression darkened but she kept eye contact with Adam. 'And what do you think? Do you think I've lost the plot?'

Adam smiled, reached down and pulled Sam from the water, then flung his arms around her soaking himself in the process. The pair of them rolled over by the side of the pool. Sam lay on her back looking up at Adam, still waiting for his reply.

'Mad as a brush, but you always have been. That's one of the things that attracted me to you. As for the Native American thing, maybe you have a point. Let's hope the old medicine man is wrong, for all our sakes.'

Sam didn't move; she said nothing but continued to stare up at Adam. She seemed to be studying the grey hair that had started to make an appearance by his temples. 'I can see more grey hair than before, and you're starting to get laughter lines. I think our adventures are having an effect on us. It's okay for you – it makes you look distinguished – but will you still love me when I'm old and wrinkly?' Adam smiled then made a face as if he was having to think about the question. 'Adam, do you still love me?'

Adam McDonald had never been one to wear his emotions on his sleeve, but Sam was looking for reassurance that if things went badly tonight she could count on him loving her. It was not a question Sam made a habit of asking and for a second it stopped him in his tracks.

'Samantha O'Conner, do you really need to ask me? We have saved each other's lives, we've had a child together, and I can't imagine you not being in my life. Of course I bloody love you, but I would love you a bit more if you got that tidy little bottom of yours into the kitchen and made breakfast.' He stood up, pulling Sam to her feet.

'Adam McDonald, just remember who you're talking to. I have killed men for less.' Sam winked at Adam before grabbing a towel and heading indoors. Adam followed her and as so many times in the past joined in with the banter.

'You just get the breakfast sorted, Mrs Assassin. Remember, I have your old pal's magic tomahawk here to protect me from evil spirits and mad women. Old Joe spoke to me in my sleep and said you should make me omelette, bacon and strong coffee.'

Sam stopped in her tracks and took a playful swipe at Adam for taking the piss out of her.

Daniil Litvak called an urgent briefing. Apart from the occasional interruption from his brother, he had his men's full attention. Before his defection to Volkov's team, Litvak had been their commanding officer for a number of years. Daniil knew if he charged into hell itself his men would be by his side; only Anton was an unknown quantity. Although a soldier, he had never served with any Spetsnaz units; Daniil was going to have to keep a close eye on his kid brother. He placed a few drawings of their target on the floor of the barn and his men huddled round, studying the pictures.

'As you can see from my sketches, the Americans have placed six motion sensors backed up by six video surveillance units here by the entrance and in these other areas. They have moved them twice to the positions shown. There are four guards but at night time only one remains on watch duty. I have marked the routes that he sticks to on his patrols. Be warned, these men may dress in suits but I have watched them and they are of high quality. They have communication equipment and so far have only carried handguns. Unfortunately something has changed and they may be moving away. A few have already left so we need to bring our attack forward or risk losing the target. I do not need to tell you the longer we remain on American soil the greater the risk of capture. Our American spy had promised us night-vision gear and grenades, but we cannot wait for them to arrive. We will attack tonight with the weapons we have. Do you have any questions?'

Daniil looked from man to man but no one spoke; they were too busy studying Daniil's map of the target and committing it to memory.

'Very well. One last thing before you prepare for the assault: the man and the woman are the targets but the woman is the priority. We cannot afford to try and smuggle her out of the country so we must eliminate her. Volkov has demanded proof of death before anyone collects the reward money, so once she is dead, remember we must take a picture of her body.'

Bill Mathews watched the handyman finish replacing Sir Neil Andrews' name plaque on his door. He thanked him and for a second stared at his own name on the door. Mathews had never thought he would sit in the hot seat at MI6, but these were days of huge turmoil in the big bad world and MI6 needed a steady hand. The prime minister had moved swiftly to fill the position and, as Mathews had performed adequately in the wake of Neil Andrews' assassination, he had been told rather than asked to take the reins permanently at Vauxhall Cross. His own position was being filled by none other than Commander Ian Devlin of the Metropolitan Police antiterrorist unit. Mathews was not a fan of the man but he did have to admit, coming from the antiterrorist unit he would come into the job with his eyes open. Mathews finished writing his final report for the Home Secretary on the Andrews bombing and the attempted bombing of Vauxhall Cross. He placed all the personnel files with his report for filing and called Jean in to pick them up.

Jean entered, smiling as she inspected the new name on the door.

'Ah, there you are, Jean. Can you make sure the Home Secretary gets our final report tonight? The bloody woman has been hounding me for it for the last week. Could you also return the personnel files to Records for me – I have recommended that Petty Officer Prentice and Captain Malden be awarded VCs for their efforts with the terrorist bomb. I fear this request will be refused by the Home Secretary on grounds of national security and the file will be sealed, but at least their military records will show they were considered for the highest honour.'

Jean nodded, picking up the paperwork and thumbing through the files before looking up. 'Adam McDonald's and Samantha O'Conner's files are not here, sir. I don't mean to interfere, but I have paperwork from the stores for Sam's file – she still has a Glock and NLB7 signed out against her name. I need to update her records, sir.'

Bill Mathews picked up two files from his desk and waved them above his head before dropping them into one of his drawers. 'Unfinished business with those two. I'll sign off the gun and the drugs – probably still in the Russian Embassy. Jean, we never did speak about your job once I found out I was staying. I take it you're not planning to retire any time soon?'

Jean stopped in her tracks and turned to face Mathews. 'No, sir. I was wondering if you still needed me or will you be bringing in your own staff?'

'My number two from Five will be replacing Peter Kent, who I'm retiring as lead agent, but I want you to stay on as my PA – that is if you want to?'

Jean replied immediately. 'I would be delighted to stay and help you, sir. I was wondering what your plans were for Samantha?'

Bill Mathews knew if she had asked her old boss that question the answer would have been to mind her own business, but he was a different type of boss.

'Yes, good question, Jean. The Russians are still desperate to have her deported and put on trial for her attack on Russian soil. I see we have a new ambassador who has taken the place of Volkov – I think it's time to put our cards on the table with our Russian friends and rattle a few cages in Moscow. Jean, can you set up a meeting with the new ambassador – in fact, tell him we want to meet in Hyde Park. That should put him on the back foot.'

Mathews was smiling as he named the location; he was going to give the Russian ambassador a meeting he would never forget.

According to Bill Mathews' research, General Alexi Mariokov was not a natural diplomat. He had been chosen by the Russian premier because of his hard-line politics and because he was a personal friend. The London embassy had clearly been a disaster since Volkov had been in charge and Mariokov would need to deal with it urgently. Mathews' sources had told him Mariokov called a spade a spade and he would sort the embassy and its staff without causing further friction with the British.

If General Mariokov was surprised by the request for a meeting with the head of MI6 he did not show it. He walked to where the meeting was to take place in Hyde Park where Bill Mathews was waiting for him with a bunch of flowers in his hand. Mathews shook hands with Mariokov, hoping the general would be curious as to why he carried the flowers. Mathews started to walk and General Mariokov joined him, walking at a sedate pace. Mathews unfolded a letter as they walked. 'I have your letter here, General Mariokov. I must apologise for not replying to it before now. Let me read it aloud then I will give you my thoughts on the matter.

'"Director Mathews, I have been asked by my superiors to remind you that we demand you hand over your rogue agent who attacked our embassy immediately. I need not remind you that what was done in our embassy amounted to nothing less than an act of war. Your government should think itself lucky that we only require the agent to answer for her actions and have not demanded your and your ministers' resignations for this disgraceful aggression." The letter goes on, but I think we have heard all the main points.'

Bill Mathews stopped walking. He had reached the place he wanted to be, and was finding it hard not to show the fury caused by the ambassador's letter.

'General Mariokov, you are new to this role, so I feel it is my duty to inform you of a few points you may not be aware of.'

Mathews stopped talking and walked over to the big tree where flowers in their hundreds had been arranged to honour the victims of the Hyde Park bombing. On his return he checked Mariokov's body language; he was pretty sure the general had little or no knowledge of what had happened here.

'General, this is where the true act of war occurred – this is where the director of MI6 was assassinated. Now I'm going to give you some facts about this. You made your points in the letter, but please listen carefully now, because you have become involved in a gravely serious situation.

'Russia would have the world believe that this attack was actioned by a Syrian warlord, but your plan failed when your patsy inadvertently dislodged a wire from the suicide vest and your hit team couldn't blow him up. The blast was meant to obliterate vital evidence that would implicate the Russian military and leave the body of a Syrian terrorist to take the blame. We knew after studying what should have been incinerated by the blast that Volkov was behind the attack, but decided to let the world and Russia believe we had fallen for your little deception.

'In truth we were doing a lot of dirt digging on your man Volkov.

'It seems Volkov had a vendetta against MI6, so much so that with the help of the Russian defence minister they planned to detonate a Russian nuclear device at Vauxhall Bridge, the home of MI6, a move that would have obliterated much of London in the process. Luckily the bombers were intercepted and the bomb removed.'

Mariokov was red in the face and attempted to speak, but Bill Mathews was having none of it.

'Forget the denials, General, just shut up and listen. We have pictures and video of the serial numbers of the nuke that your defence minister dispatched and then told the world had sunk to the bottom of the sea, only for it to turn up in London. We have documents we removed from Volkov's office implicating him, so it's not just talk. We have the proof.

'As for our "rogue" agent, I sent her into the embassy, the embassy by the way that belongs to the British government and is rented to you for the princely sum of one pound a year. I authorised my agent to use any force necessary to bring Volkov to justice. In the course of carrying out her duties she shot and killed many of Volkov's bodyguards while defending herself, and wounded the traitor Volkov before being shot and wounded herself.

'So here, General, is my dilemma. I have not submitted my report to the prime minister yet. What I don't know for sure is whether these were the actions of a madman hell-bent on revenge. Or was it state sponsored? The latter would surely be an act of war.

'General Mariokov, I am no warmonger, I take no pleasure in sabre rattling. You deal with your defence minister in whatever way you feel fit, but we want Vadek Volkov handed over to us, and a written apology to MI6 and its staff.

'Then and only then will I write up my final report stating this was an act carried out by a madman and that the Russian state played no part in the proceedings.

'I will leave you with one final thought, General. If that bomb had been detonated, knowing what we know, the UK, America and the other NATO countries would have retaliated with deadly force. Russia would strike back and this world we know would cease to exist and would be turned into a radioactive wasteland.

'I hope and I pray that no sane Russian would condone this action. I hope once you have carried out your own investigation that you decide to cast out or bring to justice the lunatics that almost caused World War Three.'

'I cannot believe that my country would be involved in these things you speak of, Director. I will look into your claims urgently and we will meet again soon. This proof you talk of – I would be interested to look at it. If you could send copies for my attention to the embassy. Good day, Director.'

Mariokov marched off in the direction he had come.

Bill Mathews waited, watching the Russian general march away joined by two bodyguards who had been lurking in the background. Mathews had done his research before arranging the meeting; he knew

Mariokov was one of only a handful of men that could pick up the phone and speak directly to the Russian premier without having to jump through FSB hoops to do so. Mathews wanted as little meddling from the boys in Lubyanka Square as possible; he was not sure how far Vadek Volkov's influence stretched in Moscow. If Samantha O'Conner's life was to return to normality it would depend on what the Russians did next; only time would tell.

Ludmilla Berkov was not sure if her cold sweat was caused by her wounds or by the fact that General Mariokov had returned from some type of meeting in a pure rage. He was screaming at his aid that there was a mole in the embassy who had handed the British classified documents. Ludmilla had only returned to work that week after recovering from her bullet wound. Initially she had been treated by her co-workers and the general as a hero; what no one had found out was that the bullet she had taken had not come from the British agent but from a Russian gun. Ludmilla was no fool; she knew the embassy would soon be swarming with FSB agents looking for the traitor. If they talked to Volkov they would find out the truth and she would be taken home where after days of torture to find out how much she had given to MI6 she would be handed over to the firing squad for execution.

Ludmilla gathered a few things from her desk then excused herself saying that she was feeling ill. She did not have to act the part; her complexion was almost grey and she was sweating profusely.

For some time she wandered aimlessly on the streets of the capital not sure what to do next; she contemplated suicide but decided against it, eventually coming to the conclusion that the only way forward was to seek asylum here in England. She had no idea how it had come to this, she was a loyal and upstanding Russian subject, yet here she was being hounded because she'd refused the advances of a scumbag who would turn on his fellow Russians for the sake of a few dollars.

Ludmilla was not sure how to go about seeking asylum, it had never entered her head, but she did have a few things up her sleeve. She had studied various MI6 directors but their PA had always remained constant. Ludmilla knew that although Jean Mitchell was on their radar she was not under surveillance. If she wanted to get a message to the top man, this lady was her best chance without drawing unwanted attention to herself. She also had information that would persuade the British to let her stay.

Jean Mitchell arrived home to find Enzo, her ginger tomcat, waiting for her in the front hall; this in itself was no major surprise – he normally attached himself to Jean's leg the minute she got in, looking for his supper. Tonight something was different; he was agitated, running back and forth in the hall. Jean sensed something was wrong and searched in her bag for her mace; slowly she entered the kitchen to find a pane of glass missing from the back door smashed and on the kitchen floor. She was about to call the office when a voice from the darkened living room spoke.

'I am sorry for the window. Please do not be alarmed – I mean you no harm. My name is Ludmilla Berkov. I am an intelligence analyst at the Russian Embassy and I must speak with your director urgently.'

Jean switched on the light in the lounge to find Ludmilla sitting by the fire wrapped up in her coat and scarf, as white as a ghost.

'Miss Berkov, why do you think I can help you? I am only a secretary – you have the wrong person.'

Ludmilla continued to stare straight ahead, not making eye contact or moving. 'I work for Russian intelligence, so please can we cut out this nonsense. You are Jean Mitchell, personal assistant to the director of MI6. You have been in this position for some time, working with the last four directors. Please ask your director to come here so we can speak, because the face of everyone entering or leaving your headquarters is beamed straight to Moscow for analysis. It would mean my death sentence if I entered your headquarters.'

Jean made the call.

Bill Mathews was mulling over the events of the day when the open-line phone rang.

'Hi, Bill, it's Jean Mitchell here. I thought I would find you still at the office. I have a surprise for you here at my house. I really think you should pop round on your way home because it won't wait until tomorrow.'

There was silence on the other end of the line. Bill Mathews hadn't worked with Jean long but he could tell from her voice something strange was going on.

'Would that be the surprise we talked about earlier today in the canteen?'

Jean agreed, then hung up. Bill Mathews had never set foot in the canteen in his life – he wasn't even sure where it was. He was sure that Jean had some sort of dilemma at home; they all had emergency call names to use. Jean's was 'Mother Superior'. If she had used that Bill would have called the cavalry, but she had not; something strange was going on. He picked up a Glock 19 from the armoury while his duty driver found the location of Jean's home, and was knocking on her front door with some trepidation thirty minutes later.

Jean said nothing but ushered him into the living room where Ludmilla had got to her feet to meet the man she apparently hoped could save her life. Jean introduced them then left them to talk.

Ludmilla explained what went on in the embassy the night she was shot and how the general had started a witch hunt for the person who had given MI6 the documents from Volkov's desk. She then sat silently waiting for the response from Bill Mathews. Mathews knew that a Russian intelligence officer coming over to them was good, but if he could turn her and keep her in her position without the Russians finding out she would be invaluable to British intelligence.

'Ludmilla, I understand that you're afraid that General Mariokov and his FSB friends will find out about you, but I fear that you have not thought this through. If you defect, what do you think will happen to your family still in Russia? No, I think you should return to your job tomorrow morning as if nothing has happened. You said yourself they think you are a hero after you survived the shooting. We will help you by laying a false trail of breadcrumbs. Sokolov, the head of security, had access to Volkov's office and he was killed in the embassy shoot-out. Dead men can't defend themselves, so we will leak that Sokolov was the mole they're looking for. That will stop the investigation.'

'Very well, Director. I have no choice in the matter, but I will only agree to go back on one condition: you send Samantha O'Conner to finish the job and kill Vadek Volkov. He knows what happened in the embassy and is a threat that must be eliminated.'

Mathews agreed, wondering whether Berkov knew of Sam's forced exile in America. Ludmilla stared at the floor, not speaking. Mathews sensed that she was having problems with her conscience. She fumbled in her coat pocket then produced a scrap of paper, moving it between her fingers, before apparently coming to a difficult decision.

'The number on this piece of paper is important – I overheard General Mariokov speaking to the person with this number. Mariokov is new to the systems in the control room and although he scrambled the call to the outside world he did not wipe the screen displaying the number. He has withdrawn all assistance for Volkov from Russia and he was telling our agent in America to stop assistance to Volkov's team in Arizona – the team hunting Samantha O'Conner. The number is a satellite phone belonging to our top undercover agent in America. Samantha saved my life in the embassy – maybe this information may save her life.'

Bill Mathews turned his driver round and headed straight back to the office leaving Jean to sort out some final details with Ludmilla Berkov before she returned to her old life at the embassy. Mathews contacted one of his old team at MI5 who had been feeding a known Russian agent the occasional bit of misinformation when required. Henry Benton was about to let slip to the Russian agent that he had been given paperwork from Peter Sokolov just before the attack on the embassy. Bill Mathews was pretty sure that this would end the witch hunt and allow Ludmilla some breathing space; he knew ultimately that for his new double agent to be safe and secure Volkov would have to go. Mathews needed Sam back so he could make use of her talents once more.

13

Death by Moonlight

Adam McDonald stood by a fallen tree listening for any tiny sound that was not normal. A stiff breeze moved the trees above him and almost drowned out any noises around him. The fallen tree had left a gap allowing the night sky to fill the area directly above him, and Adam studied the cloudless sky, watching as slowly the sky started to lighten; sunrise was not far away and with it Sam's dreaded full moon of predicted disaster would pass. An hour or so ago Adam had had enough of the tension inside the ranch house and decided to help patrol the outside the perimeter, assisting Secret Agent Brian Fellows who had pulled the late shift outside. Sam had tried to talk him out of it, babbling on about the message they had been given to stick together, but Adam's patience was wearing thin. He just wanted the night to pass.

Inside the ranch, despite being told to stay in her room, Sam had taken up a defensive position to the far left of the lounge against the back wall, which had no windows. On her left the gable end of the building also had no windows. The front of the main building had one window either side of the front door. Trudo had positioned his best marksman Pete Linn to the right of the front door by the curved wall; Dan Trudo had decided to patrol the corridor to the rear of the building that led to the bedroom section of the house himself. It was an area Dan thought would be vulnerable if attacked. Special Agent Ricky Mendez had been stationed by the barn covering the approach road to the ranch. He was armed with one of the M4 rifles and hand grenades from the circular room.

Adam glanced back at the ranch trying to stifle a yawn. To his right something caught the corner of his eye; the movement was too large to be a leaf blowing in the wind, but it was there then gone. Adam was not alarmed; he had already made contact with Agent Fellows who had been making his way from the rear of the building after checking the motion sensors. It would be him continuing his rounds. Adam moved slowly and deliberately in the direction of the movement; he did not want to spook Fellows and end up as his target.

As he approached he could see Fellows checking out the motion sensor. He decided to wait for him to complete the task before making contact. For a second or two he waited, then decided to join Fellows by the tree stump to see what was so interesting about the monitor.

It was the droplet of blood on the leaf by Fellows' ear that sent alarm bells ringing.

Adam moved to the side of Agent Fellows but already his heart was starting to race; Fellows was gone – his throat had been cut ear to ear. Adam grabbed the agent's headset, pulled it to his mouth, then whispered into it, 'Incoming. Repeat, incoming.' He was about to add 'Agent down' to his warning when the butt of a rifle hit him hard on the side of his head, knocking the headset from his grasp. He was on the ground struggling for consciousness when the second and third blows from the rifle to his unprotected head finished the job.

Daniil Litvak cursed as he picked up the mangled headset from Adam's body. He clicked on his own set; his men were not in their correct positions yet. The meddling bastard had just alerted the ranch – his attack had to be now. Two of their targets were dead; it would not take long to overcome the rest and execute the British woman. He half whispered, half screamed for his men to attack.

Two of his men were already in position and broke into a sprint for the front of the ranch house. Avoiding the front door both Spetsnaz soldiers charged headlong for the windows either side of the door, firing a burst of machine-gun fire fractions of a second before they crashed through the shattered windows. Fragments of glass and splinters of wood showered the lounge as both men dived through the frames aiming for a safe landing on the floor.

Inside, Pete Linn had got the message. Sam had no radio but saw Pete stiffen as he listened to the warning. She sat back using the wall behind her to steady herself as two Russians burst through the windows.

Sam saw Pete Linn fire as he swung round from covering the door; his shot was a fraction high, clipping the top of the Russian's body armour. The black-clad figure fired, hitting Pete in the stomach. Pete's gun was thrown across the glass-covered floor. Sam herself had her hands full. The black figure closest to her collided with the back of the sofa. As he landed he rolled to one side then got to his knees just as Sam shot him in the head, followed up by a further two shots to make sure she had eliminated him. Sam spun round to her right, firing at the black devil who had just shot Pete. She rolled onto her stomach to limit her target size but he was too quick for her and he ducked into the corridor as two of Sam's bullets thudded into the circular stone wall by the fireplace.

As soon as he heard the gunfire Dan Trudo called Creech Air Force Base on speed dial. It was time to call in his backup firepower. To his dismay the line was dead. He tried once more before his attention was drawn to the two figures in black crossing no-man's-land from the tree boundary to the rear of the building. Dan knew he had been lucky; these men were out of position when the shooting started it had given him the vital time he needed to respond to the imminent threat.

Dan used his shoulder to slam into a fire door and as it exploded outwards he picked his first target, hitting him in the throat and upper chest. The second figure started to weave while bringing weapon up but Dan was ice cool, hitting the attacker three times in the upper body. Dan was about to check his two targets were dead when he sensed movement in the shadows of the corridor. He spun round but the Russian soldier was faster and better positioned. He fired twice; the first shot was high but the second crashed into Dan's right shoulder, spinning him round in a circle and out of the fire exit. Dan picked himself up and sprinted for cover in the treeline before the Russian could line him up for the kill shot.

He watched from the treeline as the Russian soldier searched the bedrooms, presumably looking for his target. Dan was resigned to observing; he knew crossing no-man's-land to the house would bring him the same fate that he had dealt out to the two soldiers. He checked his cell phone had a signal then put a call through to the local police who, after a short explanation, agreed to send officers to the ranch. Dan was having trouble focusing; he knew too well why. It was shock and blood loss but he needed to get back in the game – his men and the Brits were in grave danger.

Sam crossed over to where Pete lay propped up against the curved stone wall. She could tell from Pete's wounds that he probably wouldn't make it unless he got urgent medical attention; she was gingerly investigating his wounds when a handful of gunshots came from the corridor leading to the rear, then silence for some time before they heard faint footsteps coming their way.

Pete and Sam made eye contact. Sam wanted to stay and face the new threat but Pete ushered her away. Reluctantly Sam ducked into the entrance to the kitchen. She had the silent figure in her gun sight when he ducked down to make sure Pete was dead. Sam could not fire; her target was obscured by a lounge chair. She was about to move to a better firing position when Pete grabbed the Russian's body armour, pulling himself up face to face with the masked assassin. He said only one word as he stared into the cold eyes of the Russian. 'Boom.' The Russian got the message and frantically tried to pull himself from Pete's death grip but he was too late; a fraction of a second later the grenade Pete was holding in his left hand exploded, killing them both instantly.

Sam knew that venturing outside was foolish, not knowing how strong or how many her enemies were, but she needed to find Adam and make sure he was safe. She loaded a fresh clip into her Glock, checked the slide and made for the door without glancing at what was left of the two smouldering bodies. She sprinted out of the front door jinking left then right; her wounded leg held out as she headed for the woods in front of the old ranch house.

Once undercover she sat for a few seconds to let her night vision improve. While she was doing this she spotted a black-clad figure to her left making his way along the barn wall by the pool. She knew Agent Mendez was probably still in the barn and about to be ambushed; from Sam's position she knew it would be a tall order to hit the black-clad figure but she needed at the very least to warn Mendez. She moved over to a big tree using it to steady her firing arm; she opened fire, emptying a full clip in the direction of the shadowy figure. She was in the process of replacing the spent clip when the Russian by the pool returned fire, confirming to Sam that her Glock was no match for an assault rifle, a far more accurate and deadly Kalashnikov AK15.

Bullets started cutting the woods around Sam's position to shreds. She ducked behind the tree to avoid being hit.

Behind her Sam heard the unmistakable thud of bullet on flesh and turned to find a Russian only ten feet behind her who had been working his way towards her and had just taken a hit in the shoulder from his fellow Russian. Sam raised her weapon a split second before the dazed and wounded Russian could react and shot him through the right eye. Her heart was still racing, fuelled by adrenalin as the black figure crumpled and fell forward only a few feet from her. She had been lucky – she had come very close to being killed.

While the gunfire raged at the left of the ranch house Daniil Litvak used the distraction to slip into the ranch house unnoticed. He had intended to start his search for the woman. She was gone but he found two of his men, one blown apart by a grenade, the second face down in a pool of his own blood. Daniil was about to pass the black-clad body when he froze, then pulled the black ski mask off to reveal the glazed eyes of his little brother staring into infinity.

Daniil had ordered him not to enter the building and to leave it to his more experienced troops to form the charge. He could feel the rage building inside him; he wanted to rip every man and woman here to pieces with his bare hands. They would pay for this with their lives – the bounty money was now not the main priority. This was personal; he would have his revenge for Anton.

Litvak continued his search of the building expecting to find the woman hiding somewhere. It was not until he reached the rear of the building and looked out onto the grounds that he realised his plan of attack was in tatters. On the grass outside another two of his men's bodies lay, cut down by the American secret service.

Daniil switched on his comms saying only one word: 'Report.'

His men knew not to speak, only click their comms on and off once so Daniil could tell by the click how many men he still had in the field.

He waited. Nothing. It was all the fault of the bastard who had raised the alarm. He was still thinking of his next plan of attack when his headset buzzed into life; unfortunately for him it was not one of his men.

'No comms clicks, Boris, looks like you're on your own. We read the Spetsnaz training manual as well, buddy. Stop lurking about the bushes and either give yourself up or come out fighting like a man. Listen to this, my friend – music to our ears.'

Daniil Litvak could hear the police sirens through his headset as he ripped it off and flung it into the bushes, unable to control his rage for a second. He wanted to set his rifle to full auto and charge the Americans down, but he knew that was exactly what they wanted him to do. Daniil shouldered his weapon and with a huge effort turned away, heading north into the treeline. Tonight was not his night, but there would be other nights … he would make sure of it.

Dan Trudo had shot the Russian by the pool but he was still alive; Dan wanted him to stay that way until he could be interrogated by Homeland Security. He pulled off the Russian headset he had borrowed, waiting in vain to see if the unknown soldier would accept his challenge and show himself. For a short time nothing stirred then, in a blaze of flashing lights, the drive filled with police cars. Trudo briefed the first police officer on the scene. He saw Mendez set off after Sam, but he had been on the edge of consciousness for some time and as he too attempted to follow he collapsed, hearing the police chief scream for medics.

Sam couldn't wait for the police to get their act together and charged back into the woods in search of Adam. She knew there was still an assassin out there and she ran the risk of being shot by the police by mistake, but no one had heard from Adam and she was now in full panic mode.

She was glad to see that Ricky Mendez was following her lead; he had handed over his Russian prisoner and charged into the undergrowth some distance behind her.

Sam spotted something shining in the distance and made a beeline for it. As she drew closer she saw it was the moon shining on Joe Hatathli's tomahawk still tucked in Adam's trouser belt. She found Adam next to the dead body of Special Agent Brian Fellows. Adam was face up and for a second Sam thought she was going to pass out. She collapsed on her knees next to Adam, tears obstructing her vision. Even in the poor light and through her tears she could see that Adam's head had taken a terrible pounding. She whispered into his blood-soaked ear, telling him they should never have split up; she cradled him to her chest, rocking gently as if he was her baby. She was devastated and couldn't get any more words out. Then she saw Adam's eyelid flicker; she'd thought she had lost him but after feverish attempts she finally found a weak pulse in his neck that confirmed he was still alive. Sam screamed at the top of her voice for help just as Agent Mendez arrived by her side.

An hour later, Adam was rushed into the emergency department of Flagstaff Medical Centre. Sam and Special Agent Mendez were ushered into a waiting room while the trauma team investigated Adam's head wounds.

It seemed like hours before anyone arrived, then the waiting room door was flung open and a tall, middle-aged doctor in scrubs marched in followed by a nurse almost running to keep up with him. He wasted no time with small talk and came directly to the point. 'Good morning. I'm Doctor David Wetherly and I am the neurosurgeon looking after Mr McDonald. Time is critical – Adam has an acute subdural haematoma. His coma is being caused by a bleed around his frontal lobe. I need your signature and consent to operate immediately.'

Sam was presented with various documents which she signed without reading or even thinking about what was written on them. Once the nurse had removed the signed paperwork Dr Wetherly hesitated before leaving. 'Miss O'Conner, your partner is gravely ill. The odds are not good. Please prepare yourself. We will do everything we can for Adam, but the chances of someone surviving an acute subdural haematoma are somewhere between twenty and thirty per cent. I need to get to theatre. I will brief you after the operation. Let's hope for a good result.'

Bruce Ellis was already up and dressed on his second day in Vegas. He had arranged to meet his next suspect that evening and was running things through his head as he strolled up and down, waiting for room service to deliver breakfast.

The view from his penthouse suite was probably one of the best in Las Vegas. He looked down on the Bellagio fountains and directly in front of him the Eiffel Tower was situated on the far side of the strip. A knock at the door returned his attention to the Bellagio penthouse. Bruce opened the door to find that breakfast had arrived; he tipped the waiter then headed back to the bedroom. At the doorway he stopped, not sure if he should wake Fiona or let her sleep on; she looked like a scene from Sleeping Beauty, her jet-black hair and pale complexion highlighted against the white silk pillows. It had surprised Bruce that even in the middle of the manhunt for the traitor Fiona Malden had managed to take his mind of things and actually allowed him to unwind for a day or two. When she had contacted him he had not wanted the distraction that she would bring to the situation, but with the benefit of hindsight he was glad he had agreed to meet her.

Bruce gently shook her awake, but it was clear to see Fiona was not a morning person. 'Jesus, what time is it?' Fiona squinted through half-closed eyes at the clock. 'It's not even nine o'clock yet – what are you doing to me? Girls my age need all the beauty sleep they can get. Come back to bed and give me a cuddle – that's an order, Special Agent Ellis.'

Bruce had grown use to Fiona's little teases and although her suggestion was tempting, breakfast was already here.

'Only a cuddle, Captain Malden? Breakfast is here. It would take a promise of more than just a cuddle to put me off my breakfast.'

Fiona Malden took the bait, jumping to her knees on the bed. 'Hey, were your ears not working when I told you I've been promoted? It's Major Malden, thank you very much. It has a far better ring to it than plain old captain, don't you think? For that you can forget the cuddle – so where's the food? I hope you got me something nice, Bruce, I'm starving.'

Fiona and Bruce had just sat down when Ellis's cell phone rang. Fiona watched as he answered the call. Suddenly he shot up, knocking over his chair and spilling his coffee in the process. All she could hear was Bruce saying 'No' over and over again. After a few minutes the call ended.

'Fiona, I need to go. That was Homeland Security – my ranch house was attacked last night. We lost two secret service agents and a third is critical. Adam McDonald is in surgery as we speak. I'm sorry, Fiona, but I need to go – please wait for me. I'll let you know how Adam is as soon as I can.'

Fiona wanted to accompany Bruce but he explained that Homeland Security were sending a helicopter for him and that they would not accept the presence of anyone who was not connected to the investigation.

En route to Flagstaff Airport Bruce Ellis went over everything in his head; how was it possible that the Russians knew where he had hidden Samantha O'Conner? There had to be a leak, but the people who knew were only a handful; the two men at the top were not in question. That only left the secret service agents, two of whom were dead. Could the Russians have killed their own agent to silence him? It made no sense – none of the agents had been in a position to know all the information leaked previously. Could there be more than one Agent X? The more Bruce tried to analyse things, the more he tied himself in knots. Bruce found the section chief of Homeland Security waiting for him at the airport. Bruce was ushered into an office and handed a telephone. To his surprise he had a caller waiting, one that for the moment he had forgotten all about.

'Hello, is that you Bruce? It's Bill here, Bill Mathews. What a bloody nightmare it is trying to get hold of you. This is very important and we're on an open line so I'll keep it short: a trusted friend of mine thinks you should look up an X friend of yours, the person you've been looking for, I believe. His satellite phone number is being sent to your office through the usual channels. Happy hunting.'

Ellis wanted to ask Bill how he had found out about Agent X – and his source – but the open phone line stopped him. He thanked Bill then called Langley.

Jimmy Mattis was Langley's communications expert. Bruce had worked with him before but not for some time, not since Bruce had transferred to the Pentagon.

'Hi, Jimmy, it's been a while – I need to ask you a big favour. Tell me first – can you track a satellite phone?'

There was silence for a second. 'Shouldn't be a problem – you can track their GPS signal ... unless it's a Russian covert unit. Their SC17 models can only be traced while searching for a phone line – once the person being called has picked up the receiver the unit cloaks itself. It's also code protected – put the wrong code in and the chip inside the phone destroys itself. Clever bit of kit.'

What Jimmy had just told Ellis made his heart sink. 'So even if you have the phone number you can't trace the phone?'

'That's a different story. Bruce. If you have the number we can load it into one of our tracking units. When the phone is used our computer can lock on to that number. Once it's cloaked you won't hear anything, but we will be able to tell where the phone call was made, if that's any help.'

Bruce thought for a second, weighing up his options. 'Okay, Jimmy, I need you to get hold of the phone number MI6 have sent my office. Find out if it is a covert phone then do everything you can to trace its owner. You've just been assigned to my team … anyone says anything refer them to the White House situation room. Jimmy, this is really important: no one, and I mean no one gets to know the phone's position. When you find it I need to know immediately, do you understand?'

'No problems, Bruce. I'll get onto it right away. Speak to you soon.'

Ellis for the moment bypassed the waiting room where Sam and Mendez were waiting for word of Adam; he wanted to speak to Dan Trudo before anyone else. He found Dan out of surgery and in a recovery room but still sleeping off the anaesthetic. He was about to leave when his phone rang; Jimmy had already checked out the satellite phone number and confirmed it was a Russian covert unit, a fact in itself that confirmed to Ellis the owner of this phone probably was Agent X. He checked to see if Dan had regained consciousness one last time before going to see Adam.

Dan opened his eyes drowsily as Bruce approached him; when he recognised Bruce Ellis he tried to sit up and shake off the remainder of the anaesthetic. 'Bruce, I'm sorry, they rushed us. Are the Brits okay?'

Ellis did not answer and changed the subject. 'Dan, the Russian hit squad found out Sam's true location – it can only have come from one of your team. Did any of them speak to someone about their mission?'

Dan Trudo pulled himself up slowly to a sitting position; he would not like the integrity of his team being brought into question and his face, although racked with pain, was also thunderous.

'My boys did not say one word to anyone – and before you point the finger at me, I told no one about the ranch other than talking to Creech Air Force Base, who agreed to supply air support if required, but I never even told them about the ranch, only that the location was in the Flagstaff area.'

Alarm bells started going off in Bruce Ellis's head, but he wanted more information before jumping to conclusions. 'Dan, who did you speak to when you called Creech?'

'The base commander, Lee Cassey. He promised me air cover if things got nasty – I called him last night but the line was dead. If you ask me it should be Samantha O'Conner you should be questioning – how the hell did she know the Russians were going to attack if she didn't have some inside information?'

Bruce Ellis left Dan Trudo with nurses fussing over him. Bruce was trying to get things straight in his head as he wandered down the corridor en route to the waiting room. He was pretty sure Sam was not Agent X, but Lieutenant General Lee Cassey was the soldier he had arranged to meet in Las Vegas; he had a gambling habit and a lavish lifestyle that even a general would struggle to afford. In his head Bruce went over the NSA file he had read on Lee Cassey; he certainly had the security clearance Agent X would have needed. Before he became base commander he was commanding officer of the development wing of Predator UAV tactical warfare. If the phone number the British had supplied originated from Nevada, Lieutenant General Cassey was going to have a lot of questions to answer.

Ellis decided a call to the White House was in order. He knew the President was overseas but he thought he would run his suspicions past the chairman. Admiral Holister was known for his no-nonsense approach to military matters; he had been widely praised for his cool head during crisis, which was one of the reasons he had been promoted to Admiral and now held the position of Chairman of the Joint Chiefs of Staff, the highest ranked military position in America.

After a few minutes Bruce was transferred to a secure line where Admiral Holister was waiting to take his call.

'Good morning, Admiral. Things are moving fast here in Arizona. I thought I'd better bring you up to speed on matters: suspected Russian special forces assaulted the ranch house but their attack was thwarted. Unfortunately during the fighting two secret service agents, Brian Fellows and Pete Linn, were killed. Dan Trudo, their team leader, was shot and wounded but is stable. Adam McDonald was also injured in the fighting and is being operated on as we speak. Five Russians were killed in the attack with a sixth wounded and taken into custody. We suspect at least one Russian escaped from the scene.

'Admiral, it would appear that one of our Agent X suspects had a hand in planning the attack. We have had intel from MI6 that may also point the finger at Lieutenant General Lee Cassey. If this proves to be the case, do you have any objections to me taking him into custody for questioning?'

For a few seconds there was nothing, but Bruce could hear the Admiral breathing; he was thinking things through before replying.

'Okay, Bruce, I'll get Homeland Security on the case of the prisoner. We need to find out if these guys were rogue agents – this better not have come from the Kremlin. In the absence of the President I will call the families of the fallen secret service agents. As for Lee Cassey, if the proof is overwhelming, yes, lift him. Damn, why did it have to be him? Lee Cassey and his team are in the final stages of producing a groundbreaking new weapon system – the Predator Genesis drone has a prop driven by nuclear cells. It's completely silent and because its main power is nuclear it can stay in the air for six months at a time. Its weapon system is a pulse, laser charged from cells covering its wingspan, so it never needs to be rearmed. It's due for evaluation by the air force next month. Cassey is putting the final touches to the machine's software at the moment – the last thing I need is him locked up. Whatever happens, the technology of these machines must not end up in the hands of the Russians. Keep me informed of progress.'

Daniil Litvak watched from the parking lot as first Adam McDonald was stretchered into the hospital followed a little later by Pavel Douchev, Litvak's team member. Litvak cursed then headed along the perimeter wall until he came to a wedged-open fire door. He crossed the corridor and found himself in a laundry room where he pulled on a set of surgical scrubs. Leaving his kit bag behind he walked along the corridor bumping into a doctor who was talking to his wife on his cell; he didn't notice Litvak removing his ID and continued his conversation none the wiser. After a bit of hunting about Litvak found a room guarded by a police officer. He walked up, smiling; the police officer was checking out his ID badge when Litvak thrust upward with his right arm. Using the palm of his hand he hit the police officer just under the nose, smashing the cartilage and pushing it backwards into his skull, breaking the officer's neck with the force. He checked he had not been spotted then dragged the policeman into the room, closing the door.

Pavel seemed to brighten when Litvak started removing the drip from his arm. Litvak asked him if he had been questioned yet. Pavel shook his head as he struggled with the bandage on his wrist; he looked up just as Daniil Litvak plunged the blade into his chest while switching off the heart monitor. He wanted to make sure Douchev was dead before the staff found him; there could be no one left to incriminate him. He was working alone now … he had taken a big risk to silence his team member. Attempting to kill the woman here would be suicide; for the moment he would have to be content with damage limitation, but soon her time would come.

Near Crookton, close to the old Route 66, Daniil watched an elderly gentleman pull his Ford F150 pickup over; the old guy smiled at Daniil as he approached his driver's door. 'Can I offer you a lift, son?' Daniil shot him in the head.

He used the old man's jacket to wipe the blood from the windscreen before unceremoniously dumping the body behind a bush not far from the roadside. He needed to get out of the area for the moment; he had almost been caught by American soldiers as he doubled back to the barn to pick up supplies. Next stop was Las Vegas, where he had a contact who would hide him and keep him informed of events.

That evening, joined by Bruce Ellis, Sam listened as the doctor explained that Adam's operation had gone well but for the moment he was being held in an induced coma to allow time for the swelling on the frontal lobe area to reduce. The doctor stressed that until Adam was awake there was no knowing what, if any, brain damage he had suffered.

Sam could feel the terror building inside her; it took all her mental strength to hold it together as thoughts of looking after a toddler and a brain-damaged partner flooded into her head. For the moment she was emotionally destroyed. Once more she walked the tightrope of life, too afraid to look down into the abyss that threatened to swallow her.

After the body of the Russian and the murdered police officer had been discovered, Bruce Ellis threw a cordon around the hospital so tight that for every employee there were two soldiers. FBI and Homeland Security turned the town of Flagstaff upside down in the hunt for Boris, as he had been nicknamed, and in the wider area special forces had been deployed to hunt the Russian down. In the middle of this circus Sam had been given a room next to Adam; for two days she cried herself to sleep as recurring nightmares of what might be their future flashed before her eyes. Would a man like Adam want to live the rest of his life disabled and broken? Would he ever see his son grow to be a man? She needed Adam to get better before she had a nervous breakdown.

He regained consciousness only for a few minutes initially; he was confused – images of people and things flashed before his eyes – he was lost, then things settled down and he found himself in a hospital room with only a pretty blonde woman sitting by his side. The minute she realised he was awake she jumped to her feet, but he was already retreating down a dark tunnel back to the land of dreams; he watched the blonde woman fade – she was speaking to him but he could hear nothing.

The darkness seemed to go on for ever … was he dead? Was this what happened after death? Then he was back in the same room with the same pretty blonde woman. She had seen him open his eyes and once again she was speaking, but this time the pain in his head made him want to scream. His body was stiff and sore but his head made him feel like the elephant man.

Only one word registered with him: 'Adam,' the woman had said. *Adam* – who the hell was Adam? The blackness returned and the pain mercifully faded.

During the next night he clambered once more from the darkness; all was quiet in the room. This time he was more with it; his head was heavy and pounded to the beat of his heart but he did not return to the darkness. At the foot of his bed the blonde woman was curled up, sleeping. He did not want to wake her so he contented himself with watching slowly as his senses returned to him. He must have dozed off until someone squeezed his hand.

'Adam, it's me, can you speak? How are you feeling?'

There was that name again – who was Adam? He tried to think but it hurt; where was he? Who was he? Panic set in and he curled up like a child.

Sam stood next to Adam's bed, tears running down her face; she had no idea what to do now. She had spent the last four days by his bedside praying for him to be alright.

The news that Adam was awake spread fast, and soon Sam found herself in the corner of the room crowded out by nurses, doctors and surgeons. Outside she bumped into Bruce Ellis who had heard the news; he had been talking to the surgeon and wanted to speak to Sam alone.

'Sam, the hospital thought it would be better if I talked with you. They're pretty sure Adam has some scarring on his frontal lobe and from early observations it would appear he has lost his memory. They reckon in time some or all of it may return – they're going to try to get in contact with a guy called Professor Paul Glen who is an expert on recovering brain function, but there's a possibility that he may not recover fully due to the damage.'

Sam's eyes were welling up as she tried her hardest not to make a fool of herself in front of Ellis. 'I already knew, Bruce, the minute he looked at me I knew he didn't recognise me. What a bloody mess this is.'

Bruce's phone buzzed in his pocket. He was about to ignore the call until he saw it was Jimmy Mattis calling. He excused himself and walked away out of earshot before hitting the green button.

'Hi, boss. I think we may have a problem. Your phone was used ten minutes ago – the call came from Creech Air Force Base. The problem is, as soon as the call was made the caller hung up and hasn't called again – either that was a signal of some sort, which I doubt because it never connected, or the phone has some sort of tracking monitor built into it. If that's the case we've just alerted the caller he's being tracked. Sorry, boss, I thought you better know right away.'

Bruce thanked Jimmy then called Admiral Holister. 'Admiral, sorry to bother you, but it does look like Lee Cassey is our man. We may have a problem though – he may know we're on to him. Can you close down Creech before he has a chance to do anything? I'm heading there now, if you could let security know. We need to get him to Langley for questioning.'

There was a short pause then Holister replied. 'Damn and blast it. Okay, Bruce, I'll tell them you're coming and that you're acting base commander until further notice. Speak to you soon.'

Bruce was about to leave for the airport when he spotted Sam sitting on a bench in the corridor staring at the opposite wall, looking dejected. He stopped by her side and put his hand gently on her shoulder.

'Try not to worry too much, we both know what a fighter Adam is. The brain is an incredible thing – if anyone can come back from this, Adam McDonald has my vote. I need to go … we have Agent X cornered. I need to make sure the slippery bastard doesn't get away. If you feel like some moral support, Fiona Malden is sitting around waiting for me at the Bellagio in Vegas – I'm sure she wouldn't mind a call from you. I need to go, and if you do talk to Fiona, tell her I'll be back soon.'

Sam watched Bruce hurry down the corridor and out into the car park. Agent X was the last thing on her mind; she needed to speak to Professor Paul Glen and she needed to speak to him now.

14

Agent X

Within seconds of his Gulfstream G500 leaving Flagstaff Airport Bruce Ellis received an urgent call from the situation room of the White House. It was Admiral Holister. 'Bruce, we have problems. I called Creech after we spoke and they have had an unauthorised take-off from one of the two Genesis drones. We're having problems tracking it due to its stealth technology. I have two F16s on their way to Creech ... when you get there you must make sure the second Genesis drone is secured. At the moment no one has found Lee Cassey – security has been told to find him and detain him for your arrival.'

As soon as Cassey tried to contact Moscow to warn Dimitri Panoz that Litvak's men had failed he was alerted by a red warning lamp on his handset that told him his number was being tracked. He hung up; he'd known this day may come sooner or later. With no fuss he moved to his already prepared escape plan.

Lee Cassey removed what he needed from his office then headed to the development hangar where both his state-of-the-art Genesis drones where stationed. Only one technician was present checking flight data recorded from Drone A. Lieutenant General Cassey informed the technician that he had conference call here with the Pentagon and that the technician had the rest of the day off.

The second the technician left Cassey activated a security programme he had installed in the defence computers. Thirty seconds later the hangar was sealed to the outside world; only the main door could be opened by the drones. Cassey crossed to Drone A. He opened a hatch in the nose of the machine and entered an eight-digit code; he then removed the hard drive, slipping in one of his own. The second the hatch was closed the drone became awake, its air screw spinning silently and propelling the Predator Genesis drone towards the closed door. Cassey opened a laptop, punched in a security code and a few seconds later cameras in the drone brought his screen to life, a read-out on the bottom of the screen telling him what the drone was up to. Cassey saw its sensors pick up the closed door and gave the command to the defence computer to open the outer door to the runway. As the door closed behind it the drone lined up on the runway, checked its radar for incoming flights and immediately applied full thrust, soaring up into the sky intent on carrying out its orders from flight control.

Cassey logged into the memory cell in Drone A's mainframe to check it still held the orders he had programmed; the orders were not complex: it was to patrol over the air base. It had been given orders to maintain security around the development hangar – anything or anyone coming within a hundred metres of the hangar was to be stopped – lethal force was authorised. Any aircraft within two miles of the airbase was considered to be hostile and was to be destroyed. The drone was a machine – it did nothing more or less than what it was programmed to do. Life or death, right or wrong, it had no comprehension; it carried out its orders and patrolled the air base as Cassey watched from the security of the hangar.

Master Sergeant Tilner saw the drone take off; he was somewhat puzzled as his flight rota showed no Genesis drone flight today. He was about to consult his log when his office phone rang. Tilner answered the call and at first found it hard to believe he was speaking to the highest-ranking officer in the United States military; he found it harder to believe what Admiral Holister was asking him to do. Arresting his commanding officer seemed insane, but the fact that the CIA were on their way to take command of the base and not the air force told him that this was very serious. Holister almost choked when the master sergeant told him that one of the new drones had just taken off, and screamed at him to get it back on the ground.

Lee Cassey punched his code into the second drone then, as with the first, he fitted the new hard drive. While he waited he noticed Drone A had perceived the movement of the pickup truck and was tracking it as it approached the hundred-metre no-go zone around the development hangar. At 105 metres it powered up its main laser, calculated the size speed and risk of the target, then at 102.2 metres it fired; the laser blast was at forty per cent of full capacity but from the ground it looked like the base was under attack from aliens. The white-blue laser pulse sent the pickup rolling sideways; its fuel tank for a millisecond exceeded the surface temperature of the sun, blowing what was left of the pickup to pieces. Master Sergeant Tilner and two of his patrol were killed instantly. Lee Cassey watched with mixed emotions; he had just proved his invention worked but now there was no way back. He had to get out of here and quickly.

Captain Frank Zeffren had been watching the noiseless drone circle the base from the car park and witnessed for the first time its laser firepower as the drone attacked its own base. Frank had been worried when he first saw the blueprints of this weapon, a weapon that needed no maintenance for six months. The laser weapon system was too Star Wars for his liking. Zeffren sprinted to his control room, flinging one of his operators out of his seat as he powered up a PD 354 Predator drone. The only way to fight this thing was with one of its own kind. He screamed at the displaced operator to get through to the Pentagon and tell them one of the Genesis drones had gone rogue.

Zeffren watched the monitor as his Predator drone lifted off; he was checking his weapon system when there was a flash.

Through the camera of Drone A Cassey watched PD354 taxi and lift off. The minute its wheels left the ground the drone complied with its orders to destroy anything flying within two miles and fired a fifty per cent pulse, obliterating the PD354 and leaving only tangled smouldering metal at the end of the runway. Cassey watched Drone A turn away, the readout on the laptop showing the drone using the power of the sun to recharge its state-of-the-art wide absorption solar cells. Cassey was proud of his achievement; his cells were fifty per cent more effective than even NASA could achieve.

Safe inside the hangar Cassey cursed; he should be on his way, but Drone B, the most up-to-date machine, had not accepted the new hard drive. Its monitor was frozen and as Cassey rebooted the system a drop of sweat splashed on the keyboard. Why today, of all days, had this happened? He still had time but he needed to hurry. Cassey was concerned. Drone A was the prototype; it had some areas a determined attacker might take advantage of, but once Drone B got into the air its systems were far more advanced and nothing America had would stop his departure. He left the system restarting and crossed over to the other side of the hangar to his Piper Seneca. He loaded his gear and checked the systems. The long-range fuel tanks were full to the brim for his trip to Cuba where his Russian friends would take delivery of their new weapon systems. It had been planned for when the Genesis project was complete, but time had run out. It was now or never.

Lee Cassey picked up his phone and called his contact, an FSB sleeper in Las Vegas. He recited the coded sentence: 'I have three books of the bible for you, my friend. Genesis, Exodus, Leviticus. Good day.'

His welcome committee would be waiting for him at a runway north of Sabalo. All he had to do was get this damned computer program working.

Bruce Ellis had been called to the flight deck by the pilot; he could see that they were on final approach to Creech Air Force Base in front of him. In the distance was the runway, nestling at the foot of the desert hills. Creech was not unlike Area 51; its isolated desert location was suited to the military's desire for secrecy. The two F16 Fighting Falcons shot past them, higher and on a steeper approach, heading for the base.

Ellis and the pilots looked out of the cockpit, watching the underbellies of the fighter jets vanishing into the distance, the jet wash from the fighters requiring Bruce's air force pilots to hang on to the controls to hold her steady on approach. Bruce was in the process of returning to his seat in the cabin when he caught the flash out of the corner on his eye.

Lee Cassey sat transfixed, unable to take his eyes from the monitor. Drone A had picked up all three aircraft on its radar and, as Cassey watched, had assigned the Gulfstream as its primary target; it was powering up its laser when the two F16s overtook the Gulfstream. Drone A changed primary targets and altered its laser pulse to match the threat, setting it to eighty per cent.

Captain Eugene 'Tex' Carlin was a F16 instructor with the 8th Fighter Squadron; his wingman Ross Stein was new to the F16. They had been heading back to Holliman Air Force Base in New Mexico when they got the call to proceed to Creech Air Force Base and await further instruction. Carlin was about to contact the tower at Creech for permission to land as their fuel levels were low when his world turned upside down; just as he noticed the black drone below him there was a blinding flash and his wingman exploded in mid-air. Tex Carlin had flown combat missions over Iraq and was a veteran of Afghanistan; he thought he had put all that shit behind him. Instantly the fighter pilot instinct in him was awakened; he threw the F16 onto its side using full reheat then pulled the stick over. The F16 Falcon responded like its animal namesake; under full power Carlin held his breath, fighting against the incredible G force the F16 was producing in the turn – and that threatened to cause him to black out. He watched out of the corner of his eye as the black drone slipped out of sight under his port wing tip, but just in time to see the unknown aircraft fire a white-blue pulse, the same pulse that had just killed his wingman. Carlin twisted round and watched in horror as the pulse hit the Gulfstream that had been heading for Creech Air Force Base.

Cassey watched in horror as Drone A reacquired the Gulfstream as its new primary target. Cassey knew this was a tactical error by the drone but he was helpless to intervene. The F16's quick reactions had pulled it out of the target zone. The drone recalculated speed and size of the target and reduced the laser power to fifty per cent.

The Gulfstream was on final approach to land when it was hit by the drone's laser. Cassey smashed his fist down on the desk, making his laptop jump into the air. The prototype drone had fired without waiting for its batteries to recharge; in the heat of battle it had not called on backup power from its nuclear generator. The Gulfstream ploughed into the runway but withstood the impact, arriving in a shower of sparks. Both pilots must have been blinded by the pulse but had held on to the jet.

Cassey breathed a sigh of relief. The Gulfstream was as good as destroyed. Now Drone A would reacquire the fighter jet that could do so much damage to his plans. As he watched his drone started the turn to bring its laser to bear on the F16.

Carlin in a fit of rage had turned the F16 Fighting Falcon back towards the airfield. He was not heavily armed, only two medium-range sidewinder air-to-air missiles and his guns; he didn't know if he had authorisation but he had little time to make his move. Tex was not sure why, but his weapons system could not acquire the black aircraft as a target. Carlin couldn't wait any longer and fired both sidewinders; he watched in horror as both missiles passed by the black bastard, exploding by the perimeter fence of the airfield. Carlin had no options left; he was closing rapidly on the black drone, and he did what any self-respecting Texan would do: gritted his teeth and went for his guns.

The shells from the Vulcan Gatling gun firing from just behind Tex Carlin's left ear on the port side of the F16 tore into the electrical heart of Drone A. Tex closed his eyes, preparing to ram the menacing unmarked black aircraft, but with no electrical function the drone plunged towards the desert, missing the screaming F16 by only a few feet.

Captain Zeffren and the fire crew arrived at the stricken Gulfstream; as the fire crew tried in vain to help the pilots, Zeffren watched the black drone plunge to earth out in the desert. There were no flames or explosion, only a loud thud as the inhuman angel of death met its fate.

Zeffren watched the F16 circle and drop its landing gear. He made a mental note to buy that guy a beer – he had outmanoeuvred and outfought the artificial intelligence's version of a fighter pilot.

In the passenger cabin Bruce Ellis had no idea what had just happened; he felt like he had just been electrocuted. His chest was heavy and he was having problems breathing. He tried to unbuckle his seat belt, but his arms wouldn't do what his brain told them.

His seat was in an unusual position – his feet were level with his chest and his seat was canted over to the left; the smell of aviation gas and burning electrical circuits filled his nostrils and with some effort he eventually managed to throw his belt off, fearful that the plane could burst into flames at any second. With adrenalin pulsing through his veins he tackled the cabin door; its normal opening mechanism was stiff and he struggled to move it. There were shouts from outside and crowbars appeared through the gaps around the jammed door; seconds later Ellis staggered from the wreck of the Gulfstream. He turned to go back in to help the two pilots but he was stopped by a captain who said his name was Jake Zeffren – there was no hope for them. The cabin had folded in on them as they tried to control the crash; they had lost their lives doing their duty to the end.

Bruce was a mess; his ears and nose were bleeding, he had a nasty gash in his right leg, his trousers were in tatters. Only the adrenalin was keeping him standing, but he was still asking questions. 'Where is General Cassey? I need to get to Cassey – where? Tell me where?'

As if on cue they heard the hum of the hangar doors opening, but that was drowned out as two hundred metres away the nose of the Piper Seneca slipped out onto the runway. Zeffren pointed to the plane, but Ellis needed no explanation; before anyone could stop him, Ellis leapt into a rescue truck parked next to the crash site. Selecting reverse he thumped the throttle to the floor just as Captain Zeffren jumped onto the driver's step, grabbing the mirror.

A plume of smoke belched from the exhaust stack and the rescue unit careered backwards in the direction of the escaping Piper aircraft. Zeffren was holding on for dear life. Ellis was not for giving up, even though he knew there was no way the rescue unit could catch the Piper going forwards never mind in reverse. As they approached the hanger the long black nose of another Genesis drone was a menacing sight as the machine started to follow the Piper out on to the airfield. Bruce Ellis spotted the drone and screamed at Zeffren to jump.

Zeffren must have realised what Ellis was about to do and jumped for his life just as Ellis swung the steering round. He had aimed for the drone but missed, hitting the gable end of the hangar and stopping with a lurch as the rescue unit stalled.

Debris from the door fell, blocking the drone's path. Bruce Ellis's gamble paid off. The drone had obviously used some type of emergency protocol to shut down its command program to avoid a collision with the crashed truck and debris.

Lee Cassey cursed as he watched over his shoulder. The crash tender had collided with the hangar, blocking the way for his Genesis drone to escape. There was nothing he could do about it now – all that mattered was escaping to Cuba. He had the plans and blueprints with him and would help his Russian friends build a new Genesis drone, even better than the one he had left behind. He turned his attention back to his take-off just as he spotted the F16, which had completed a circuit of the base and was on final approach and just about to touch down at the end of the runway. He judged the distance and increased the throttle to full; he had flown the Seneca for some time now and knew he could get it into the air before the F16 arrived. The Piper built speed as the F16 grew bigger in his windshield – he had forgotten to take into account the extra weight in the long-range fuel tanks. At the last second he pulled back on the stick and the Piper Seneca leapt into the air.

Lee Cassey almost made it; if it were not for the high tail fin of the F16 he would have been gone, but the tail of the fighter sliced off the port tailplane of the Seneca and it rolled to starboard, out of control. He fought with the Seneca controls, trying to minimise the inevitable collision, and braced himself for impact as his plane careered off the runway heading for the car park. The final impact knocked Cassey out and for precious minutes he lay in the cockpit. When he regained consciousness he had no idea how long he had been out. It took him a few seconds to get his act together before struggling out of the Seneca carrying the blueprints and cash in a holdall in his left hand. He needed to get to his car so he could reach his friends in Las Vegas who would smuggle him out of the country. The only problem was that although he was in the car park, the perimeter fence of the runway was wrapped around the nose of the Piper Seneca; the fence had slowed the plane and saved his life, but now it acted as a trap.

Jake Zeffren watched as the tailless F16 completed its landing while the Seneca touched down on two wheels before careering off into the scrub, smashing through the boundary fence and heading for one of the car parks. Zeffren had expected a ball of flame, but all was quiet other than sirens going off and men shouting. There was no explosion. His attention returned to the lunatic who had stopped the second drone taking off. He was in a bad way, trying to hold himself together; he slipped his wallet out of a blood-soaked jacket pocket. Zeffren took it, opening it to find his ID card. He was Special Agent Bruce Ellis, Department of Defense, with a Langley phone number; he was CIA. Jake went to hand it back as Ellis handed him his Beretta. 'Stop Cassey,' were his last words as he passed out.

Captain Jake Zeffren shouted for medics to get the special agent out of the wrecked truck and took off at a sprint to where he had seen the Seneca crash. He arrived in the car park to find the plane resting against a Dodge pickup. As he approached the door was thrown open and Lee Cassey stumbled out, intact other than a bad cut above his right eye.

'It's over, General, you're going to have a lot of explaining to do. The CIA would like a word with you.'

Zeffren spotted the Glock in Cassey's right hand just as his arm swung up; Cassey fired, hitting Jake in the chest. Zeffren fell to his knees in a state of shock – he had just been shot by his commanding officer.

Jake's vision was going dark at the edges as Cassey turned to make his escape. Jake lined Cassey up in his gun sight. He fired six shots before his finger stopped working; the gun slipped from his lifeless fingers but he died knowing he had stopped a madman. Lee Cassey was too close for him to miss and took three bullets through the heart. He let go of his precious money and blueprints and before the holdall hit the ground he was dead.

Admiral Holister's hand was shaking with rage as he waited for his call to Air Force One to be put through. The President was silent as Holister briefed him on events at Creech; true, they had succeeded in finding and stopping Agent X, but they had paid a terrible price: three ground crew and four pilots killed. Thankfully Agent Ellis would recover, but they had lost millions of dollars' worth of equipment and the Genesis project would be delayed indefinitely. At least they had stopped it being handed over to a foreign power. The President instructed Admiral Holister to bury the events at Creech; no one needed to know how close they had come to disaster. The official story would be that a drone had crashed, tragically killing a number of onlookers – end of story.

15

Vegas

Sam was in a world of her own as she made her way through the usual crowds on the Las Vegas strip. Her son was with two virtual strangers in Los Angeles while she wandered around Vegas looking for the elusive Professor Paul Glen. She had just been to his hotel room but had been informed by the concierge that he had left for a medical seminar; she thanked him and followed his directions to the venue on the opposite side of the strip. She was done with beating herself up for being a bad mother – she needed to fix Adam so they could get back to being a family once more.

Sam was glad to find that she was in the right place and after a bit of digging around found that the man on stage addressing the audience was Professor Glen himself. She sat at the back of the room studying the small man on stage; he had thinning grey hair and an out-of-control beard. Before she had even spoken to him she knew she would have a task on her hands trying to get the professor to come and look at Adam. The lecture seemed to go on forever. Sam checked her watch; she was due to meet up with Fiona Malden in an hour at the Venetian, but she was sure that Fiona would wait if necessary.

The lecture eventually ended and after Professor Glen had met a few people he headed for the exit. Sam cut him off before he could escape; he listened to her story but she could tell he was not interested. She offered to pay whatever he wanted but his lack of eye contact told Sam she was fighting a losing battle. She tried again – she wanted to grab him and scream at him – but still he was not interested and he waved her off. 'My dear, your time would be better spent holding your fiancé's hand. He will need your support now and in the future – go back to him. You are wasting time here.' And the little professor headed for the door without looking back.

Sam was upset; the gamble she had taken had failed. She had wasted valuable time here; she needed to get back to the hospital and regroup.

She didn't know how she got there but after some time she found herself standing looking down into blue water and the gondolas outside the Venetian. Sam made her way inside, resisting the attempts of sales people trying to tempt tourists into their shops. She crossed a bridge and found Fiona Malden drinking coffee surrounded by tourists in what Sam reckoned was a replica of St Mark's Square. Fiona waved to Sam as she crossed the bridge, and Sam threw herself down on the seat next to her.

'Hi, Samantha, I take it you've had a hard day?'

Sam shook her head, almost in tears. 'Life was so much simpler when I only had myself to look after. Sorry, that didn't come over very well, did it? I love what I have now, it's just … life is so bloody complicated. I know Bruce will have told you what happened.'

'When you called you said you were going to try to meet up with a doctor who was in Vegas and might be able to help Adam, but your call was short and sweet. How is he doing? Bruce said he had a head injury but didn't go into any detail – that was a short but sweet call as well, come to think of it. I feel like a dummy sitting here in Vegas twiddling my thumbs – tell me about Adam.'

Sam didn't really want to talk about it; she wasn't sure if she could hold herself together and this was too public a place to have a meltdown. 'Would you mind if we headed back to your room? I could do with a freshen up, then I'll bring you up to date before I head back to the hospital.'

In the foyer of the Bellagio Hotel Daniil Litvak positioned himself in the centre seated area, making himself comfortable. His contact had been able to tell him the hotel that Agent Ellis had booked, nothing more. It was not perfect – it was the woman he was after – but Litvak knew the CIA agent would know where she was. He did not want to draw attention to himself by asking for Ellis; he decided he would wait for the agent to appear, tail him to his room, find out where the woman was, then eliminate him. There was little chance of anyone noticing him; the foyer was the hub of the hotel and the busy reception staff had enough to deal with without wondering why he was sitting there for so long.

Litvak bought a paper and observed the comings and goings of the hotel guests and staff. His main concern was that in the crowded foyer he might miss his target, although he had memorised the agent's face from his many reconnaissance trips to the ranch house; if he spotted him he would not mistake him for another. Litvak had been waiting for two hours and was about to go in search of a bathroom when two women appeared at the reception desk. He waited until they had left then approached the same receptionist they had just spoken to.

'Excuse me, but the two ladies you have just spoken with – one of them has just dropped her credit card. I am heading to my room – if you tell me their room number I'll drop the card with them.'

For a second the girl on the desk hesitated and Litvak thought his deception had failed.

'Our guest is in Lake View, one of the penthouses. I can get one of our porters to take the card up, sir, it's no problem—'

Before she finished the sentence Litvak was gone.

It was getting late. Bill Mathews was about to head home when his phone rang; he wanted to ignore it and get out of the office but he knew it would play on his mind all evening if he didn't answer the damned thing. With a loud sigh he picked up the receiver.

'Hello, Bill, thought I would still catch you at the office. You need to slow down and go home, old buddy.'

Bill Mathews sat back in his chair smiling to himself. 'Well, Special Agent Ellis, that is exactly where I was heading until the bloody phone rang. What can I do for you this evening?'

'I'm stuck here in the hospital with a doctor who's related to Attila the Hun – she won't let me go home so I'm making a few calls to keep me from going stir crazy. Thought I'd bring you up to speed on things here. I have a thank you for you and a kind of request you might be able to help me with. Things have been going a bit crazy over here. Sam is fine but Adam took a bit of a beating – he's okay, but he's having some memory issues because of a head wound he received. He's still getting checked out. The good news is thanks to your information we have removed a security risk with the help of your agents. I'm sure my boss will be calling your boss to thank him but I thought I would say thank you anyway. Sam and Adam are free to return when you need them once Adam is back on his feet.'

'Thanks for the update, Bruce. I'll need to have a think about things before they come back – the last I heard the Russians were still demanding we hand Sam over to them.'

There was a pause before Bruce Ellis spoke next. 'Bill, you do know, once Sam sorts her family out, no matter what you say to her she is going to go after Vadek Volkov.'

Mathews sighed. 'Yes, I know, that's why it may be better for the moment if you hang on to her for me. Not that it would be a bad thing for Volkov to meet his maker, but it can't be Sam who sends him on his way – she's in enough trouble with the Russian authorities without killing their ambassador and proving to them it was her intention all along. Anyway, enough of this, wasn't there a request? Not that I want to hurry you, but if I don't get home soon my wife will think I'm spending yet another night at the office.'

'Ah, yes. I have Major Fiona Malden here on holiday – she's due to fly home this week. I know I shouldn't mix business with pleasure, but the poor girl has been sitting waiting for me in a hotel room for most of her trip. As you can imagine, me being stuck in this damned hospital is not helping matters – do you think you could speak to her commanding officer and see if you could swing her a bit more time off so I can get out of here and spend some time showing her around? Hey, I understand it's a tall order, but it would be appreciated if you could have a word, buddy.'

Bill Mathews rang off, promising to do his best with the MOD. He grabbed his raincoat and his attaché case full of low-security-risk paperwork and headed for the door, switching off the light on a mission to get home. Just as he was about to close the door his phone rang again. He was beginning to wish he hadn't let Jean slip away on time tonight – normally she would have deflected the call away from his desk to allow him to escape. He re-entered the office, flinging his things onto the spare chair, and lifted the receiver to find the switchboard on the line.

'Good evening, sir. I have a General Alexi Mariokov holding on line one – do you want to speak to him or shall I tell him you have gone home for the evening, sir?'

Since Bill Mathews' fiery meeting with General Mariokov in Hyde Park he had heard little from the Russian Embassy, other than an email to say they had received the documents sent to them and that they would be in contact soon. Mathews had heard nothing since then but his contact in Moscow had noted more than the usual number of visits to FSB headquarters in Lubyanka Square. Also Russian navy dive teams equipped with deep-sea submersibles had visited the site of the sunken nukes, allegedly to make sure they were not damaged and leaking their contents into the sea.

This was a call that Bill Mathews would not have missed for anything; he told them he would take the call. He switched the light back on, removed his jacket, taking his time, and then sat down and pressed line one.

'Good evening, Director Mathews. I see we are both busy men working long into the night. I hope you are in good health, my friend?'

The relationship since their last meeting had apparently changed; the general was trying hard to be very pleasant. Mathews could have torn into him for not getting back to him but he decided to play the general's game.

He sat back to wait and see what this call was really about. 'I am in good health, General, as I trust are you. Are you settling into your new position at the embassy?' Mathews could almost cut the air with a knife; he sensed tension and apprehension from the general's end of the line – he was obviously not used to being diplomatic.

'I am settling in as well as a soldier can in these circumstances, but orders are orders, my friend. I would like to talk about the reason for my call this evening. It would appear that your observations made at our last meeting have some elements of truth to them. It would seem that our defence minister, aided by Vadek Volkov, colluded with the war criminal Tarek Attar to attack London. Neither Moscow nor any of her military personnel played any part in this terrorist attack, you have my word on that. Russia strongly condemns this cowardly attack and will be taking strong action against those who have betrayed Mother Russia.'

Bill Mathews stopped the general – he had reached a point where he had more than a few questions for Mariokov. 'Thank you for your frankness, General, but you must understand I need to know what action you are taking against these men. A slap on the wrist will not do, General. You must be clear about what is to happen to your defence minister, your ex-British ambassador and the Spetsnaz unit that aided them.'

There was silence for a second before the general spoke again. 'It will be announced tomorrow that Russia has a new minister of defence. Dimitri Panoz has shown his desire to work with nuclear material so I have organised a new job for him at the Zvezda shipyard dismantling nuclear submarine reactors and as a lesson, my friend, I have instructed his supervisor not to issue him with protective clothing. I think it only fair that the good defence minister find out at first-hand what he was prepared to inflict on London – they tell me he should be able to do six weeks hard labour before the radiation poisoning finishes his sentence. As for Volkov, for the moment he is in hospital in Switzerland … when he returns home I assure you he will be given a similar sentence. Anyone assisting him is now an enemy of the state and will be treated accordingly. As for Tarek Attar, he has been moved to the top of our wanted terrorist list and we will double our efforts to bring him to justice.'

'Very well, General, I will take your word on it that Russia had nothing to do with the attempted bombing and that you will keep your word on the fate of these criminals. As for Attar, we have already dealt with him – he was eliminated as he attempted to leave the country. I take it in the light of the situation you have dropped your calls for our agent to be questioned by yourselves over events at the embassy?'

Bill Mathews had let the general off lightly, both men knew it. Mathews held his breath waiting on the Russian's response.

'I think it would do neither of our great countries any good to drag this out any further, Director. I accept that your agent was doing her duty, but in future should you need to enter our embassy for any reason it must be authorised by Moscow and no one else. I look forward to our next meeting and hope that it will be on a more friendly subject. I bid you goodnight, Director Mathews.'

Bill Mathews said goodbye and hung up the phone, thinking things through. He pulled the plug out of the back of the bloody phone – it was time to go home. Yet again Samantha O'Conner had dodged the bullet; Mathews still had no idea what he was going to do with the woman, but for tonight at least he could forget about her.

Sam took the opportunity to hop into the shower while Fiona pottered about in the kitchen making coffee for them both; Sam was heading to the kitchen when there was a knock at the apartment door. Sam shouted to Fiona to ask if she was expecting anyone but the water boiling drowned out Fiona's answer. Sam undid the latch and opened the door slightly, looking out into the lobby.

She walked back into the lounge area of the penthouse carrying the biggest bunch of red roses she had ever seen.

'Fiona, the porter knocked on the door – he had these for you. There's a card with them – do I get to read it out or do you want to look at it first?'

Fiona arrived with the coffee and read the note before handing it to Sam; the flowers were from Bruce. In the note he apologised for leaving Fiona on her own and asked if Sam had met up with her. He had been tied up but hoped to get back soon, adding that he might have a surprise for her when he got back. Fiona, although she looked pleased with her flowers, changed the subject.

'Okay, Miss O'Conner, here is the coffee. Now, park your backside and tell me what's eating at you. Don't even think about saying nothing – you didn't speak a word all the way back from the Venetian and you have a face like a bulldog chewing a wasp – so spill the beans. I'm your personal agony aunt for the day.'

Sam was close to tears as she explained how Adam had no recollection of her; she raised the subject of her being a bad mother but Fiona was having none of it.

'Sam, hiding Luke for his own safety doesn't make you a bad mum – get a grip, girl. Your family need you to be strong for them right now. It's bad luck that your past has come back to haunt you, some would say it's karma, but that's the life you chose – you can't change it now – so just get on with it. I'm not talking through my arse … I know how low a person can get.

'When Paul, my first husband, was killed in Iraq I just wanted my life to end – there was no point to it anymore. But I kept my head down and got on with it and looking back at it now I know Paul would be proud of me. I've pulled many soldiers out of situations that were about to end badly and I've stopped their loved ones feeling as I did. If I die doing it well that's the life I chose.'

Sam wiped away an escaping tear before replying. 'You said Paul was your first husband – does that mean you're looking for a second one? Looks like someone has a crush on you and you've come all the way to Las Vegas to see him – do you have Brucie boy in your gunsights, Major Malden?'

Fiona Malden had a wicked smile on her face as she turned away to look out over the water and the Eiffel Tower on the opposite side of the strip, but wasn't able to hide her blushes from Sam.

'Just good friends, Samantha.'

Sam brightened up a bit – she knew she had Fiona Malden on the ropes over this one. 'Sure, Fiona, just good friends – that's why the second bedroom has never been used. Nice one … how about another cup of coffee while you think up an excuse as to why you had that twinkle in your eye as you read the note from Bruce Ellis? You've got it bad, woman – husband number two might just be on the cards, I think.'

Daniil Litvak had decided against risking anything inside the hotel; his FSB contact in the casino had informed him of the true identity of his target. Litvak was not impressed that Volkov had never mentioned the fact that the woman his team had been sent after was an MI6 agent – it may or may not have changed the outcome but for sure Litvak and his men would have been more cautious in their approach to matters. Litvak was worried that the hotel may have been set up as a trap for him and decided to back off and do a bit of recon before making any attempts.

He watched a small chubby balding man wave goodbye to the other receptionists to head home after his shift. Litvak followed him to his car and as he was about to leave climbed into the passenger seat.

The little man turned to see who had just opened his door. Litvak read the staff badge on his waistcoat as he turned to find a silenced gun pointing at his stomach.

'Drive me to your home, little man, or should I call you David? No fuss or anything stupid if you want to stay alive – do you understand?'

David was clearly not about to argue with a loaded gun and nodded to his new passenger.

After a fifteen-minute drive they pulled up at a dusty bungalow on the outskirts of the city. Daniil followed the hotel receptionist into his hall. Suddenly Litvak's prisoner made a lunge for something by the coat rack in the hall. Daniil spotted the baseball bat as it was swung at his head; he stopped the swing, which was limited in power due to the lack of space in the hall, with his left hand while using the pistol in his right hand to hit the receptionist square in the mouth. David fell onto his hall floor spitting out blood and teeth as Daniil Litvak brandished the captured bat above the unfortunate receptionist's head.

'Tell me, David, have the FBI or the police set up a trap in one of the penthouse rooms? Tell me the truth or it will become more painful.'

David's terrified eyes looked back at him blankly.

'David, do you know a man called Bruce Ellis?'

'I have no idea what you're talking about – there are no police in the hotel,' David said.

Litvak brought the bat down with a resounding crack on the top of the receptionist's left knee, shattering his kneecap. David screamed through clenched and broken teeth, then sobbed into his hall floor, begging Litvak to stop. 'Please, no, stop, there are no police, I swear. I don't know anything.'

Litvak weighed up the situation; this little man was not battle trained. Litvak was sure he was telling the truth. 'It's okay, David, sit up. I believe you. No more pain, I promise. Now sit up and pull yourself together, man.'

With some effort David pulled himself up, his damaged leg twisted under him. He was trying to move his lower leg back into position when Litvak brought the baseball bat down with full force on his now unprotected skull, killing him where he sat.

Litvak went through his pockets removing a few dollars and his car keys before dragging David's body into the kitchen. Daniil wandered round the house until he found what he was looking for in the utility room. Litvak was pretty sure the man lived alone – there were very few things that he would have considered a woman's touch – but on the off chance of a cleaner or someone coming into the house, Litvak decided to dump the receptionist's body in his chest freezer. It would stop the smell attracting the neighbours, because it would not take long in the Nevada heat for the man's body to start to decompose. Litvak cleaned up the hall floor and walls, removing the blood spatter and any signs of a struggle, then made himself a meal, lifted what cash he could find in the house, and headed back to the hotel. He was still not sure about eliminating the woman inside the hotel; even if there were no police it was too busy and had too many cameras. He needed to give himself a good chance of getting out of town before her body was discovered. One thing was for sure – he knew he couldn't waste too much time and lose her again. The attack would have to be soon.

Sam had wanted to leave for the hospital that evening but Fiona talked her into having supper and staying the night, then heading back fresh in the morning. Sam sorted her hair and touched up her make-up while Fiona booked a table. She returned to the lounge ready to head out as Fiona hung up the phone.

'The table is booked, Sam. That was Bruce on the phone – he's wangled some kind of deal with the MOD. It would appear I'm on loan to the CIA as some kind of special advisor … he must have a bit of power to pull that off. He was asking how you got on with the professor. I told him, and said you were heading back to the hospital first thing in the morning but not before I got you pissed tonight.'

Sam smiled as she lifted her handbag. 'Let's go then. Looks like I'm going to be dining with Major Fiona Malden, special advisor to the Pentagon – you'll need to ask if you get a salary increase with the job. Maybe you could stay out here for good?'

Sam followed Fiona out of the hotel. She was shocked at the temperature; even with the sun vanishing over the dusty horizon the air they breathed was still hot – whoever thought up the plan to building a city in the middle of a desert must have been at least half mad. Sam and Fiona crossed over a footbridge high above the Vegas strip; even as evening arrived the crowds and the traffic remained constant. The concierge of the Bellagio had been correct with his opening statement as Sam had arrived: 'Welcome to the city that never sleeps.'

Fiona led the way, navigating through the barrage of ticket touts and beggars who lined the sidewalks of the desert oasis. On the far side of the strip a huge man-made volcano complete with fire roared into the desert night; Sam was so busy looking at the volcano that for a second she lost sight of Fiona and turned 360 degrees until she spotted her by the doorway to a restaurant, waving to her to follow.

Once inside, out of the heat and the crowds, Fiona headed up to the second floor were their table awaited them. While Fiona ordered cocktails Sam sat in a world of her own; something was bugging her, something that had just happened. She couldn't put her finger on it and sat analysing the last few minutes in her head; she had seen something – or someone – that had triggered something in her subconscious mind.

She came to as Fiona engaged her in conversation; she was saying something over the music but Sam had not picked it up first time.

'You were away on your own little planet there – I said I've ordered you a cocktail I think you'll like, but knowing what you are, you'd probably prefer a vodka Martini, shaken not stirred.'

Fiona laughed at her own joke and Sam smiled, but her mind was still analysing the last few moments outside on the sidewalk.

The waiter appeared, muscles rippling as he handed over the two cocktails and took the girls' orders for supper. Fiona ordered two more cocktails, clearly intent on getting Sam to relax and enjoy the meal.

'What do you think, Sam?'

With some effort Sam replied, still thinking. 'Yeah, good, is it *crème de menthe* that's in it?'

Fiona was laughing again. Sam had been so distracted – she realised it was the young waiter Fiona was talking about, not the drink.

'Sorry, I thought you were talking about the cocktail. Yes, nice body, he looks like he could lift a ton, but I doubt if he could spell it. Not my cup of tea, sorry.'

Fiona rolled her eyes. 'Samantha, no one is asking you to sleep with him, it's just a bit of eye candy to go with the meal. Loosen up, girl, for god's sake.'

As the meal progressed and the alcohol took effect Sam relaxed a little, forcing herself to let go of her concerns. The pair talked about Bruce and Adam and what the future held, but Sam found it hard to look into the future, not knowing how Adam would recover from his head wound.

Sam soon wanted to head back; tomorrow was going to be a busy day and she did not need a hangover to go with it. Fiona excused herself to visit the ladies' and square off the bill. Automatically Sam's thoughts returned to earlier events; for some reason her mind took a step back in time: she was back at Vauxhall Cross and Bill Mathews was telling her to memorise some faces because her life might depend on it.

Suddenly her memory kick-started as if given an electric shock: a face from the pictures jumped out at her, then she remembered the man in the grey T-shirt who was half turned away from her as she looked for Fiona in the crowd. Her agent's mind had clocked the actions of someone trying to make themselves look invisible, and it had almost worked ... the man on the sidewalk was one of the men from the pictures. The Russians were here. Sam was worried; for the second time in only months she found herself confronted by an enemy and no gun to back her up. Her mind was racing as Fiona rejoined her.

'Are you okay Sam? You're a bit pale?'

Sam said nothing, grabbing her handbag and heading for the exit at some speed with Fiona trailing in her wake.

She walked out into the busy sidewalk then turned to wait for Fiona. She stepped back into the doorway just as Fiona arrived – her action had been planned and had allowed her to check who was outside. She grabbed Fiona by the arm and pushed her back into the entrance hall of the restaurant.

'We have a big problem ... you need to listen to me and do exactly as I say. We are being tailed by the Russians – they're outside right now. I want you to walk with me for a bit then lag behind so I can turn to hurry you up – act drunk – it will let me turn and check who's following without giving away that their cover is blown. When I squeeze your hand I want you to get away from me – they're not after you. If you stay in busy public places you should be safe, and when you're sure you are safe call Bruce and tell him to send the cavalry. Do not, I repeat do not go back to your hotel room until Bruce sends help. We need to go before our Russian tail becomes suspicious.'

Sam led a shaken Fiona Malden out onto the sidewalk, turning to make sure Fiona was in her footsteps and checking that grey T-shirt was still there; he was studying the volcano on the other side of the strip. Sam's brain raced as she walked; she was angry that she had dropped her guard and taken alcohol – she needed a clear head.

This was not some small-time drug dealer; Spetsnaz operatives were to be treated with great respect. They were well trained and fanatical about their missions; Sam had picked a deadly opponent to tangle with this time.

She forced herself to stop panicking. She had to outwit her Russian friend, and the first thing she needed to know was if he was alone.

She had to perform a number of moves and observe the people around her before she could take a calculated guess as to how many she was up against. The opinion of Homeland Security was that only one Russian had escaped the ranch house attack, but Sam was pretty sure there must be others; if not soldiers there must be some type of backup for a unit operating so far from home. Sam had turned to talk to Fiona a few times – she was doing a good job of looking tipsy – and checked that grey T-shirt was in tow with them. He was tucked up behind a huddle of tourists some distance back, working the crowds to his advantage. Sam stopped outside Harrah's Hotel and squeezed Fiona's hand to let her know it was time for her to get out of the hunt.

'Time to go and do some gambling, Fiona. Remember what I told you.'

Fiona was pale but smiled at her. 'For god's sake, Sam, be careful. I'm shaking like a leaf here.'

Sam squeezed her hand, giving her a hug and whispering into her ear. 'I'll be fine – this is what I do. You fly helicopters, I kill people. Now go and call the cavalry for me.' Sam walked away without looking back, giving Fiona a wave as she left.

Daniil Litvak watched the dark-haired girl head off into the casino before returning his attention to Samantha O'Conner. If she took one of the side alleys he would have her; he could tell by her walk that she had been drinking heavily. If the worst came to the worst he would have to follow her to her room and eliminate her there, but he was hoping to finish his task in a dark doorway or car park. He rotated the handle of his commando dagger in his pocket impatiently as he watched the woman make her way through the sea of beggars.

She crossed over a side road then continued straight on. For a second Litvak was confused; if she was going back to the Bellagio she should have turned right and crossed the strip by the second road bridge, but she kept on going. She was either going someplace else or was so drunk she had missed the bridge. Suddenly she turned back, cursing to herself. Litvak threw himself on the ground between two sleeping beggars, curling up in a ball as his target staggered passed.

Sam checked out the shop windows, watching the reflection of grey T-shirt and those around him. So far she hadn't picked out any other targets; grey T-shirt had not been replaced by a stand-in, which pointed to him possibly operating alone, but she wasn't sure yet … she would play the game a little further before deciding on a course of action. As she walked she searched her handbag for a weapon – no nail files, scissors or anything. Only the ring box in the bottom of her bag gave her some hope.

She opened the box inside her handbag and slipped the ring on; it gave her a slight feeling of comfort to know she was wearing her favourite piece of jewellery.

For a second she thought she had lost her tail but just as her heart began to race she spotted him lying between two sleeping men pretending to be a down and out. Sam crossed the bridge, looking down to see the space he had been occupying was now vacant. She was almost certain now that the Russian was working alone.

Reaching the opposite side of the strip Sam walked towards the Bellagio lake. Outside the hotel she started hatching what normally she would have considered as a very risky plan. She knew if she entered the hotel the Russian would have no option but to act; if she waited outside she still held the element of surprise.

She propped herself up against the railings surrounding the pond, and was quickly aware of someone to her right. She glanced round to find the Russian not far from her staring into the water. Sam tensed up, flexing her fingers in anticipation of the attack just as a group of tourists moved in between them ready for the Bellagio's evening fountain show.

In the heat of things Sam had forgotten about the fountains and, as if on cue, the spotlights and music started. People flocked from the sidewalk to witness the nightly spectacle performed by the dancing fountains accompanied by floodlights and music, one of the few beautiful things that Vegas had managed to achieve in its miles of concrete in the desert.

Sam grabbed the chance with both hands, slipping back behind the crowd then cutting back into them directly behind grey T-shirt, pushing her way to the front where she hoped the Russian was still standing.

Grey T-shirt had been taken by surprise as the fountains kicked into life. He was hemmed in by the sudden surge of tourists to the railings and seemed about to try to make his way out when Sam arrived beside him and wrapped her arm around his neck … it took a fraction of a second for recognition to appear in his eyes. She could feel his grip tighten on something in his pocket but he was too late; she smiled, looking at him with her own cold, grey, deadly eyes.

The Russian was so occupied with the situation he could not have noticed the tiny prick behind his right ear caused by the tiny needles on the underside of Sam's ring. As a result, NLB7 would course through his veins causing every muscle in his body to instantly enter a state of paralysis; he was awake – he just could not move, not even to blink. Sam had won; she propped his body up by the railings as the music burst into Ennio Morricone's 'The Good, the Bad and the Ugly'.

Sam cuddled into the Russian intent on looking every bit the loving couple as she searched his pockets for a weapon. She removed the razor-sharp dagger from his lifeless fingers.

The crowd were captivated by the beauty of the fountains as they danced to the timeless classic western's music.

Sam had used the nerve agent supplied by the boffins at Vauxhall Cross before, and knew the drug would last for twenty-four hours. She could hand the Russian over to the CIA, but he was just one more nightmare that could come back to haunt her. She whispered in his ear as she turned the dagger upwards. 'Time to go to hell, my friend. When you get there be sure to keep a place for your boss Volkov because as sure as day follows night, he is next.'

Sam stared into the Russian's eyes as she pushed the dagger upwards. Her own eyes never flickered as the knife cut under his ribcage. She twisted the blade in his heart to make sure not even the most talented surgeon could repair his torn organs, then cleaned the knife on his T-shirt and wiped her hands. She slipped the blade into her handbag just as the music finished and the fountains died down, then turned with the ebbing crowds and walked away in the direction of the Bellagio's side entrance. As she entered a woman screamed down by the pond. Sam never looked back as she made her way through the hotel lobby. In the ladies' room she calmly cleaned herself up and checked her appearance in the mirrors, then headed back out into the lobby. Outside the music from the fountain display was drowned out by sirens and shouting. Sam wanted to head up to her room but she was still not sure if the assassin by the fountain was alone, so she decided to play it safe and keep an eye on who was coming and going from the busy hotel.

As her adrenalin levels returned to normal she started to feel cold and tired; tonight's dice with death would have broken the resolve of some people, but it had proved to Sam that she was MI6 first and a mother second. She had missed the adrenalin highs of being an MI6 operative; being a mum gave her a warm glow inside, but when you had lived on the edge as Sam had done for so long the quiet life was difficult to get used to.

Some considerable time later Bruce, with Fiona hot on his heels, entered the hotel lobby heading straight for the penthouse, presumably searching for her. Sam waved, catching Fiona's eye, and the pair rushed towards her through the busy lobby. Bruce stopped a manager and showed him his badge and credentials and minutes later Sam was ushered into an office where they could talk without fear of being overheard.

Fiona was the first to speak as she gave Sam an unexpected hug as. 'Thank god you're okay. Did the bastard touch you? I was worried sick – how you do this shit I will never know.'

Sam was about to reply as Fiona relaxed her grip but Bruce wanted answers and cut in before the two women could continue.

'Sam, I have the strip crawling with FBI agents. We have one dead male by the fountains – were there more following you?'

Sam shook her head. 'No, I don't think so. I worked my tail pretty hard – no one relieved him and I saw him signal no one. I'm ninety-nine per cent certain he was alone. Volkov has failed once more – there will be no next time, I'm going to make damned sure of it.'

Bruce cursed quietly while Fiona looked on in bewilderment. Sam knew why he was unhappy but understood why Fiona hadn't got it yet. Fiona came from a different background, but Sam was streetwise; she knew that Bruce was raging because she had killed someone who could have unearthed further Russian spy networks – or there was always the possibility of turning them into a double agent. Sam's job was a nasty one but spooks, whatever country they worked for, had no scruples: they would do anything to achieve their goal, including letting a killer go free in exchange for information.

'Sam, I'm pretty sure someone helped Agent X and these men who came here for you. Did you really have to kill this one? He could have had valuable information we could have extracted.'

Sam had half expected the lecture but after the night she had been through and the worry about Adam it was too much. She exploded at the unsuspecting CIA special agent.

'Maybe one of your agents would have hung around and bought him a coffee while they waited for the cavalry to arrive, but I don't work like that.' Sam rumbled about in her handbag and pulled out the commando knife. In one fluid action she sent it whistling through the air, missing Bruce's right ear by inches before it buried itself in a noticeboard behind him. For a second there was a stunned silence before she continued. 'Excuse me for not giving a shit about your information network – I was too busy trying to stop a professional killer cutting my throat with that little beauty. I took him out cleanly and quietly with no collateral damage in the middle of a crowd of tourists.

'Before you start shouting your mouth off, Bruce, ask yourself how they found us. Tell me how you managed to get a penthouse suite at the height of tourist season – did you do your little CIA trick and flash your badge and your eyes at the staff to get the room? Maybe if you'd done your job instead of trying to impress your new girlfriend you would still have someone to question. Now get out of my way before I get the urge to use the knife for a second time tonight. I'm going to bed. I need to get back to my partner who is struggling to recover from another attack that happened on your watch.'

She threw the office door open and stormed out leaving Bruce and Fiona in stunned silence. Tears were welling up; her emotions had overtaken her once more.

Sam woke the next morning to the smell of strong coffee. She was not feeling her best as she headed to the kitchen to find Fiona up and making breakfast.

'Hi, sleepy, the toast is on and so is the coffee. We need to get a move on – my boyfriend, as you so delicately put it last night, has a chopper waiting to take us to the hospital as soon as you're ready to move, so eat up and get moving.'

An hour later, after passing on the toast, Sam and Fiona were airborne watching Las Vegas vanish below them as the Bell helicopter climbed into the desert sky. Sam could see Fiona was finding it strange to be in a helicopter but not flying it, possibly a sign of things to come, although she knew Fiona would resist any attempt at trying to give her a desk job. Sam remained quiet for the rest of the trip; she was still not feeling at her best, and the thought of what she would find with Adam did nothing to help. She prayed for an improvement in Adam's condition.

16

Mac

The flight was short and on landing Sam was surprised to be ushered into the hospital by waiting FBI agents. Bruce, fresh from his ear-bending the previous night, met Sam in the corridor and stopped her from entering Adam's room. 'Sam, we better hold up here for a minute. Professor Glen is just finishing a few tests on Adam, he'll be out shortly.'

Sam was at a loss for a second. 'Professor Paul Glen? But he refused to help – what the hell is he doing here now?'

Bruce Ellis exchanged knowing glances with Fiona Malden before he spoke again. 'You gave me a hard time last night, but not as hard a time as your pal Fiona. It would also seem you have a fan in the White House. I briefed the President on events down here last night, including your Vegas adventure. He was concerned that we had overstepped the mark with your family. On behalf of the President I would like to apologise for dragging you and your family through the mill over this operation … it was the President who last night contacted Professor Glen and explained that he needed his help with Adam – you have some heavy hitters on your team now, that's for sure.'

Before Sam could answer, the door to Adam's room opened and Professor Glen and two doctors emerged. The professor spoke for a second with the doctors then turned to Bruce, Sam and Fiona. He nodded to acknowledge Sam's presence but stopped short of saying hello; instead he addressed them as a group. 'I have examined Adam's file, and of course Adam. The good news is he is healing well and I would expect him physically to make a full recovery. Mentally he is confused by his loss of memory.

'With help, patience and the passage of time, I think Adam will make a recovery, but the brain is both fragile and remarkable, so even for me it would be a guess how much of a recovery. I have spoken to the doctors and we're changing Adam's medication and his diet. In time this should help a little. I have some information on brain exercise and therapy which I'll pass to the doctors, but I recommend that Adam goes home. He needs to be in a place that will jog his memory, not here in a hospital surrounded by strangers – but no flying, not for the next six months. I would recommend a cruise ship so Adam can get to know you again.'

Professor Glen did not hang about, advising that he would recheck Adam in a year's time to assess his condition.

Sam was miles away in her own little world as she entered the hospital room. Although Adam looked much better and the swelling around his eyes had gone, Sam still found it difficult to make conversation with a person she had lived and breathed with for the last six years, but was now a stranger with a familiar face. She dug around in her handbag and produced a picture of Luke; she reckoned this would be a good icebreaker for them both. Adam studied the picture of a son he didn't know; Sam could tell he was upset and was trying hard to remember the cheeky little face that stared up at him from the photo.

'Samantha, he's lovely – he looks so much like his mother. I find it hard to believe I have a lovely wife and son and can't remember a thing. I'm sorry for causing all this trouble – where is Luke now?'

Sam squeezed Adam's hand. 'He's safe. I sent him away to Los Angeles. We'll get you up on your feet and then we'll go and get him together – he'll be missing his daddy.'

For the next hour Sam answered Adam's questions. She was careful to steer clear of explaining either of their past working lives – things were too complicated for Adam's wounded brain to burden it further with the knowledge that they had been and still were MI6 operatives.

Sam was in the process of trying to explain to Adam that they weren't married when the hospital room door opened wide and Bruce and Fiona entered, followed by Lauren with Luke perched on her shoulders. Sam could see Bruce was shattered – he looked fit to drop. Sam was not surprised when after only a short time Fiona took charge and ushered him out of the room. It was clear to see he was not fully recovered from his plane crash.

Sam was relieved that the room was starting to empty. She had been watching Adam, who was struggling to cope with all the new faces in the room. He talked to Luke, who sat on the end of the bed glowering at his father while Sam hugged Lauren and thanked her for all her help. Although glad to see her wee boy back where he belonged, Sam was struggling with strange emotions. In her head she was trying to pull herself together but for some reason she was jealous that her time alone with Adam had been interrupted.

It was madness, but the hour she had spent with Adam had almost felt like a first date. They hadn't had a first date before because of the unusual way they had met; they had never shared that experience. Sam felt in the last hour she had reformed a bond with Adam, but the intimacy of the moment had been shattered with the arrival of junior and co.

Luke stole the show, as he had a habit of doing, when he announced to all present in the room that Dada had a painted face, pointing to the black-and-blue bruises around Adam's eyes. After a few minutes Lauren excused herself and left in search of Cheveyo, who had travelled back with them from LA.

Sam and Luke stayed with Adam until two doctors accompanied by a nurse arrived to run more tests. Sam excused herself and headed to the waiting room. Fiona and Lauren took custody of Luke and went in search of ice cream for the toddler. Sam decided this was the perfect time to hatch a plan that had been building at the back of her mind since she arrived at the hospital. She did not want to try to rebuild a shattered family while looking over her shoulder for the next attempt on their lives by Volkov; she needed to take control of the situation and finish this madness before she would feel safe enough to relax with her son and partner once more.

Sam found Bruce Ellis nursing a huge mug of coffee while studying a laptop in the hospital canteen.

'Hi, Sam, how is your better half getting on … any progress?'

Sam pulled up a chair and sat down opposite Bruce. 'Hmm, he's almost someone I don't know – we need to get him home. That's why I'm here – I need you to organise a few things for me. I need Adam, Luke and Lauren booked on a sailing to the UK and I need a flight as soon as possible to Dublin.'

Bruce had been glancing at his laptop while Sam spoke; it was only when she mentioned Dublin that he looked up.

'Dublin? Why not cut to the chase and fly into Switzerland? You and I both know that's where you're headed. Karma's a bitch – Vadek Volkov sent a team to assassinate you and it ends up with him being hunted by arguably the West's deadliest assassin, the very person he tried to assassinate. I take it from your route you know the Swiss police still want to question you about the massacre of the gun dealer and his men at his castle? They don't know who you are, but I know they have CCTV pictures of you. Six has obviously pulled your Interpol file to protect you.

'A word of advice, Sam. Do what you have to do, but do it quietly. You've already caused a political storm by attacking the Russian Embassy – don't make Bill Mathews have to explain himself to the Swiss government, he can only take the heat for you for so long.

'Of course, Switzerland and America being close friends, my superiors will not let me help you. For example, I can never tell you that Volkov is staying at a private hospital in Lucerne situated on Sankt Niklausen Strasse, so don't ask because I won't tell you.

'Now, I suggest you go and talk to Lauren. She was just telling me she's about to head back to LA. You get her and the Navajo boy sorted and I'll sort out your travel arrangements. You owe me big, Samantha.'

Sam stood up, pushing her chair back under the table. 'No, Bruce. We helped catch Agent X – we are even, my friend.'

Sam turned and was about to walk away when a thought struck her. 'Does LA have a university that offers law?'

Bruce nodded. 'UCLA Law, why?'

'Bruce, I need you to pull some strings and get Cheveyo a place. I will pay for his course, and before you say a word, we are still even. Just remember, I'll be going home with a partner who paid a high price for your success.' Sam walked away without waiting for a reply.

Cheveyo and Lauren sat in stunned silence while Sam outlined what she wanted to do. Sam was praying that her plan would work; she was pretty sure Cheveyo would go for it but it all rested on what Lauren thought about it.

Eventually the silence was broken by Lauren. 'Okay, Sam, let me get this right – you want me to come back to Scotland with you to be your PA-cum-nanny. This will be for a minimum of four years. Cheveyo will rent my apartment in LA while he studies at UCLA Law.'

Lauren stopped for a second. Sam could almost see her mind working things out – no doubt there would have to be some bargaining done if she was interested in the proposal.

'Okay, Sam, you're on, but I have a list of must-haves before I say a definite yes. A salary of fifty thousand pounds a year, a car, a house, and the rent money for my apartment in LA at the going rate.'

Sam knew Lauren was no fool; she also knew that back in Scotland she could employ someone for half the fee Lauren wanted, but she liked her and she needed her now, not just anyone back in Scotland.

'Your prices are a shade on the high side, Lauren, but okay, fifty grand and the rent for your apartment. You buy your own car and we sort you out with a house. We'll loan you transport and put you up in our home until we build you a house – we live on the top of a cliff and there are no houses nearby. Deal?'

Lauren at first said nothing while Sam and Cheveyo waited for her answer; her mind made up she turned to Cheveyo. 'If you even think about having a student party in my apartment I will be on the first flight back and I'll use that tomahawk of yours to remove your man bits. Do we understand each other, young man?'

Cheveyo grinned, apparently hardly able to believe his good fortune. Sam bent down and pulled a cloth-wrapped object from her handbag; she unwrapped it and handed over the shining tomahawk to Cheveyo. He tried to stop her but she insisted.

'Cheveyo, when Adam lay in the forest, his life draining away and unable to call for help, it was the moon shining on the tomahawk that led us to him. I'm sure that's why Adam was given the weapon. Just think what it's called: Life and Death. It saved Adam's life.

'We're finished here and are going home. Remember the story of your relic: it has been passed from one Native American to another, to brave men who carried the hopes of a nation on their shoulders. Take the tomahawk and use the knowledge of law to help your people, then you will be the worthy custodian of Life and Death. Old Joe had second sight – he knew it would find its way back to you. Honour him and your people and live up to the challenge ahead.'

It took until the next afternoon for Bruce Ellis to comply with all Samantha O'Conner's demands. Sam used the time to walk in the grounds with Adam and Luke, Adam stopping every twenty paces to ask Sam another question about the past while Luke clung to his leg like a puppy. While Adam was undergoing a final scan to recheck his frontal lobe damage Sam sought out Bruce who had managed to scrounge the use of an administration office where he could check on his work and the ongoing repairs to his poor old ranch house.

'Ah, there you are, Samantha. Boy, did you set me some tasks. Listen up – here's the timetable. Adam, Luke, Lauren and Cheveyo will be taken to LA along with Adam's nurse, who has agreed to accompany him as far as the ship. I've booked them on an Amtrak train with a holiday company … they'll travel from LA to San Francisco, then Denver, Chicago and then New York. It stops in each city so Adam can rest. The next stage of the journey is aboard the *Queen Mary 2*. She leaves from New York in ten days' time, giving Adam and the team a day to recover from his rail journey. The ship gets into Southampton seven days later – do you think you'll be back from your little trip by then to meet them and get them home? Oh, by the way, when they drop Cheveyo off in LA he has an interview at UCLA Law that evening, so not bad organisation, you see. I think I should go into the travel business – life might be a bit safer for me, don't you think?'

Sam bent over and gave Bruce a peck on the cheek before turning and heading for the door, where she turned on her toes as Bruce called her back. 'You need to go and say your goodbyes, by the way, your flight from LA to Dublin leaves tomorrow morning – you need to leave here in a couple of hours.'

Sam's first instincts were to find Luke and go to Adam, but she needed her business head on for the moment. She found a payphone and made an overseas call to France; she wanted to have things in place for her arrival in Ireland. It only took a few minutes to sort. Her next call was to an old contact of her sister's in Ireland – all she needed to know was that she was still around. Sam would sort out the details once in Ireland – she didn't want to broadcast her business to the wrong people.

Content for the moment she had done all she could she headed for Adam's room. She was still not sure what she was going to tell him as she entered the room; she didn't want to lie to him but at this stage in his rehabilitation she wasn't sure if he could handle the truth.

Adam smiled as Sam entered the room; he patted the side of his bed for her to join him and she obliged. She was still searching for the right way to tell him she was leaving.

'Samantha, does that look mean bad news – are you okay?'

Sam smiled, avoiding eye contact. Adam very rarely called her Samantha, it was a symptom of his brain injury, and once again she felt she was in the presence of a stranger. She brushed his mop of dark hair away from his bruised forehead; other than the discolouration it had returned to its normal shape and size.

'You've lost your Frankenstein forehead – you're tall, dark and handsome once again. I have some good news: you're going home in style – a train trip then a cruise ship across the Atlantic. Should be good fun.'

Adam had been watching Sam closely and removed her hand from his hair and clasped it between his hands on his lap. 'Listen, Samantha, I may have lost my memory but I'm not a complete idiot I note that I am going on a boat trip, not we are going on a boat trip. I take it you have something else you want to tell me – something I sense you're struggling with. Listen, I get it that you never signed up for looking after me. If you want to cut and run I understand – better to do it now. I hope that helps with your Dear John speech you're about to make.'

Sam's mood lifted on hearing what Adam was thinking; it made her task somewhat easier than she had previously thought. 'You are an idiot, a big Scottish idiot. No one is leaving anyone. I do need to deal with a couple of problems, so while you relax and let that brain of yours recover, I'm going to sort out things then meet you when you get off the boat in Southampton. You might have forgotten for the moment but let me remind you we have a son and we're in love. Get to know your son on the boat trip and you can get to know me again once we get home to the glass house.'

Adam squeezed her hand. 'Okay, Samantha, you're the boss.'

Sam found herself once more brushing away tears as she hugged little Luke; her driver had arrived to take her to the helicopter for her flight to Los Angeles and then her flight to Ireland.

Sam finally handed Luke over to Lauren; she was struggling to find the words to say to her. Lauren spotted Sam was too choked up to speak and came to her rescue.

'Don't you worry about the two men in your life. I'll take care of them both until you get back – just make sure you do make it back. Don't do anything daft, woman, remember your family and my money. Now, enough of the tears – you've got a job to do. Go, before I change my mind about going back to rainy Scotland for four years.'

Sam managed to give Fiona and Lauren a quick hug before being whisked away to the waiting chopper. Hopefully the next time she saw her family it would be when she picked them up in Southampton.

17

Ireland

The helicopter flight was uneventful and Sam picked up her connection to Ireland with time to spare; it was only once the flight was underway that she had time to think of her moves in Ireland. It had been many years since she had talked to Martha O'Donnell; once upon a time she had been her sister Mary's handler in Ireland and after Mary had been assassinated she had become a mother figure to Sam whenever her work took her to Ireland. Sam did not want MI6 involved in what she was about to do so – she was praying Martha could help her without involving Bill Mathews and the team at Six.

As arranged Sam made her way through customs using the false identity of an American police officer who was on vacation. She avoided the CCTV cameras where possible; when she had to pass one she made sure her LA Dodgers baseball cap was pulled down low over her eyes. Sam made her way past the inevitable rows of shops but before heading for the rendezvous point she visited the toilets, using the privacy of a cubicle to swap tops, lost the baseball cap and ponytail and added glasses. Her body language changed from tourist wandering along to businesswoman in a rush. Sam had been away from the sharp end of the spy trade for some years, but her training kicked in as if it was yesterday. Sam bought a paper and ordered a latte; she used the paper to shield her face while scanning the people around her for any sign of Martha or any unwanted attention.

Sam spotted the old woman making her way towards her and for a second she dismissed her; but when she smiled and reached out Sam realised that Martha had arrived. Sam hadn't seen her for almost twenty years and it took her a few seconds to adjust to the older Martha in front of her.

'Hello, kid, long time no see – you still working for that shower of conniving bastards in London?'

Sam smiled; she may have been older, but Martha's sharp tongue had lost none of its unique style. 'On and off, Martha. I'm trying to give it up, it's a bad habit, but I'm on my own on this trip – just me, no governments involved.'

Martha nodded, looking around the coffee shop as she spoke. 'Come on, girl, let's get out of here before some Paddy with a grudge and a sharp eye makes us. My car's outside – follow me.'

Sam was not sure which type of Paddy Martha was referring to. Martha was born in America to Irish parents; her mother was Catholic and her father Protestant, which was the main reason they'd left their homeland. Martha, like Sam, had lost her parents at an early age. It was the CIA who returned Martha to her homeland and the CIA who exchanged her with MI6; Martha had never been a true British agent, preferring to play the field with all parties and looking after her own interests first, a dangerous tightrope to walk during the troubles.

Sam was not that impressed with Martha's mode of transport as she left Dublin Airport. Luckily for Sam the road trip did not take long. She studied River Valley Road in the village of Swords as Martha O'Donnell parked the battered old Micra in front of a respectable home on the edge of a park. Once inside Martha busied herself making coffee while Sam made herself comfortable in the lounge, shouting through to the kitchen to compliment Martha on her choice of watercolour pictures hanging on the walls.

Martha appeared, carrying a tray with coffee and homemade cake. 'Right then, Samantha, cut out the bullshit and tell me why after all these years I'm now your number one friend.'

Sam knew better than to hold out on Martha; she needed her to do a little job for her, one that Martha excelled at.

'I need you to do me a French passport and I need a new face for it, and I need it within the next twenty-four hours. I have a plane to catch tomorrow.'

Martha scoffed at the suggestion, rolling her eyes to the heavens before replying. 'Those days were long ago. I deal in rare art now – you've come to the wrong person, young lady.'

Sam reached down and retrieved a white envelope from her handbag, slapping it down on the coffee table and letting the notes inside spill onto the tea tray.

'Five thousand pounds can buy a lot of paintings, don't you think?'

Martha picked up the envelope and scooped the money back into it. 'It's not easy to fake a passport these days, you know, it takes skill and some very special equipment.'

Sam smiled sweetly before her next comment. 'You know, Martha, I can remember reading a file at Six about a raid on some nasty terrorists who were doing naughty things with that very type of equipment. Funnily enough I believe it was you who raised the alarm. They found lots of grade A forged passports, but the equipment was never found. Six were going to look into it but the file went missing – I may have misplaced it. Shame it was never backed up on computer … looks like I'm the only one who can do anything about it.'

Martha knew she had been outmanoeuvred and the look on her face confirmed the fact. 'Okay, madam, you've made your point. I take the money and you destroy the file. I do your papers and we are even, deal?'

Sam smiled, shaking her head. 'No deal. You get the five thou and I keep the file out of the way – you never know when I might need your services again. You're too valuable, so I'll keep the file as a type of retainer, deal?'

Martha rolled her eyes but Sam knew she had her in checkmate. 'Your big sister would have been proud of you. That bastard Andrews taught you too well, god rest his twisted soul.'

After tea Sam followed Martha upstairs to one of the bedrooms. Sam watched in the mirror as Martha cut away her blonde locks, trimmed her short hair then dyed it red and added the final touch – coloured contact lenses, changing her eyes to a deep green. It wasn't until the transformation was complete that both women realised they had created a carbon copy of Mary, Sam's older sister. Sam studied herself in the mirror, saying nothing about the haunting image that looked back at her from the grave.

Martha was not so silent. 'Jesus, pet, I didn't mean to do that, but as god is my witness Mary O'Conner has come back to life. No time to change it, now let's get your passport pictures done for you.'

Martha worked on the European Union French passport while Sam brushed up on events through the news channels. After two hours Sam had a new French passport, driving licence and fake credit cards; her new identity was Marie Delamere, a senior nurse working for Médecins Sans Frontières. Martha had stamped the passport to show Marie Delamere had visited some of the darkest places on earth, among them Rwanda, Sierra Leone, Uganda, Yemen and Libya. Sam's new passport read like a list of all the places in the world any sane person would avoid, but it gave her identity papers credibility. Sam studied Martha's handiwork looking for flaws but, as she had expected, there were none. When it came to forgery Martha prided herself on her work, coming as close to the real thing as possible.

Martha watched in horror as Sam dropped the passport on the floor of the kitchen, using her foot to scrub it into the ground. Sam spotted Martha's look of disbelief.

'Nice work, Martha, but it's too new. My passport would be well worn if I'd visited all these hellholes, don't you think?'

Martha smiled for the first time. 'You know, Samantha, Mary would have been proud of you. You have proved over the years you're just as smart as your big sister. Now do yourself a favour, girl, and prove you're smarter than her – get out of this fool's game while you're still alive. It's the one thing your sister never managed, god rest her soul.'

As planned, Frederick le Combe waited by the car rental desk people watching as he waited for his VIP passenger to arrive. Dublin airport was not a place he had been for some time and his memory of Sam was fading – he hadn't seen her in four years. He was still looking for the blonde Samantha when a stunning redhead tapped him on the shoulder. It took Fred a second to realise the redhead standing in front of him was Samantha O'Conner.

'My word, young lady, you've changed so much and so sophisticated now. Tell me, are you still a photographic model?' Fred had a twinkle in his eye as he spoke; he had worked out long ago that Sam was far from a model. He had never pursued the matter further, preferring to go with the saying 'ignorance is bliss'.

Sam winked at Fred. 'Too old for that now. I run my own model agency now and I have a shoot in Switzerland. Did you manage to find me transport to get me from the airfield to the shoot?'

Fred nodded, picking up Sam's luggage and heading for the exit. 'All sorted, young lady, now let's get moving and we can talk more once in the air, yes?'

General Mariokov was tired of waiting for his dinner guest and made the executive decision of ordering for them both. He did not need to look at the menu of his favourite Moscow restaurant; while in England he had been deprived of his favourite food and was determined to make up for lost time. The general ordered two large portions of blini topped with sour cream and ground steak mince; he was secretly hoping Lev Aristov was not a lover of his favourite pancakes and would leave them for his second helping, but minutes after the waiter left Lev Aristov arrived. Mariokov did not like the man but he had to admit that Aristov's track record was impressive – as section leader of the FSB's black unit he had overseen many Russian undercover operations. Although he held the military rank of colonel, he was a quiet man who preferred to work alone with the minimum of help from his team. His father was Russian and his mother German, which meant that Lev had a German passport and could travel through Europe unhindered. Interpol had never discovered that Russia had a hit man with immaculate European credentials – a huge bonus the Kremlin had used to their advantage on numerous occasions.

Without even looking at the menu Lev Aristov came straight to the point. 'Good afternoon, General Mariokov. I believe you have requested my assistance. What can I do for you today?'

Mariokov tossed over a computer memory stick then took a sip of his water before explaining. 'Comrade Aristov, the memory device is code-word protected. On the device you will find the FSB files of two people. I have spoken with our premier and we are in agreement that for the good of our country these two must be eliminated. Your primary target is Vadek Volkov ... he has brought our country into disrepute. The premier has asked me to warn you that this man has information that could compromise our government, and will use it if he finds out he is our target, therefore it is imperative that when you move to eliminate him you must carry it through and make sure you are successful.

'The second person is the British agent who desecrated our embassy in London. The British secret service think we have lost interest in her, which should make your task a little easier. Obviously the Kremlin cannot be seen to be targeting British agents, so you must be tactful when you eliminate the woman. Latest intelligence on the agent has her travelling to Ireland on an American passport. Concentrate on Volkov for the moment and we will keep an eye on the woman until you are ready to deal with her.'

As Mariokov finished speaking the waiter arrived with the two portions of blini.

Aristov got to his feet, scooped up the memory stick and placed it in his inside pocket. 'Very good, General. I shall get to work on the project immediately. I will leave you to your lunch – good day, sir.'

'Aristov, can I not interest you in a spot of lunch?'

Lev Aristov shook his head, turning and walking away without speaking.

Vadek Volkov roared at the top of his voice; he had woken in a foul mood, screaming at the nurse as she attempted to help him dress. His left side was weak and that, combined with his shattered right ankle, made him for the moment wheelchair dependant. Volkov knew he did not make the ideal patient; his nursing staff over the months he had spent at the private Swiss clinic had changed regularly as staff grew weary of his endless temper tantrums and had left. Only the large sums of money he was paying for his care kept the clinic from asking him to leave. He shouted once more for his bodyguard.

Senior Sergeant Balakin was being very well paid for his services; why was he not here? Volkov did not feel in charge of his own destiny in this place; it was full of people who had given up. He had not given up, and it made him mad that for the moment he could do nothing other than direct operations from his sick bed. Where the hell was Balakin? He roared once more like a mad bull.

Yury Balakin finally appeared and after an earbashing from his boss pushed Volkov out onto the large lawn by the side of the main building and under the canopy, while listening to a string of commands Volkov fired at him. His bad temper showed no signs of abating.

'Why have we heard nothing from Litvak? I need to know if he has killed the O'Conner bitch, and if not, why not. I want you to contact Minister Panoz. He will be able to find out the truth for us.'

Balakin placed the wheelchair in the shade from the morning sun and was locking the brake when for no reason Volkov's temper erupted once more. 'Don't just stand there like a fool – go and get in touch with Moscow. No wonder Litvak left you behind – you are slower than a snail.'

Yury Balakin said nothing. He left and headed in the direction of the hospital entrance.

As Balakin departed he was replaced by Dr Rymer.

'Good morning, Vadek, how are feeling this morning? Nurse tells me you have had a restless night.'

Volkov had never been one for small talk and today was no exception. 'If you were doing what I paid you to do I wouldn't have restless nights, Rymer. How many more X-rays, pills and injections do you plan to torment me with before I can walk out of this geriatric shit hole, or are you waiting until you have bled my bank account dry before you tell me I'm fixed, is that the plan, my good doctor?'

Dr Rymer was used to Volkov's foul tongue and took the insult in his stride. 'Vadek, as we have told you before on many occasions, the fragments of bullet that we removed from your upper torso unfortunately damaged nerves in your spinal cord. You are lucky that you were not paralysed from the neck down. We can sort many things but we do not have the technology to repair your nerves. Your lung is mending well and the damage to your heart has been repaired, but only time will tell if you regain the full function of your left side. You must be patient, and please remember we are all here to help you, so a little cooperation would be good, my friend. Now, is there anything I can get for you – a sedative to help you rest a little, possibly?'

Volkov was not hearing what he wanted to hear and waved the doctor away, scowling at him as he retreated to the safety of his office.

To Sam's surprise she was shown into the cabin of the Falcon 900. She had expected to sit up front with Fred as usual but he had company in the form of his co-pilot Geena.

Fred had obviously moved upmarket and, although Sam had never asked for a price, she was pretty sure Fred's fees had moved upmarket to match the transport. Mate's rates were about to be replaced with executive prices, Sam reckoned.

Once airborne Sam had time to let her mind wander back to her family; she so wanted to contact Lauren to find out how Adam was doing, and talk to Luke. She had to wipe away a tear before she became angry with herself. Self-pity and worry were not good – she had a job to do and an important one. She needed to focus fully on the task at hand, not only for her own but for her family's safety she had to stop Volkov, and she knew the only way was to wipe him from the face of the earth, but she needed to do it in a way that did not point to her or MI6.

Sam had brought no weapons or gadgets with her. She thought through things once more in the peace of the Falcon's plush cabin; this job was going to be completed using her core skills and knowledge acquired from years of undercover work with Six.

At Bourg-Ceyzériat airfield, not far from the Swiss border, Fred escorted Sam to the car park behind the main offices to where her hire car was waiting for her. Sam thanked Fred for all his hard work and settled the eye-watering bill with him before giving him a peck on the cheek, warning him she would be calling him in the near future for a return flight to the UK once her photo shoot was complete. Fred nodded knowingly; he was more than happy not to know the truth in case there were questions asked.

Although Sam had travelled the route previously she punched in Geneva on the satnav. The BMW M3 snarled into life as she pressed the starter button; the journey via the back roads into Switzerland was going to be entertaining to say the least.

She arrived in Geneva faster than she had ever done the journey before thanks to the Bavarian hot rod.

Tomorrow was going to be a busy day; Sam dropped her gear off at her chosen hotel then found a chemist only a couple of blocks away. After only a few minutes browsing the aisles she found what she was looking for: on a rack were rows of spectacles of various of lens strengths. Sam picked a ruby red pair with the weakest lenses available – she was not sure how well Vadek Volkov would remember her, but she was going to use the glasses as well as her short red hair and green eyes. Hopefully this would be enough for her to get close to Volkov without him recognising her.

She was about to head for the sales counter to pay for her glasses when a thought that had been lurking in the back of her mind surfaced once more. Sam retraced her steps a couple of feet and stood thinking over her next move. She was tired and she needed a bath – standing about like an idiot was not her normal behaviour. She picked up a box from the shelf and without checking placed it in the basket with her glasses and some vitamins.

Back at the hotel while she ran her bath she unpacked the items she had bought, stopping to study the pregnancy test kit. There was no way she was pregnant, but for some reason she had to prove it to herself. True, since her injuries her body had not returned to its normal cycle and her moods had been all over the place, but her mental state had been tested to the limit over the past few months. She wasn't pregnant; she just needed to sort the Volkov problem and her body would sort itself out. She wasn't sure why she was trying to reassure herself but the kit would be the judge; it would put her mind at rest so she could get on with the task at hand.

Ten minutes later Sam sat by the running bath holding the instructions and the test kit, too shocked to read the instructions for a second time. The truth was she didn't know whether to laugh or cry; she looked at the test sample one more time. There was no mistaking it: the test was positive. Luke was going to be a big brother.

Sam's hand was trembling as she placed the test kit on the floor and gently slipped into the bath. Her mind should have been on tomorrow's goals but tonight's revelations had wiped everything from her mind. How was she going to cope with a toddler, a new baby and a partner with a brain injury? Her discovery should have been a joyous occasion, but Sam curled up in the bath and wept; there was a deep feeling of her past exploits coming back to haunt her private life. Karma had knocked on her door.

Although Sam had not slept well she was up early and was one of the first hotel guests to be served breakfast. She had not been idle while she waited in Ireland for Fred to pick her up; she had found out where the head office for the Freda Larsen care clinics was situated in Geneva. The company had twelve clinical care homes scattered around Europe; Volkov was a resident at the Freda Larsen home in the city of Lucerne. Sam had been well warned that any attempt on Volkov's life would have to be subtle – she couldn't go in as she had at the embassy, all guns blazing. She would still finish Volkov off but to do it she needed to find out more about the hospital in Lucerne; this was going to be the object of today's little exercise.

Sam finished her tea and croissant. She was still finding it hard to believe she was pregnant; when she had been carrying Luke she'd had bad morning sickness to start with, but at the moment there were no symptoms. If it was true and she was pregnant there was little point wondering what had gone wrong – it was highly possible with all the drugs she had been taking they had weakened the effect of her contraceptives.

Sam forced herself to snap out of it – she needed her wits about her today. What had happened couldn't be undone, but the future was a different story. Sam knew she had to dictate what was to happen if she wanted safety and security for her family – even more so now it looked like there'd soon be another member.

18

The Hit

One hour later Sam stood outside the offices of Freda Larsen. She checked her reflection in the front window before entering the building – her new glasses made her look a bit of a nerd but changed the shape of her face. Sam was satisfied that this was a good enough disguise.

Inside, the office manager, who introduced herself as Sandra, took some details about Sam's alias, Marie Delamere, and the position she was looking for. Sam was glad to find she didn't have to do too much digging. Sandra was very talkative and chatted away about the systems and the people in the organisation. She told Sam about a local outfitter who could provide uniforms off the peg if she was offered a position in the Freda Larsen homes. Sam left with a number of brochures and a list of names, promising to send her full CV into the office for Sandra to look over.

Sam found a local coffee shop and stopped for a breather and to regroup before her next task. During their conversation Sandra had told her she would not be able to look at her CV for a week as she was going on vacation in Vienna and the office would be closed. That fitted in perfectly with Sam's plan. She needed to kit herself out with a uniform so the outfitter was going to be her next port of call. She asked the coffee shop owner for directions, paid her bill, and set off on foot following the directions she had been given.

Sam presented the sales woman at the outfitter with the brochure for the Freda Larsen care home. Sam explained that she did freelance nursing and was going to be working at the home but did not want to look out of place. The woman took little notice of Sam's explanation, she was too busy measuring her for the uniform, which appeared with military precision after only a few minutes. Sam bought two of the nurse's uniforms, thanked the woman for her speedy assistance and left the shop. She was ahead of target for the first day of the operation; things had gone well. Tomorrow, when Sandra the manager would be travelling to Vienna, Sam would introduce herself to the staff of Freda Larsen in Lucerne.

Although she tried for an early night, sleep would not come; Sam's brain was racing with hundreds of different problems. Finally she gave up on sleep and in the early hours of the morning, after overdosing on coffee, set off on the three-hour trip from Geneva to Lucerne. The sun was coming up when Sam pulled the BMW into the car park of a big motel on the outskirts of Lucerne. She booked in, dumped her stuff and headed for a well-earned breakfast followed by a successful couple of hours' sleep before heading out to find the route to the convalescent hospital.

The hospital was located on the outskirts of the city overlooking the lake and the town of Meggen on the far shoreline. Sam parked some distance away and walked the last half mile along Sankt Niklausen Strasse to the hospital. The hall was deserted, so Sam wandered into the main lounge. A young girl in blue scrubs was attending to six patients who were dotted around the large room; Sam noted that none of them were her friend Volkov. The girl spotted her and headed her way.

'May I be of assistance, madame?'

Sam smiled, shaking the young woman's hand. 'Good morning – my name is Marie. Head office sent me. I start work here tomorrow, and I thought I would pop in and introduce myself. Is the supervisor Linda around?'

The young girl's face lit up at this news. 'Oh, thank goodness for that – we've been so short-handed since Sabrina left. Linda will be so happy you're here. Please wait in the hall and I will run upstairs and get her – she's doing room calls at the moment.'

Linda arrived a few minutes later, her face sombre and businesslike. Sam's first impression of her was that she wouldn't want to burn her toast. It only took a second for Sam to discover what was eating at her.

'I have not been informed of any new staff members. Sandra always asks for my input before offering anyone employment – this is most unusual. Do you have any papers or documentation with you?'

Sam had been half expecting this and was ready for the question. 'I was a nurse in Dijon then I joined Médecins Sans Frontières. I worked all over the world with them – Sandra has all my documents and certificates. She said she will return them next week when she returns from Vienna – she said in the meantime I was to start as soon as possible to help here.'

Sam sensed Linda was still not sure but decided not to push too hard and arouse suspicion.

'So Marie, if you've been with MSF all over the world what made you want to work in a place like this?'

Linda was fishing and Sam knew it. She paused for effect then reached down and lifted her shirt up as high as her bra, revealing her stomach and the deep purple bullet wound in her side.

'On my last trip to Syria I was shot by a sniper as I tried to save a child shot by the same sniper. After I was discharged I decided it was time to play it safe … the next time I might not be so lucky. So here I am, ready to get back to work.'

The bullet trick worked a treat. For the moment Linda had been won over by Sam's story and offered to show her round, then asked her to start the following morning. To Sam's surprise, after asking if she had the training to dispense drugs, Linda handed her a spare key to the medical stores, a building that stood alone in the large grounds of the hospital.

As Linda gave Sam a quick tour of the building and grounds Sam spotted the figure of Vadek Volkov sitting in a wheelchair in the middle of the lawn under a parasol. Not far from where he sat a man on the steps of the veranda was watching Sam with interest. Sam was pretty sure he was not medical, a fact she confirmed as she walked back indoors past the man. Tucked in the rear of his trousers was a holstered Sig Sauer pistol. Sam said her goodbyes, promising to be in early to start the morning shift.

Sam slept very little that night. She was going to do nothing tomorrow, just sort out a few parts of her plan. She had to get this one right – she could not afford to fail – the future of her family depended on it.

The next morning for the first couple of hours she shadowed Lucy, who she had met the previous morning. Lucy was a cheery young girl who never stopped talking. Sam chatted away as they did the rounds, paying particular attention as they entered the drugs store while helping Lucy to collect what she needed for the afternoon rounds. Sam spotted many drugs that she could weaponise, but for the moment was content to know she had everything she needed here to carry out her mission. On the way back to the main building Sam pointed to the solitary figure under the parasol in the middle of the lawn.

'Do we need to sort that gentleman out? He looks so lonely sitting there by himself.'

Lucy shook her head, not looking in the direction of Volkov. 'No, Linda will sort him out. Best place for him, sitting out there. He is a nasty man with a foul temper … he is Russian. His bodyguard doesn't let anyone other than Linda or the doctor see him. Come on, Marie, time for a coffee break – let me show you where the kitchens are.'

Later Sam helped serve lunch then, when Volkov's bodyguard was having his own lunch, she wandered out unnoticed to Volkov who was dozing in the sun. Sam needed to test her disguise out – if Volkov didn't recognise her, no one would. Although Sam spoke Russian it would raise eyebrows if a nurse spoke to him in his native tongue; she could have used German, but she was more comfortable speaking French.

'Excuse me, sir, have you finished with your lunch? May I take your tray away?'

Volkov squinted up at Sam who was silhouetted by the afternoon sun.

'Is there no peace in this dump? Take it and get out of my sight, girl.'

Sam lifted the tray and discarded napkin, said a swift sorry and turned to leave, just as the sun was blocked out by Volkov's bodyguard. He said nothing, but his stare spoke volumes; Sam was aware his eyes never left her as she made a hasty retreat to the kitchen with the dirty dishes.

The next morning Sam's plans were turned on their head. She arrived as normal and parked the BMW some distance away, but in the hall she was met by a tearful Lucy who informed her one of their patients, Countess Zermental, had passed away during the night. Sam listened to the young nurse as she explained that the countess was a Swiss VIP; her husband the count had been informed and was on his way. He had talked with Sandra who had cut short her stay in Vienna and was on her way back to take charge of the situation.

Linda asked Sam to help Lucy with the daily tasks while she waited on the doctor's arrival to issue the death certificate and deal with the body. Sam's mind was racing as she handed out breakfast and sorted out the morning medication while Lucy concentrated on changing dressings and updating records.

While Linda was otherwise occupied Sam took the opportunity for a second visit to Volkov, who had just been wheeled out onto the lawn by his bodyguard. She headed for the Russian but the bodyguard stood in her path. Sam waved him away, telling him Linda was unavailable to carry out her duties and that she would look after Volkov. The bodyguard hesitated for a second then moved aside, watching Sam closely. Sam had been thinking on her feet; she knew her time had run out. She needed to get the job done here and now. Luckily, the bodyguard was too busy paying attention to Sam's actions to notice Volkov had two sleeping pills instead of his normal medication. Sam waited while Volkov swallowed the pills then washed them down with water; the first part of her plan had worked. She was satisfied with her first move as she walked past Volkov's bodyguard without making eye contact.

Dr Rymer arrived in a mad rush and Lucy accompanied him

upstairs to the countess's suite. Sam seized the opportunity and headed for the medical store – she needed to sort out her little present for Vadek Volkov and now was the time.

She searched for the container she had seen on her earlier visit. Quickly she emptied the potassium chloride onto the counter, broke up a number of capsules and used the back of a spoon to grind the chemical into a fine powder; as part of her MI6 training she had been given the assassins' course in concocting various ways of killing people with chemicals.

In the medical store there were hundreds of drugs that would kill if used correctly, but Sam favoured an overdose of potassium chloride given intravenously. The right amount would stop the heart beating and, as Volkov had had work done in that area, there was a chance it would be mistaken for heart failure at the autopsy. Sam added water to the mix and filled a syringe with the milky-looking solution. She was in the process of tidying up the evidence when the door of the store flew open. Volkov's bodyguard stood in the doorway looking at Sam, who was holding the potassium chloride container above her head as she returned it to the shelf. She knew it would only take seconds for him to realise what she was up to. She had hoped to sidestep the bodyguard but he had forced her hand – she had no option other than to deal with him. It had to be now, this very second while he was still off guard.

Sam's move was cat-like; she launched the container at the startled guard. She watched two things as she leapt forward: her left hand grabbed the bodyguard's right hand, finding the target just as his fingers gripped the Sig Sauer in its holster. She applied full force downwards, stopping him from drawing the weapon; her right hand raked the workbench, grabbing the only weapon at her disposal, and her body crashed forward throwing them both towards the now closed door. Sam brought her right hand up holding the packing scissors from the bench just as the bodyguard slammed backwards into the door, his free hand trying stop his fall backwards. He was still desperately trying to draw his obstructed weapon as Sam rammed the blades of the scissors through the soft flesh just above his Adam's apple. The back of his head hit the door and Sam used her momentum to cut through tissue and muscle until only the curved handle of the large packing scissors protruded below his chin. Sam felt the life leave his body as his legs gave way and he slid down the storeroom door, air gurgling in his lifeless throat, his limbs twitching as his brain gave out its last signals before shutdown was final.

Sam was shaking as she stepped back. She cursed the guard for this mess – he had ruined her chances of keeping things quiet. She needed to deal with the body then carry out her mission and get the hell out of Switzerland fast.

She grabbed a couple of bin bags and pulled them over the dead guard's head and feet, trying to stop him bleeding all over the concrete floor. She opened the door and gave the grounds a quick check – in the heat of battle she was not sure how much noise there had been. Luckily nothing was stirring … for the moment she had got away with it. She spotted a row of three wheelie bins, and it took only a few minutes to load their contents into two bins before wheeling the empty bin into the medicine store. Loading the dead weight of the bodyguard into the bin proved challenging. She had to lay the bin on its side to load the body, then used a length of washing line over one of the roof beams to get it on its feet. She loaded potato peelings from one of the other bins on top of the body to cover up her handiwork and placed the heavy bin back in the line with the others. She cleaned up quickly, discarding her blood-spattered tunic, aware that time was running out rapidly, and gave herself a quick check in a dusty old mirror.

Sam tucked the bodyguard's Sig Sauer handgun in the back of her scrub trousers, grabbed a tray with the syringe full of potassium chloride and headed across the yard to the grass and the figure of Vadek Volkov. Three unknown cars had arrived during her time in the medicine store, although thankfully no one was around at the moment. It was time for Vadek Volkov to meet his maker.

Lev Aristov made a couple of final adjustments to the telescopic sights of his Orsis T5000 sniper rifle, but then picked up the movement of someone approaching from the main building. A slight movement of his shoulder brought the person into focus.

A nurse with short red hair and glasses arrived and started to roll up a sleepy-looking Volkov's sleeve in preparation for an injection.

Aristov fiddled again with the lens – he had never seen this nurse during any of his recon runs. Studying her again there was something familiar about her, then suddenly it all fell into place. It was the British MI6 woman – that was why she had attacked the embassy. Volkov was her target, and here she was about to complete her mission. Lev Aristov grinned to himself as he watched her injecting him. *No no, my dark angel, it is I, Lev Aristov, who will decide when he dies, and the second your pretty little head lines up with Volkov's, I, the greatest marksman in Russia will send you both to hell with one shot*, he thought.

Sam finished injecting the potassium chloride into Volkov's vein. She should have walked away and left the injection to do its work but for once she let personal matters cloud her decision. She bent down, putting her mouth next to Volkov's ear. 'Time for you to go and visit your drug-dealing sister in hell. Tell her Sam O'Conner says hi.'

Sam could see from the look of terror on Volkov's face that her words had got through to him. Her fingers noted his pulse but it was her trained eyes that caught the muzzle flash and, like the true pro she was, she reacted, helped by her already pumped-up adrenalin levels. She had just started to move as the shot hit Volkov in the middle of the forehead, went through his brain and continued on its deadly path, carving its way out. Sam heard the crack of gunfire as it followed a fraction of a second later. She threw herself towards the ground, and felt the disturbance in the air from the bullet as it passed what must have been a millimetre from her ear. She was covered in Volkov's blood and had been so close that splinters from his skull had cut her cheek.

It took Sam a second or two to realise the sniper had missed her, and only milliseconds later for it to dawn on her that she had been targeted along with Volkov.

Aristov saw Volkov's head explode and the O'Conner girl hit the ground covered in blood. He ducked down, recovered the spent shell, then folded up the legs of the rifle before placing it in a ski bag. He left the old barn at a leisurely pace. He had parked his van behind the building, out of view from the road; he had done this many times – running about like an idiot would only attract attention. Slow and steady was the way to go.

Sam could feel the rage building as she got to her feet – some bastard had just tried to kill her and ruined her attempt at a clean kill of Volkov into the bargain. She took off like an Olympic sprinter in the direction of the muzzle flash. About half a mile away an old derelict barn stood by the lakeside, the perfect place for a sniper. Sam was pretty sure if he still had sights on her she would have been dead by now – she was willing to gamble that he was packing up to get clear of the area. Sam vaulted the hedge at the bottom of the garden without losing a stride. On the far side of the hedge a minor road wound its way around the shoreline. Sam kept up the momentum; closing in on the old barn she pulled the blood-spattered glasses from her face with her left hand, throwing them in the direction of the lake. She used her right hand to draw the Sig Sauer. The adrenalin was fading and the old wound in her leg was starting to throb … only the rage in her heart pushed her on.

Sam was closing in on the barn when an engine fired up and a Volkswagen van appeared, trundling onto the road from the back of the barn.

The driver had spotted her and immediately the van sped up. Sam knew she needed to take a shot now, but she was still over a hundred metres from the van. She dived forward onto her belly, trying to bring her breathing under control; if she had any chance of hitting the speeding van she had to control her body.

What made things worse was there was a corner in the road ahead. She would only have a few seconds until the van was round the bend and gone.

Sam fired a single shot, but it was wildly off target. She regrouped and fired three shots spaced by her breathing. The first two bullets arced and hit the ground by the van, but the third hit the sidewall of the front offside tyre as the van sped into the corner.

The tyre exploded, causing the van to skid straight on, missing the corner and careering down an embankment by the lake before ploughing into a large tree, stopping with a sickening crunch.

Sam checked how many rounds she had left in the Sig then set off once more, her leg stiff and sore but still working. Sam arrived at the scene of the crash. There was no movement from anyone in the shattered van, only the sound of escaping steam from the burst radiator. Slowly she walked down the embankment, Sig raised ready for round two with the unknown assassin.

Sam found the driver trapped and still dazed. He had not been wearing his seat belt and had probably been knocked out for a few seconds by the blast of the airbag. Sam watched as it dawned on the sniper he was trapped; his ankles were broken and his twisted legs were trapped by the mangled foot pedals.

Sam stared into the cabin of the van. She was shattered from her run, but also finding it hard to believe who she was looking at. 'Aristov. Colonel Lev Aristov, the pride of the Russian army, your number is up this time, my friend.'

Aristov spat out blood and a tooth and groaned as he tried unsuccessfully to free his shattered leg. 'Shut up, MI6 bitch. Put a bullet in me and get it over with.'

Sam stood for a second, thinking before replying. 'No, I have a better idea, my friend. I think it would be better if the world thinks you died in a car crash trying to escape from your latest hit.'

She leaned in through the open window and with one expert move snapped Lev Aristov's neck. She watched the Russian killer twitch and shake until he became still, then she positioned him to make it look as if the airbag had broken his neck.

Sam removed a waxed jacket from the passenger seat, pulled it on over her filthy and blood-covered clothes, and headed back along the road towards her parked BMW.

On the walk back Sam found a black beanie in the pocket of the jacket. She pulled it on and adjusted it just to cover as much as possible of her red hair. In the distance she could see a group of people gathered in the garden of the hospital – no police had arrived on the scene yet. Sam decided to take a detour that took her behind the gardens of houses bordering on the grounds of the Freda Larsen hospital. She emerged just opposite the main entrance of the hospital grounds at the opposite end of the site from the shooting just as a refuse lorry and three workers on foot left the premises. There seemed to be no fuss – it looked as if no one had investigated why one of the bins was particularly heavy. Sam quickened her pace after the refuse truck was out of sight; she wanted to get clear of the area before the police arrived.

She had pulled up at a crossroads in her hire car and was turning left towards her hotel when three police cars passed, sirens wailing. She continued her manoeuvre, heading back to the hotel. Her hands were shaking but she was breathing easier, knowing she had cleared the immediate danger zone.

It only took Sam minutes to clean the hotel room of prints. She bagged the blood-covered nurse's clothing, changed into jeans and T-shirt and then settled the bill with cash.

She called Fred from the bus station payphone. She was glad to hear he would be at the airfield in a couple of hours. She filled the BMW with fuel, dumped the bin bag with the nurse's uniform, grabbed a sandwich and headed for the French border via the back roads. After some hard driving Sam passed the empty border checkpoint just about on schedule to get to Bourg-Ceyzériat airfield for her flight back to the UK.

19

Heading Home

At the airfield she could see the Falcon sitting on the apron waiting for her arrival, steps in place and cabin door open ready for action. Sam parked the M3 by the gate then used a cloth to remove her fingerprints before taking her gear out of the boot. She pulled the Russian assassin's waxed jacket on and as she did something dug into her; a quick inspection found the root of the problem was a computer memory stick tucked into the lining of the inside breast pocket. Sam studied the device thoughtfully, wondering what secrets a Russian hitman might have stored on a memory stick as she wandered across the car park heading straight for the side gate and access to the waiting jet.

'Good evening, young lady, how did the photo shoot go?'

Sam continued to walk to the aircraft as Fred chatted. She was desperate to get into the air and as far away from the area as soon as possible.

'Snowy mountain shots and lots of fur coats, models with attitude – can't wait to get home, Fred. Do you think we can go soon? I've had it with travelling for the moment.'

Fred stopped by the Falcon's nose, gesturing for Sam to lead the way onto the aircraft.

'We'll be airborne the minute you tell me where we're going. I have full tanks and you have the big cheque book so where will it be tonight?'

Sam stopped and turned after checking out the cockpit. 'What, no

Geena tonight? Looks like I'll have to keep you company in the cockpit, Captain. It's Heathrow tonight, by the way, nothing exotic I'm afraid.'

While Fred logged his flight plan with French air traffic control, Sam had a few minutes to think. She was desperate to find out how Adam and Luke were doing and desperate to run a second pregnancy test. There was also the matter of the computer memory stick – what secrets would that hold? She had a couple of days until the cruise ship arrived in the UK, time enough for her to sort things out.

She spent the flight chatting with Fred with the occasional interruption from air traffic control. She was curious about Fred's change to upmarket jets and after questioning him was saddened to hear that her friend Madame Chemolie, who had been Fred's boss, had passed away, leaving him the Falcon 900 in her will.

Sam was happy for Fred, but at the same time devastated to hear of the old lady's passing; it had been Madame Chemolie who had spotted that Sam was pregnant with Luke.

Fred was busy talking to air traffic control, leaving Sam alone with her thoughts. Her hormones were in overdrive. She wanted to cry for the old lady, then reminded herself that only that morning she had killed three men without even a second thought.

She looked out of the cockpit into the darkness of the evening sky, tears welling up in her tired eyes. She had thought killing Volkov would be the end of it, but now she was not so sure.

Aristov was Russia's top hitman; he had tried to take both her and Volkov out with the same shot. His arrogance had been the undoing of him and Sam now knew where she stood with the Russians. She was going to have to come up with something or be on the run from the Russian machine for the rest of her life.

Frederick le Combe escorted Sam as far as the VIP lounge where she handed over the keys for the hire car and payment for her return trip and the car. Fred said goodbye and Sam gave him a peck on the cheek before heading for the exit.

She was thinking on her feet as she left Arrivals. The last thing she expected was her French passport name to be called out; at first it didn't register, then for a second time the American voice called out 'Marie Delamere.'

Suddenly like a bolt of lightning it struck Sam that she was being spoken to. She turned, following the voice. Dan Whittaker was standing smiling at her; she jumped straight back into character, answering him in French for the benefit of anyone watching them. She recognised the big American but it took a second for her to realise she had just been busted by the CIA.

In a quiet part of the hall Sam interrogated Dan. 'Jesus Christ – how the hell did you find me? MI6 don't even know I'm here yet.'

Dan was grinning, obviously enjoying pulling one over on the Brits. 'Oh, it wasn't that hard, especially when you pick a CIA asset to fly you around. Old Freddie boy is a good friend of the CIA. Don't get sore at him, he didn't give you up, we just like to keep tabs on people we do business with. Anyway, the reason my boss wanted me to talk to you is nothing to do with Freddie.

'The cruise ship is busted so your family had to fly home. Bruce wanted me to get hold of you the minute you landed. I reckon you'll need a ride, so here I am, your knight in shining armour once again, but this time, lady I ain't pullin' you through no hedges or pluggin' bullet holes. Got it?'

Sam agreed to meet Dan in the short stay car park. She had a task to perform and did not want him around. She made her way to the lost baggage area of Terminal 3 where she wrote out a note and handed it to the baggage clerk. He read the note, for a second was puzzled, then slowly the names and numbers Sam had written down clicked and he vanished without saying a word.

A few minutes later he reappeared with a brown leather case. He ushered Sam into an office then left her without speaking.

Sam jammed a chair against the office door then opened the case. Inside there were bundles of cash in various currencies, two new Glock 19s, ammunition, spare mags and two silencers. The password and numbers were given to all MI6 field agents in case of emergencies. Every lost baggage office at all the main airports carried one of these cases, all with different passwords.

Sam helped herself to some British currency, a Glock, a box of ammo and two spare mags. Outside the office a CCTV monitor looked down on the desk; Sam thanked the clerk, handed back the case and smiled up at the monitor. There was no point trying to hide – someone at Vauxhall Cross would already be watching the footage, alerted by the airport staff.

Outside Sam found Dan waiting by a Ford Galaxy people carrier.

'Where to, lady?'

Sam climbed into the passenger seat before speaking. 'Have you any idea where Adam and my son are now?'

'Yip, sure do. It was me who picked them up and took them home. Big glass building looking over the sea, way up on the coast in Scotland. Beautiful up there, ain't it?'

Sam didn't answer … she was lost in thought. Her heart told her to go home but her brain was still in MI6 mode. Deep down she knew she had to sort the Russian situation out once and for all, and now was the time. She needed to strike while the iron was hot.

Dan dropped Sam at the security gate of Vauxhall Cross then left, giving her a wave as he pulled out into the evening traffic. As Sam expected, news had reached HQ she was back in town and she was ushered downstairs to Bill Mathews' office, security escorting her all the way.

Sam was surprised to find Mathews was not in his office. Instead she found Jean sitting at his desk studying a letter.

'Samantha, it's good to see you are still in the land of the living. Unfortunately you've missed the director – he's on holiday with his wife in York. What have you been up to since we last met? I think Bill Mathews suspects you've jumped ship and joined our American cousins.'

Sam smiled at the comment. 'Jean, does Billy still work late in IT? I have something I need him to look at urgently, then we can have a chat over a cup of tea and I'll bring you up to speed on things.'

Jean nodded, lifting the director's phone. Five minutes later Billy had the Russian's memory stick in his hot sweaty palm and was on his way back to his office to see what he could find out from it. Jean poured the tea while Sam filled her in on the last few months in America. She drained the cup and asked Jean for a refill, and then hesitated. She'd missed out Ireland and was about to start talking about Switzerland when Jean interrupted.

'Tell me, Miss O'Conner, were you anywhere near Lucerne? Interpol seem to think that the Russians had Vadek Volkov eliminated. Seems their plan went wrong – their hitman crashed fleeing the scene and was killed, giving the game away. Interpol are still searching for Volkov's Russian bodyguard. They think he was in on the plot and has legged it back to Mother Russia – they want to talk to him urgently. Of course it's good news for you – almost too convenient, some would say.'

Sam refilled the teacup, draining the remainder of the pot. 'Let's hope they keep thinking it was the Russians – that works for me. Let me tell you I clutched victory from the jaws of defeat with that one. The Russians are still after me, I'm sure of it – I need to know what was on that memory stick. I pulled it from Lev Aristov's jacket. They sent their top man – the team leader of the FSB black unit, probably the most famous assassin of modern times – to take out Volkov but he waited until I was directly behind him before he fired. He almost got me, the bastard.'

There was a soft knock on the office door and Billy reappeared, holding a laptop in his arms.

'Billy, I bet you're going to tell us that both my details and Volkov's are on the memory stick and we were to be eliminated – am I correct?'

Billy nodded in amazement. 'Spot on, Samantha. The memory stick belongs to a dude called General Mariokov, big hitter in Russia but not so clever with computers. Relied on his password and a cleaning tool to keep his info safe – the silly man's password is Maria 1956, his wife's name and birthday. He put the hit on you both. There's more stuff on the stick that he's wiped – it will take weeks to piece it together, but we'll get there. I'll keep you informed. Thought you might want to know pronto – going back to get on with it. Catch you later, guys.'

Billy vanished, apparently eager to find out what other gems he could extract from the general's memory stick.

Sam had started to formulate a plan in the back of her head. She needed to sort out a few things here, but foremost she needed Jean to play ball.

'Can I offer you a bed for the night, Samantha? I doubt you have had time to sort out accommodation. I'm about to leave, we can share a taxi.'

'Sounds like a good idea, Jean, thank you. I have a few things here I need to sort out so I'll come over a little later. You send the taxi back for me and I'll be with you shortly for some more tea. Do I still have a desk upstairs or has Mathews removed me from his Christmas card list?'

Sam could see Jean was tired; she probably knew Sam was up to something but for the moment at least she let it slide and agreed to head home.

Sam finished her phone call with the new MI5 director, Ian Devlin, then headed to the stores in the hope that they were still open.

Sam arrived at the stores just as Bernard Davis finished doing a weekly stock check. She knew her request would probably send Bernard into orbit but she had worked with him long enough to know he usually came up with the goods.

'Good god, young woman, what do you think this is – the bloody commandos? What in god's name would make you think MI6 stocked hand grenades? This is the twenty-first century, my dear, we do our warfare with phones and laptops nowadays. Let me tell you it would have to be an extraordinary quartermaster who could get you hand grenades.'

Davis had a twinkle in his eye as he turned round, walked to the back of his office and opened a filling cabinet. 'You'll have to sign a request form for me – how many do you need? You know I don't even know if I should be handing these over without prior authority – they were only bought in for field tests on our body armour, not standard issue for field agents.'

Sam smiled at him as he handed her a grenade. 'One is all I need, Bernard. You come up with the goods every time – you're an angel.'

Sam signed the paperwork then headed to the security gate, her work for the night done. Now all she needed was to get Jean to sign off on her plan and she was in business.

Sam sat quietly as Jean poured her tea out.

'Samantha, you seem to have acquired quite a taste for tea. I don't recall you drinking it much previously?'

Sam took a sip of the tea before replying to Jean. 'No, I'm normally a coffee person. I suspect it's a craving – should go away after seven or eight months, I would think.'

Jean almost spilled her tea all over her Persian rug. She stared wide-eyed at Sam for confirmation. Sam burst into a beaming smile without saying a word. Jean put her cup down, crossed the room and gave Sam a hug before returning to her chair, her face full of concern.

'Samantha, you have to finish with us. You cannot be expected to be an active agent with two children – even Bill Mathews must know it would be impossible.'

Sam nodded, taking another mouthful of tea. 'Jean, I'm finished, believe me – this is the end. I have one final thing to do then that's it, I'm out of here, but I need you to do something for me so I can draw a line under the Russian problem for good.'

Jean put her teacup down on the table. 'No problem, Samantha, if I can help you I will. What do you need?'

Sam took a deep breath; she knew before she asked this was going to be a tall order. 'I need you to set up a meeting between General Mariokov and me. He will not want to meet me, so he has to think he's meeting with Bill Mathews. I know it's a lot to ask but I must get to him.'

Jean was speechless for a few second while the task that Sam had asked of her sank in. 'Samantha, you know I would do it if I could, but that's too much. I would be sacked on the spot when Bill found out what I had done.'

'Jean, I have a baby on the way, a toddler and a partner with a brain injury. I can't fight the Russians. I need to sort this now. I need Mariokov out in the open so I can speak to him.'

'Sam, with the greatest respect, you're not a negotiator – you're an MI6 assassin. I've seen your negotiation before – I can't be responsible for more bloodshed. You will go and get yourself killed, girl. No, I won't do it – I can't do it. The spare room is made up for you. Goodnight, Samantha.'

Before Sam could reason with her Jean took off upstairs.

Sam spent a restless night. She badly wanted to go home but she had to sort things out or live in fear for her family's safety, always looking over her shoulder.

In the morning Sam made her way down to the kitchen where she found Jean already up, dressed and waiting for her cab. She sensed right away that Jean was a different person this morning.

'You'll find tea in the pot – it should be infused and ready to go. There's porridge cooked and on the hob. I need to get going. Please for once do me and yourself a favour and do what I say. I want you to stay here until I call you, and for god's sake stay away from the Russian Embassy.'

Sam made a face. 'Porridge, yuk, can I make some toast instead? I need to pop out to a chemist, but I'll be back here for your call.'

'Very well, there's a chemist first left then first right. It opens in half an hour. Eat the porridge and make toast, your little one needs you to eat properly. Remember what I said, Samantha, do nothing until I call. I mean it.'

Sam bought some vitamins and a second pregnancy test kit which she used as soon as she got back to Jean's house. The result was once again positive and, as if on cue, Sam felt sick. The thought of porridge did nothing to help – only cups of tea seemed to move the nausea. Sam passed the time stripping down the Glock and loading and unloading three magazines until she was sure there would be no jam-ups with the new equipment. Just after ten the phone in the hall rang. Sam was there before the second ring.

'Sam, it's me. Twelve o'clock in Hyde Park. I ran your request past Bill Mathews' number two – he isn't quite as switched on as Bill. Let's hope he doesn't call his boss. Be careful, Sam. Remember, only talking.'

'Thank you, Jean, you are one in a million. We're just going to have a cosy chat. By the way, the porridge was lovely. Speak to you later.'

Sam hung up the phone and immediately called Ian Devlin. 'Hi, Director Devlin, it's a go. I will meet your men at the Hyde Park gates on Speakers' Corner at eleven forty-five. Thank you for your assistance – I owe you one.'

Sam pulled on the waxed jacket she had acquired from the dead Russian hitman, slipped the grenade, spare magazines and Glock into her handbag, then headed out to find a cab.

Sam found Devlin's men had already arrived and were waiting outside, looking somewhat lost.

'Hello, gentlemen, I'm Samantha O'Conner. What I need you to do for me this afternoon is keep General Mariokov's protection detail away from me so I can have a quiet word with the general without any rude interruptions. I'm sure you have a few things that will keep his men out of my way for a bit.'

The tallest of the four, a man with sandy blond hair, stepped a little closer to Sam so as not to be overheard by any passers-by. 'Ma'am, you do know the general has a panic button? We can keep his men busy – loitering with intent to commit a crime, permit check for any firearms, that type of thing – but if he presses the button we won't be able to do jack shit about it. We're not far from the embassy – he'll have backup here in minutes and they will mean business.'

Sam paid little attention to her friends from Five's fears. 'You let me worry about the panic button. Just take his men out as I spot them for you – probably two, maybe four – I'll do the rest. Now spread out and follow me at a distance.'

Sam had passed the spot where Neil Andrews was killed and was checking other pathways when she spotted a distinguished gentleman wearing a black overcoat consulting his watch. Sam passed him without looking in his direction; her eyes were scanning the path behind him for his bodyguards. She spotted two right away, and a third was jogging at a leisurely pace while a fourth was off the path studying the trees.

Sam passed them all then turned, pointing to all four men. The tall blond agent nodded then spoke into a hand mic. Each of the four MI5 agents took up position on a different target and stopped the men, flashing warrant cards at the startled Russian protection team. Sam turned, making for Mariokov. As she approached she was glad to see he had not noticed his security team had been compromised; she also noted his right hand tucked in the outer pocket of his overcoat. Mariokov had reached the Italian Gardens in the park before he turned to check for his backup.

There were a couple of people by the garden's ponds but some distance from Mariokov's position. Sam waited until Mariokov lifted his right hand out of his pocket and pounced, leaping the last few feet and ramming the barrel of her Glock into the general's throat.

Her nose almost touching his, she glared into the startled general's eyes as she hissed instructions. 'I will blow your head off, General, if your right hand so much as twitches. Keep it exactly where it is for me.' Sam slipped her hand into the pocket of the waxed jacket and removed the grenade. She placed it in the general's right hand and, to his obvious horror, pulled the pin, leaving only his grip stopping the grenade arming itself.

'That's better, General. As long as you don't let go the grenade it is safe, and it will stop you from alerting your pals at the embassy.'

Mariokov was clearly playing for time until his bodyguards got to them. 'I am sorry, I do not speak much English.'

'Rubbish, General Mariokov, but if it pleases you we will speak only in Russian.'

Sam could tell Mariokov was shocked that he had been answered in his native tongue; she watched his eyes narrow as the penny dropped. He had not recognised her at first with red hair but now it was clear he knew who he was dealing with she saw his grip on the grenade tighten and a cold rage infuse his face.

'There is no point waiting for your protection detail to show up – I have taken them all out, my Russian friend. I am sure you're used to giving orders while others listen, but today you will listen. I have a proposition for you.'

The general roared at her in a fit of rage. 'How dare you threaten me? Do you know who I am, woman?'

Sam removed the Glock, tucking it in her waistband but never taking her cold grey eyes off the general.

'No, General Mariokov, the question is: do you know who I am? Shut your mouth and listen. You are looking at the person who eliminated your best assassin, also Vadek Volkov, and made it look like an accident. You're talking to the agent that took out a Spetsnaz unit in Arizona and eliminated a Russian hitman in the middle of a crowd in Las Vegas without anyone knowing, and if you're not careful you're looking at the angel of death who will take you to meet your maker.

'This is Lev Aristov's jacket I'm wearing, and in the inside pocket is the memory stick you gave him with the details of the two people you wanted eliminated. MI6 broke the password … by the way, Maria 1956 is a shit password. Not only that, they have earlier information you tried to wipe off but failed miserably.

'So, General Mariokov, you're in big trouble. You are at the mercy of the person you tried to have killed, and your boss won't be happy that you've handed MI6 classified information on a plate. I should put a bullet in your brain and send the Kremlin an email letting them know how much of an idiot their general was. I see you are lost for words, General, in either language.'

Sam paused for effect, letting what she had just told the general sink in. Mariokov's usual bravado was gone; he was chalk white and breaking out in a sweat.

'Here is what's going to happen, my good General. You are going to pretend this meeting never took place. Call off any attempts on my life or my family and go about your business as normal. I am finished … I have a second child on the way and my MI6 days are over. Do this and we shall all live happily ever after. But I swear on my sister's grave if anyone, Russian, Syrian or even Mickey Mouse tries to eliminate me I will assume that you have put them up to it and I will find you and send you to meet your friend Lev Aristov in hell. Look into my eyes, General, and tell me if you think I'm kidding?'

Mariokov was avoiding her cold eyes, still lost for words, as Sam took his hand and returned the safety pin to the fragmentation grenade. She put it in her pocket and replaced it with the memory stick she had taken from Aristov's jacket.

'Go, General, before you are missed at the embassy. Go and enjoy the rest of your life, but remember who it was that let you live when you should have been dead.'

Sam turned and walked away from the Russian general before he could say anything.

Mariokov turned in the direction of the Russian Embassy covered in a cold clammy sweat and his legs shaking. He had studied the MI6 agent's file previously and knew she was not to be underestimated, but after meeting her in person he knew he had just been in the presence of a cold-blooded killer who, for the moment, had let him live. His mind was racing as he tried to recall what information had been stored previously on the memory stick he had given to Aristov; he may have bigger problems than the girl to worry about. Maybe it was time for him to return to the safety of Moscow.

Jean Mitchell was nervously checking her wall clock. She had heard nothing from Sam since this morning; twelve o'clock had come and gone and it was now almost five.

Jean was contemplating listening to the news to hear if anything had kicked off in Hyde Park today; she checked the clock once again just as Sam walked into her office. She was shocked at the transformation: gone was the red hair, replaced by her natural blonde, she was wearing designer trousers, shoes and jacket, and her look was topped off with expertly applied make-up.

'That's things sorted out with the Russians, and Neil Andrews' killer has been dealt with, so I'm just here to tie up some loose ends then that's me done. Do you have notepaper I can use to write my resignation, Jean?'

Jean handed Sam a notepad and pen, not sure what to say, then watched as Sam started writing. 'Do you not think you should wait and speak to Bill Mathews before you leave?'

'No, Jean, there's no point – it will change nothing. I'm going. Bill threatened me with a lot of nasty things if I tried to leave MI6 – let's hope he was bluffing. I'm a far better friend than an enemy, let's hope he realises that and leaves us alone. My Scirocco was still in the car park so I had it brought up to the gates for me. Could you ask Bill Mathews to send me the bill for the car and also the money I borrowed from the emergency case at the airport? Jean, I need to get going, so could you return these for me?'

Sam placed the unused Glock, the spare magazines and the hand grenade on the desk. Jean recoiled when she spotted the grenade and Sam smiled. 'Don't worry, it's safe as long as you don't remove the pin. This is a thank you from me for all the times you pulled me out of the shit.'

Sam placed a black leather case in front of Jean on her desk and opened it to reveal a three-strand diamond necklace. Jean put her hand over her mouth to muffle the gasp she let out.

'If you don't like the design the gentleman at De Beers will be happy to change it for you. Here is my resignation and if you need me here in my new mobile number. When Mathews calms down tell him you want a holiday – come up to Scotland for a visit.'

Sam gave Jean a hug then, before she had a chance to say anything, left at the same speed she had arrived.

20

Suicide is Painless

S am had picked the wrong time to try to get out of London, but she
was happy just to get moving. After a couple of hours in heavy traffic Sam eventually found a clear road ahead and pushed the Scirocco
up past the speed limit, trying to make up for lost time, although it was
clear unless she wanted to drive well into the night she was going to
have to stop at some point.

She could feel her eyelids getting heavy and decided it was time to
find a place to stop for the night. A sign flashed past, telling her the
closest hotel was at Junction 21, Warrington, in a couple of miles. Sam
backed off the throttle, pulling her car into the slow lane. She was hoping this place would have a room; the last thing she needed tonight was
to have to go hunting for a hotel.

Sam was in luck and, after a quick bite to eat at the attached restaurant she booked an early breakfast, paid in advance and headed to
her room.

Since leaving London Sam had been waiting for her new mobile
phone to charge. Several times she had lifted the phone from the passenger seat to check its charging level – it was only when she pulled
into the hotel car park that she noticed it was fully charged. She'd un-
plugged it and popped it into her pocket, and ever since then she had
been desperate to call home. She sprawled on top of the double bed
and punched in Sue's mobile number, praying she hadn't changed her
phone or switched it off. There was an agonising pause as the phone

connected then rang out; Sam was about to hang up when a puzzled voice burst into her earpiece. 'Hello?'

'Sue, it's Sam, boy is it good to hear your voice. I hope you and Bob are doing okay. Sorry to bother you at this time of night, but do you know if Adam and Luke are okay?'

There was a pause for a second as Sue caught her breath.

'My god, Sam, where have you been? We're all worried sick, especially when you didn't turn up with the boys. Where are you, girl? Your little boy is missing you badly – you need to get back here – your family needs you. Hold on a second, I have Lauren here. I'm up visiting at the glasshouse – she can fill you in better than me.'

There was a rumble in Sam's ear as the phone was transferred to Lauren.

'Samantha, when are you coming home? Your wee man needs his mum. Sam, I take it you are coming home?'

Tears were welling up in Sam's eyes as she tried to hold it together; she would soon have her son back in her arms but tonight she felt she was the loneliest person on the planet. 'I know the wee guy will be sleeping, but let me speak to Adam at least. I'm on my way home, will be back tomorrow, but put Adam on the line for me.'

Again there was a pause; Sam assumed they were getting Adam.

'Sam, Adam has been having a rough time of it. We've tried to help but he's been strange … when he's awake he's withdrawn and quiet and when he sleeps the nightmares come. He has been waking screaming, covered in sweat. We'd been holding off on calling in a doctor, waiting for you to come home. We thought he was missing you, then last week he announced he was leaving and that he needed some space to think things through. We tried to talk him out of it – hell, even Bob tried to stop him – but he was having none of it. He left in the middle of the night in your Beetle after a particularly bad dream – he woke little Luke with his screams. Bob confronted him about not taking his medication but it only made things worse. I'm sorry, Sam, but there was no way of contacting you. We're very worried for him.'

Sam was in shock; she thought all she had to do was drive home, but now the love of her life had vanished. 'Okay, Lauren, don't beat yourselves up over it – it's not your fault. Change of plan. Looks like you're going to be in charge up there for a little longer until I can track down Adam. I'm really sorry to do this to you, but I need to find Adam and get him some help. Have you any idea where he might have gone?'

'He spoke to Bob and talked about getting back to the cottage, if that makes sense. We were wondering if it was his place on Arran he was talking about. I hope that helps. If you find him, Bob did manage to put his pills in the glovebox of the Beetle.'

Sam thanked Lauren and promised to keep in touch. The sleep she so badly needed eluded her for much of the night; she tossed and turned and finally fell asleep in the early hours of the morning. When she came to she found that she had missed her breakfast slot and the traffic was already queuing for the morning rush hour. Sam cursed as she dived into the shower – breakfast was the least of her worries – she was feeling squeamish as she dried her short blonde hair with the cheap nasty hairdryer the hotel had supplied in the room. She grabbed an energy drink from one of the vending machines in the lobby before flinging her belongings in the boot of the Scirocco and joining the long queue heading to the roundabout above the motorway. At least where she was headed there was none of this traffic nonsense to put up with.

It was late afternoon when Sam rolled up to the kiosk at the Ardrossan ferry terminal just as the big ferry cleared the harbour wall heading out on its crossing to Arran.

The Cal Mac official in the ticket office must have seen that Sam was tired and stressed out and promised, although she was not booked, to find a place for her on the six o'clock boat. Sam parked the Scirocco in the first column for boarding, picked up a coffee from the canteen then headed back outside. She had been sitting all day and needed to stretch her legs. She strolled out through the car park following the sea wall until it came to an end by the harbour lighthouse, then leaned over the railing and watched the ferry disappear into the distance, dwarfed by the hills of Arran in the misty blue distance. The sea wind whipped around her head and she clasped her coffee with both hands to keep them warm. Now she had stopped she had time to think about what lay ahead, if indeed this was where Adam had headed. That in itself posed Sam another question: she hadn't reminded Adam about his cottage on Arran; this, coupled with his dreams, although worrying, was also intriguing. Adam must have had some type of memory event for these two things to have happened. The concern was that Arran held so many memories – some good, some bad – would Adam's poor brain be able to cope? Sam crossed her fingers and stared longingly over to the island in the distance.

Adam woke with a violent lurch. His heart was racing and for a second he could still hear the muffled thud of a helicopter blade as it lifted off. He jumped to his feet and charged for the cottage door; without hesitation he threw it open and sprinted outside. A stiff breeze hit his face but there was no helicopter; he searched the skyline, his heart still racing, then cautiously he made his way to the beach, his heart filled with dread. He somehow knew he was going to find a body. The wind was cold on his sweat-soaked body as he worked his way right along the beach towards Machrie, but there was no body. He was confused, tired and full of despair – he was almost in tears as he turned back towards the cottage – then he noticed an object on the beach in the distance, and something in his memory clicked. Above the object was a cliff face that dropped to the beach; his eyes filled with tears and his heart once more with dread as the adrenalin kicked in and he ran barefoot along the beach to the object. Was this the body he had been looking for?

As he reached the object his legs gave way and he collapsed. A large chunk of driftwood had become entangled in a black bin bag. He was shaking – he was losing what was left of his mind. He closed his eyes, trying to clear his head. His heart was still racing as he opened his eyes; for a second the open eyes of a pretty girl stared lifelessly up at him, then there was only the driftwood.

Adam could not explain what was happening to him. He had not slept without the nightmares; even dropping off in the chair this afternoon had caused them. Ghosts haunted him whenever he closed his eyes – now they were tormenting him when awake – he was losing his mind. He'd thought coming here to this place alone would allow him to fight the demons, but for some reason this place that was his and that he had dreamed of was making things so much worse.

He had a terrible urge just to walk out into the water and end it all – he needed to stop the torment before it drove him insane. There was something familiar and so inviting about the cool, calm water; he almost felt that he had done this before, and the more he thought about the waves flowing over him the more appealing the idea became. A man appeared before him. It wasn't until he spoke that Adam realised it was his old buddy, Sergeant Ferris. 'Come on, laddie, what are you waiting for? Do it – go for it, son.'

Adam was not sure how long he had been standing up to his waist, but his lower half had stopped shivering. He was starting to feel an inner warmth; it was such a comforting feeling he wanted more and stepped forward. Suddenly the nightmare was back – a vision of a screaming woman tried to stop him. He was angry – he wanted to keep going, he wanted the warmth and peace – no ghost was going to stop him. The ghostly figure of the woman was screaming as she struggled to stop his advance into the waves. Adam was too strong for the ghost and she hit him hard across the face.

For the first time that afternoon he knew that this was no ghost – his eyebrow was cut from the blow and the saltwater stung like mad, bringing him back from the brink. There was something familiar about her face and he stopped walking – no ghost could have done this. She clung to his chest, sobbing. Was this the woman who had been with him when he first woke up or the ghost of Samantha, his wife.

'Samantha, are you real? Please, for god's sake tell me you're real and not another nightmare – I can't take this anymore. I'm finished. I need this to stop.'

Just when Adam thought she must have been an illusion she spoke, still clinging to his chest.

'It's me, Adam, it's Sam. Please get out of the water. Do you under-stand – we need to get out of the water. Please, for me – I swear I will never leave your side again. Please turn back … we need to get you better … you're not well. Please, Adam, I'm begging you – don't do this.'

Adam still felt he was walking in a dream as he turned round to head for the beach. Sam clung to him like a child, whispering encouragement in his ear. He was still not sure if this was all part of a bad dream as he made his way out of the water, expecting any second for the dream to end and to find himself once more covered in sweat, screaming into the night. He reached the cottage door and still Sam clung on to him for grim death. He could feel the warmth of her body next to him and her heart beating against his chest; this was no dream: she was the real thing, for sure.

They both sat wrapped in towels in front of a roaring fire. Adam had said very little while Sam had stripped him of his soaking clothing and lit the fire. She was not sure where to start with him. Eventually it was Adam who spoke first, confident now that Sam was no hallucination.

'You've changed your hair, Samantha – it's short now.'

Sam pulled back from him, staring into his eyes. 'There you go, that memory of yours does work. Yes, I've had it all cut off, well spotted.'

Adam took her hand and kissed it. 'Thank you for being real, Sam. I think I'm going mad. I heard a helicopter today, then I started looking for a body, and when I couldn't find it I turned back. Then I spotted what I thought was a second body of a girl that turned into driftwood. It's not my memory that's the big problem – I'm insane. Back at the glass house I dreamt that I found a girl with her tongue cut out. I got out of there before I started killing people – you should have let me drown, it would be easier for everyone.'

Sam shook her head as she grabbed him by the shoulders, making him look into her eyes. 'I'm going to make you a deal, Adam McDonald. If I can explain some of these things to you will you promise to get back on your meds? Luckily for you, Bob had the good sense to hide them in the Beetle. I checked and they haven't been opened. You can't stop taking them, Adam, not until the doctor says so.'

Adam shook his head as he looked into the flames. 'They were having no effect. I think they were causing the dreams. I don't need them.'

Sam wanted to explode at him but she held it back. 'You don't need them? So suicide was a better option? Listen, Adam, I think – no, I know – your memory is coming back. You've had one hell of a life, so lots of things you dream about are not going to be pleasant, but you are going to have to deal with them. I will be here to help, and I'll explain the dreams where I can.

'The girl with her tongue cut out did happen. You were a special forces soldier working in Ireland during the troubles. The girl was my sister Mary, your undercover partner. The IRA got to her and cut her tongue out before executing her for being an informer, so you see it was terrible, but it makes sense.

'You know for memories the worst thing you could have done was come back here. When you left the army you fell for a lady doctor who was doing research here for MI6. She was assassinated because of her work – you found her body below the cliff. As for the helicopter noise, it was when our friend Smithy was shot and left here by the Americans almost four years ago – again it was you who found his body. You were devastated by his death – your son is called Luke because Luke was Smithy's first name – you named your son after him.

'Adam, I'm no doctor, but these dreams are your memories coming back. This coupled with you coming off your meds has caused the hallucinations and breakdown, I'm sure of it. There will be many more things that will come back to haunt you, but if you get back on your meds and I help talk them over with you I'm sure we'll get through them together.'

Sam handed Adam two pills and he swallowed them without arguing; suddenly he seemed tired and more exhausted than she had ever seen him before. She watched over him through the night, shattered herself but too afraid to fall asleep.

The gulls outside woke Sam the next morning; her body had given in and she had dropped off just before dawn. Adam was still curled up in her lap where they had both fallen asleep next to the fireplace.

Sam got to her feet but not before kissing a still sleeping Adam on the forehead. She went to the kitchen in search of food, ravenous after yesterday's efforts.

Adam joined her shortly afterwards and after breakfast they spent the day walking and talking, Adam describing memories and Sam helping to place them in his jigsaw puzzle of a brain. By evening with his meds working and Sam's help he was a different man. They spent the evening in front of the fire, Sam telling him stories from his past, Adam clinging to her like a lost child. But that night she knew they had turned a corner; she fell asleep in his arms thinking of baby names. She wasn't going to tell him about the baby just yet – that was for another time.

Sam was up bright and early the next morning. For a second night Adam had slept right through. Sam let him sleep while she cooked bacon for their breakfast, only calling on him when the food was on the table.

'Come on, lazy bones, time to get up. We need to hurry – we're going home to the glass house today – if I don't see Luke soon I'll go mad. Coffee and bacon rolls then we're out of here, so let's go, Captain, get your finger out.'

Adam polished off breakfast while Sam called Sue from the bedroom.

Sam finished her call updating Sue; she'd also talked to Luke and Lauren. It was only then that she realised that Adam was missing and panic stabbed at her heart. She sprinted out of the cottage door towards the sea. She didn't have to go far – Adam was only a few feet in front of her. He stopped in his tracks, a startled expression on his face.

'Jesus, Adam, don't do that to me – are you okay?'

Adam smiled, but it was a strange smile. 'I didn't tell you I had a dream last night. Don't worry, it didn't wake me, it was a nice dream. I dreamt it was Christmas. I dreamt you kissed me on the beach, and I am pretty sure it was our first kiss. Was I right?'

Sam nodded but said nothing.

'You used this, I believe?' Adam produced a clump of seaweed from behind his back and Sam smiled; her memory went back to that fateful day when she had to improvise and use seaweed because there was no mistletoe.

'Sam, I know it's not Christmas and this still isn't mistletoe, but could you do me a favour and recreate the moment? I need to try and jog my memory.'

Sam wrapped her arms around his neck, kissing him passionately before finally letting him come up for air. 'Adam, I don't know if I ever told you, but that was the moment I finally realised I had fallen in love with you. How was the kiss, did it help with your memory?'

She could see that Adam was trying desperately to keep a serious face on but was struggling.

'I'm not sure, Sam, I think we need to try that a few times more just to be sure I've got it.'

Sam grabbed the seaweed and flung it away. 'Funny guy. Get your backside in the passenger seat of the Scirocco – we're leaving now.'

Adam's gaze transferred from Sam to Herbie the Beetle. 'What about the Beetle?'

'Leave it – we'll pick it up next time we're here. I'm not taking my eyes off you until I get you home, now let's go.'

'Admit it, Sam, it was the kiss … that's why you can't leave me alone.'

Sam shook her head. 'You're getting better – your sense of humour has returned. Now, get in the car, you big Scottish idiot. We have the rest of our lives to get on with and the clock is ticking. Let's go home.'

Printed in Great Britain
by Amazon